REDEEMER

S.L. LUCK

For Chris, Rebekah, and Laura

Acknowledgements

I've wanted to be a writer ever since I was thirteen, back when I first read S.E. Hinton's *The Outsiders*. My thirteen-year-old self also happened to have a thing for Emilio Estévez at the time and, after watching him in *Young Guns*, I proceeded to write a terrible Western. All thirty or so handwritten pages are still somewhere in storage, but I haven't forgotten that feeling of putting pen on paper and letting my brain flow out. Since then, I've written five novels, which I shelved as *practice* novels, and many short stories, some of which actually see people from time to time. This novel is the result of an encounter I had in a second-hand bookshop in early 2020. To the stranger who warned me against picking up a *haunted* book, thank you. Of course, it takes a team to make something like this happen. My husband, Chris, has unfailingly supported my writing endeavours, for which I am forever grateful. Chris and our two tiny cheerleaders make the long days and the writing headaches so much more bearable. I am blessed because of them. My first and most eager reader, however, is my sister Jennifer. Thanks Buddy. Bookending my smooth days are many days where I struggle, many days where I wonder if I'm doing the right thing. Crystal sets me straight. Every. Single. Time. You rock Sista. Lastly, to my readers, thanks for sticking with me. I can't promise perfection, but I think we'll have fun together. Read on.

PROLOGUE

.

"Get up Vanessa! You have to get out now!" Beneath the smoke, Betty dragged her legs over the floor. She crawled on her elbows toward where the girl lay writhing, Vanessa's head a mess of blood, her eyes a terrible scramble of confusion and horror. Wisps of smouldering ash floated onto Betty's skin and into her hair, igniting the thin strands from her ear lobes to her forehead. She smacked her skull here, there, everywhere, unsure if the flames were out because the pain was bad, so very bad, she was sure the membrane that held her insides together for eighty years had erupted wide open. But the girl. The girl! Betty heaved herself toward Vanessa, her elbows splitting wide and wet where they scraped against the confetti of broken glass dusted over the floor. Her night gown, splotched with blood and ash and flame, seemed to evaporate off her body, disintegrating upward above her, and far into the cracks of the old floorboards beneath. Then, searing pain on her foot; a hot thump of something which halted her slow drag. Betty glanced back. The wobbly china cabinet Stan poorly fashioned during one of his more productive drunken stupors lay in a fiery heap, toppled over her ankle. She always knew Stan would be the death of her. Alight with angry red flame, the cabinet held her, clenching with its weight and its heat, but no matter how hard Betty pulled, she could not free herself. Soon, the cheap slippers Stan bought her for Mother's Day ten years ago caught fire and broiled her feet. "Now! Get ... out ..." she croaked but the heat took that opening, too, and whooshed down her throat and into her lungs. The scorch spread from her center and filled her insides with the hot soup of death. Coughing, she reached for the girl. Then Betty wailed as the cabinet seared into the soft tendons of her ankle. She cried out. Again and again and again she cried until the girl finally moved.

Then Betty heard a crack.

She gaped upward and saw that the fire had torn through the roof, wrenching lumber and shingles and insulation down into the fiery maw of the attic. The midnight sky, upwards and out and full of stars, promised safety and the end to her pain and Betty thrust her hands toward the good, clean air, but then a breeze drew the flames higher. Through all this, she heard a moan. Squinting, the woman looked toward the window. There, in the terrible haze, Vanessa was trying to get to her feet, her awareness slowly, too slowly waking. "The window! Jump!" Betty barked, before the support beam that sturdied her attic for sixty-one years collapsed onto her back, killing her instantly.

Through the rags of smoke, Vanessa watched Betty die. The vision of the naked and charred woman reaching out before the column of lumber shot into her back brought vomit to her throat and she retched uncontrollably. Awakened with nausea, Vanessa took in the burning furniture and flaming drywall and ashen floor and dead woman, suddenly aware that she, too, was about to die.

On her feet, Vanessa coughed as smoke enveloped her face. She hacked and heaved, and it was only when she dropped back to her hands and knees that she was able to breathe again. The hot air hurt her throat, dried her eyes, baked her skin. Vanessa gagged and felt for the window. Eyes watering, she lurched forward, feeling for the attic's front wall. She was stung by ash and then something larger and hotter fell onto her shoulder. Gasping, she brushed it away, but then there was another sting and another, two more, ten, the burns coming fast, faster, and she realized with horror that the attic had become a raging crematorium—and that she was trapped inside.

Sucking the last bits of air that hovered over the floor, she plowed forward, dying but still alive. Still alive. Still … her hand struck something soft and Vanessa realized it was one of the pillows that she remembered on the couch beside the adjacent wall. She had gone too far. The smoke grew denser, a molasses-like black that flowed overhead, churning angrily. Vanessa lowered her head further so that her chin brushed the floor. Her chin bled as she snagged herself on a shard of glass, and there it remained as she blindly reached out. Vanessa patted and tapped glass and wood, locating Betty's pub table only when the hot metal scorched her palm. Vanessa screamed. The fire raged.

I can't die like this, she thought. *I can't. I can't.* "Please God," she prayed aloud. "Please." Spit erupted onto her chin and mixed with her tears. Her blood ran. The fire closed in. With a last look at the room, Vanessa caught sight of Betty's smouldering and broken body and turned away. Fear clutched her now and she winced as she hooked her foot around the leg of the chair, dragging it behind her as she crawled to where she knew the window would be.

Quickly, she felt her way up the wall, tentatively tapping for a different sound, a different material that would signify her way out. When her fingertips hissed against the glass, she knew she had found it, still intact. Vanessa cursed and punched the window with both fists, but the glass held. Above, another beam fell from the roof and Vanessa knew that she had only seconds before she would be crushed by the roof or strangled by the smoke. With great effort, she slid the chair beneath the window with her shoe, then howled with pain when her fingers clamped over it. Once, the chair screeched against the glass, but the thick windowpane was part of that well-built era that never wanted to die. Her fingers burned, and Vanessa willed her strength into the chair. Smoke unfurled lower, and Vanessa coughed relentlessly. Stars pricked her vision and she knew that soon, the blackness would take her away for good. With one last surge, she thrust the chair and all of her body weight at the window.

The last thing she remembered before she fell was the baby.

1

Vanessa Penner was halfway into another lane of traffic when she was startled by the blast of an angry horn. She flinched, spinning the wheel too far left and got another blare from a red-faced truck driver, who swerved wildly to avoid her. Jabbing a middle finger out of his window as he passed, the man cursed. Vanessa tightened her grip on the wheel and thought of returning one of her own single-finger salutes but realized with embarrassment that she probably deserved that finger. The 401 wasn't a place for daydreaming. That could get you dead. Responsibly, she centered herself back into the middle lane, shrugged her shoulders apologetically at the trucker who was now far past her small Toyota Echo, and sighed. She turned on the radio, went through the entire gamut of available stations, and flicked it off again.

The three-hour drive from her small apartment in Toronto's east end to her parent's house in Garrett was something she usually took with enthusiasm. The monthly trips gave her the chance to stock up on groceries at her mother's insistence and cash at her father's because he still was not convinced she'd chosen the right career. "Graphic designer?" Nick Penner scratched his head every time his daughter reminded him that, yes, people made money from the profession. In truth, she made a respectable wage, but that was before the pandemic reared its terrible jaw and clamped down on the world. Who needed a graphic designer to help sell gourmet food when the world only cared about toilet paper and sanitizer? In the strange days of the pandemic, design simply didn't matter and designer food didn't matter, so it was not long before business stagnated. While her boss Maury had lost almost everything during what he called "that goddamed corona racket", he'd labored tirelessly to keep his people working. The man had given up his own salary, rolled out an admirable work rotation plan, wrung every penny he could from the government, and negotiated lower rent, machine, and service costs, but three months of forced shutdown and an excruciatingly slow resumption of consumer spending decimated the business. He couldn't hold on any longer and that meant Vanessa, along with a handful of others from accounting, finance, category management, and marketing had to go. Maury's tears were the worst part of all and she couldn't look at his blubbering face when she collected her purse and sweater from her cubicle on her way out the door. Sweetly, he offered to carry her things to her car, but she politely declined. She didn't need the pictures of Curtis at her desk. It was better to make a quick separation, even if half the bandage still dangled in the air.

Losing her job was difficult, Vanessa reflected as she drove, but the timing of her separation with Curtis was downright terrible and it gnawed at her now. Hadn't she tried so many times before to break it off? Call it quits? Tell him she wouldn't be needing his midnight services in the quiet of the night or at any other hour, for that matter? Over the two years they dated, Vanessa broke it off with

Curtis no less than a dozen times. Yet with each occurrence, when she waded into the river of testosterone flowing her way over the grimy streets of Toronto, at once overwhelmed by the aggression and conceit or, just as often, the timidity, she found herself back with what she knew. And that was stifling old Curtis.

The frayed rubber of a popped tire appeared on the road and the bump sent the bags on her overstuffed back seat cascading to the floor. At once, smells from her emptied fridge bloomed inside the car as takeout containers burst open. Of course. Karma was coming to bite her in the ass. Presently, she regarded Reggie, the small green-eyed Bombay cat snoozing on her jacket in the passenger seat and scratched his head. Reggie stretched his paws, sniffed the chicken korma behind him, yawned, and promptly went back to sleep. He was the only part of her relationship with Curtis that Vanessa was willing to keep.

"Now? You're doing this now?" Curtis bawled like a baby when she told him those few days ago. That inward pucker of his face made him look like one pale and giant, quivering rectum, something she couldn't help thinking whenever he pouted, which was often enough. He beat his chest one, two, ten times, assailing his body until angry red welts peeked from his pale belly under the hem of his shirt. This was his game, hurting himself until her concern overrode the sense in her heart. Only now, with the recent deaths of both his mother and father from Covid-19, Vanessa knew Curtis was particularly vulnerable. He threw a half-eaten orange at her face when she told him it was over. Then he struck himself. Then he grabbed handfuls of spaghetti from his dinner plate and threw that at her too. That just made it easier for her to walk out the door. A pouty partner she could manage, a violent partner she could not. But then Curtis ran after her, catching her halfway down the walk, and curled himself around her leg. Vanessa, already smaller and thinner than every other girl she knew growing up, lost fifteen pounds over the course of the pandemic, too stressed to do anything but drink wine and search the internet, so she had no hope of budging even one ungodly inch of Curtis' 250 pound frame. She stayed put and listened to his sobs and self-deprecation and insults until his neighbour arrived home from work and gave the pair of them a concerned look. Only then did Curtis reluctantly release her. She was already in her car, backing out of the driveway when he tore a rose bush from the ground and hurled it at her windshield, the dirt from which was still clumped against her wipers.

The last of the bandage ripped off, Vanessa was free. Free and what? The rest of it she didn't know, but was headed toward home, to what she knew, and that couldn't be all that bad, could it? Reggie mewed and Vanessa tugged a bag of cat treats from the console and set a fistful in front of him. They were only twenty minutes from her parent's house, and she didn't want to stop. Better to keep Reggie happy than have him howling in her ear like Curtis for the rest of the drive. The cat ate greedily while Vanessa pulled off the 401, north onto Dutton. The sudden drop in traffic was like being spit from a current, which, she supposed, she was. A little regurgitation from the smoggy city into the bright blue of languid Garret, Ontario's southernmost 15,000-strong farming community.

She casted off from the highway, away from the surge, far from the populous clot, beyond the parasitic clutch of the city that held her these past six years, since she was a younger girl of twenty-one. Now an inky drop returning to the otherwise clear pool of her childhood, Vanessa was older, more mature, more than a bit jaded, and she wondered now if this latter development could be changed. She wasn't so sure.

Vanessa let down her window, feeling the warm summer air veil her skin. Bags rattled in the back, papers and loose pictures flew like dry leaves, dusting up the interior of her car but she didn't care. She just didn't care. For a moment, she closed her eyes and let the sun heat her eyelids. Her grip on the wheel loosened as memory carried her home, and when she looked toward the gold fields on her left and her right, Vanessa's uncertainty faded away. So peaceful was her re-entry that she didn't notice the police car behind her until the flash of blue and red reflected in her rear-view mirror. That bastard Karma again.

Easing her foot off the gas pedal, Vanessa suddenly realized she hadn't reduced her speed since exiting the highway. What was the limit here? Fifty? Sixty? She couldn't remember passing a sign but then she hadn't been looking, she had been in her own damned head. To the cat, she said, "Well, Reggie, looks like we're making quite the comeback, aren't we?" Reggie lifted his head, regarding the slowing scenery around him, the long chestnut furrows sunk between the dark green ropes of soybean crops, the handful of small farmhouses set back from the road, the reflecting, peaked tops of massive grain silos, the green and red dots of resting equipment in far away fields. When she pulled her car to a stop on the shoulder of the road, a dog bolted from his slumber in front of a garage, barking wildly as he dashed toward them.

Vanessa lowered her window further and waited as the officer took his time in his cruiser, which was now parked behind her, lights still flashing. Then he was out of the car, approaching with a slight limp. He leaned over her window and said, "License and registration please." The sun beat brightly from behind the man's face, obscuring all of his features except for the thick shape of his body. Silently, Vanessa pinched the corner of her wallet out of her purse. The officer accepted her identification, looked from her licence to Vanessa, from Vanessa to her license. "Hmm," he said. "I'll be right back with these, you just hang on here for a moment, alright?" Vanessa nodded and watched his retreat in her mirror. He dragged his right foot across the gravel, dusting up his shiny shoes as he waked. Then he got in his car and tapped Vanessa's information on his laptop. She knew there would be nothing to find. She never had a speeding ticket or other traffic violation, no unpaid fines, no misdemeanors, no indiscretions, large or small. Nothing except her shitty breakup with Curtis. *And for that*, she now thought smugly, *I should get a fucking medal.*

Before Vanessa knew what was happening, the dog that raced from the garage was now in her window, front paws half inside the car, barking and trying to lick her face. His bronze coat and friendly whimpering suggested a retriever cross of some sort and she tentatively pet the dog's head, to which it happily thumped a hind leg against the gravel. Inside the car, Reggie hissed, the fur on his arched back splayed and spiked, then he threw himself deep into the folds of clothing on the floor. Two more muffled hisses came as the dog whined again, now clattering his back legs against the door as he tried to enter the window. "Awww!" Vanessa heard the officer yell as he toddled toward her, documents in one hand, overworked belt in the other. He hitched up his pants and then grabbed the dog's collar. "Stanley! Off Stanley! You know better than that, now, don't you boy? Come on, boy, let's leave these folks alone." The dog called Stanley gave Vanessa one final lick, pulled out of Vanessa's window, and dropped to the gravel, his tail wagging furiously as the officer rubbed head and scratched his ears. "Sorry about that. He's a good old boy but the Coopers let him run free and he likes to travel some. Picked him up near Boomer's just last week, best coffee in town so I couldn't be too upset with the little fella. Got him another ten clicks past the dump only the day after, busy buggar. It's a bit of a trick to get him in the car sometimes but thankfully we've got nothing much else going on, so we don't mind. Do we?" he was cooing to the dog now. "Do we Stanley? No, we don't." Stanley barked and Reggie yowled, and the bundles on the floor beneath the glove compartment rustled madly. "Oh my! You got a cat in there, miss? Why didn't you say so? I would have locked Stanley in my car had I known you had a feline in there." He palmed the top of his hat apologetically, grabbed Stanley's collar and hauled him away from the road, sending the dog toward home with a friendly pat on his rump.

The officer was back in a minute. He set an elbow on her roof, resting his tall frame against her car. "I'm assuming you came in from the city, young lady?"

Vanessa nodded. "I'm sorry. I guess I didn't see the sign. There used to be one about a minute or two off the highway, but it must have been removed since the last time I visited." Vanessa hadn't been home in almost eight months, the pandemic had saw to that. There was still snow on the ground when she last entered Garrett but now the fields were in late bloom.

"Sign's still there, miss, but I'd have to admit you're not the first and you won't be the last to have missed the damn thing. That virus took out our best road crew. Three of them dead and another still too weak to work. City's been hiring but ..." he shrugged. "Well I suppose it's just going to take us some time to get back to normal, you know?" Vanessa nodded. *Time*, she thought, *that which shall not be rushed.* "The crews that we do have are working like dogs trying to catch up, so I can't blame them for not cleaning the ditches or trimming those branches yet. I'd do it myself if my leg here would let me." Vanessa peeked over her door at the officer's leg. "Knee replacement," he said, patting his thigh. "Almost new again. Another few weeks and I'll be running faster than Stanley," he chuckled.

By now, Vanessa's full bladder made her squirm. "I'm sorry, Officer. I didn't realize ..."

"Ah, now," he said. "It's not all your fault, miss. Sure, you were speeding like the dickens and had that sign been as visible as it was supposed to be, you would be getting more than a warning right now. Now, if you'd been caught by an actual speed trap, you wouldn't be getting off so easy. As luck would have it, I was tending to a call out near McGuinty's and just happened to spot you shooting into town like a firecracker in a coffee can."

The tension that had congealed in Vanessa's veins thinned with this news and the red-hot blood that collected and settled in her cheeks finally abated. "I'm so sorry."

"You don't remember me, do you, miss?"

Vanessa's head went up, finally brave enough to get a good look at the man. She squinted into the light and regarded him. Though his black hair had gone grey, he had the same caterpillar brows, moustache, and long forks of genial creases near his eyes and a spray of boyhood pink still on his cheeks. His wireframe glasses were new. "Mr. Beatty?" she eyed him.

He smiled. "I was wondering if you'd remember. All those years Wendy sat for you, watching you grow from diapers to those teeny bopper dances, when you didn't need watchin' any more. Sheesh. What's it been since we last saw you? Ten, fifteen years?"

"Almost fifteen," Vanessa warmed to her parent's old neighbour, before she entered junior high and the Beattys moved to a small acreage south of the bridge. "Gosh, it's so good to see you Mr. Beatty. How is Mrs. Beatty these days?"

"Holdin' up as good as can be expected," he said. "She's been lonely ever since the boys moved out but she's puttering around in the garden a lot more, cooking like the devil, as you can see from my waistline." He patted his stomach, chuckling. Then the strong scent of ammonia wafted up from the floor to their noses and they knew the terrified cat had peed. "That's my cue, little miss. Sorry for keeping you so long. Be sure to pass a big hello to your parents and do everyone a favor and ease up on that gas pedal from now on, will you?"

"Sure thing. And sorry again," Vanessa said. With a friendly double-tap to Vanessa's roof, Horace Beatty ambled back to his cruiser.

Slowly, Vanessa returned to the asphalt with her windows open, gagging as she released the stench of cat piss into the open air. Her bladder now screaming, she took the direct route home alongside the fast blue water of the Collingwood River. She passed the grey slabs of Garrett's water treatment plant, the brown towers of its industrial clump, and the damp green of adjacent little league fields. Then she went over the Hoggarth Bridge, where she slowed for another look at the charred stumps of the former Holy Redeemer, known for the last twenty-two years as the *haunted church* by locals old enough to remember the fire. She was a pig-tailed, scabby-kneed, five-year-old when that fire took the church, and the story became the stuff of legends even in her small kindergarten circle. Presently, Reggie mewed, and with one last look, Holy Redeemer faded away in Vanessa's rear-view mirror.

2

The summer sun was still high in the sky when Nick Penner and Steve Rikkes cracked their third beers on Penner's front porch. With a lip full of tobacco, Rikkes spat into an empty beer bottle before taking a long pull on the beer Nick handed him. "That shit's gonna kill you one day," Nick said. "And look at your goddamned teeth, will you? At least spit it out before you drink."

Rikkes smiled, his tan teeth speckled with tobacco. "It's better this way, Nick. You get a real buzz this way. Don't need no drugs, you know? The combination of the two … boy! Ain't nothing like it."

Nick said nothing. He remembered those blackout highs of long ago; *those* were the real highs. Lynn changed all that. Before Lynn, Nick couldn't remember his own name some days, even recognize his own goddamn face. Had Lynn not come along, well, Nick's own teeth might have been as brown and jagged as a bottle shank. At least Rikkes' teeth wouldn't disintegrate like sandcastles during high tide. The men sat, looking over the street where the treetops met, alive with birdsong and summer wind and white clouds of dandelion fluff. A pack of boys skittered by on scooters and hoverboards and undersized bikes, hurling boyhood dares faster than softballs. "Betcha can't ride with no hands," one said. "Do it with your eyes closed," said another. "Race ya!" ventured the smallest. Nick and Steve watched the younger and more innocent version of themselves tearing up the street, remembering, drinking. Steve said, "Ten bucks says one of those fellas end up in Lynn's office tonight."

Nick shrugged. "Wouldn't be the first, won't be the last." As Garrett's head pediatrician, Lynn Penner had stitched more knees, set more bones, punctured more abscesses, tempered more fevers, soothed more throats, gave more vaccinations, controlled more asthma and prescribed more birth control than there were weeds along Dutton. She was on call at the hospital tonight, which made it the perfect time for the two construction workers to unwind on Nick's front porch. Settling into this peace, Nick let out a long breath, closing his eyes, letting summer's inertia relieve him of his workday's frustration, his marital inferiority. He listened to the far-off voices of children, the chatter of neighbours behind backyard fences, the eager squeal of tires reaching homes, the sludgy hawk of Rikkes' wayward tobacco. A horn honked and Nick opened his eyes.

"Hi Dad," Vanessa pulled into the driveway beside Nick's truck, calling out from her window. She turned off the ignition, closed her window, and turned her shoulder to retrieve something from the passenger seat floor. When she finally opened the door, Nick saw that she was cradling a non-too-happy cat in her arms. "Mind if I give him a quick bath before I unpack the car?"

Nick slapped Rikkes' leg. Rikkes removed his outstretched legs from the porch railing, tucked his spit bottle behind the leg of his chair and sat up. "Thing looks right pissed," he whispered to Nick.

16

Vanessa made her way up the porch steps toward the front door. "My girl!" Nick said proudly, reaching to hug her. Then, catching the strong sent of cat pee, turned his nose, and said, "You just go on in the house, hun, but wash him in the downstairs bathroom, okay? Towels and clean sheets are already waiting for you."

"Thanks Dad," she said, quickly ducking into the house when Nick opened the door.

Rikkes watched the girl go inside, admiring the thin legs beneath the short shorts and the smooth spine of her toned back suctioned to her tank top. He licked his lips. "Your girl don't like me much."

Nick slapped him then, not hard, but hard enough to make Rikkes stiffen. "Can you blame her? You look at her like a goddamn piece of ripe fruit. She's my fucking daughter, Steve. I don't know what shit you've got going on at home with Shannon, but you don't go looking at another man's daughter like she's fucking porno material, got it? I wouldn't like you either, sweating and eyeing her all up like that. How many times do I have to tell you?"

Rikkes blushed, dragging a hand through his thinning, greasy hair. "Aww, now, Nick. You know I don't mean anything by it. Just appreciating her beauty, is all. I think I'm just not used to seeing her all grown up, you know? Just yesterday she was twelve, man, and then she goes away and now there's this beautiful woman you got there. Shannon doesn't have anything to do with it but, I'll tell you, it's not easy to marry someone who once looked like your daughter and wake up almost thirty years later to a gorilla. I suppose I'm just remembering." He took his beer bottle again, spat, and, with one long throw, scored the bottle in Nick's open trashcan beside the garage.

"Next time you see her, you look at her eyes, asshole, her fucking eyes, got it?"

"Got it."

By the time Vanessa had scrubbed and dried Reggie, Rikkes was gone and Nick began to wash vegetables for supper. He was peeling a potato when Vanessa entered the kitchen. "Where's the cat?" Nick asked.

"Hiding somewhere. He'll be mad at me for a while for the bath and the new place, but he'll get over it." She came up behind her father and squeezed tightly around his belly.

"Now that's more like it," Nick said. He rinsed his hands, rubbed them on a towel and hugged her long and hard around the shoulders, his petit daughter only a scratch shorter than himself. "It's been way too long, Vanny."

"Still can't believe I'm here," she said. "Thanks for the room, Dad."

"Hey now!" Nick released his hold and looked at her, catching for the first time the depressions beneath her eyes, the faint stretch of pimples on her chin, the dim pallor of her skin, like the sunlight that was always there, always shining, had been scoured away. A thin film of tears coated her eyes and she looked down at her shuffling feet. Nick pinched her chin between his thumb and forefinger, tilting her to look at him. "Aww, Vanny. It's going to be okay. All that crazy is behind us now. It's going to be okay. *You're* going to be okay. Don't you go frettin' about anything, you hear me? This is your home, Vanny, and you'll always have room here. There's nothing to worry about. You'll get another job and I bet it'll be even better than anything in Toronto."

Her cheeks reddened as she released him. "Thanks Dad."

"Aww, you know what I mean, Vanny. That cesspool's no good for you. You've got everything a person could want right here. Fresh air. Miles of nature. Border's just," he snapped his fingers, "this close. Best of both worlds, Vanny."

She took her hands to her face, circling her temples. "I don't know what to do with myself anymore. I mean, before all that happened, I was okay, you know? Loved my job, still *had* a job, had a cool apartment, small, but still it was mine and it was close to everything I needed. Curtis was kind of a shithead, but it wasn't terrible. Could have been worse, but it was okay, Dad, it really was."

"Sounds like heaven." Nick began peeling potatoes again.

"Uggh, why is this so hard?" Vanessa groaned.

Nick fished in the drawer beside the sink, rustling around until he found another peeler. He handed it to Vanessa and said, "People think more clearly when they're working."

They finished the rest of the potatoes in silence. After a while, Vanessa said, "How's Mom been with everything?"

Nick shrugged. "Good as can be expected. This past month as been a lot better but before that, Vanny, it was real rough for a while there. She's lost some weight, still not sleeping well, working thirteen-hour days and even when she's here, her mind is elsewhere. It's good that you're home, Vanny. I think she needs it, hell, we all need it." He set to coating chicken in flour before placing a frying pan on the stove. Vanessa prepared a salad while the potatoes boiled and the chicken fried. Soon, the kitchen was filled with the familiar smells of home cooking and Vanessa realized she was starving. Even Reggie, still scowling, tentatively brushed against Nick's calves as he worked the stove. "Look, he's already at home." Nick shooed the cat away with the tip of his toe.

"Give him food and he'll be happy anywhere." Vanessa scooped Reggie up and dropped him before his food and water bowls in the back porch while Nick filled their plates. Vanessa had just sat down when the front door swung open and her mother, arms outstretched, squealed toward her.

"Vanneeee! My girl! Oh! My girl!" she threw her purse down and clutched Vanessa hard, squishing the air from both of their lungs until they were panting and gasping and on the verge of bruising. On she held, rocking and swaying, dabbing at her eyes, leaking from her nose and mouth, twisting the sunglasses she hadn't yet removed. "Let me get a look at you," Lynn swiped her cheeks with her wrists, tugged her glasses off and dropped them in the bowl of mashed potatoes before she realized what she had done. "Oh Nick. I'm so sorry about that, yeesh I don't even know what I'm doing right now. Look at me, I'm shaking. I think I need to sit down." She pulled out a chair and sat, plucking her frames from the potatoes. Nick passed her a towel, thought better of it, and took Lynn's slimy glasses into his own hands, cleaning them thoughtfully. Then Lynn began to cry, not the happy tears she had shed minutes before but rivers of tears, oceans of them, so many tears that the front of her beige jacket had grown dark with wet and the cavities under her eyes had filled like rain puddles, every new splash sending a torrent of water down her cheeks and into the skeletal crevice below her neck.

Nick put a hand on Lynn's shoulder. "Lynnie, it's okay Lynnie. She's home now."

Lynn smoothed her hair and Vanessa saw for the first time that she had gone almost completely grey. The look was not entirely unbecoming on her otherwise youthful face, but it aged her mother in a way that Vanessa did not particularly like. It worried her. "Mom," she ventured carefully, "you look sick."

Lynn howled now, letting the worry and frustration and misery of those long, cursed months wash out and away and into the open, onto the table, onto their plates. "Oh Vanny," she sniffed, finally removing her shoes and her jacket, which Nick dutifully scooped up and put away. "We've had such a rough go of it. Both of the nursing homes wiped out, half their staff, a handful of our best teachers; why, I think Tom Widlow lost five of his guys— four constables and that cross-eyed woman from dispatch— Arlene, Mona, Nancy …"

Her mother's childhood friends. Vanessa gasped. "Why didn't you tell me?"

"You had enough on your plate already and I didn't want you to worry and rush home like you always do. You think I wanted you here in the middle of it? No way, Vanny, no way in hell. How crazy is it that you were safer in Toronto than middle-of-nowhere Garrett? I don't understand it either, Vanny, but there it is. I'm just glad you're home. Give me a moment," Lynn let out a slow breath.

Vanessa looked at her father. "Had I known …"

"We know, Vanny. That's why we didn't say anything. Believe me, it's a blessing to your mother that the news around here isn't so interesting to anyone once you pass the corn fields. Saved her a lot of heartache if you can believe it."

"Oh Mom, I'm so sorry." Vanessa leaned toward her mother for another hug.

Lynn stretched an arm out. "Don't. Not just yet when I've started to dry up or I'll go on blathering again. There will be plenty of time for hugs and I intend to get every single one I can. You'll be sick of me before you know it."

Nick reset the table and warmed the food again and they ate, gathering the time that separated them, roping days, coiling months, tying moments back together into a uniform life. Afterward, they relaxed on the front porch, settling into their new, comfortable collective, sipping full cups of sweet wine. Lynn stroked Reggie's head and the cat purred affectionately, sleepily from her lap. "Any idea what you're going to do, Vanny? With a job, I mean?"

Vanessa shrugged. "Either of you need a graphic designer?"

Nick grunted. From beside him, Lynn smacked his chest, spooking the cat. "Enough of that."

Rubbing the sting from his torso, Nick's levelled his eyes at Lynn as he rubbed the sting from his torso. "Come on, Lynnie, you know how I feel about this. Couldn't she get a real job? It's not something people do for their whole lives. Maybe when you're young, but not when you're sixty and looking at retirement. There's just no security in that."

"I'm right here," Vanessa glared at her father.

"I'm just saying."

"Well stop saying, Nick. She's got a degree and she's happy. Isn't that what matters? Anyway, there's plenty of opportunity here in Garrett."

Nick scowled. "Since when? We lost half our businesses with that virus shit, and I'm pretty goddamned sure no one here is going to need some fancy schmancy designer to sell them toilet paper."

Lynn chugged half her wine then shook her head. "Every single time, Nick. Every single time you get into this trash of yours. Not everyone wants to be an accountant or a doctor or lawyer, Nick. Some people are happy doing other things, even if it might not make as much money."

"Like construction?" Nick asked, tingling with a long-simmering burn. He put his glass down as his rage turned his stomach.

"Whatever makes us happy, Nick. Isn't that what we said when we got married?" Lynn said resentfully, letting her wine roll up, over, under her tongue and down her throat. "Whatever makes us happy."

"Us. Lynn. Us!" Nick shouted. He turned to Vanessa, annunciating with the waving of his arms. "See, Vanny, this is the problem if you don't get educated before you get married. One person gets the short end while the other follows their dreams, then when your turn comes around, well, sometimes it's too damn late for any more dream chasing."

Lynn stood, rocketing her glass at the wall to the right of Nick's head. The glass shattered, the rupture of brilliant crystal and red hemorrhage coming down against the grey siding like the house itself had been mortally stabbed. Reggie howled and scrambled back into the house. "Enough!" Lynn shrieked, venting the poison that simmered all these years and ripened alongside the virus. "You had your chance, Nick, just like me. But then you caved like you always do because it took work, Nick. You were happy being the doctor's husband because you had an excuse *not* to be anything else. 'Oh, she's too busy. We need to save up for tuition. When we get a little more ahead.' Bullshit, Nick! You could have gone into engineering any time you wanted but … that's the thing! You didn't want to work for it, Nick, so you blame me! Well I damn well won't be your excuse anymore." She tugged at the hem of her shirt, squaring her shoulders, and turned to Vanessa, who sat open-mouthed looking at both of them. "Sorry Vanny. But this has been a long time coming."

Vanessa drank. Her father shook his head, biting his lip as though to hold back a torrent, then he stomped toward his truck. He had just turned the key in the ignition when the door flung open. Nick stepped out onto the running board and said, "Fuck you, Lynn. Sorry Vanny, but fuck you, Lynn." Then he pealed out of the driveway and the only remaining arguments were from the crickets in the evening heat.

3

Her father didn't return. Now, several days later, with Reggie more at home and her mother starting to look more like the woman she remembered, Vanessa's old worry began anew. She recalled that before she left for university, there were many angry nights when her father had gone off with Steve Rikkes or Gus Steeger, sometimes cheap old Wally Gund, too drunk to be dragged home and too muddled to be talked straight. His fragile ego galvanized with alcohol, she often found him at Boomer's, the 24-hour diner in Old Town near City Hall, or losing to Tuck Gruber at the bowling alley that sat like a wart along the otherwise beautiful riverfront. Most often, though, Nick's ass would be planted on his favorite barstool beside both Steve and Gus at Shooters, the country bar under the bridge on the slimy side of the city. Back then they found him quickly, so this delay troubled Vanessa. Presently unpacking the last of her clothes, she heard a soft knock on her open door. Vanessa turned to see her mother with two steaming mugs of coffee in her hands. "Come in, come in," Vanessa pulled the empty boxes off her bed and Lynn sat, handing her the mug with her five-year-old handprint on it. "Cute," she grinned.

"How are you settling in, Vanny?" her mother asked, tucking her legs underneath her as she settled onto the bed. Her hair was always tied up at work but it was now down for the day and Vanessa was struck by how thin it had gotten.

Vanessa took a tentative sip from her mug. "Better now," she said. "I really don't have much to do. Everything is put away and Reggie doesn't need anything from me. I might just sit here and freeload and get fat," she laughed.

Her mother's eyes slipped over her lean arms and thin legs. "You could use another pound or two, hun, but enough of that. You can sit here and do nothing but gain a hundred pounds if you like, I'm happy to have you home, but you know it's not your style. You'd go crazy by the end of the week. Have you seen any of your old friends yet? Do they know you're home?"

Vanessa shrugged. "Not yet. I was going to call Stacy later."

"And that Briggs boy? The one who owns that car dealership?" Her mother eyed her naughtily.

"Owen?" she cringed. "He's a player, mom. Besides, that's not the kind of action I'm looking for. I need a job."

"You'll get to that later, I suppose. There's lots of time for that now that you're back. Speaking of which, I did some digging for you. Now, this is one of those times that your father is right, Vanny. There's just not much in the way of graphic design work around here. I'm not saying that won't change, but today it's just not the case." Vanessa opened her mouth to speak but her mother put a finger out to hush her. "Don't get me wrong; I'm really proud of you, and I'm glad you're happy. That said, I think there's plenty of work around here that can keep you busy until you find something you really enjoy."

"Like what?"

"Well, there's always my office, you know we could always use you at the computer since you're so good at that and, truthfully, Elaine isn't what she used to be. Between you and me, I think she's starting to lose it a bit; just the *idea* of technology scares her. She almost fainted during the last upgrade when she lost half our patient records and it took three hundred dollars and an IT tech to recover them. Anyway, I'm not offering, Vanny, because I don't think you'd be too happy being at my hip all the time. If you want to, it's yours but only if you really want to. Your father also mentioned he might have something for you, but I think you'd have a hell of a time trying to set those boys straight. Too many cocks in the henhouse if you ask me." She spread her free palm up placatingly. "Nothing against your father, of course. It's just … I don't think you'd be happy there. So," she let out a long woosh of air, "I did some digging and I think I have two good options for you."

Vanessa said, "Let's hear them."

Her mother blushed. "Well, now I don't think you're going to like the first one very much but I mentioned Owen because I was talking to his mother and she said that they were looking for an admin person, someone to run the books, maybe some filing. They'd also need you to answer phones, of course, but there could be an opportunity to do some advertising for them, too, mostly fliers like you were already doing in Toronto. That might be alright, no?"

"And the second one?"

"Do you remember Katherine Beecher?"

Vanessa thought. She vaguely remembered her mother spending a lot of time with one of the Beecher kids. "Sure. She worked in your office for years. Doesn't one of her kids have autism?"

Lynn nodded. "Grandkid. Tanya and Phil's middle one, Christopher. Sweet boy. Anyway, with this whole virus nonsense, we brought Katherine back for a while there to help. Her son Phil owns that newspaper, the Garrett Gazette, you know that old brown building on the hill across from that church? Well, she told me he's been looking for someone. Seems he lost a few people, too." Lynn looked away, the half moons of her eyes falling to the downy hide of the blanket at the foot of Vanessa's bed.

She wasn't about to tell her mother that newspapers were a thing of the past, that people didn't read them anymore, that by the time the paper was printed, there was newer news, and by the time the ink dried, there was breaking news, and by the time the papers landed on doorsteps and in mailboxes, they were yesterday's news, good only for kindling or the washing of windows. She couldn't tell her this. Not with her looking like that, crumbling like that. So Vanessa took Phil Beecher's number and set off to find a job and her father.

It was almost noon when Vanessa left the house, shedding her sweater before she was even two steps off the porch, the heat coming down in a fever on the brittle grass, the blistering sidewalk, the broiling pavement. Her car had been parked for days and now, when she opened the door, heat bloomed outward and into her face, the fog of days-old cat pee shrouding her skin like unwanted aerosol repellant. Coughing, Vanessa got into the car, turned the ignition, and immediately opened the windows. She pulled out of the driveway and sped down the block to ventilate the car, slowing only when she could breathe without gagging.

She turned left onto Hillsdale, swooped around Garrett's only traffic circle, and exited onto Mitton, where Garrett's wide lawns and fat houses gave way to the beige squats of strip malls and the grey wedges of mechanic shops, tire centers, gas stations, and parts stores. A left turn took her to Hachette's Car Wash, the glass cube between Blackstone Gas and Harper's Auto Repair, where she stopped at the end of a long line of cars. The air conditioning died once she cut the engine, but she was thankful for the slight, albeit warm breeze that carried the plume of ammonia out her passenger window and away from her face. Within seconds, she was sweating as the heat coiled through her hair, around her neck, down her back. The sun burned through her windows and stung her thighs, then it warmed her sandals and blistered her toes. She had just turned the car back on for another blast of cool air when a horn honked. She proceeded up the line and kept the engine running. Her mind was in the dim lit spaces where her father might be when another blast of an impatient horn dragged her off of her imaginary barstool and out of the bar. Vanessa returned and saw that the line hadn't moved, so she gestured to the driver behind her that she couldn't proceed no matter how much he wanted her to. Now, she the radio on and listened for anything that might once again remove her from the stagnant line and the stench crawling from her floor. Vanessa leaned back, resting her head against the doorframe as her radio captured the bing-bong beat of Billie Eilish's *Bad Guy*.

> *… on your tippy toes*
> *Creepin' around like no one knows*
> *Think you're so criminal*
> *Bruises on both my knees for you …*

It took her little time to mentally remove herself and soon she was settling into her own drink at her own bar when there was movement in her side mirror. The man behind her had exited his truck, his belted waist all that she could see as he quickly neared her car. Before she could react, the man knocked on her roof. "Excuse me, ma'am?" He lowered his head, bending over to speak to her, recoiling as Reggie's scent hit him.

Vanessa punched the radio off. "Oh! Sorry! My cat peed in here. It's terrible, I know."

"I—" the man started, stepping backward with one hand over his nose.

Embarrassment bloomed on her face. "I'll move up when I can. They're just so slow ahead of me. Sorry again."

He waved her apologies aside. "You've got something hanging out your hatch. I though you should know." He pointed at the back of Vanessa's car.

Turning around, Vanessa saw Curtis' sweater trapped in the trunk door. Deflating with the realization that she must have dragged the damn thing all the way from her parents' house, Vanessa collapsed against the steering wheel and lamented the strain that pushed too many times from too many directions. She bumped her forehead against the steering wheel. "I need more coffee," she said.

"One of those days, huh?" the guy laughed. He took his hand from his face and Vanessa was instantly struck with a feeling of familiarity, something about those white teeth and the way his eyes narrowed when he smiled, but she unable to immediately place him in the past periphery of her life.

He tilted his head, leaning toward her, squinting. "Vanessa?" he said. "I thought that was you! Man, I haven't seen you in years. It's Trevor," he grabbed his cap with both hands, fanning his elbows out, and she saw the entirety of his face for the first time, his eyes and mouth spreading wide. "Remember me?"

Of course she did. Trevor Williams, Alexander Mackenzie's vision board for teen impulse and adult nostalgia. Trevor Williams, athletic demigod and intellectual cardinal, owner of the world's greatest ego and Garrett's smallest conscience. *The smartest bully who never got caught,* as her mother always said, having had to mend his silent victims on several occasions. "Trevor?" Vanessa hooked an eyebrow up, hoping he didn't catch the disgust she felt.

"The one and only," he said, now removing his cap and slapping it against his knee. He dragged a hand through his flattened hair, smiling so wide Vanessa thought his teeth might just fall out of his mouth. An SUV behind Trevor's truck honked to let them know the line was moving again. Trevor held a finger up, signalling the driver to wait. "Say, since this line's going to be a while, why don't we just leave the keys inside and let them take care of it for us while we go grab a coffee. Sound okay to you?"

"I—" The driver honked again. "I have a few things to do." She rolled her car forward slowly, so that Trevor walked alongside her window as her car moved.

He was wringing his cap in his hands and Vanessa couldn't tell if this was an old spark of anger or something new, like apprehension. The way he blushed, she suspected it was the latter, until the horn blared again and he threw up his arms in frustration then moved his truck into her previous spot. Seconds later, he was back beside her door. "Come on, it's a beautiful day and we haven't seen each other in years. Just a coffee. You can throw it in my face if you want to, but just sit with me for a few minutes, please?"

She laughed. "Twist my arm, why don't you?"

They gave their keys to the wash attendant, an old friend of Trevor's family, paid, and began walking toward

Java, a small artisan coffee shop that roasted its own beans and sold specialty desserts and fresh juices. She tried not to look at him as they walked, fearing an unintended and severely delayed reaction to any of his old antics. Instead, she clenched her teeth and held her tongue and looked at the rhythm of her feet slapping the hot sidewalk which was annoyingly in line with the chuff of his sneakers as he walked beside her. "It's good to see you, Vanessa. You know, you're the first person I've seen since I've been back? Been here almost two weeks now but my dad has me so busy with the farm that I haven't really been out. It's a nice surprise." The wind had picked up, their shadows making strange, elongated spikes above flapping coils of darkness near their feet.

"I've been here since Wednesday," Vanessa said, pulling hair away from her face. "Seems like the car wash is the place to meet. You're the first person I've seen since I've been back, too."

"Yeah?" he looked at her.

"There will be more people coming home now, with the vaccine blitz. By this time next week, we'll probably have enough people for a high school reunion. At least that's what my dad says."

He cringed. "Not sure I'd go if we had a reunion. I was such a shit in high school I don't think anyone would want me there."

"I'm sure that's not true," she said, hoping he didn't catch the insincerity she felt, but she knew better than to tell him how many of her high school days were spent trying to avoid him.

"Liar," Trevor said, "but thank you." They crossed the street, pacing toward the trendy spots near the river, and hopped onto the sidewalk in front of Burt's Barbershop. Soon, they passed the organic produce market, the second-hand bookstore, and the kitchen supply boutique before taking chairs under Java's big green patio umbrellas. Enjoying the pleasant current of cool air sweeping over them from enormous overhead fans, they ordered iced lattes and cheese scones. Vanessa was watching a man across the street trying to coax a new puppy back onto a leash when Trevor said, "I'm glad you came, Vanessa. I can't tell you how hard I've tried to find you over the last few years. That night before we left for university …"

She shook her head. "We were drunk, Trevor."

"I know, I know," he said, putting his palms out apologetically. "But that doesn't excuse what happened after. I was an ass, Vanessa, and don't say I wasn't because I was. I know I was."

"You definitely were," she said, offering a slight smile to the waitress delivering their order.

Trevor nodded. "I was a jerk in school. To you. To everyone. Shallow like you wouldn't believe … or *would*. That last night, I was trying to make amends."

Color bloomed in Vanessa's cheeks as she picked at her scone. She said, "So you figured you'd give everyone an apology fuck?"

"That's not what it was, at least not with you. It was, I don't know, different. Those girls from Chartwell just tackled me and by then I was too drunk to do anything about it."

"You fought *so* hard."

"I blacked out, Vanessa. I still don't remember anything from that night. Only a few moments from when we were in Dunner's truck." He blushed and she looked away.

"Anyway, you probably won't believe it, but I'm not the person I was back then. Not even close."

She sipped her coffee while he fidgeted with a napkin. "What have you been doing since then?"

He shrugged. "My dad cut me off after my first year away. He was right, though. I was partying too much, my grades sucked. One of my profs told me I'd never have a career in geochemistry because it would bore me and that's why my grades were so bad. That part was my own fault, but he was right. I would have been bored. I did some soul-searching over the first summer then switched my major. Had to work three jobs to pay for tuition but it was worth it. I'm glad I did."

"What do you do now?"

"Aerospace engineer," he laughed when her eyes went wide. "It sounds cooler than it is. Really, it's just a lot of research and analysis but sometimes we get to build things and that's pretty neat." He was tapping his thumb against the table and bobbing a knee so that Vanessa could hear a faint squeak from his shoe. "What have you been up to?" he finally asked.

"Nothing as impressive as that. I was working as a graphic designer in Toronto, but they just let me go. Now I'm here."

"Me too," he said, draining his coffee. "Well, at least for a while. I'm furloughed for a few months while they figure things out, but I still have a job at least. I should be going back soon now the vaccine is out, but since I'm off I figured I'd come back and help my parents on the farm. Any idea what you're going to do?"

She sighed. "Not sure yet. I could work for my parents—in my mom's office or at my dad's work—but I think it would drive me crazy after a while. I'd like to do something on my own, you know? Apparently, Owen Briggs has something for me."

"That asshole?"

"I didn't say yes. In fact, it's the last place I'd work. I think my mom is trying to set us up, but he gives me the creeps." She cringed.

Trevor caught the movement and snorted. "When's the last time you saw him?"

She considered this. "Maybe five years ago, just before I bought my car. I went to his lot with my dad. He offered me a discount if I agreed to have dinner with him."

Trevor leaned forward. "Did you?"

"Let's just say I was taught that sometimes the lowest price doesn't mean the best price."

"Good decision," Trevor agreed. "So the dealership is out. Any other options?"

Their waitress came with the bill, which Trevor insisted on paying. Vanessa said, "I'm supposed to go to that paper, the Gazette. My mom knows the owner's mom and she said they were looking for help. It might be something to keep me busy while I'm here."

"Phil Beecher is the best," Trevor told her as they stood to leave. "You couldn't work for a nicer guy. My parents have been friends with the Beechers forever. His wife Tanya is my mom's best friend. They've had quite the rough go over the last few months; I'm sure they could use someone with your skillset."

They took to the sidewalk again, returning to the unprotected streets which reflected burning heat onto their exposed skin and singed the delicate coating on their eyes. By the time they were back at the car wash, both Trevor and Vanessa were sweating. They were exchanging phone numbers when one of the wash attendants called to Vanessa, "Nasty smell there, ma'am. We got most of it out, but the heat might stir things up a bit and make it worse. Might want to keep your windows open for a few days if you can." Little did Vanessa know, that wasn't the only nasty thing coming her way.

4

Red. That's all Phil Beecher could see. No matter how much he hacked and slashed, how often he quieted the desperate pleas of his creditors, or how he strategically manipulated the books—he was losing money. For fifty-one years, his family had owned the Garrett Gazette, the brainchild of his father, until it passed to Phil's own hands with Ray's unexpected death from that terrible fall nineteen long years ago. Barely a man himself, he wasn't ready for it, wasn't prepared for the dark mornings and darker nights, when pressure compressed his young days into thin slivers of progress and great bulks of failure. He hadn't had time to learn, to hear that sweet song his father called the 'hum', when the great orchestration of efficiency and creation wound into profit and pleasure and progress. No, with Ray's fall from that ladder, Phil had been shucked from his studies in literature at the University of Windsor and thrown into a business he wasn't prepared for nor wanted. Now, nineteen years later, Ray was on the verge of losing a business he had very much come to enjoy and depend on. The idea sickened him.

Tough times weren't new to Phil Beecher. He'd learned the hard way with the death of his father. Phil had been the one to find Ray at the bottom of that ladder with a coil of holiday lights still stuck in his bloody hands, the light frosting of new snow turned to pink slush on the driveway beneath his stiff body that cold November. That was bad enough for a kid of twenty-four. But his eyes. His father's goddamned eyes. Bugged out like veined golf balls, his father's eyes looked on the verge of falling out of his very head. His face had taken on a pale, liver-like sheen, through his blue lips peeked a bloated tongue, and a pale line tracked across his neck where the cord had caught him before the strain was too much and finally broke, sending his father two stories to the ground. His father had lay there, stiffening and bleeding out, halfway done his overzealous annual Christmas display, while Phil's mother shopped for presents, his eighteen-year old brother Rick got stoned at Tommy Guthrie's, and Phil himself was in Tanya Billings' dark basement trying to coax her panties off. That woman had become his wife.

His poor father. Too kind. Too smart. Too everything for this undeserving town, Ray Beecher observed Garrett with his newspaper, sparing no kindness to its people, no wrath to its adversaries. Garrett *was* Ray Beecher. The first man in church and the last man home from every city council meeting, food drive, community run or shelter benefit, his father was Garrett's voice, its legs, sometimes even its savior. It was his father who had pulled the first body out of that church fire. It was his father who gave CPR to Father Pauliuk's wife. It was his father who first saw the flames licking the church's blackening roof through the window of his office at the Gazette when Phil was twenty-one and Rick was just fifteen years old. Responsibly, Ray Beecher dialed his friend Kurt Noonan, Garrett's Fire Chief, and told him to get the hell down to Holy

Redeemer. Then Ray put out his cigarette and ran like the devil toward the church.

Phil opened his drawer, plucking the mickey he deployed for times like this, and set the bottle on his desk. Still half full, the bottle was as old as his father's gravestone. Normally, Phil preferred to do his drinking at home with Tanya or at Boomer's with Rick. Long ago, his father ingrained in him that drink was sometimes a reward, sometimes a bloody curse, and that there was no in-between. Like many things, this always stayed with him. When Ray was alive, he kept a bottle of Jack in his desk drawer, still full enough to get Phil blinding drunk the day after his funeral and Phil hadn't had more than three drinks from the replacement bottle in all the years since his father passed. Now, Phil emptied his water glass and poured himself two fingers of whiskey. He sipped the warm liquid and strode to the wall of framed articles and decorations behind his leather couch, letting his fingers rise and fall over his father's awards. He closed his eyes, reading from memory Ray's plaques, trophies, and medals. 1996 Canadian Journalism Foundation Award for Excellence in Journalism, Small Media — The Garrett Gazette. 1999 Canadian Journalism Foundation Award for News Literacy —— Ray Beecher. 1995 Garrett Citizen of the Year Award — Ray Beecher. 1992 Order of Ontario — Ray Beecher. 1989, 1993 & 1999 Ontario Volunteer Service Awards — Ray Beecher. 1998 Medal of Bravery — Ray Beecher. Phil thumbed the small glass case with the blue and red ribbon, opening his eyes to study again the maple insignia in the laurel wreath on the silver medallion, the medal that declared his father a hero. The medal that his father hated the most of all.

"Heroes keep people alive, Phil," his father had told him, sulking and half-drunk as he tossed the small box into the fruit bowl on the kitchen table that evening after the ceremony. "Two people dead don't make me anything but late. That Stu fellow, the curate, I still picture him, you know. It's a terrible fright, I tell you, to see a man with flames on his back, his hair gone up like kindling." He snapped his fingers. "I thought I'd been quick enough, but he just lay there, his body spitting fire and I knew he was dead then, Phil, I *knew,* but … instinct I guess." His father shrugged, letting his head hang. "He was so hot, like holding a campfire. His skin … his hair … he was long past saving, but I keep thinking the preacher's wife might have had a chance, you know? There was something there, Philly, there was *something* still in her when I opened those doors. When I heard her cry, so faint, it was like the whisper of the wind, the sound pollen being whisked away. It was there and then it was snuffed out. I can't describe it anyway but that, I know it's weird, but that's what it was, a *harvesting.* I felt it in my bones. Evil, Phil, it was evil and it wanted that woman dead. If I'd only come a few minutes earlier …" But Phil was glad his father was late. Something told him that had Ray been on time, he would have been harvested, too.

Phil drained his glass and said presently to the empty room, "I'm glad you weren't on time, Dad." Then Phil opened his laptop and considered how to save his father's business. After a time, the bell over the front door jangled, then he heard the click of Cynthia's heels against the laminate and knew his assistant was scraping her way toward his office.

She knocked lightly before poking her head through the gap she pushed open. "Phil, hun, there's someone here to see you." The doe-like blankness on her face told Phil that Cynthia had no idea who the someone was. She looked at the bottle still on Phil's desk, pressed her lips together in a sympathetic smile and said, "I can tell her to come back later if you want." She popped her gum, waiting.

"No, no. Send her in. Nothing I'm doing that will be solved in the next five minutes." While Cynthia lead the visitor to his office, Phil stowed the bottle back in his drawer, wondering if it would still be there for one of his own sons, after his own funeral.

"You just go on in here, hun," Cynthia said to a young woman, maybe no more than twenty, in what looked like beach wear, indicating to the chairs in front of Phil's desk. Behind the woman's back, Cynthia's eyes surveyed the young, lean body with distaste and wide, disapproving eyes. *Of course*, Phil thought. *She's almost sixty. She's forgotten what it's like to be young.* He grinned at the two women, asked Cynthia to bring them coffee, and shook the woman's hand before welcoming her to sit.

"What can I help you with, ma'am?" Phil asked curiously.

"It's Vanessa, actually," she said. "Penner. I believe your mother was a nurse in my mom's practice."

Phil's smile grew wide. "While I'll be! Lynn's daughter. You know your mom delivered all three of my kids? My wife Tanya just adores Lynn. All those knee scrapes and fevers, our middle son's autism, I think Tanya has her own seat in your mother's waiting room." He laughed. He could tell the girl wanted to say something but that maybe she didn't know how to say it. She looked uncomfortable.

"I'm sorry for coming in like this, Mr. Beecher—" she started.

"Please, call me Phil."

"Okay, Phil, it's just that my mom spoke to, Katherine, is it? Your mom?" Vanessa tugged at a hair elastic around her wrist.

"The very one," Phil said.

"I'm not sure but she said you might need some help. I know I don't have an interview or anything but—" Color spread on her face but she looked him in the eye as she spoke.

Cynthia entered with hot coffee and a plate of vanilla cookies, careful to offer Vanessa a large napkin to place over her lap. "For the crumbs, dear," she said with superiority. Phil shot Cynthia a look that Vanessa missed, still stirring sugar into her mug while the older woman quickly, gloomily departed.

Phil took a biscuit and dipped it in his coffee. "I'm not a cream and sugar guy but I haven't had lunch yet, please forgive me."

"Not at all," Vanessa said. "I'm the one who should apologize. I normally wouldn't dress like this in an office but it's so hot out there I think I'd just bake if I were wearing sleeves or pants. People are staying inside like the pandemic is happening all over again, just for the air conditioning, I've never seen it this hot before."

Phil nodded. "They're saying it's a fifty-year event. Not sure how many more of these rare events we can take." She didn't respond, both of them unsure of how much people actually *could* take. They had taken so much over the last two years; the heat wave was just the vomit on the dog-shit sundae, Phil reflected inwardly. "So, tell me about what you're looking for."

Vanessa straightened. "Well, I've been home for a few days now and I think I'm already starting to go half-mad without something to do. My mother suggested something at the Ford dealership, for the Briggs family, you know the one?" Phil nodded, his smile faltering slightly. "It's mostly menial work but I'd get to design ads sometimes so it's somewhat close to what I was doing in Toronto."

"And that is?"

"I designed flyers and ads for Saporelli's. Not the most creative work, but I liked it."

"The gourmet food chain?" Phil asked.

She nodded, sipping her milky white coffee. "We had seven locations until the virus hit. Four in metro Toronto, two in Mississauga and one in Oakville. We were going to open an eighth but then, well, you know."

Phil thought, pressing a finger to his lips, letting his chin perch on his thumb. The Gazette already had two designers. As Editor-In-Chief, Phil quite liked that Ronnie and Suzanne knew exactly what he was looking for without having to spell it out for them. They'd been with the Gazette going on twelve years for Ronnie and nearly nine for Suzanne and Phil didn't like that he could barely afford to pay them now as it was, let alone adding a new employee to the mix. He thought of his copy editors, both contract and so easier to upend, but he didn't believe the girl would be happy with such a role. She'd mentioned that she liked creative work, much like Phil himself, and copy editing wasn't a mecca for creative endeavor. He briefly considered replacing Cynthia, thought of his scratched floors and all the missed calls with her extended lunches and smoke breaks, then remembered that his father hired her all those years ago. She was as much a part of the Gazette as his own father had been. A giant pain in the ass, no doubt, but Cynthia was the *Gazette's* pain in the ass. Phil looked to his father's wall again, wondering. "Ever thought of being a writer?" he asked.

Vanessa blinked. "A writer?"

"One word in front of another sort of thing. After a while, you get enough for a sentence, then a paragraph, and before you know it you've got a story in there. I've been down two writers for the last eight months."

"I—I don't think I'd be any good," she stammered, wiping the sweat off her forehead.

"Ever put words on paper?"

"I took a creative writing class in university, but it was just for fun—"

"Good enough for me," Phil said. "My graphic designers don't just make things pretty, you understand, they make thinks work, they solve puzzles, they compress a whole lot of information and inputs from all directions and sharpen it until it shines. Just like you would have done with your design work, I suppose."

"Well, I—"

"Would be working with one of my best writers, that would be Amy, as well as one of the worst, that would be me," he chuckled.

"I mean, it's not that I haven't—"

"Anything better to do?"

Vanessa set down her coffee. She shook her head. "It's not that at all, Mr. Beecher—sorry, Phil—it's that I don't think I would be any good, and I haven't lived in Garrett for years, I'm not that familiar with the city as I used to be. Practically a stranger now," she trailed off.

Phil leaned forward and slapped his desk. "That's exactly why I want you. A fresh set of eyes can give us a new perspective, a new lens to look through. Something different from what we're used to. I think it's exactly what we need after everything that's happened, all the crap we've had tossed at us." Phil could feel his pulse thrumming now, hard and fast, the way it did whenever he was onto something. Yes. Yes. Something new. Something different. Bold. A new story to follow.

Vanessa twisted her fingers in her lap, considering. "What would you want me to write about? I can't promise I'd be any good."

"And I can't pay you a lot, not even full-time work but if this works out, we might even figure a way to keep you." The last part wasn't exactly true, Phil knew, because he had no idea if the Gazette would survive past the summer, but he would try, dammit, he would try. "I'm not sure how familiar you are with the paper, but we generally focus on local stories, business, sports, feel good stuff. We try to stay away from negative press, not that we don't have it, not at all, it's just that, well, my father's philosophy was to always tell the truth and don't embellish for the sake of shock. We've more or less stuck with that and people seem to like it around here."

Vanessa nodded. "My parents read the Gazette every day, online though."

"There used to be a time when folks couldn't get enough of the paper, they'd be raging against us if their daily paper appeared even a minute after the crack of dawn, God forbid. Now, they expect news every five minutes so they're not away from their phones. World's most expensive drug."

"Most addictive, too," Vanessa agreed.

"What a world," Phil leaned back in his chair, crossing an ankle over his knee, and tapped his kneecap thoughtfully. "So, this leads us back to what you can do for us. I've been doing some thinking about a project that predates your time by many years. Goes back twenty-two years."

"I'm twenty-seven," she said, with no hint of offense.

"Well then, maybe you know something of it. Most everyone around here does. Tell me, what do you know of the church across the street?" He swivelled his chair around to look out the window, tipping his head at the tall grass where the grey stump of Holy Redeemer's campanile once rung its holy bell to summon Garrett's devoted. To its right, there was a great show of nature reclaiming itself with wild crab apple trees sprouting from blown-out windows and cottonwoods shedding the last of their seeds through the charred floor of the open vestibule. Somehow the old building still stood. A resistant frame with broken skin. The scorched face with its crippled front porch. The crumbled pulpit where once raised the resonant voice of young Father Pauliuk, beyond which today a collapsed backside lay tumbled and rotting into the soil.

Vanessa craned her neck to see past Phil, where she, too, looked out the window. She shifted in her seat then said, "When I was growing up everyone thought it was haunted. My cousin once dared me to touch it, just touch it, but I couldn't do it. I was too afraid. Probably silly, but I was young. And the way kids talked, well, it gave me nightmares for years. Didn't actually know anything about it, but the stories ..." she shook involuntarily, smoothing her hands over her bare legs.

He looked back to Vanessa now. "My father wouldn't let me or my brother go anywhere near it. I was already a man when it happened, twenty-one, and my brother Rick was not far behind. Fifteen. Still, we knew not to touch it. My dad said it was not right. Unholy. At first, I thought it was because he'd been the one to take those two bodies out. But over the years things just didn't seem right with that site. They rebuilt Holy Redeemer not two-hundred meters away on the other side of that field," he turned and needlessly pointed toward the current church, its wide narthex and brick bell tower peeking from the far periphery of the church ground. "And it's fine. Nothing wrong with it. Tanya and I were married there. Our kids were baptised there. I think I know every inch of that church, daises to Jesus, faucets to stained glass. No problems at all. But the old church …"

"I've heard of kids trying to have seances there and one time a girl went missing."

Phil gritted his teeth, recalling the story about the girl from Mitton who went missing for over a week. He'd featured the story on the front page of the Gazette over a decade ago and could still recall the relief he felt when one of the parishioners found the girl as he was mowing the church lawn. Phil said, "That was an overdose. They found her unconscious in the bushes behind the fence, more track marks on her arms than there are stars. She said she went there looking for God or the devil, but I think she found a bit of both. She's a librarian now."

"Why don't they knock that building down?" Vanessa asked. "It can't be safe to have it up like that."

Phil pursed his lips, remembering the debate, how hotly he had insisted the death trap be dismantled, even offering to take John Hebner's dozer and do it himself until Ada Tilbury and Frances Gosmer, vinegary church ladies from before even his father's time, shrieked that the old building must stay. They had been baptised there, *their* parents had been baptised there, and if it wasn't down already then God *wanted* it to stay, and bad things happened when you went against God's will. Phil didn't believe it was God's will. A religious man, Phil *did* feel that God's role was inseparable from man's, but he did not believe that God wanted such a temptation to be left around for children to cavort in or for the city to be reminded of one of its greatest horrors. No. Phil believed the fire was an act of evil against the Creator, against Donna Pauliuk and Stu Kline and his own father. He was definitely for demolition, campaigning for it until the bitter end, but had been voted down by no small margin. He said, "The church refuses to tear it down, saying it's a testament to God's will, that He works in mysterious ways and had it not been for the fire, the new building—which fits more parishioners, mind you—wouldn't exist. The parish council forbid its demolition exactly for this reason. The fire brought more believers together and while I *do* think that's a good thing, I think the reasons for keeping it now are misguided. You see that fence there? I wouldn't exactly call it as secure as Fort Knox. The opposite, if anything. You might as well put up a sign that says 'free candy', for all the traffic I see sometimes."

"Kids," Vanessa said, as though it had been decades since her own youth.

Phil sighed. "Anyway, it's more than a bunch of kids trying to scare each other. Sometimes … now I know this is going to sound completely insane, but I swear I've seen someone inside there at night. Alone. Just standing there."

Vanessa shuddered. "You want me to do a story on the church?" Garrett was in the middle of a record heatwave, but she had suddenly gone cold.

"My father believed there was something to it, that fire, but nothing ever came from the investigation, you know. They interviewed every member of the church, one hundred and twenty-one people, and nothing. Tried looking into it myself, mind you I was just a kid and could barely pump gas let alone figure out how that fire happened or who did it. Now," he patted his waist and looked up, "I'm wider and balder and maybe just a bit smarter. That's where you come in. A fresh set of eyes. Not too familiar. I'm wondering if you can find whatever it is that we've been missing."

"But the police—"

Phil held up a reassuring palm. "Tom Widlow will let you see the reports. They've released more information as they've received it, hoping to solve the case, but nothing's worked yet. We've had a few local sleuths who've investigated it, trying to be the first to uncover the mystery and all, but no one's really gotten anywhere. Lord knows we haven't tried."

Vanessa was silent for a time and Phil was convinced he must have terrified the girl. "My parents talked about the old church when you printed those memorials back then."

"Still have them every year. I was figuring that maybe we could run your piece on the anniversary, three weeks from now on the twenty-fifth. You're welcome to write about anything else you can dream up, of course, but this the big one, if you understand me. Maybe you write something that spurs a memory. We'll never know unless we try, right?" There was a lapse of silence when Phil finally said, "If this is not for you, there's always the Briggs gig."

Vanessa looked at his sideways smile and bit her lip. "When do I start?"

5

"Unit Thirty-One this is Unit Thirty-Three. What's your twenty? Over."

The radio crackled with the hypnotic drum of activity Tom Widlow had grown to love over the last twenty-seven years. "Seventeenth and Old Town," Tom responded. "10-24, over." Tom waited while Dan Fogel answered his request. His radio beeped, indicating that the communication between Tom and Dan's cruisers was now private.

"You at Boomer's?" Fogel's voice trilled over the radio, loud and high-strung, like the sergeant was in real-life.

"Thirty-seconds from the parking lot. Want to join?" The invitation was habit. How many times had Tom and Dan drunk too much coffee and ate too much pie in their corner booth at Boomer's? Tom figured if it weren't for their business, Boomer's wouldn't have been able to hire the extra cook or the skeletal cashier, Bonnie, who doted on them like Tom and Dan were God's gift to the city. If it weren't for Tom and Dan and the rest of the department's preference for scuffed floors and worn vinyl chairs and the uninhibited view of their eggs spitting on the grill behind the counter or their hot coffee sloshing into their favorite cups, well, Boomer's would have become another fatality of modernism. It was the grit that made Boomer's special and that was simply something that couldn't be washed away or made new. Tom needed that nostalgia today, more than ever. On any other day, the company of his best sergeant would have thrilled him. But today Tom needed nothing but the feeling of his favorite seat, hot black coffee, and a slice of cherry pie, enjoyed alone.

"Negative," Dan said. "Up to my ears in paperwork today. Got to get back and take care of that *adminsturbation* shit you keep piling on me."

Tom cringed. That word again. "Is it really so bad?"

"Keeps me from important things like convincing Billy Hart's wife to change the sheets." Fogel roared with laughter so long Tom envisioned splashes in his eyes.

"Can you repeat?"

Fogel's words rushed from the radio. "Stiles and Hinshaw's call. Billy wouldn't let them in unless I was there." Tom pulled his cruiser into Boomer's narrow parking lot, waiting. It was a rare weekend when the department wasn't summoned to the Hart residence. A childhood friend of Dan Fogel, Billy Hart had once been decent. He had good grades and was once a respectable athlete, participating alongside Dan in every football game and track and field meet, and was the only player present for every hockey game ten years straight. Those years, Billy had promise. Then late puberty came crushing down on him like a slab of cement. Billy developed moods that Dan didn't much like and a terrible drug habit that Dan couldn't handle. Time simply widened the distance between them, elevating Dan into the police service and dropping Billy inside the parasitic maw of addiction.

Tom shut his eyes, squeezing the bridge of his nose. "What is it this time?"

"Dispatch was Tomlinson's. Something about screaming from their house. Stiles and Hinshaw were already in the area so they took it but, Tom, I tell you they could barely speak when I got there. Last night I guess Billy'd been with Gus Steeger at Shooters, drunker than hell, so bad that Randy was scared to throw him out, thinking Billy might come after him, you know how it is. Well, Randy convinced Gus to take Billy home. No one in their right mind would pick those drunk assholes up so they took a short-cut through Clay Elliot's manure field and wouldn't that asshole go marching through his house without taking his shoes off. I swear his wife must have been on something because she didn't notice it until she woke up with Billy yelling at her to clean it up and then she went nuts. Christ have mercy, the *smell*, Tom," Fogel's breath came out with great heaves of laughter.

"I can only imagine," Tom shook his head, thankful for his own distance from Billy and Misty Hart. "Look, I just got to Boomer's. Want me to pick you up a coffee or something?"

"Get me something green. A salad, maybe."

Tom waited for the punchline, but Dan remained silent. "Who are you trying to impress?"

"Brandy's been on me again."

"Enough said." Tom turned off the ignition, promising Fogel the best salad Boomer's could make, the bagged garden special, and ended their transmission. *Anything to keep the wife happy*, Tom thought, and then recalled how he had left Irene in tears just minutes before.

His wife of thirty years had never looked so sad. Her usually smooth face was puffy and streaked, having cried her makeup away in a great wash of tears, relinquishing the bursts from her nose and mouth down Tom's chest, his shirt, his tie. Those green eyes, his favorite eyes in the world, now red and lined. Irene's pupils dilated wide to take him in, all in, where she could hold him and he might stay forever. They lingered like that for an hour, Irene desperately clutching him, Tom sentinel, trying to find the right words.

But there were no right words. There were only wrong words. And they were written there on paper for both of them to see: *Stage 4 Small Cell Lung Cancer*. His family doctor for as long as Tom had been a police officer, Greg Huxley's eyes were as wet as Irene's when he first told the two of them. Stooped shoulders and fidgeting hands were abnormalities for the confident physician but when Tom took his seat in Huxley's office yesterday, Tom could *feel* the man's regret. This is when he knew. The hard conversation and the sobering letter were just formalities.

Tom settled into his favorite booth and ordered coffee and cherry pie, reflecting how terribly his stubbornness sealed his death warrant. Hadn't Irene nagged him to quit smoking? Hadn't he suspected something was funny those months ago when his chest began to hurt like he had inhaled needles, his back stinging as though scissors were tearing him up every time he took a deep breath? World news told him it might be Covid-19, but that was back when everything from a hangnail to diarrhea implied a Covid-19 infection. Once, Tom even *hoped* for it because he knew the infection was something he could survive. But the fever never came. What came instead was the wheezing, his lungs whistling like a spring draft through an old window. This itself wasn't necessarily strange, however. Like Tom, many an officer gained enough spare tires to mount a semi, so a bit of wheezing down the station's halls wasn't alarming. Also, unlike what he knew of typical cancer patients, Tom didn't appear to have lost weight. He would have heartily welcomed the warning, of course, but he now understood that what he lost in fat was retained in water. So there was no senile panic, no morbid concern, no restless anxiety. There was only the pain and then the cough and that first bloody Kleenex two weeks ago.

Back then, he hadn't the heart to tell Irene. Not until he knew. But Irene was more perceptive than any of his officers; she could sniff out a lie, and so she grilled him relentlessly. By the time she finally wrestled it out of him, Greg Huxley had Tom's diagnosis: Lungs. Spleen. Liver. Kidneys. All with lethal inmates.

"Refill, hun?" his usual waitress, Nina, asked. Tom nodded while Nina overfilled his cup, apologizing as she plucked a handful of napkins from the dispenser and mopped up the mess.

"Thanks," Tom said.

"You alright, hun? You don't look so good." She backed away slightly, like people always did if they suspected a Covid infection, even after the vaccine blitz.

Tom cleared his throat. "Allergies and diabetes catching up, I suppose. You got to stop bringing me all those sweets, Nina. Only salads from now on, you hear?" She laughed, having heard it before. He added, "Doctor's trying to put me on a diet, damn stick-in-the-mud."

She smacked his arm playfully. "Aww, now, Tom. You know he's just trying to keep you around longer. We just can't do without our Police Chief."

"You want my job, Nina? It's yours if you want it."

"No thanks. I put up with enough shit as it is," she smirked.

"Ain't that the truth," Tom said. Nina floated away toward her other tables which were filled with diners, distanced for so long but now happily sardined with company. Picking the last few crumbs off his plate, Tom watched them, when the bell above Boomer's front entrance clanged and a harried-looking Phil Beecher scrambled in. Tom raised his palm. "Phil!"

Phil put up a finger in a *just a moment* gesture. He went to the counter and spoke to Bonnie, giving her a fistful of cash before making his way to Tom's table, his arm outstretched. "Tom," he said, shaking Tom's hand. "Good to see you. How are things?"

"Can't complain, as you can see by my waistline," Tom chuckled.

"You're not the only one," Phil patted his stomach. "That quarantine business did a number on my closet. Every one of my belts have shrunk."

"Mine too, but that was about twenty years ago. Think the virus was around back then?"

Phil grinned wide. "Let's say it was." The men laughed. Tom motioned to the opposite seat, indicating that Phil was welcome to join him. Phil sat on the edge of the bench and said, "Maybe just a minute. I was on dinner duty today and plain forgot about it. I got to run home once our food's up or the kids are going to start eating the dog. Glad I caught you, though. I have a favor to ask."

Tom's eyebrows knitted upward. "What's that? Another speeding ticket? You got to slow down when you're getting off Mitton, Phil." Tom watched as Phil's face twisted in disgust at the idea of visiting Garrett's worst area, where a handful of spindly women in wisps of dirty clothing stumbled into back seats and out of consciousness alongside dozens of emaciated, delirious men with spotted faces and broken teeth. "Don't mean to spoil your dinner."

Phil snorted. "Too late."

From across the diner, Bonnie called out, "Two minutes, Phil."

"That's my cue. Anyway, Tom, I'm glad I got you. I've been thinking of a new project. Well, it's not really new, actually, but I've hired a reporter and I'd like to have her eyes on the Redeemer file you've got." He held up his palms before Tom could protest. "Just what you've already shared publicly, of course. I'll give her what I know of it, but I was thinking that maybe she could sit down with you, get the official story and all."

Tom sipped his coffee, now cold. "*Another* memorial story?"

"Something like that. You know, with the way the world turned upside down over the last while, I think people are ready for something different. Get them thinking about something else for once."

"Like a story you've already told a hundred times? One hundred and one going to make any difference?" Tom questioned, though both he and Phil knew Tom would do whatever he could if it meant closing the Redeemer file. Information sharing with the city's only newspaper wasn't exactly unusual. Tom and Phil had exchanged intelligence perhaps thousands of times over the years. Small-time robberies, an infinite chain of assaults, the roving whereabouts of Garrett's greedy pushers, the ubiquitous missteps of an entire city. The Redeemer case, however, gave Tom an ache so deep he wasn't sure it would be wise to revisit it now, given his diagnosis.

"Look, it's not just the memorial. My dad …" Phil started.

"Was a great man," Tom said solemnly. Ray Beecher had been a good friend to Tom. Ray had even been at Tom and Irene's wedding. Where many law enforcement relationships with media were fraught with challenges, Tom was immediately taken with Ray's sincerity and compassionate ideology and he was grateful their professional reciprocity passed along through Phil.

"He was," Phil agreed. "And I know he would want me to figure this out, Tom, to find the real story. Damn, the last year's been hard on everyone, makes a man think more than he needs to, you know? I was holed up with Tanya and the kids so long and all I could think about was if I got the virus and died, who would find out what happened? Who would do it? Tanya keeps telling me to let it go, says it's not good for my health to fret over something this long but I can't help it, Tom. All I'm asking is for one last shot. Maybe she'll see something we didn't."

"And just who is this new reporter of yours? A writer friend of Amy's?" Tom asked.

Phil shook his head. "Vanessa Penner."

Tom screwed up his face, retrieving from memory Irene's graduating lists and the faces of the kids she instructed at Garrett High. He knew the name, of course. Lynn Penner was a respected pediatrician and Tom had collaborated with Lynn on Garrett's drug and alcohol awareness programs for adolescents many times. Lynn was simply a jewel in the community. Tom also knew of her husband, Nick, though just from the rough company the man kept.

"Class of 2011? Lynn's daughter?" Phil nodded. "I thought she's in Toronto."

Phil shrugged. "Came back."

"And a graphic designer." Tom glanced to where Bonnie was waving two large brown paper bags at him. He tipped his chin to Phil who looked toward his dinner in the cashier's hands.

"Not anymore. Don't think I don't know it might be an exercise in futility, Tom. Sure I do. But just talk to the girl for me, please. That's all I'm asking."

Tom said, "Have her drop by the station on Monday." Phil thanked him, took his food, and left. When Nina returned, Tom ordered a chicken Caesar salad to go and settled his bill. Then he walked to his cruiser, trying to figure out which gave him more heartache: dying of cancer or reopening the Redeemer file. Irene would be livid, he knew, because just like Phil's wife, Irene hated the times when he worked that case, mining for a resource that just wasn't there, not sleeping, not eating, almost as dangerous to his health as if he *was* in the airless underground with miles of overhead rock threatening to crush him and leave him pummelled in the dark. With the diagnosis, Irene begged him to submit his resignation and that was something Tom just couldn't do, hence today's fresh batch of tears. If he continued working *and* reopened the file, well now, he believed his wife might just end up beside him in the graveyard.

But …

But how many nights had that God-forsaken case kept Tom awake? The answer seemed infinite. Was it better to worry about dying or worry about dying knowing his beloved city had a murderer on the loose? That's what it was, what it had always been, even if Tom had no way of proving it. He was no stranger to fire fatalities. Garrett had seven others in the years since Tom joined the force: one faulty plug, two incidents of arson by scorned lovers, and three misplaced cigarettes. In all, three children and four adults had died, not including Donna Pauliuk, or Stu Kline in the Redeemer fire. They were citizens of the cloth, a preacher's wife, and a curate, but it wasn't their posts that troubled Tom. It was that in all the fires in all the years, these two were the only victims who had been locked in. From the outside.

6

"They are returning, Lord," Father Robert Pauliuk spoke as he prepared his sermon. Alone in his office, alone but for the great company of the Almighty, Father Pauliuk beseeched his Father for the right words, that they may make His broken church whole and unite Garrett's children of God once again as they returned from their far places. He'd known they would return, of course. Once the commercial clutches of the world cracked into a lattice-work of layoffs and loss, with death striking households like firstborns in Egypt those many years ago, Father Pauliuk, through the grace of the Lord, knew the disbanded citizens of Garrett would return. As the pandemic raged on, he extolled the love of the Lord, His patience, and His mercy and His purpose, charging his parishioners to lean on the strength of the Lord for their physical and spiritual survival. Now, these months later as post-pandemic life began and sons and daughters restored themselves in the city, Father Pauliuk had a new message for his repatriated congregants: *Return to the Lord*. He decided that he would begin with Hosea 6:1: *Come, let us return to the Lord. For He has torn us, but He will heal us; He has wounded us, but He will bandage us.* With their attention, he will then cite Nehemiah 1:9: *But if you return to Me and keep My commandments and do them, though those of you who have been scattered were in the most remote part of the heavens, I will gather them from there and will bring them to the place where I have chosen to cause My name to dwell.* And before he releases his faithful, he will remind them once again of God's unerring mercy with Joel 2:13: *And rend your heart and not your garments. Now return to the Lord your God, For He is gracious and compassionate, slow to anger, abounding in lovingkindness and relenting of evil.* The last part was important. Sending them away with hope, Father Pauliuk believed that they were more likely to *want* to return if he showed them a merciful God, a forgiving God that not only welcomed them back but implored them to come, come with all their flaws and faults and misdeeds, which could only be cleansed by the Lord. He would remind his congregation how, in these times, our sanitized world would only flourish once again if we kept it that way. And so, we must be good houseguests to the Lord if we want to retain the sanctity of His house. Let your return honor the Lord, Father Pauliuk will say.

He put his pen down, rubbed the pinch in his wrist, and removed his glasses to wipe the mist from his eyes as was his habit when he worked with the Lord. Then he stretched his back, feeling the strain of many years and many hardships rise toward those sealed surfaces of his skin and of his mind that resisted release. A ball hitting the outside wall brought him back and he hastily scooted from his chair to the window to see a group of children playing soccer on the parched lawn; six boys and three girls from the youth ministry, using splayed bicycles as goalposts, a set of which Robert could see directly below his office window. He released the catch to open the screen door and was immediately caught with an oven-hot plume of air. He quickly closed it again and found his way to the lower kitchen in the basement where it was still cool. Robert opened the freezer, counted ten popsicles, and pocketed a pair of scissors before progressing in full to the day's fever. Seeing the rainbow of treats in the good Father's hands, the children ran toward him, abandoning their game. "Who's winning?" he asked.

"We are!" Gordie McRay, a thin, shirtless boy panted. "Eleven to four. Thanks Father." He accepted a grape popsicle and sucked at it noisily.

"Gordie's cheatin'," said a red-cheeked girl. Robert couldn't quite place her name. One of the Sleuter children, he knew, but there were five girls in the family and Robert always had trouble remembering which *A* was which: *Alice, Ava, Alix, Alexandra,* or *Avery.* He guessed the indignant girl was the latter, but he preferred not to attempt it.

"Did not!" Gordie cried. "I can't help it if you don't have a goalie."

The girl that could be Avery licked her lips. "It's not fair if you start kickin' the ball before we're on the field."

"Then get on the field so I don't score," he stuck his tongue out at the girl, reddening even more when Robert cleared his throat. The boy said, "Sorry Father," and looked away, popsicle dripping from his mouth.

Robert unwrapped his own popsicle now, savouring the chill on his tongue while the rest of him broiled beneath his clothes. He looked at them looking at him, the way they always appeared uncomfortable when he wasn't in cloth, like there simply couldn't be a regular person beneath his vestments but some alien they couldn't quite figure out, his collar both a beacon for their curiosity and ingrained respect. Their hot faces, blotched from game and impending burns, worried him. "How long have you been out here?"

Three little ones shrugged in answer. Another boy, Tim Lackowski, said, "We came out after the treasure hunt. Paisley said we could go." He swiped his forehead with the hand holding his popsicle and a trickle of neon orange fell onto his nose. The boy swiped it away with his other hand then rubbed the mess onto his shorts.

Robert frowned. The maddening heat was no place for anyone, let alone children in his ministry's care. He said, "You kids look redder than tomatoes. Go on inside now and tell Paisley to start the movie so you can finish it before your parents pick you up. It's cool in there." He watched them collect their bicycles and set them in the stands beside the rear entrance, cheering when the church's air conditioning wrapped itself around them, welcoming them like Jesus. Robert stood, finishing his treat, watching the warblers and the flycatchers and the sparrows swoop and crest, darting through trees between outcroppings of elephant grass and wildflowers. He listened to their songs, a canorous salve for his tired mind. They liberated his tension with their throaty crescendos and staccato soliloquies, and Robert breathed the warm air while he untied his shoes, pulled off his socks, and placed his bare feet upon God's carpet.

Robert wiggled his toes, settling in past the dry prickle of the lawn until he felt the good rub of God's soil. Just then, a bird pierced his peace with a cackling intrusion somewhere off to his left. He squinted through the sunlight and caught two crows fighting over something at the far end of the field near the old church. He put his hand to his forehead to block the sun and watched the birds pluck with their sharp beaks at something too buried in the grass for Robert to make out. When the fighting went too long, Robert gingerly padded barefoot past the rear of the church and the coupling of picnic tables that sat beneath the salmon-colored dogwood blooms, toward the fenced enclosure of his former parish, wondering what sort of rubbish the local adolescents could have gifted to the parish lawn this time. The ominous area near the old church was a collecting ground for the grey-brown nubs of cigarettes or joints, used condoms and all sorts of dirty plastic. Just as often, Robert would find the casings of unpopular school lunches: wrapped sandwiches, things with raisins, the dreaded handful of raw broccoli or something ethnic and, Robert was sure, was once quite edible, if not delicious.

Hearing him come, the birds drew back, holding a short distance to their meal until Robert waved his arms to shoo them away. Closer now, he knelt down and surveyed the stretch the crows had guarded. What he saw made him catch his breath. There, in the sun-baked embers of the field, the bloody, chunky residue of an eyeball swelling with an accumulation of flies. He turned his head and retched, his once very welcome cool summer treat now a slimy expulsion near his feet. Robert crossed himself, closing his eyes to the evil fright, and turned inward to God. He stayed like this, safe with his Father for a few moments, until he was soothed and collected enough to investigate. He held his nose and leaned in, quickly identifying that it was not human. Larger than a ping bong ball but smaller than a baseball, Robert believed the eye to be that of a cow, maybe even one of the llamas from Roy Botcher's farm near the fairground. He noted with disgust that the crows had been pulling on one end at the ocular nerve and, on the other, right in the middle of the cornea. He stood, clenching his fists not in anger but in frustration at the adolescent trick, then he tilted his head skyward. "Please forgive me, Father," Robert said and blew out a long breath as he looked toward the cauterized stub of his former parish.

How lovely the former Holy Redeemer had been. Robert fondly recalled its wide pearl sandstone porch, the flat ivory envelope of the nave, and the dark stone arch of the chancel vaulted toward heaven in a brilliant kaleidoscope of stained glass with a mighty assembly of saints and angels alongside Mother Mary and the saviour Jesus Christ. An endowment from Cecil and Emily Brooks, long-retired venture capitalists from Garrett, had enabled Robert's predecessor Father Johnathan Borst to oversee Holy Redeemer's path from conception to completion, with a much younger Robert eventually stumbling around as one of Father Borst's altar servers for almost seven years and then later as his curate for the better part of four years. When Borst retired, Robert was only thirty-three and though he felt had not yet matured in his canonical competencies, Robert dutifully accepted Bishop O'Driscoll's appointment of Holy Redeemer's pastoral care. He knew the parish, he knew its parishioners, all of whom welcomed him and Donna enthusiastically and without pause. There had never been a regret on either side and all these years later, Robert's pastoral existence gave him nothing but gratitude. His personal province, on the other hand, imparted a heartache so deep he felt the shred in his soul.

God had always been Robert's first love but Donna held that part of inward part of him that was inseparable from his manhood, that part that made him first appreciate her beauty and then allow himself to unburden his very real and very human desires by taking her as his wife. He was surprised that with their union, he found himself better able to serve God and, thus, those in his pastoral charge. How better to extol the virtues of Godliness in a marital union than with the model of his own? He and Donna had understood that their marriage was the providence of God and so endeavoured to represent its sanctity on Sunday mornings, in which their relationship was often the relatable example in his homilies. With their laughter and the way they would straighten their slouched bodies, he also knew that his congregants loved these talks and, with Donna's encouragement, Robert loved giving them. As human relationships go, Robert couldn't have asked for a better partner, he only wished that they had been blessed with children. But whether they would have had one child or five, he would never know. He only knew that Donna had gone to God before they could find out.

Robert would always remember Donna on that last day. They met in the vestry as he attended to the first leaks in the church roof. Heavy rain had fallen for the better part of a week and though Holy Redeemer was solidly built, it was nearly forty years old by that time and the building was beginning to show its age. Despite the scuff of considerable traffic, the floor was still intact and the windows had yet to accumulate condensation or cracks, so it took that relentless downpour for Robert to really register the building's antiquity. He had gone to fetch his robes for the morning's service, only to find them dripping, the spare box of hymnbooks beside them leaking from the inside and spilling onto the carpet. He had been on his knees inspecting the damage to the floor when Donna came up behind him.

"Oh Robert!" she had said with that birdsong voice of hers. "Your robes! The books! The floor!" He turned to see her hands over her mouth, her usually rosy skin ashen and still wet from the morning's rain.

"I suppose it was only a matter of time," he said. "We've had many good years in these walls, it was only natural for it to start weeping eventually. Oh well. Better a good cry than a drowning, don't you think?" And then Donna did something he hadn't expected. A great splashing of tears swept her eyes and a low, guttural sob erupted from her throat. He realized then that her face hadn't been wet with rain but that his wife had been crying. He stood and went to her, his wet vestments in one hand, a damp piece of baseboard in the other. He put his arms around her and soon water was coming off her shoulders in quick aortic pulses as she wept into him. "Oh, come now, dear, it's only a leak, not even a big one. I bet we can get this fixed up and it'll be good as new. You know that Gil Elias won't charge us but a penny. Few shingles and some plywood won't cost much." But Donna didn't stop crying when he said this. Sure, Holy Redeemer's finances were tight but with his Business Administrator Ed Norman's watchful eye and the careful management of the Finance Committee, Holy Redeemer was by no means in financial distress. Donna knew this and so her reaction puzzled him.

"Robert—" she started and then her face was lost again in his chest. He swung his arms toward a chair and emptied his hands onto its seat, now taking Donna fully into him as he wrapped himself around her.

He kissed her head, inhaling the soft smells of cucumber and mint from her favorite shampoo, and let his fingers smooth her autumn hair. "What's wrong Donnie?" he called her by his pet name for her, hoping to calm her but she trembled in his arms. How small she felt then, her thin frame almost disappearing in his hold, even the waif-like mewls from her mouth sounding like that of a kitten.

She sniffed and cleared her throat, looking him full in the face, her green eyes blazing emeralds of grief. "Robert, I—" and then the half-closed door swung open and Ed Norman appeared in a mess of water and soaking drywall and pink insulation.

"Narthex is leaking, Father. I was posting the newsletter when I heard a pop and she just came down on top of me."

Robert squeezed Donna's arms and turned toward Ed while she composed herself. "Are you hurt?"

"Thank the Lord, no, just mighty wet. Lucky for us it's not a big opening yet. I figure if we get Gil in here, we might be able to save it. But we'll have to cancel the service, we just can't chance it. Rain's still coming down and the roof is sagging pretty good there in some areas." Ed brushed at the insulation on his jacket and shook away the white bits stuck in his grey hair.

Robert breathed deeply while he collected his thoughts, then he said, "Let' reschedule the service today. Hun, can you reach out and let everyone know what happened and that we'll gather at the house later today?" Donna nodded. "Ed, get Gil over here as fast as he can manage, and maybe Roger or Wayne. They might be able to help. I'm going to see if there's anything else about to come down." Ed dashed away.

Robert turned back to Donna, who was now more composed, her cheeks regaining their healthy peach. He softly squared her in front of him at arm's length, kneading her shoulders and tilting his head to invite her to speak. "I'm sorry, hun, please, what's bothering you?"

"Robert, the church—"

"Will be fine, Donna. Our foundation is Christ, not the building, remember?"

She nodded, giving him a weak smile as she cited the scripture he proselytized every time their own small home had a leak or cracked window or broken appliance. "Ephesians two, nineteen and twenty: '*you are fellow citizens with the saints and members of the household of God, built on the foundation of the apostles and prophets, Christ Jesus himself being the cornerstone.*'"

"Amen," Robert said and then Ed was back in the room.

"Gil's on his way over with Wayne. Roger said he'll pick up some plywood and shingles before he comes, but he's waiting for them to let him know if there's anything else he needs to bring. Roger also insists on paying for it, Father. He went on about those months you visited Ruth in hospice and said Ruth would have wanted him to."

"God bless him," Robert said, remembering the one time he had almost succumbed to tears himself while he performed the Holy Unction by anointing Ruth's forehead with oil as she lay, thin as smoke, in her bed at St. John's. Roger, a former boxer and Combat Engineer in the army, had seized the key ring where the consecrated chrism on Robert's hand waited to be anointed. Stunned, Robert pulled his hand away and tightened the lid of the oil stock. Roger reached out again, pulling at Robert's hands as though the initiation of the sacrament was the very thing that would kill Ruth, instead of committing her to the Blessing of God. Then Roger's hands were quivering, and his body was trembling with volcanic eruptions of agony, moaning to such a pitch that a nurse asked him to settle. Robert took the man's hand and prayed with him, then they prayed together over Ruth's departing body as Robert finally initiated the sacrament. Roger had been subdued ever since, quickly at Robert's hip whenever help was needed. The Lord worked in mysterious ways, Robert reflected.

"I need you in the kitchen," Ed now said. "We've also got some water near the freezer, but I can't tell if there's a leak or Mary's defrosting it again. Still plugged in so I'm not too sure." He scratched his head.

Donna straightened, flattening her wrinkled skirt. "You go. We'll talk later, okay?" Then Robert kissed his wife for the last time.

He touched his lips the way he always did when he remembered that moment before the day pulled him in too many directions. Robert hooked his fingers onto the chain link fence that kept trespassers away from his former parish, feeling like a bit of an interloper himself. The old building held more mystery to Robert than it ever held clarity. God was the answer to all, but Robert felt the fire was the provenance of the devil, and there were no answers with that one, only pain and suffering. He rested his arms over the fence, letting them hang, feeling the jut of the steel fabric deep in his armpits, and looked into the blackened corridors where he once served his congregation. The aisle he and Donna had walked on their wedding day was the same aisle Ray Beecher barrelled down with Donna, unconscious, over his shoulder.

Robert had arrived that night just as Ray was setting his burning wife down, her scorched body making a sizzling sound as it hit the damp grass. Donna's long auburn hair singed to crisp bristles, her back blistering through her nightdress and the exposed dark muscle of her right calf forced Robert out of himself, out of time and space and then he was falling, falling into a blackness that enveloped him so thoroughly and so quickly, Robert hadn't had time to seek God before he hit the ground. He was covered in vomit when he awoke a short time later, and by then Ray Beecher was on his knees beside him, coughing violently. "I tried, Father," Ray barked through the smoke and the ash. "I goddamn tried." And then a flash of medical attendants were on Ray, forcing oxygen into him, wiring him up and strapping him down and then whisking him away. Before they got to Robert, he had lain watching the dried remains of his still wife, who was not yet covered, and noted that the peach was gone from her cheeks.

He sunk into himself, eroding inward with grief until Tom Widlow sat him down and asked Robert if he knew of anyone, anyone at all, who might have wished harm to Donna or Stu Kline, his quiet curate. Robert flinched first at the ridiculousness of the question and then at the suggestion that the fire had not been an accident at all. When Tom related that Ray Beecher had first pulled the long handle of a shovel from the brass loops on Holy Redeemer's double front doors before entering the burning church, Robert got sick in Tom's office. He knew of no one who would harm another human being, let alone his kind wife and good curate, in such a manner. The idea set Robert into such an emotional collapse, he'd quietly been prescribed sedatives. In the weeks that followed, Tom Widlow aimed his attention at Robert and Donna's teary conversation in the vestry, pushing Robert for every detail, from the pitch of her voice to the direction of her gaze to the fidget of her fingers. There had been no argument, Robert insisted, but there had been something she wanted to tell him. This had been verified by Ed Norman, Tom reluctantly revealed to Robert.

"Just doing my job," Tom said apologetically, a touch of color on his face. Robert understood Tom's position but what he couldn't understand was what Tom Widlow and his team found through a search of his house—a positive pregnancy test.

7

It was Monday morning before Vanessa's father returned home. She had just slid into her shoes for her meeting at the police station when she heard his truck pull into the driveway. He had turned the ignition off and Vanessa waited for him to come inside but he sat there, heatwave and all, alone in his vehicle for many minutes, seeming to stare at the closed garage in front of him. Worried, she went outside. The click of the screen door closing behind her seemed to finally convince her father to exit his truck. When he lifted his face, Vanessa was horrified to see a nasty cut beneath his eye, something that might even require stitches. "Dad!" she gasped as she went to him.

Nick's hands immediately went up. "It's okay, Vanny. Looks worse than it is."

She hovered over him, fretting like an anxious bird. "Did you get it checked? It looks like it might need stitches. What happened?"

Nick hugged her and went to the porch, where they sat shoulder to shoulder on the highest step. He sighed, "Your father is an idiot, Vanny. That's what happened. I shouldn't have left like that the other night. You didn't need to see it and I wasn't thinking straight, Vanny. No, don't make excuses for me. I had no right to react like I did. Your mother's right. I could have gone and went to school any time I wanted. Hell, I could open a bloody theme park and your mother would have supported me, I know that. It's just sometimes I see your mother and the way everyone in this goddam town exalts her like she's the next coming of Christ and I—I don't know. I'm so damn proud of her, Vanny. But being the idiot that I am, I suppose I'm a little jealous of my own wife. How's that for stupid?" He tightened his lips, raising his eyebrows. "And I guess there's a part of me that feels not quite good enough. Some days are better than others but with the pandemic and all those kids she saved, I feel like an asshole for saying it, but I seem be having a lot more of those bad days."

She said nothing about his revelation as it was nothing new. Vanessa had known of her father's feelings for a long time. She had felt the downdraft of his inadequacy since she was a child. Temper. Argument. Great flings of insult filling the house like swarms of insects. Her father's devices only served to deepen the imbalance between her parents, and Vanessa was keenly aware that *she* had been the reason they stayed together. However much she preferred their union as a child, their misguided intention nauseated her as an adult, and she vowed she would never do the same. Sitting here with her father, however, it occurred to her with palatable disgust that she *had* done the same thing with Curtis and that had she married the spaghetti-tossing child, she would have endured the same marital discomfort her mother had. This was not to say that she didn't love her father. She loved her father very much. His spousal deficiency did not parlay into parental deficiency, so she adored him with that near blind adoration most children had for their parents.

Near blind but still able to see. She nudged her father's knee. "Tell me how the idiot got his face smashed in."

Her father dragged his hands through his hair then plucked a cigarette from his pocket. "Don't tell your mother," he said, and whether it was about the cigarette or about how he had gotten himself cut up, Vanessa didn't know but he eventually went on. "Well, I guess this is what happens when you try to do the right thing, Vanny. We were down at Shooter's having a few, maybe more than a few I suppose, when Randy asked us to leave. That went fine until Steve tried to get into his truck. He hit me when I took his keys away." He rubbed his face and took a long drag on his cigarette. "But you should have seen *his* face," he finished slyly.

"Barfight Dad? Really?" she tugged at the hem of her skirt.

"Sorry Vanny. Old dog and all that. And where are you off to dressed up like that?"

She stood, fiddling with her car keys. "I got a job."

He brightened. "Really? You talked to Owen?"

She soured. "Didn't even try. I'm going to try writing for the Gazette."

"You're not a writer, Vanny," he inhaled, holding the smoke inside. When he finally let it out in a slow, controlled seep, he said, "No offence, kiddo. It's just that your degree is in art, isn't it? I heard you could design something for the dealership, their ads or some shit like that."

Color flushed into her face. "I'm going to try some other shit this time." She popped off the stairs and started toward her car.

"Vanny! Vanny, I'm sorry. I'm an idiot, remember? Nothing I say is worth listening to. I'm proud of you, I really am. Please don't go off like that."

"I'm going to the police station. I don't want to be late." She threw open her door, cringing when her legs touched the smouldering leather of her seats.

Her father got to his feet, a hint of concern on his face. "What business do you have at the station, Vanny? You get a ticket already? Is there trouble, Vanny?"

She started the car and unrolled her window, poking her head outside. "I have a bar fight to report."

"Oh Vanny, don't be like that. C'mon. What are you going there for?"

"Remember that church fire?"

Nick dropped his cigarette. "You're writing about *that*?" He wiped his mouth and stuck his hands on his hips.

"It's nothing, Dad," she said. "The anniversary is coming up and they just want to see what I can dig up. Maybe nothing, for all I know, but I'm going to try. And then I have to write a story about it. They probably won't even print the crap I write but at least I won't have Owen breathing over my shoulder or trying to get in my pants. I'm interviewing Chief Widlow in twenty minutes, so I've got to go." As she pulled out of the driveway, Vanessa saw her father kicking up grass on the front lawn.

Once again, Vanessa took Hillsdale, this time turning left on Central. She crossed the bridge and was struck by the level of the river. The banks expanded dryly upward, exposing typically submerged tree roots. The rocky shallows, once marinated with slick ecosystems of biofilm, now dried and as powdery as a blanket of dead moths. New islands topped the river like heaps of sand and, on the other side of the bridge near City Hall, an old cluster of discarded shopping carts popped from the water near a graffiti-clad abutment. *Every city has its warts,* as her grandfather would say.

She rolled past Garrett's municipal center, where the red brick and pale limestone facades of the main library, community services building and City Hall functioned as historic bookends to the vibrant palettes of produce stands and watercolor kiosks and exotic oil and vinegar booths. Vanessa slowed, watching the discordant scurry of children and saunter of adults, and noticed a newly erected splash park at the end of the block. Half-naked infants and bare-ankled mothers negotiated unpredictable squirts while larger children joyously drenched their shirts and shorts in coveted torrents of water then maniacally chased their dry guardians, who wanted nothing of their embraces. Past this, Vanessa navigated through a throng of sandal-clad jaywalkers with reusable bags slung over their shoulders marching toward the outdoor pavilion. Three blocks down, she entered the parking lot beside the station, rolled up her windows and exited her car, notebook in hand.

Vanessa wasn't two steps into the building when she heard, "Ms. Penner!" Tom Widlow issued a large hand from behind the front counter, which Vanessa shook warmly.

"Want me to take your cup?" Tom asked the seated officer beside him.

"Go on, Tom. I got this," the officer responded, taking Tom's coffee mug, and holding both their empty cups in one hand. "Thanks for the chat." She smiled comfortably at Tom, then scooted to the half-door that lead into the inner office, pressing a button and opening it for Vanessa.

Vanessa thanked her and followed Tom through a maze of cubicles to a large office set along the perimeter of the building, where Tom gestured to a pair of chairs in front of his desk. "Have a seat," he said.

She sat, putting her purse on the floor. "How did you know it was me?"

"You're the spitting image of your mother," Tom smiled as he took his own seat behind his desk. "I've worked with her off and on for many years and I thought you were your mother when you first walked in. Strong genes in your family." He coughed and when she backed away slightly, he knocked his chest with a closed fist. "Strong genes in mine too. My grandfather was a smoker. My father was a smoker. Can't tell you how much I wish that proclivity skipped a generation."

Vanessa relaxed. "My dad caught me smoking when I was fourteen. I was with two of my friends down by the river and he happened to be driving by on his way home from work. It was our first cigarette. We wanted to see what the fuss was about, so we made a pact to try it together. He stopped to pick up something from that butcher shop behind the pool hall and heard us hacking like we were dying." Vanessa crossed her legs, exhaling with the unpleasant memory of her father's punishment. "He made me smoke the rest of the pack in front of my friends, to teach me a lesson. Didn't make it past another cigarette before I threw up, but he wouldn't let me stop."

Tom frowned. "Sounds like a terrible experience."

"Well, I never smoked again, so there's that."

"Want him arrested?" Tom gave her a crooked smile.

She laughed. "I think I'm over it, but there is an ex-boyfriend who might need a talking-to."

"Say the word and I'll have someone on it."

They lingered in their new companionship like old friends while Vanessa explained Phil Beecher's assignment. "To tell the truth, I'm really not the right person for the job. I've never really written anything beyond my creative writing class at the U of T, and even with the work I was doing before the pandemic, the only words I had to put together were basic. Granny Smith apples, ninety-nine cents a pound. Two percent milk, gallon, three-eighty-nine. Nothing I did after university was especially creative or required more than a few words."

Tom removed his glasses, pointing the tips of his earpieces at her. "That's probably why Phil wanted you. Let me tell you a story. We had a rather nasty hit and run a few years back. A mother and a small boy were walking home from a birthday party out near Craig's Valley, you know that skiff of land between the fairgrounds and the treatment plant, over near those apartment blocks?" Vanessa nodded. "Well, a car jumped the curb and hit the two of them then ended up in the patio of one of the first-level corner units. Somehow the driver managed to get his car back out and onto the road before we arrived. It was near dark so we couldn't get a good description. Both of the mother and her son survived, thank God, but neither of them could tell us anything helpful about the car, and the old lady in the apartment could only say that she thought the front of the car looked like it had one of those old radiators for a nose, but thinner. Not much help, right? We were stumped. We had a team of specialists from London investigate and, I tell you, they were just as lost as we were with this one. We must have showed that woman two hundred cars, all makes and models, but nothing clicked. It was maybe ten months later during the Canada Day parade when half-way through, there were a bunch of classic cars riding through and I got to talking to the guy next to me. He was one those die-hard enthusiast types, living for those A&W show-and-tell meet ups and Sunday drives where they show-off their cars. It was nothing at all, but I figured I'd ask the guy about the radiator-nose and guess what?"

Vanessa slapped Tom's desk. "No way!"

"Uh-huh. 1970 Mercury Cougar Eliminator. He'd given me a few other suggestions but when I showed the old lady a picture of the car, she knew it right away. Rare enough of a car that there was only one registered in the city. The driver could have come from elsewhere, but we didn't think so, so we pulled his record, and wouldn't you know that the guy had two DUIs and was waiting for a court appearance on a third. His other car had been impounded but he had his Cougar wrapped up in his garage, until the day he hit that woman and her boy. It took a while, but he got the justice he deserved, which brings me back to my main point. You better believe we've had our best people working on that church case. Our own detachment, specialists from London to New Brunswick, consultants out in BC, techs from Alberta, even a handful from the US had their eyes on it. Kurt Noonan, our Fire Chief, must have had a dozen departments from across the continent look into that fire, but we're no closer to figuring it out. Hell, sometimes I think we're digging backwards with this thing. Anyway, my point is that sometimes you need another point of view and, who knows, maybe you're the one who finds out what the goddam radiator nose is attached to."

She breathed heavily, opening her notebook. "No pressure …"

"Phil knows better than anyone how important perspective is. The guy runs a paper for a living. If he thinks you can do this, Vanessa, I think you should give it a shot. There's nothing to lose and I'll help you as much as I'm able. Unlike court records, much of what we have is not public. I can show you most of the physical evidence, go over the time frame and all that, but as for our conversations with individuals, well, I have to let you know that's not for public accord."

"Because no one has been charged." Vanessa said, her face squished with consideration.

"You've done some reading, I see," Tom set his glasses on his desk and sat back into the familiar shape of his chair.

"It's all everyone talked about when I was little," she said. "And I like to do my homework. I went through so many of Phil's old papers yesterday that my hands were black. I had to wash them five times just to see my fingernails." She stretched the strain from her shoulders, then rubbed the back of her neck, the tension not from poor posture but from the terrible things she had read. In the late evening of August 25, 1998, Ray Beecher attended to an alarm at the newspaper. He arrived at approximately 11:22 p.m. and found the large picture window behind his chair shattered, a pool of rain rapidly spreading from the new opening downward onto his floor and toward the cables beneath his desk. A sizeable rock lay half-inside his Dell computer monitor. Stressed, Ray lit a cigarette, quickly working to protect what was left of his workstation. He hadn't seen the smoke rising from the Anglican church until he turned back toward the window. Ray immediately dialed his long-time friend, fire chief Kurt Noonan, and told him to get down to Holy Redeemer. When asked why he didn't call 911, Ray Beecher said that since it was near midnight, he didn't believe anyone would have been in the church and that Kurt *was* the fire department, for heaven's sake.

Call made, Ray then rushed out the door and across the street, bolting over Holy Redeemer's saturated lawn and then using his jacket against the hot handle of the front entrance. Ray quickly identified the unconscious body of Donna Pauliuk and lifted her up. By this time, Father Robert Pauliuk had seen the flames from his own home across the green and came running, arriving at the church just as Ray Beecher was carrying his wife out, when sirens could be heard in the distance. Ray left Donna with her husband and went back into the inferno, looking for any other occupants. For several minutes, Ray went deeper into the church, calling out to anyone who might hear. When he couldn't see more than an arm's length ahead, Ray was about to give up when his foot hit Stu Kline's calf. Ray Beecher hauled the heavy man over his shoulder and was met by a fireman half-way to the door. The fireman, later identified 28-year-old volunteer firefighter Ben Sibley, would go on to report that, "When I first saw Mr. Beecher, flames behind him, I thought a ghost was coming at me. Then when I saw Mr. Kline over his shoulder, I realized Beecher wasn't a ghost—he was a warhorse." Of course, Ray Beecher's efforts, from which he himself nearly died from smoke inhalation, were all for naught, as both Donna Pauliuk and Stu Kline were beyond saving by the time Ray arrived. Still, articles in the Gazette as well as others in the London Free Press, the Sarnia Observer, the Windsor Star, the Toronto Sun, and those in papers as far as Vancouver, Saskatoon and even Yellowknife, rightly posited the tragedy as horrific but feverishly extolled Ray Beecher as a hero, two minutes delayed. Many papers morbidly impressed the idea that had Ray not pull the bodies out when he did, Donna Pauliuk and Stu Kline may have only been identifiable by their dental records, and this was affirmed by mortician Karl Wobbler, of the Blundy & Ashurst Funeral Home. "We were fortunate that Mr. Beecher recovered Mrs. Pauliuk and Mr. Kline when he did," he was quoted as saying. In the early days following the fire, with the city in a frenetic panic and its citizens now outraged firebrands of justice, then mayor Joseph Stelleran held a press-conference, vowing full support for the investigation and swift and unrelenting punishment for any responsible party, should investigators determine a cause of arson. "Can I ask you a question?" Vanessa presently said.

"Shoot," Tom replied.

"Why weren't they able to determine the cause of the fire?"

"Well, I'm no fire chief but I can tell you what I'm sure Kurt Noonan would tell you. Investigators won't identify a cause unless they can confirm without a doubt what the cause is. Sometimes, as when accelerants are present in a location where they shouldn't be, say, gas in a library or baby's nursery, then they may make that judgement, providing the evidence supports it. But if there is any doubt—any at all—they simply won't do it, legal ramifications and all. You read that the fire started near the altar?" Vanessa nodded. "And would you say it's possible to assume someone forgot to douse the prayer candles at the end of the day?"

"They didn't have a service that day. It was raining and…"

"And did you know that they found water in an electrical panel and resorted to lighting candles to help them see so they could make repairs?"

"No, but—"

"But what?" Tom pressed.

Vanessa flushed. "But why would they go to the church in the middle of the night?"

Tom leaned forward on his elbows. "Are you suggesting Mrs. Pauliuk and Mr. Kline of something improper?"

"Didn't you?" Vanessa frowned. "You must have. You …" and then she understood. Tom had thought of that, had likely homed in on the possibility of infidelity from the start.

"Rubbed that preacher raw, I'm afraid. Clean as a whistle, as godly as a saint. He hadn't known Donna was out of the house until the sirens woke him up. He assumed she was in bed with him but when he woke, he realized that he was alone. He called her name and did a quick search of the house then went to check to see if she was on the patio outside. He said Donna went there sometimes to pray when she was stressed. The church sustained some pretty significant water damage that day so he figured she must be talking to God outside."

"But she wasn't there."

"No," Tom sighed. "But he saw the flames coming out of his church and put it all together."

"Do you think there was something going on between Stu and Donna?"

Tom shrugged. "That's always our first thought, wrong or right, but I don't think so in this case. First, Stu was a large man. That don't mean he didn't deserve love, by all means, but I don't think a woman as thin as a sparrow would go prancing about with a man likely to need a seat-belt extender on an airplane. Second, Stu was quite a bit older than Donna."

"Almost thirty years," Vanessa agreed. "So why were they in the church?"

"That's the question now isn't it? Father Pauliuk believes his wife might have gone to talk to the curate about the church finances. My understanding is that things were tight for the church. No payment delinquencies or anything but tight to the point they had to have ultimate discipline with water and power usage, discount supplies and all that."

Vanessa read that Stu Kline had been a member of the church finance committee but that the committee itself was headed by a man named Ed Norman. She said, "But Stu didn't run the committee."

Tom shook his head. "No, that would have been their administrator, Ed Norman. Your thoughts align with mine that way. Wouldn't it have made more sense for Donna to talk to Ed Norman rather than Stu Kline if she wanted to discuss the church's finances? Perhaps, but we believe that Donna Pauliuk didn't want to disturb Ed. They'd had terrible trouble with the roof leaking and he was in the rain most of the day trying to help patch it up. Father Pauliuk said that Ed didn't look so good by dinner time and sent him home. By then, Ed had been outside for maybe eight hours. The man had early onset diabetes, type 2, so his condition worried the Father."

Vanessa uncrossed her legs, feeling a tingling sensation that her right leg had gone to sleep. She rubbed it, thinking. "Do you really think she went to talk about finances at eleven thirty at night?"

Tom pressed his lips together, feeling that old curiosity bubbling inside. "I don't know. My guess is no, but that's not on record anywhere. Earlier in the day Donna had gone to her husband, upset about something, but the roof started leaking before she could tell the Father. He was convinced she was worrying over the church's money troubles but at the time, he didn't know she was pregnant." Tom let that bomb do its work as he watched Vanessa's eyes go wide, wider, her hands drawing to her mouth in disbelief, an airless gasp caught in her throat. She grew so still, he thought for a moment the girl might faint, then he said softly, "We found a positive pregnancy test during a search of the house. Three of them, actually, like she really wanted to be sure."

"They were Donna's?" Vanessa asked.

"None other. We ran a DNA analysis, but we knew it wouldn't come back with anything but a positive match on Donna."

"I'm going to hell for asking this but," she hesitated, "was the baby his?"

"I don't know about your Bible, but in mine, God doesn't demand you believe a preacher's wife. Maybe there's an eleventh commandment I missed." He smiled. "But I know what you mean. They were both people of the cloth and some of the best citizens this city has ever seen. That said, while I'd like to believe Mrs. Pauliuk only had eyes for her husband, I can't confirm or deny she didn't. We have no reason to suspect she strayed, but stranger things have happened. The thing is, they had been trying for some time to conceive. Two or three years. They'd even talked about fertility treatment or adoption, but only in conversation, nothing committed enough to book an appointment. We believe she was about seven or eight weeks pregnant and before you ask, yes, we considered DNA analysis on the fetus, but Father Pauliuk wouldn't hear of it. We could have pushed but our techs but didn't believe they'd get much from it anyway. Her body was badly burned and she wasn't far enough along in her pregnancy for accurate testing. Am I scaring you?" He gestured to her hands.

Vanessa looked down and realized she'd been clutching the arms of her chair so tight that her fingernails had gone white. She released her grip. "I'm sorry, no. It's just a surprise. I didn't read about a baby."

"There was no baby to read about," Tom said. "Out of respect for Father Pauliuk, we kept that part pretty silent. Releasing that kind of information would likely have put a mighty dark cloud over the Father and we had no evidence to suspect he was tied to that fire in any way. In any other city, we might have had issues with the local snoops, but Ray Beecher put most of it to bed before it could spread. When the only paper in town isn't reporting on it, well it doesn't sound like news worth spreading, am I right?'

"But the rumours ..." she started, unsure of how to finish, if she even wanted to finish. As usual, the rumors were more terrible than the facts, but if they were true, God, if they were true—

"Like Donna and Stu had tried burning down the church for insurance money?" Tom opened his fingers as if to express that his appreciation that Vanessa was open to all possibilities, dark and horrid as they could be. "While it would have put a tidy close on the case, we don't see any truth in that. As I mentioned, Holy Redeemer might have been struggling but it was far from underwater, pardon the comparison. Plus, the church had quite a few patrons that were well off and willing to toss a few bucks to the church whenever needed. The church did get a small settlement, but it wasn't enough to cover a complete rebuild. They had to fundraise for a long time to get the second building built."

Vanessa had heard tales of a potential insurance scam, but she had grown up in the church. She knew of no one that had any bad or even questionable memories of either Donna or Stu and couldn't reconcile their impressions with the gossip or flings of doubt she overheard. She bit her lip. "There was another one, though. Something worse. I remember adults talking about it when I was little, and when I was a teenager kids would scare each other and tell the story at sleepovers and at their lockers and around campfires. It's ridiculous, but I remember it scared me so much that I wouldn't shut the door when I went to the bathroom or took a shower, I was so scared someone was going to lock me in and keep me there. Even in malls or restaurants, you wouldn't find me shutting the door. I had to know I could escape if I wanted to. I peed in public for quite a few years," she laughed uncomfortably. "My dad went nuts over that." Tom seemed to stiffen, then steepled his fingers in front of his mouth, resting his chin on the pads of his thumbs. Vanessa watched him as he seemed to turn something over in his head, his face suddenly swabbed with a great coat of solemnity. He remained silent. "But it's a rumour, right?" When he didn't immediately answer, she said, "Tell me I'm crazy. There's no way…" but Vanessa couldn't finish. That terrible rumour couldn't be true. It simply couldn't.

"The doors weren't chained and, no, there wasn't a mob of atheists trapping them inside. We had an unfortunate uptick in hate crimes due to that particular ditty, I'm sad to report. Those have died down some over the years, but every once in a while, we still get some hot-headed zealot trying to run an agnostic off the road. I used to think Garrett was above all that. We never had a hate crime, not a single one, until that fire. Sometimes I think it would have been better if we'd caught Donna cheating, however much it would have broken the preacher's heart."

Vanessa steadied herself then asked, "*Were* the doors locked?"

"The old church had one of those rounded-top double-doors you'd see in quiet little paintings and scenic fieldscapes, the kind people like to use as wedding picture backdrops. Something straight out of Europe. You probably saw it in the papers you were reading." Vanessa nodded, then Tom went on, slowing his explanation as though every word projected spikes that caught and tore at him. "When Ray arrived, a shovel handle was pushed through the loops of the door knockers and he had to pull it out to get into the building. Donna had been scratching the door from the inside…I'm sorry, should I stop?"

Vanessa swallowed. "Could I get a glass of water?"

Tom nodded. "Of course." He picked up his phone, requesting coffee and water for both of them. A tall man in a shirt and tie brought a tray of refreshments in and Tom waited for the door to close before he continued. "Better?"

Vanessa gulped her water down, then poured herself a half a cup of coffee from the decanter. "Much better. Sorry about that."

Tom raised his palms. "No need at all. My reaction was the same as yours. It still disturbs the stomach, even now."

"What I don't understand is why they didn't go out any of the windows? I know the fire started near the back, which would explain why they went for the front, but there were several windows they could have jumped through. It just doesn't make sense."

Tom tipped his head in agreement. "Stu got the worst of it. Our best guess is that he was unconscious before the flames got him. Him being close to sixty, he wasn't exactly a teenager anymore, if you get me. Thankfully, he died from smoke inhalation, as terrible as it is to say it. And as for Donna, well, your guess is as good as mine. Four windows on either side of the aisle, but she didn't go for any of them. Why not? I would think that she could have jumped through any one of those glass saints and God would have forgiven her."

"Why wasn't that reported?"

Tom shrugged. "Same reason as for the pregnancy test, but also because we thought it might cause more harm than good. We didn't want it to rile anyone up. People were already uneasy over the situation and we didn't want to agitate them anymore. You've seen what the pandemic has done to some people; just a little nudge and they go from reasonable to needing straight-jackets."

Vanessa finished her coffee, taking care to write everything in her notebook. After a time, she said, "I don't even know where to begin. It's all too much."

"Start—" Tom began, then a high whistling cough flew from his mouth. Vanessa turned her head while Tom wheezed and chortled and snorted his breath back into him. When he saw the concern on her face, he said, "Survived the damn virus to get hit with my own stupidity."

Again, she relaxed. "You had Covid-19?"

Tom nodded, coughing into a tissue which he quickly pocketed. "My wife and I were the first ones in the area to get it. We didn't get it as bad as others. If anything, my smoker's lungs make that virus look like the hiccups." He took a long drink of water and said, "As I was saying, you can't start anywhere but at the beginning. You wouldn't open a book and start reading halfway through, would you?"

Vanessa shook her head. "Of course not."

"Then start by talking to the people who might know something about it. The preacher. Ray Beecher's long passed but his wife and sons might know a thing or two. Ed Norman has been in Southbridge for a few years but I'm sure you could call the home and they'd let you see him now they've lifted visiting restrictions. Kurt Noonan is retired but he's one hell of a guy and I'm sure he'd talk with you. The firefighter that found Ray and Stu in the church is gone, I'm afraid."

Vanessa raised her eyebrows, remembering what she had read of Ben Sibley. "He would have only been in his early fifties."

"Uh-huh. But his lungs were as bad as mine by the time the virus got him. He was one of the last ones to go around here."

"Strange times," Vanessa said, and closed her notebook.

8

Rain fell in the early hours of the morning, bringing a shock of cool air and a burst of deafening thunderclaps that shook the windows and lit up the lawn, terrorizing Reggie until he urinated on Vanessa's bed. She would have to get his incontinence checked with a veterinarian but seeing the clock beside her bed radiating 4:17 a.m., it would have to wait. In the meantime, she struggled out of her wet and smelly sheets and found one of her empty moving boxes in the closet. She laid one of her old sweaters at the bottom and carefully put the trembling cat inside. Then Vanessa stripped the sheets off her bed, scrubbed what she could in the half-light of her bedside lamp, and set a wet towel over where Reggie released himself to soak up any areas she might have missed. By the time she was finished, the rain had slowed to a much more pleasant drizzle and the sun had already begun pushing its way through the departing clouds. She wrung out another wet towel and used it to clean Reggie, to which he angrily meowled and pawed at her, and Vanessa received a sizeable scratch that would need tending. Curtis would have thrown Reggie out in the rain had the cat done the same to him, but Vanessa was not her ex-boyfriend. If she were a cat, Vanessa thought her reaction to the storm might be the very same and so instead of tossing Reggie outside, she dropped a few of his favorite treats into the box. Soon, Reggie was purring and Vanessa reluctantly understood that, whether she liked it or not, the day had started and, more importantly, that coffee was definitely in order.

She went to the kitchen, scooped fresh coffee into one of the single-serving baskets her parents used, and watched while the life-affirming hot liquid filled her mug. It was almost finished brewing when she heard shuffling from down the hall. A moment later, her mother appeared, showered, dressed, and perfectly ready for another day of tending babies and saving lives. "Can't sleep hun?" Her mother asked, squeezing Vanessa's shoulders, and smelling the top of her head the way she always did since Vanessa was a child.

"Reggie went crazy from the storm," she said.

"That cat. He's sure been through a lot, poor thing. I thought he was doing better lately."

Vanessa sighed and tucked her messy hair behind her ears. "He was, he *is*, but did you hear the thunder?"

"Baby, there's no one that didn't hear it. God knows we needed it, though. Hasn't been this dry since I was your age." She removed a coffee mug from the cabinet. "Want to make me a cup while I fry us some bacon?" Vanessa prepared a latte and sliced oranges while her mother dropped strips of bacon into the frying pan. They ate, laughing when Reggie appeared, enthusiastically rubbing against their legs. Vanessa deposited some bacon in front of him, and they were both watching the cat when her mom said, "I'm thinking of leaving him, Vanny." Vanessa looked up and what she saw on her mother's frame was not quite sadness but the resigned face of someone who has given up.

"You probably don't want to hear about it, but I wanted to tell you in case things got weird around here."

"It's always been weird, Mom."

"I know it has, Vanny. God, I can't tell you how hard I tried and it's terrible of me to say this, but I know I should have left him ages ago. We've really only had a few good moments, not even months or years, but I just kept telling myself it would get better, you know? He'll find his calling, he'll follow his passion, whatever that is, he'll be … I don't know … maybe *satisfied* is the right word? I'm not sure if he's ever been *happy*, Vanny, and I guess I'm done trying to figure out how to do it for him."

Vanessa chewed her bacon, letting the salt fortify her for a conversation too long coming. "Why did you stay with him? I mean, don't get me wrong, I love him too, but it's not like he's ever been that good to you. I think I lost track to the times the neighbours called the cops because of your fights."

"I'm sorry Vanny," her mother shook, convulsing in sprays of tears. "Oh God, you have no idea how I hated for you to see that."

Vanessa took her mother's hand, squeezing her love into it. "Don't be. If anything, you taught me resilience. Besides, I don't ever remember you starting an argument with him. It's not your fault."

"Well, I definitely never *tried* to start anything with him. He just has this … this *way* of making something out of nothing. Stupid, but it was the first thing I loved about him when we were younger. He'd *breathe* energy, Vanny, just suck it right up and spit it back out like a tornado. Didn't matter what he was talking about, good, bad, anything at all. Anything he said could pick you up and make you feel like part of his storm. He'd rile me up with the way he saw things, the way he talked, like everything, every experience was something meant just for us, only for us, out of all the people on earth. I loved it so much that I guess I looked past it when the miracles became some sort of curse or slight against him, until it was too late, when everything pissed him off." She had stopped crying and now wiped her eyes, carefully dabbing a tissue around the shadows of her makeup.

They cleared their plates and Vanessa sipped another cup of coffee while her mother washed dishes. "Whatever you need," she said, finally feeling the welcome stir of caffeine. "I'm here, Mom."

The last of the dishes in the cupboard, her mother whirled around and said, "Well, aren't we two sour grapes in the morning, huh? Gosh, it's no good to start your day like this, hun. Let's change the subject. How's that writing project of yours going?"

The day she returned from her first meeting with Phil, her confusion bracketed by doubt and more than a little fear, Vanessa's mother poured her a full glass of wine and said, "You got this, Vanny. Maybe you find something, maybe you don't, but I know you'll give it a good shot, no?" Presently, as she filled Reggie's food and water bowls, thinking about her conversation with Tom and everything she read, Vanessa wondered if a good shot was possible at all. Ray Beecher, dead. Ben Sibley, dead. Donna Pauliuk and Stu Kline, dead. Father Pauliuk would be her best, if not only, hope of uncovering anything that might help Phil Beecher honor the memory of his father. She didn't doubt Phil's motive in this regard, but it did make Vanessa pause and cause her to wonder if she'd have the same commitment to her own father, had their positions been similar. She wanted to believe that her own obligation would run as deep as Phil Beecher's, she really wanted to. To her mother, she raised her shoulders with great uncertainty. "Not sure yet. There's just so much to think about, Mom. I mean, it was terrible the way it happened and I'm not sure if what I learned so far makes me want to give up or keep going. Maybe a bit of both. Would it be strange if I said I think it's kind of interesting?"

"Not at all. People make millions off of whodunnits, or whatdunnits, in this case. You're not the first and you won't be the last to try to figure out a mystery but I think you might get a parade in your honor if you figure this one out." Her mother smiled and patted her shoulder. "But you shouldn't be hard on yourself if you don't get any closer, hun. I think a memorial story would be nice, too. Fresh perspective, nothing lost."

"I suppose," Vanessa said, not believing the words as she said them.

Three hours later, Vanessa leaned into Holy Redeemer's empty parking lot with a box of fresh doughnuts on her passenger seat, enjoying the slight temperature dip as she drove with her windows open. She parked, turning her engine off, craning her neck to see the massive cross atop the black pyramidal roof of the bell tower. On cue, its hammer tolled one, two, five, nine times against the bow, resonating from the open casing here, now there, then there, outward with its canonical melody, raising the hair on Vanessa's arms as she listened with an open spirit. "Help me, Lord," she said to the heavy ceiling of the sky, leaving the windows down as she took to the sidewalk in search of Father Pauliuk and Phil and Rick Beecher.

Nearing the building, Vanessa noted the doors on the new church were more abundant and, predictably, harder to secure from the outside. Layers of red brick and tan limestone abutted four glass doors with waist-level interior push bars, and staggered recesses fell away on the sides, veined with crystalline panes etched in peacework from ground to sky. It was the work of a building that welcomed people in but also ensured their release. Of this, there was no doubt. She scooted into the open doors and saw Father Pauliuk, in collar, with Phil and whom Vanessa believed was his brother Rick. One hand piously resting behind his back, Father Pauliuk was pointing with the other to the upper corner of one of the roof's scissor trusses where a nest of birds was tucked tightly near the ceiling. "It was up before we could do anything about it," Father Pauliuk was saying. Hearing Vanessa approach, he turned and extended both of his hands to embrace her. "Vanessa, hi!" She accepted his hug, feeling both comforted and guilty at her inconsistent attendance over the years. Though she had moved to Toronto years ago, she hadn't exactly been absent from the city since she left. Still, he hugged her with the forgiving zeal of holy understanding.

"Hi Father," she gave him a warm squeeze.

"I was just showing them our new little visitors," Father Pauliuk said jovially. "Barn swallows. You can tell by the nest. See there?" He pointed at the grey half moon jutting high above the apse. "They use sticks and mud to make their homes. We've had the doors open quite a lot in the evenings to help cool the building down. With the river behind us, we get all sorts of wildlife around here, but I confess we've never had an actual nest before. The birds usually fly out soon enough, but these little guys seem to like it here." As he said this, something dribbled from the nest, their four heads following it as it plunked into a shallow plastic basin on the floor. A cluttering of droplets that had missed the bin were splashed this way, that way, against the wall, and on the leaves of nearby artificial foliage.

Rick Beecher grunted, "Your floor!"

"Will recover," said Father Pauliuk. "Unfortunately, their species is threatened so we must do what we can to protect them. Besides, the children love seeing them here. They've even given them names. Chirpy, Burpy, Slurpy, and Lou from what I can last remember. The parents are just mom and dad." He laughed.

"We don't get much of wildlife in Toronto," Vanessa said. "Mostly rats and pigeons, sometimes coyotes."

"All God's creatures," the Father said, smiling. "Now, I see from the box in your hand, you've come to fatten us up. Shall I make some coffee to go with that and we'll sit in my office to chat?"

"Just tea for me," Vanessa said, having felt the uncomfortable churn of too much caffeine in the chambers of her heart.

"Tea it is. Shall we?" The Father gestured back at the vestibule which was hemmed with sunlit hallways to its right and left. He conducted them to his office where he left them as he went to make coffee, having politely rejected their offer of assistance. When he returned, there was something in his countenance that suggested he was not altogether as comfortable as he appeared to be when Vanessa first saw him. The tray he carried trembled and by the time he set it on his desk, the napkins he had placed on the bottom were soaked through. "Please forgive me. It's been many years, but my heart still likes to prod my nerves when I think about it."

Phil rose from his seat and poured their drinks while Vanessa plated donuts for everyone. Then Vanessa looked at Phil, who dipped his chin almost imperceptibly. She said, "Thanks for having us, Father, but we can do this at another time if you like."

He sniffed. "No, no. Not at all. You are here and I am leaning on the Lord. So," he stuffed his donut into his mouth and washed a large bite down with gulps of his still-steaming coffee, "we must go on but with full stomachs. Two vices I have been unable to beat, but I think God would understand in this case." The corners of his eyes creased into deep fissures as he grinned sheepishly then he saw Rick looking at his watch impatiently. "I'm sorry, you must be pressed for time."

"Sorry Father, not trying to be rude. My boss has me on a pile of properties he wants done yesterday. He's trying to make up for lost time, you know?"

"Aren't we all," said Phil. "It's going to take a while yet for the economy to get back where it was, but we'll rebound. We always do."

"Last I heard, you were going to try mining, if my old brain is working properly," said Father Pauliuk.

Rick used a napkin to scrape the chocolate from the top of his donut before picking at the sides. His fingers worked restlessly and soon the donut was completely dismantled without him having taken a single bite. "You have no idea how bad I want to eat this donut," he said to no one in particular. "Gloria's got the whole house on a diet; said we all got a little too fluffy from being locked inside so long. She's got the girls drinking spinach smoothies and I've had nothing but egg whites and kale for the last three days. No sugar, no gluten, and no dairy for a week. Sometimes I feel okay, but I get jittery every now and then. Damn, it looks good," Rick eyed his plate like a wolverine at a rabbit. "Oh man, I did it again. Sorry Father."

"*We rejoice in our sufferings, knowing that suffering produces endurance, and endurance produces character, and character produces hope, and hope does not put us to shame, because God's love has been poured into our hearts through the Holy Spirit who has been given to us.* Romans five, verses three to five," the Father pronounced. "It's been one of my favorite passages even since before the fire. I would think you've suffered, yes?"

"Yes Father," Rick said.

"And yet you've endured?"

"So far, that's if I don't faint on my way to my truck."

The Father sipped his coffee thoughtfully while Vanessa stirred her tea. "You know, I commend your perseverance. Here I am leaning on my vices and you're fighting your own to the point of impairment. Ah, well. Some crosses are smaller than others, I suppose. Can I get you something else that might help? We might have some fruit juice in the fridge."

Rick shook his head, retrieved several small crumbs from his plate, then quickly stuck them in his mouth, his lips venting the room with the sound of complete and utter satiation. He took another piece into his mouth while they watched, amazed at the speed of his ingestion as much as his sudden lack of restraint. When he was done, Rick's head swung like an inverted pendulum, the sudden rush of sugar surging through his veins, his arteries, his blood, from neuron to neuron so violently that they could see him tremble. "Oh man, oh man. I'm sorry Father. Vanessa. I needed that so much. Please don't tell Gloria, she would kill me."

"We'll have to remind her of the Ten Commandments, then," said Father Pauliuk, deadpan, and soon they were all were all giggling and wiping their eyes.

"I feel better now," Rick said. "Yes, to answer your question Father, I was thinking about switching to something in mining, but that was before the pandemic. The world got so crazy I stayed put. I'm still in surveying."

"Ahh," said Father Pauliuk knowingly. "Scut Merrill still runs that?"

Rick nodded. "He's got his hand on a bid from a company out of Vancouver for a master-planned community out past Dutton. Apartments, high-end condos, retail, all along the river near Jack Fischer's farm. You know him?"

The Father nodded. "We used to see him quite often. Scut, too."

Rick blushed uncomfortably. "I'd convince Scut to come but he doesn't take lightly to suggestions. Tore a strip out of me when I told him I needed a few hours off today."

"Well, let's not tempt the devil anymore that we need to. How can I help you?" Father Pauliuk's spine was straight and stiff as he prepared himself for this part of their meeting.

Phil said, "We're going to try again, Robert." Vanessa was surprised at Phil's use of Father Pauliuk's common name but neither man seemed uncomfortable with it, so she settled. Phil pulled his seat closer to Father Pauliuk's desk, resting his elbows on his knees with his arms folded in the crook of his arms. He spoke slowly, softly. "I know it's hard, Robert, and I can't promise you it's going to be easy, but I want your blessing on this. Twenty-two years without answers, Robert. Twenty-two years without knowing, without justice."

"God's justice is the most just of all. It will come," said the Father, looping his hands into a skin-twisting knot. "But that's assuming it wasn't an accident."

Phil's mouth tightened. When he finally spoke, he reached out and put a hand on the preacher's pressure-white fingers. "Robert—"

"There was a lot going on that day, Phil. I don't know, what if someone had stuck it there by accident. A child, someone who wasn't thinking. Maybe—" His awareness of the tragedy struck Vanessa. Obviously, that Donna and Stu had been trapped inside Holy Redeemer was not entirely a secret and Vanessa wondered how many people *were* actually aware of it, whatever Tom Widlow told her.

Phil squeezed his hand. "Let's hope that's what we find, huh?" Vanessa and Rick busied themselves with studying the floor, the walls, the windows, their own shoes, briefly looking at each other uneasily until Phil said, "Vanessa isn't some big city reporter, Robert. She's one of us but she's been away enough that she might just see something that we don't."

"Sorry Phil, but I'm with the Father on this one," Rick said, leaning back and slipping a thumb under a beltloop as he stretched his legs. "You think she's going to find something that thousands of experienced manhours haven't been able to? No offense at all, really, but I think it's just stirring things that don't need to be stirred, Phil. You remember that memorial you did, when was it, 2007 for the ten-year anniversary?"

"2008," Phil said.

"2008, then. When you printed that article suggesting it wasn't an accident, you got those diehards all gung ho again and put Boyd Melnyk in the hospital for two weeks because a group of kids saw him burning a brush pile at night and they thought he looked suspicious."

"I don't want any trouble," said Father Pauliuk.

Phil sat back, exasperated. "There won't be any trouble, Robert. We do a memorial every year. The article is not really new, and Rick is right, she likely won't find anything new at all."

"Can I speak?" Until now, Vanessa had been silent, but she looked at all three of them when she said, "We all know I'm not a reporter, but I'd like to find out just as much as anyone else. Yes, people are crazy. If anything, the pandemic has proved that. But I do think this would be a change of pace. All we've talked about for the last year and a half has been that blasted virus. Cover your face. Keep your distance. Stay home. Wash your hands. I think people are ready for this, maybe now more than they ever have been *because* of what we've been through. Honestly, I can't promise I'll do a good job. I'm not an investigator. I don't have a clue what I'm doing. But from everything I read, Stu and your wife seemed like pretty amazing people. I was only five when it happened so I never got to really know them, but I would like to. It's not worth not much at all, but I promise I'll at least try." Color flushed her cheeks as she spoke. The corners of Phil's mouth rose slightly while Father Pauliuk's head bobbed up and down and Rick fingered the short whiskers of his dark beard, considering. Vanessa went on. "I've been thinking. I'd like everyone to meet them again. The way they were back then. Simple things that we can all relate to like what Donna's favorite breakfast was. What Stu's favorite shirt was. Did they like animals? Did they have any pet peeves? Guilty pleasures like adventure books or gossip magazines or, I don't know, *The Walking Dead?*"

A groan escaped Father Pauliuk's mouth. "Zombies. Televised spawns of Satan?"

"Sorry Father, not like that. I'm sure Donna would never, but I think you know what I mean. I think people would be interested who they were. Who they really were, you know?"

By now chewing his bottom lip, Rick said, "They were good people."

Phil opened his mouth to speak but Vanessa interrupted. "With your permission, Father, I'd like the world to meet Donna again."

They sat silently as the Father deliberated for a long while. Then he stood and said, "Take a walk with me."

Outside, the sun was once again broiling the grass and what rain fell over the night had long since evaporated. Dust whipped around their ankles, their legs, their faces as new winds pushed, shoved, scratched this way, that way, against their eyes and twisted their hair. They followed Father Pauliuk away from the cool cover of the church and the shade of its surrounding trees out into the open and through the field toward the remains of the old parish. Not even a quarter of the way there and Vanessa could see the beginnings of sweat marks on both Rick and Phil's shirts, and Father Pauliuk's own shirt wasn't far behind.

"So much for the rain," Rick complained, wiping his forehead.

Ahead of them, Father Pauliuk said, "It was a beautiful storm, but the sun wasn't quite ready to rest yet. It will come. In the meantime, God gave us wind so we could deal with it."

Phil shook his shirt, letting the wind inside to coil around his body and balloon out his sleeves.

Rick rubbed the sweat from the back of his neck, looking as red and uncomfortable as Vanessa felt. "At least if I get heat stroke Scut can't holler me back to work," he moaned.

"This won't take long," the Father said. "I just figured we should all go back to the place where it started. It's certainly a shock when you first see it, but I think we're all generally familiar with what it looks like."

As they neared the ghostly remains, Vanessa noted with disgust not one but two used condoms on the grass near the fence. She let out an involuntary groan, taking a few wide steps sideways to keep her distance. Father Pauliuk stopped and shrugged hopelessly. "A common occurrence, I'm afraid. The building draws the voyeurs and exhibitionists from time to time and it's a veritable circus around Halloween."

Vanessa's nose wrinkled at the filth near the old church. "I'm sorry to bring this up, Father, but can I ask why the building hasn't been torn down? Terrible to say, but these kinds of things are big temptations for kids. I think half of my friends climbed that fence when I was in high school."

"My graduating class took a class picture in front of it," Rick said with a sigh. "The fence wasn't up yet and they marched across the field in their heels and dresses and tuxes, drunk and posing like clowns in front of it in the dark after the dance. I didn't go with them. My dad would have killed me, and it wasn't right, you know?" Phil put an affectionate hand on Rick's back as they stopped closer.

"My, there's a lot of killing in your family," Father Pauliuk said but this time no one laughed. They had stopped short of the fence and the sight of the building came upon them like night terrors, black and ominous. The swift wind seemed to die at the entrance of the building, as though it would dare not enter and risk mingling with the darker energies inside.

Father Pauliuk reached into his pocket and produced a key. "I would have preferred it removed years ago but our planning committee voted against it, mostly for nostalgic reasons but I suspect some of them wanted it as some kind of testament to the church's resilience. I'm not sure I would agree with that as our cornerstone is and will always be Christ. We don't need a building, sacred as it is, to prove the Everlasting, but it would have caused quite the stir among some of our older congregants. It took some time, but we came to a resolution with the fence and it more or less keeps the trouble out." He pulled a hanging padlock into his palm, eyed the bottom, blew into the keyhole, and clicked the key inside, jingling it until it caught and the metal loop released upward. He stepped forward with Rick and Phil but, this close to the black and terrible maw of the old church, Vanessa hesitated. Sensing this, Father Pauliuk drew back and put his hand on her shoulder.

"I just need a minute," she said.

"We don't have to go in." Father Pauliuk rubbed her back, drawing his forehead toward Vanessa's. "I'm sorry, I just see this so often that I sometimes forget what it's like for others to see it for the first time."

"I've seen it before," Vanessa took a deep breath, entering the gate. "It's just been a long time but after everything I read, it almost seems new to me again, if that makes any sense."

"It's not something that grows on you, Vanessa," Phil stuck his hands in his back pockets, surveying the wreckage with a long sigh. "My dad used to cry every time we passed it. I still remember that."

Off to the side, Rick sniffed. "You think you can handle this? No one would be upset if you decided it wasn't for you. Phil?"

"Not at all," Phil agreed. "There's other work we can have you do. I'm trying to build up my flyer business anyway."

The four of them naturally sought the spire, their eyes lifting upward over the punctures and gashes, past the violations of smoke, the spoils of spray paint, the chiseled names of too many lovers, and found the cross unspoiled and still broadcasting against the cloudless sky. Vanessa shuddered, not with fear, but from respectful awe that the cross had survived. Father Pauliuk took them in a slow circuit outside the building, pointing to where the lectern once was, where they believed the fire began. The windows, first broken by firemen then finished by vandals, granted them an unobstructed view of the interior, where the contrast of catastrophe intermingled with the sprouting of ivy, moss, dogwood and aspen. Above, three-quarters of the roof had collapsed, permitting a stretch of sunlight from the apse all the way to the narthex, illuminating the wide length of the aisle. Vanessa carefully navigated through a tangled row of thorn bushes and made her way to one of the windows to get a better look inside.

"Careful," Rick used his boot to crush down some of the thorny tangles beside Vanessa.

"I—I've never been this close to it before," she said into the window, and the church absorbed her voice as though she hadn't spoken at all, as though the fire was still seeking, consuming, eating what it could to stay alive until the next cull. Why she had expected an echo, she wasn't sure. The walls had been ravaged, the windows were now cavities, and the roof had been blown off. Twenty-two years of disintegration and what remained of the church was being slowly engulfed again, this time by Mother Nature's cavalry.

"I used to love coming here," Phil said from his own window. "Most of my friends were too busy drinking and chasing girls, but up until it burnt down, I don't think I ever missed a Sunday service."

Father Pauliuk's lips pulled up in a slanted smile. "Admirable devotion. I daresay Miss Tanya Billings never missed a service during that time either."

Phil blushed. "Guilty as charged."

As they drew back from the windows, Father Beecher clapped Rick on the back. "But there were no younger Billingses for our Rick here and yet I believe his attendance was just as spotless as yours, if I do remember correctly."

"True disciple," Rick grinned.

"And one of our best altar servers," Father Pauliuk said as the stood back to survey the building one last time.

"Those were good times," Rick said.

Father Beecher led them back through the gate, the others silently watching him lock up. Then they started back across the field; the intense heat now padded with humidity so dense that their clothing was sodden by the time they returned to the newer building. Vanessa's dress clung to her legs and she pulled at it while Rick took to fanning his face with his hand and Phil unbuttoned the top few buttons of his shirt. They continued like this as Father Pauliuk led them back inside to the cool air of the church, rolling up his sleeves as they sat back down. "Since I believe we're all ready for showers, I'll ask you your thoughts on proceeding, Vanessa."

"I don't have a choice," she said quickly. "To give up before I start wouldn't be doing anyone any favours, but I want to do it right. Even if we get another memorial piece, as Rick mentioned, I'd like it to be different." *We.* It wasn't lost on Vanessa that she'd already begun to see the Garrett Gazette as something of her own and as she spoke, she saw Phil's acceptance in the way he nodded, urging her on. "So, with your permission, I'd like to continue by interviewing everyone who was there that night and anyone who had anything to do with the church at the time. You three and Ed Norman. I'm already working with Tom Widlow and he's getting me in touch with Kurt Noonan, the Fire Chief." She opened her book and checked her notes. "If I'm understanding correctly, there were at least five other people there that day who were helping with the leaks. Is that right?"

Father Pauliuk nodded. "Gil Elias, Roger Semple, Wayne Turner and two of our other altar servers. Agnes Clarke and Patrick Lewis. They helped Rick wipe up all the water while Ed and I helped the others fix what we could but I'm afraid you'll only have Agnes to talk to. Patrick drowned a few years back."

Detecting her surprise, Phil said, "He was on a fishing trip up near, was it Tobermory, Rick?" Rick quietly tipped his chin. "They were in rough waters and his canoe tipped. Didn't make it to thirty. It was a sad situation for his wife and daughter."

"God only takes the good ones," Rick said, sniffing.

"Amen," said Father Beecher.

"So just Agnes, then," Vanessa sighed. "Okay, just for a second, I'm going to ask you to treat me like I don't know anything or any of you. I want you to walk me through this. The church was sustaining water damage, so the service was cancelled. There were ten of you in the building that day." She dragged her finger down the page as she spoke to Father Pauliuk. "You, Donna, Stu, Ed, Gil, Roger, Wayne, Agnes, Patrick and Rick. Is this right?" He nodded. "And it took you how long to fix everything?"

Without having to think about his answer, the Father said, "I sent the kids home around three and the rest of us left at seven."

"So, Rick, Agnes and Patrick leave and then there are seven of you. Did you leave at the same time?"

Father Pauliuk shook his head. "I sent Ed home earlier because he wasn't looking to well, and Gil left shortly after that to pick his kids up from their friend's house. They were both gone by maybe four and Donna left around five to make dinner."

"Which left yourself, Stu, Roger and Wayne left. Is that right?"

"Correct. They left with me at around seven."

She could connect nothing from the fire to any of the earlier arrivals, so Vanessa was stumped. Instinct pressed her toward the Father's conversation with Donna in the vestibule and to her pregnancy, but she felt that those were private questions for another time. As Father Pauliuk had said, Vanessa also didn't want any trouble, nor did she want to cause it.

9

Shit, Nick Penner thought, *shit, shit, shit*. He downed the last of his beer, now warm, and ordered another. He looked around. Middle of the week and Shooter's was packed. Having been closed the better part of a year due to the pandemic, the bar was making up for lost time. Rowdy men and loud women were crammed into booths, crowded around the pool tables, huddled beneath the wall of televisions, and swarming the dance floor as they two-stepped to Luke Bryan's "Most People Are Good". The smell of many perfumes and spilled beer wafted through the dim light and the sounds of high laughter and loud conversation pushed too hard at Nick's ears. He cringed, settling deeper into his barstool, waiting for Gus.

"Can I get you something, hun? Maybe something a little stronger?" The bartender leaned over so that Nick could see down her shirt. The move was purposeful, he knew, anything to squeeze another dollar for the tip jar, but her breasts were nice and Nick did, in fact, have money for her tip jar, as she knew he always would.

Nick placed a twenty on the bar, taking his time. "I'm not sure what I feel like, Lana. Why don't you tell me?" He leaned in.

Lana bit her lower lip and tossed her hair behind her shoulders. She bent her elbows so they rested on the bar beneath her breasts, which were now threatening to escape the deep cut of her shirt. "Hmm. I don't know, Nick. What kind of mood are you in today? That might help me decide."

Nick thought, and a sly grin came upon his face. "I'm feeling a little nasty today, Lana. Got anything for that?"

"Maybe I do," she said, but her eyes told him there was no doubt at all. Her eyes wanted to f—" A hand clapped him on the back and Nick turned around.

Gus Steeger, beer in hand, burped not too quietly as he took the stool beside Nick. With his belly protruding from the bottom of his tight red shirt, Nick could see a dark trail of hair leading toward the wide outline of Gus' navel underneath. Seeing this, Gus lifted his shirt, picked at the hollow, inspected his finger, and grudgingly pulled his shirt down. "It was a hot day, man, got sand from my asscrack to my tits, see?" He proffered said sand by digging beneath the fingernail that was in his bellybutton.

Lana swiveled her breasts toward Gus, who gave them a quick look. He held up two fingers in a wide V. "Jack for me and my boy." Nick slumped as Lana turned away. "Hey man, what's the problem? Lynn nagging you again?" He swallowed a throatful of beer and wiped the bit that trickled from the corner of his mouth with the back of a sunburnt hand.

"What else is new?" Nick said, but that wasn't the reason he wanted to see Gus today. Usually, their visits were innocent, nothing more than barroom blather or weekend steam vent. Sometimes a drink, more often near a dozen, but there was nothing Nick ever really needed from Gus besides to bitch about his marital headaches. Today though …

A shot of pain ripped through Nick's shoulder as Gus cuffed him a little too hard. "Man, you just got to do it. Rip the band aid off, then you can let loose, you know? Dip in the pool, share your shit like I do." At this, Gus grabbed his nuts and gave them a little squeeze. Lana returned with their shots, her eyes following Gus' gesture below. "Want some?" he asked. Lana rolled her eyes and said to Nick, "I'll check you later."

Nick elbowed Gus in the side and Gus grunted, finally settling. They lifted their shooter glasses, tipped their chins to each other, and drank their shots quickly, to which Nick hissed at the burn. He said, "You still good with Jolene?"

"Aww, now, man. You know I can't let you go there. Max would kill me. It ain't right." Gus shook his head and turned toward the football game where the Edmonton Eskimos were crushing the Toronto Argonauts 47–13. He cursed at the screen, pounding his fist on the bar. "Run, goddammit, run!"

By the time Nick looked at the screen, the play was over. He said, "I'm not after your sister-in-law, shithead." In another life, Nick felt that maybe he would, in fact, have gone for Max's wife. At 40, she still had the ass of a twenty-year-old and her skin resisted age as much Lynn's welcomed it, the dichotomy of their youth all the more prevalent with their attire. Lynn was no slouch, Nick reflected, but neither did she take it upon herself to get familiar with spandex and lace, as Jolene and others of her type had done. The common thread between the two was their professional success, he knew, which was mostly the reason Nick never treaded that way. He'd already suffered enough of those waves and he preferred not to get caught in them again. "Jolene still run that agency?" Nick said casually.

"Huh? Yeah, at least I think so. Max said they were slow there for a while, you know, with everything, but I think it's going better now."

"You think she might be looking for people? Like help, I mean."

"She don't need no work done, if that's what you mean," Gus said dismissively. "And their building is practically new so …"

"Not for me," Nick said, annoyed at having to spell it out for Gus. "For Vanny. She's got something with the Gazette but I'm not too sure about it."

"Yeah? She's working for Beecher? Can't be all that bad, can it? Wasn't she working for some hot shit paper in Toronto?"

"Grocery chain," Nick said. "It's not the same thing. I just think she'd be happier doing what she's used to. Now that she's home, we would give anything to keep her here. I don't now, maybe things would be different with Lynn if Vanny stayed." Nick hoped he sounded adequately disquieted.

Gus didn't bite. "Keeping her here would change things how?" He drew so close to Nick's ear that Nick could feel Gus' alcohol-thick breath brush his lobe. "You going to keep it in your pants, now, Nicky? You goin' Mormon on me, fucker?" Nick shoved him away and Gus laughed. "You'll never change, Nick. Even if Vanny *did* stay here. Remember before she left, who was there?" Gus scratched his chin. "That Tori chick, Melissa, Rhonda, Fiona …"

"Whatever, man," Nick said, standing.

"Hey! Hey now! Don't be like that. Sit your ass down and tell me what the fuck is going on. That virus get to your head?" Gus signalled Lana over and ordered two more beers.

"Maybe it did," Nick shot back. "It's not right what I've done, how I've treated Lynn. All that time got me thinking that maybe what I've got at home isn't so bad, Gus. Lynn's smart, you know." Nick gritted his teeth, needing Gus to believe him.

"Too smart for your ass," Gus agreed.

"Look, there's nothing for Vanny here, but I figure that maybe there could be something, something that will make her want to stay. If Jolene had anything Vanny could do, I think we might have a shot at keeping her this time. We'd be better if she stayed, Gus. Lynn would finally have someone to bitch to who actually cared." He sniggered, reluctantly sitting when his beer arrived.

They drank, watching women, watching the long-awaited resumption of normal, fan-packed sporting events. Gus burped, and finally said, "I'll ask, man, but don't get your hopes up."

When Gus left an hour later, Nick was pleasantly plastered. He stumbled off his stool when it was apparent that Lana wasn't going to allow him another drink and made his way into the humid night, kicking up gravel as he walked. Fucking Beecher couldn't let things lie. That night, that never ending night, still fresh in his memory, had died with the preacher's wife and his fat assistant. Why dig it up now? And why bring Nick's goddamn daughter into it? He brought up the burger he'd had at Shooter's and wiped his mouth with the collar of his shirt, then fumbled with his zipper as he walked toward the bushes. Sufficiently hidden, Nick urinated, his forehead pressed against a tree to keep him from falling forward. Finishing, Nick felt for his zipper, but the slider was stuck in the bottom fold and he was too drunk to fish it back out. "Fuck it," he gruffed to no one and, with great effort, stepped forward toward home.

The air was too hot, too goddamn hot, and even in his disordered state Nick felt the impending storm so deep in his bones he figured they just might split from the pressure. Maybe not tonight, maybe not tomorrow, but it would come, Lord it would come, when hell opened up on Garrett and whether it spilled rain or blood, Nick Penner knew he was in for a flood.

He thought of the women Gus spat at him and reflected not with a little bitterness that those encounters meant little to him, then and now. How could they? He hadn't enjoyed a woman's lips since the night of the fire, hadn't been driven to extasy without humiliating amounts of prodding, hadn't wanted the prodding in the first place, even with Lynn. Especially with Lynn. Not like that, never like that again, because if Lynn knew, well, any penetration on his part without her knowledge of who Nick truly was would be tantamount to rape. Nick was many things, but he was not a rapist, so their marital bed had only one function, with just the occasional slip up.

He went on, unable to clear his mind of his hands on those breasts that night, where the two of them were tucked away so no one could see. How she teased him! Nick was delirious with ecstasy when his hands travelled inside her thighs, hers between his, then her lips, her tempting lips on … "I can't do this, Nicky," she had whispered into his ear as she sucked on his lobe. But she did do it. Over and over and over again until Nick came with such force that he felt he might never be full again. Then the flames came and Nick was out the door, running, running, running … and now Nick was running again, wheeling past the river bank, scrambling over the bridge, charging past the graveyard, careening through one yard, two, so close to home until the squawk of a siren sounded behind him and Nick whirled around into a psychedelic curtain of red and blue lights, passing out before they could cuff him.

10

Scents of lavender and seafood greeted Vanessa as she entered the garden where she was meeting Ray Beecher's widow, Katherine, along the downtown riverfront on a very welcome cloudy morning. Orchestrated with the ping of wineglasses, the clattering of dish and silverware, and the low hum of chatter, the patio around the old Victorian restaurant presented a quaint and calming backdrop for an otherwise difficult conversation. Vanessa made her way through a maze of billowy topiaries and spiraled cedars toward the center of the courtyard. There, a green ceiling of hanging ferns and ivies united with bright sprays of flowers and strings of glowing lights. From the far left corner, Katherine Beecher waved. Beside her, another woman was on her cellphone, studying the drink menu.

"I hope you don't mind," Katherine said, gesturing toward her friend. "But I like to have Betty around whenever I discuss these things. It gets hard sometimes …" she didn't finish. "But let me look at you, kiddo!" She stood, taking Vanessa's wrists and holding her at arm's length. "My you've grown. You know, I watched you grow up all those years in your mother's office and I always knew you were going to be such a beautiful woman. If either of our boys had been even a little younger, I would have stolen you for myself, not that I don't like my daughters-in-law, mind you," she giggled. "It's good to see you, dear." Now Katherine was hugging Vanessa, her thin arms drawing her in tight and long. Katherine smelled of rosewater and cigarettes and Vanessa politely held her breath until the older woman released her. Vanessa took her seat, admiring at once Katherine's dress, a black and white striped arrangement with an off-centre V neck. Unlike Vanessa's own grandmother, whose sparse hair was tightly permed, Katherine's hair was short but chic, swept to the side above bright blue eyes and peony-pink lips. She said, "I'm glad Phil called me, though I don't know how much help I can be. I wasn't there the evening of the fire, so I can only tell you what Ray told me and *that* has already been told to the police."

"And it got you nowhere, Kathy," Betty set her phone down, and summoned the waiter with the flick of a bony gray finger. Beside Katherine, Betty looked almost dowdy. Her oversize tan dress, covered by a thick floral sweater and accented with several strands of milky-white plastic baubles, seemed to devour her small frame. Large black sunglasses consumed almost the entirety of her face, save for the small chin and crumpled mouth. The waiter appeared. "We're expecting my grandson, can we get another place setting?" With a quick nod of his head, the waiter disappeared.

"Poor boy's been working all week in the heat, I told Stephen to send him my way so he could work on the house but," thick eyebrows crested from behind her glasses and she huddled toward them, "I don't need anything done. The boy just needs a rest and what better place for that than with me at my house." Betty slapped the table and guffawed victoriously. When she settled, she said, "Oh dear, where are my manners, going on like an old bird without introducing myself. I'm Betty, hun, and you must be Vanessa. Kathy just loved working for your mother, you know that?"

Vanessa smiled. "My mom always said that Mrs. Beecher was the best nurse that ever worked for her."

"Call me Kathy, dear."

"Now, let me get this straight," Betty said, pausing for a moment to beckon the waiter back. "Glass of whisky, half full, no ice. I'm old enough and I can handle it so don't be stingy." Vanessa and Kathy quietly ordered a bottle of white wine to share and then Betty went on. "So Philly, that's what we call him, Vanessa, at least that's what I've called him since he was in diapers; Philly wants another story and he thinks you are going to write it?"

Her chair squeaked against the floor as Vanessa fidgeted. "I know, I know, it's strange because I'm not a reporter. At least, I've never been hired as one before this."

"That's not the strange part, dear," Betty said. "You could've written the constitution, for all it's worth, gotten one of them fancy Pulitzer prizes but that doesn't mean anyone around here is going to talk to you about the fire."

"Betty!" Kathy chided.

"You know as well as I do, Kath." Betty turned to Vanessa, annunciating each word with the flapping of a hand. "Oh, they'll talk to you all right but they won't *talk*, if you get what I mean. If they did, well, I'm not sure any of us would be here, would we? We'd be toasting to long prison sentences and ripped assholes." Kathy put a hand to her forehead, churning with embarrassment. "What?" Betty whacked Kathy's arm. "You know that's what they do there."

"So you don't think it was an accident," Vanessa interrupted.

"No I certainly do not think it was anything of the sort," Betty swiped the glass of whisky from the waiter's hands before he had the chance to set it down. She took a sip, brooding, while Kathy spoke.

"I'm inclined to believe the same thing," Kathy agreed. "Ray told me there was a—I'm not sure how much you know—" she looked sideways at Betty as her voice trailed off.

"I know that Donna was pregnant and," Vanessa hesitated, "I know about the shovel."

Kathy's chest expanded as she took a long swallow of air. "There's that, but also … Ray said there was something odd about that night, something he was never able to quite place. He just felt it, I don't know how to put it any better than that, but it scared him more than the fire itself. Here he was, the building was coming down around him and he thought, well, he thought there was something, *someone*, there."

"Besides Donna and Stu?" Vanessa asked, noting Kathy's comments in her book.

Kathy nodded. "Yes, but there were no other bodies, so that's impossible."

"What's impossible?" said a familiar voice behind Vanessa. She turned and there was Trevor, appearing just as surprised to see Vanessa as she was him.

"My boy!" Betty leapt from her seat, scooted around the table, and threw her arms around Trevor, who hugged her gently.

"Hi Grandma," he said, his eyes swinging from Kathy to Vanessa and back again.

"Grandma?" Vanessa was surprised.

"You two know each other?" Betty asked, but the question seemed false to Vanessa's ears. The sly smile on the woman's face suggested the meeting wasn't at all coincidental.

With a raised eyebrow, Kathy turned and said, "Betty?"

The uptick of Betty's name at the end made Betty shrink slightly. She said, "What? He's young, she's young. They'd make beautiful babies. Why not?" Betty's small head pivoted between Trevor and Vanessa. She sipped her whisky then lifted her glass. "Cheers to grandchildren!"

"Grandma—" Trevor blushed.

Betty slapped the table. "Can't an old lady dream? Is it so bad at my age to want something to hope for?" Trevor relented and Betty yanked his wrist. "Then sit and show her your handsome face."

Obediently, he sat across from his grandmother and buried his face in his hands. Kathy slid a menu toward him. "The sooner we order, the sooner this is over," she said. "And a drink might help."

They ordered and Trevor listened quietly while Vanessa reviewed her notes, jotting down what she could of the present conversation. "Kathy, can we go back to what you said about Ray thinking someone else was in the building? Did he ever tell you why he thought that?"

Kathy sipped her wine, then shook her head. "He couldn't put his finger on it. The building was filled with smoke and, now he was never sure about this, but he thought he saw a face, just for a second, but he could barely see and there wasn't much time for him to go looking around. I told him it was probably just the smoke playing tricks on him. He was in such a state when he found those two that I wouldn't have doubted if he'd seen the Dalai Lama."

"There's no chance that the fire burned a body to ashes?" Vanessa asked. "I didn't get the chance to go through all of the files yet, but maybe I missed something?"

"It would have to have been burning for hours for that to happen, at least that's what they told us, but the fire department put it out long before that," Kathy said.

Their food arrived and Betty and Kathy feasted on creamy scallop linguini and candied pecan salads while Vanessa and Trevor pushed maple-glazed salmon around their plates, occasionally risking glances at each other, then dove back into their food until it was safe to glimpse again. "I take it you took that job with the Gazette," he finally said quietly.

"I did. I couldn't bear working with Owen."

"And you're writing about the fire?"

Vanessa nodded. "At least, I'm trying to."

Trevor thumbed a finger at his grandmother, who was busy hailing another drink. "Look no further. She's lived that story for as long as I can remember."

"I can tell." They chuckled to themselves while Betty drank and Kathy nudged her food around, the coiled noodles never leaving her plate. After a time, Vanessa said, "This must be so hard for you, Kathy. I'm so sorry to bother you with it."

Kathy set down her fork. "Please don't be sorry, Vanessa, really, it's not so much the fire that bothers me, tragic as it was. Not to diminish the loss at all, not at all, but all this talk reminds me so much of Ray, you know. There was no other man like him. I know other women could say the same about their husbands but with Ray, there really wasn't. He just shone everywhere he went, right until the end, and even … oh you'll think I'm morbid for saying it but even with his fall … those Christmas lights shining all around him, it was a perfectly *Ray* way to go. Gleaming to the very end." She toyed with the stem of her wineglass, staring blankly into the crystal as she spoke. "You know, if he was here today, I think he'd have been just as devoted to figuring the fire out as Phil has been. They were so much alike. You would have liked him."

"My mom and dad still talk about him. He seemed like quite the extraordinary person," Vanessa smiled warmly.

"He was," Kathy said, and Betty patted her arm.

Their plates removed, they ordered coffee and dessert, tucking into creme brûlée and strawberries while Vanessa considered anything she might have missed. She scratched her chin, thinking. "I'm honoured by all the information that's been shared with me, but I don't think I'm any further than I was before all of this. I still have so many questions. It's agreed that the fire started after eleven because Ray had an alarm go off at," she flipped through her notes again, "11:22 p.m. He gets to the building and sees his window smashed in. Did they ever find out who did it?"

"No," Kathy said. "Our security cameras were down for the week. There was some construction on the road in front of the building, from Simon all the way to Weller. They were replacing some cables under the road and they accidentally hit a line that knocked out power to the lights in the parking lot. The cameras were hooked up to that part of the grid and unfortunately, we didn't have battery back up at the time. We went through this with the police."

"But Ray still got an alarm from the building?"

"Uh-huh," Kathy said, stirring a packet of sugar into her coffee. "We had sensors on the windows. We had problems with vandals in the past. Whenever Ray would run something provocative or sensitive or polarizing, we could almost always count on a threat. Mostly angry letters threatening to drop their subscriptions but sometimes they called, sometimes they showed up at the office, sometimes they would take it out on the building. Someone smeared excrement all over the front door when Ray wrote about the referendum, that was in the fall of '95, I believe, then there was a ... a pig's head left on the hood of Ray's car when he wrote about the import of European pigs being a potential threat to the environment. Ray said those things were just part of doing business, but I never got used to it. The night of the fire was our fourth broken window in less than a year, so it wasn't all that unusual." Trevor and Vanessa, eyes saucer-wide and mouths agape, looked at Kathy. "What? The paper was Ray's life, his other soul besides me, I'd like to think, so we took the good and the bad and I know I haven't painted the nicest picture of it, but there is so much good there. Really, there is. People can be cruel, yes, but they can be so kind, too, and Ray knew that. Most responses he had were overwhelmingly positive and I think that's part of what kept him going over the years."

"Can I ask what stories may have prompted the vandalism the night of the fire?" Vanessa asked.

Kathy put a finger to her lips, considering. "Well, that week Ray published an article about the Catholic priest sex abuse scandal that was happening, where was it ..."

"Where *wasn't* it," Betty croaked, spilling her coffee. Without hesitation, Trevor swiftly remedied to mopping it up with his napkin, giving Betty a stern glance.

"Well there was that and, oh yes, he wrote one about the Gay and Lesbian games in Amsterdam, Ray was for all causes, dear, all of them. He simply could not stand for anyone being marginalized for any reason. There was something about the mayor's office that week, too, but there always was," she giggled.

"That man did more good by dying than he ever did by living," Betty spat with a swipe of her hand. "That's Gilbert, hun, not Ray, of course."

Vanessa returned to the vandalism at the Gazette. "So the articles were nothing new and had the rock been a response to one of them, something from an angry reader, it wouldn't have raised any red flags beyond what you would have normally expected."

"We figured it was business as usual," Kathy agreed. "And the police thought so, too."

"Did they ever look into it? Get fingerprints or anything?" Vanessa asked.

"They tried," Kathy hailed the waiter and asked for their bill. "If the cameras were working, they figured they might have known how the fire started, or who started it, and as for the vandalism, they didn't find anything in or out of Ray's office. The rock was big but quite porous, you know those bumpy and rough types? Like sandpaper almost, and they said it likely would have already been wet when it was thrown at the window. There was so much rain that night, they told Ray not to expect them to find anything. Had it not come down so hard the way it did, there could have been a chance. Nothing was on our side that night."

Trevor said, "What if they were wearing gloves? I mean, if you're going to throw a rock at a window, you probably don't want to be caught anyway, right?" All three women looked at him and he shrunk a little under their collective stare. "I mean, I'm just saying that's what a smart person would have done." He shrugged and sipped his water.

The waiter arrived with their bill, which Kathy quickly snatched away. At once, Vanessa and Trevor protested, while Betty hurriedly added another drink to the tab. Kathy nodded to the waiter and slid him her credit card. "Ray would have been appalled if I let you pay," she said. "Besides, talking about it is therapeutic for me. I talk poor Bet's ear off so much, I wouldn't blame her if she started spiking her coffee in the morning."

"Been doing that since I met you," Betty said.

"Drive her home, Trevor, will you? I've got some shopping to do yet and I'd prefer not to smell a distillery beside me when I do."

"You ain't living, Kath," Betty raised her new drink in toast.

"I got her," Trevor said, standing. Then Betty's elbow shot him in the side with such force he doubled over. He felt the run of fluid down his shirt and saw that half of Betty's drink had spilled onto him. He swiped a napkin from the table and blotted the scotch from the front of his pants. "Careful, Grandma," he said.

Betty flung the rest of her drink down her throat and stuck her hands on her hips. "What are you waiting for, boy? Invite her over."

"Easy, Grandma," Trevor sighed. "We don't want to bother her. She might be busy." His face congealed with collegial irritation as he was obviously used to Betty's ribbing.

Slipping her notebook into her purse, Vanessa stood and adjusted the strap on her shoulder. "Does a bit later work for you?" she asked, if only to save Trevor from Betty's pestering. "I'm meeting Tom and Kurt at the marina this afternoon, but I can swing by after that. Maybe I bring dinner, if that works for you?"

"Scared her off already," Betty huffed as Trevor helped her out of the restaurant. "I knew it wouldn't last long." She hiccupped then walked into one of the topiaries, which Vanessa caught and steadied back into place.

Guiding Betty to his car, Trevor said over his shoulder, "I'll text you the address."

11

Through the fever of the late afternoon heat, Tom passed over the bobbing docks of the Garrett Marina alongside clusters of cattails, back toward the shore, and waited for Vanessa. Halfway along, Tom was suddenly struck with pain and he clutched the ribs below his heart. He leaned strongly to the right, trying to stretch away the pain that grew worse by the day. Pulling in for the afternoon, a nearby boater called out, asking if Tom was okay. Tom amiably raised a palm and continued walking, lest the concerned boater scuttle after him. He didn't want to explain it, didn't want to impart his troubles, his sorrow, on anyone. Already, the residue of his passing would cling like darkness to Irene and Tom was a firm believer that those feelings boomeranged back around, and he would be damned if he let out any more sorrow in the world for Irene to bear. He took a Kleenex from his pocket and wiped his forehead, sweaty from trying to help Kurt isolate the cause of a recent leak in his boat. They'd just narrowed it to a seal in the stern when Tom's watch beeped, indicating that he had to meet Vanessa in the parking lot near the boat launch, and Kurt sent him away with the keys to his truck and instructions to pick up the cooler of beer Kurt had left in his back seat. On land, Tom slowly swerved between a multitude of trucks and large SUVs and mostly empty boat trailers, and found Kurt's truck blessedly parked in the shade between Waves, the lakeside breakfast go-to and Sunset, the romantic evening spot favored by Garrett's well-to-do. Tom plucked the cooler from the floor of the back seat and peeked inside to see if the beer was worth lugging to the boat. He was pleasantly surprised to find six bottles of Canadian plunged deep in a slush of ice and water. The beer would be ice cold and well worth the effort. He snagged the cooler in the crook of his arm, smiling.

"You taking me fishing, Tom?" Vanessa said from behind him, gesturing to the cooler with a tip of her head.

Tom hoisted the cooler. "This? No, we wouldn't need an ice box for that. Haven't caught anything from this lake in years but weeds."

"Really? I thought there were lots of fish in there. My dad goes all the time." She caught up to him and they made their way toward the docks.

"Could be." Tom maintained an easy pace as he tapped a finger to his temple. "But these fish are smart. It's like they know when I'm coming and then they dart to the other side of the lake until I'm gone. Irene can catch them no problem. Walleye and perch practically jump in the boat for her, and she caught a big bass not two weeks ago but the second I drop a hook in the water, they scatter like I've fouled the water. No kidding. It's not so bad outside of the city, so I get my revenge there." He laughed as he led her past a marine store and a fiberglass repair shop then onto a long wooden dock that led out onto the water, making a sharp left turn when the reached the end of the platform. He pointed to a small boat docked at slip 11 where a man in a red t-shirt and jean shorts waved at them.

"Ha!" Vanessa laughed at the name scrawled on the boat's side: *The Extinguisher.*

"He thinks he's pretty smart over that one, makes his ego as big as that fat head of his," Tom said.

"Took you so long," Kurt said, wiping his hands with a towel and stepping onto the dock. "You're excused Vanessa. It's this old fart I'm talking to." He jerked a thumb at Tom. "I'm surprised you didn't have to carry his ass here. You got a beer for me, man?" He thrust out a black hand and shook Vanessa's own vigorously. "And one for our friend."

"Thanks," Vanessa said, accepting a beer from Tom. The three of them clinked the rim of their bottles together then drank long, slow mouthfuls of the cold liquid. She had never really been acquainted with Kurt Noonan. Previously, her only encounters with him were those of busy church gatherings when she was younger. So she looked at him now, his warm black face, the cheerful wrinkles at the sides of cheeks, the way this skin between his eyes puckered upward as though he was always on the verge of smiling. She enjoyed the comfortable way he conversed with Tom, peppering him with good-natured pats and spirited insults. Unnecessarily, she asked, "You two know each other long?"

"This asshole?" Kurt scowled playfully at Tom. "Oh, what's it been now, Widdy? Fifty years?"

"Fifty-three, unfortunately," Tom said, helping Vanessa onto the bow so they could sit. She took the bench opposite the two men, setting her purse beside her feet and drew out her notebook.

Kurt said, "My family moved here when I was in kindergarten and he was the first person I met. He kept coming over for this chicken stew my momma used to make and by the time I really got to know him, it was too late to poison him. People would have known."

Tom grunted. "Good stew, terrible company."

"Garrett's finest, right there," Kurt said and before Vanessa knew what was happening, something was licking and scratching at her ankle. She looked down to see a young beagle pup scampering along the deck, now fully engrossed in discovering the contents of her purse.

"Flick, get out of there," Kurt said, gently shifting the dog away. Undeterred, Flick's tail wagged happily as he playfully charged Vanessa's legs with his curious wet nose.

"Oh!" she cried, and merrily pet his head. "How old is he?"

"Just over six months," Kurt said. "Retirement gift from my wife. Apparently, I was moping around with nothing to do, so she gave me a list a mile long and a dog to help me with it."

"Not a bad plan," Vanessa smiled, now scratching Flick's offered belly.

Kurt nodded. "It was the dog or Widdy and the dog smells better."

The retort was on Tom's tongue, but he was suddenly snared by a violent coughing fit as pain spidered from his lung to his shoulder blade. It seized him, pulling him into a haze of stars and fog that threatened to overtake him. *Not now*, Tom thought, *not yet*, and as if it had listened to him, the pain and darkness retreated, temporarily slinking away into the periphery where they would lurk until Tom's next unguarded moment. He cleared his throat. "Pollen," he said. "My allergies have been so bad this year." The way that Kurt and Vanessa looked at him told Tom that they were unconvinced, but he waved their concern away with a flip of his hand and took another long swallow of his beer. "I'm fine, I'm fine. It's probably a bit of the heat, too. It's hotter than a bastard out here."

Vanessa took this as her cue. She patted Flick's bottom to get him off her purse and retrieved a pencil. "Mind if I take notes?" she asked.

"Be my guest," Kurt said to Vanessa, but his eyes were narrowed on Tom.

Vanessa noticed an unspoken conversation between the men, something she felt was not intended for her, so she turned her attention to her notes and the happy thumps of Flick's tail on her foot. "I'll try to speed this along so we can all get out of here sooner. I'm guessing Tom filled you in on everything?" Kurt nodded. "Okay, I know you've likely gone over this a million times, but can you take me through what you remember of that night?"

Kurt rubbed his chin, sighing as he sat back in his chair. He set a towel on the seat and patted it and the empty space beside him was quickly replaced with fifteen pounds of squiggling puppy. He scratched behind Flick's ears. The dog settled and Kurt seemed to settle with him. "That was a tough call. I won't say my toughest because nothing is worse than when there is a kid involved but this one still haunts me, you know. You remember my wife Diana?"

Vanessa nodded. "She would always bring those cinnamon buns to the potlucks. Still my favorite."

"I'll tell her you said so." A slight smile touched Kurt's face, but it was overtaken with the gradual tightening of his jaw and the clenching of his teeth. "That church was everything to Diana, still is, but it's been different since then. We were members and I'll be the first to admit that, at the time, it meant more to Diana than to me. Not that I didn't, or don't believe—my momma taught me right that way—but it was something really special to her and she hasn't really been the same ever since. She's still at every luncheon and all the Bible studies, but it's like she's always waiting for something to come and wreck it for her. I try to help her with it ..." Kurt trailed off, staring at the dog. When he finally looked up, he said, "Don't let anyone tell you that time heals all wounds, Vanessa."

"Sap," Tom interjected, and nudged Kurt's foot with his own. Of course, Tom knew that Kurt was referring to more than just the fire. Kurt was the only person besides Irene that knew of his impending death. Yes, Diana struggled with fire, just as Tom's own wife Irene had, but not as bad as Kurt made it appear to Vanessa. Kurt was hurting because Tom was dying. Ever since Tom confided in Kurt just a few days ago, Kurt had acted as though he'd been struck with terminal cancer himself, dying alongside him, and had gotten uncharacteristically philosophical at least once during every conversation. This time was no different.

"Just telling it like it is," Kurt rebutted, then went on. "Anyway, that fire was hard because we were so close to it, much like the rest of the city was at the time. I can't profess to know everyone in Garrett but it's not unusual for me to respond to a situation involving someone I know. Your typical small town, limited resources sort of situation. I was never a good sleeper and had been in bed watching TV that night when Ray called."

Vanessa interrupted. "Did you find that unusual?"

Kurt pursed his lips and shrugged. "Not really. For many people, 911 still isn't their go-to in case of emergency. Sounds strange, but it's true. In this case, I really think it's because I had seen Ray only a few hours before. Diana and I were replacing the pot lights over the island in our kitchen and ran into Ray and Kathy in the lighting section at Canadian Tire. They were looking for some motion-activated security lights for the Gazette and we ended up going for a quick coffee, nothing long but it was probably just top-of-mind, you know? Anyway, Ray calls me, quite calm, but told me that the church was on fire. I specifically told him not to enter the building and that help would be there in minutes."

"But he went anyway," Vanessa said.

"Uh-huh," Kurt said. "That was Ray for you."

"He was one heck of a guy," Tom agreed.

Rested, Flick bounded off the towel and went foraging once again inside Vanessa's purse. She laughed, lifting her bag onto the seat while Kurt fished in his pocket and produced a dog biscuit which he then tossed across the deck. Flick went scrambling after it, his nails clicking wildly against the floor. "Needless to say, we got to the building after Ray did, not by more than a few minutes, but by then he'd pulled Donna out and had just gotten a hold of Stu. Our first guy in was Sibley, with Johnson just behind him. It was about a bad a situation as you could get. The rear, that's what they call the apse, was fully developed. Perimeter and center aisles were not yet caught, but the building was well ventilated, which is the exact opposite of what you want when a fire happens. You know about the leaks they had that day?"

Vanessa said, "Father Pauliuk told me."

Kurt stood and went to the Bimini frame, unzipping a large canvas canopy the color of the sea. With a pull, Kurt unfurled the top and then clicked the sides into place, giving them all a much-needed reprieve from the sun's direct heat. Sitting again, he said, "We believe they fixed the leaks that presented themselves but that they were likely indicative of other failures, maybe not big, but enough for a significant amount of movement that otherwise shouldn't have been there. All of this is our best guess, of course."

"So the fire started near the back and Donna was found near the front, which was blocked, meaning that she couldn't escape from the doors. What has me confused is that there were a number of windows on both sides of the aisle that Donna could have jumped through to escape, but she didn't. Have you ever seen a situation like that before?" This was the crux of the visit today. It was the one thing that couldn't be reasoned away, no matter how much Vanessa tried. Tom himself had never been able to understand it either, though he'd heard Kurt's possible explanation many times. They both waited for Kurt's expertise, which he gave in short order.

"From the outside, it definitely would look unusual. You see a window, you escape. But it's not that easy. I've seen it before with a mother and her children. She tries to save them, realizes she can't, but by that time the smoke is too thick for her to see her way out, if she even wants out by then. Most would rather die with their children unless they've already saved at least one of them. There's been a few dozen cases like this since I started fighting fires in my twenties. Not all in Canada, of course. Most of them were in the U.S., they tend to get more fires than we do, but it's an occurrence we can't ignore."

Vanessa wrote furiously as Kurt spoke. She asked, "So you think that Donna tried to save Stu?"

"Most likely," Kurt nodded, finishing the last of his beer and pulling another one from the cooler. He offered Vanessa and Tom another but both of them declined. "We need to remember that Donna was a small woman," he said, "no bigger than you, Vanessa, and quite a bit shorter. Stu was packing around three hundred pounds at the time. Even with a surge of adrenaline, that would have been a terrible feat for her. Father Pauliuk is convinced they were meeting about the church's finances. If that were the case, it would make sense that they met in the office to go over paperwork, but perhaps they lit a candle or two at the altar, praying for a solution. A natural thing to do. But if the candle tipped, it would have lit the altar. It was draped in fabric, which would have gone up like that." Kurt snapped his fingers. "The smoke alarms *were* operational. They weren't wired to alert outside sources or connected to each other, unfortunately, but we do know that the one in the vestibule above the front entrance went off because it was still ringing when we arrived. It was definitely loud enough to alert Donna and Stu, but my guess is that they were too consumed with trying to put out the flames to call 911. This is also a common occurrence. People try to tackle it themselves and by the time we're notified there is much more damage or even fatalities that could have been minimized or avoided. This could have been the case here, unfortunately. It would make the most sense that Stu and Donna tried to put the fire out themselves but by the time they realized they couldn't do anything, Stu, who was already in poor health, collapsed from smoke or exhaustion or a combination of both. If Donna tried to pull him out, she would have had a hell of a time trying to lift him. Adrenaline can give people some pretty intense power, but I don't believe it would have been enough to help her carry him out. I believe that when she finally realized she couldn't save him, she would have went for the front door because the fire hadn't reached the vestibule yet. Only, it was locked and by then the smoke behind her would have been too thick to see the windows. She was trapped."

Vanessa rubbed at her temples. "Okay, but what about the shovel? Why were they locked in? It would have been a terrible practical joke and insanely poor timing. Do you not believe the fire and the shovel are related in any way?"

"I wish I had an answer for that," Kurt said. "Without the shovel, I would have bet my life that what I just told you was God's honest truth. But with it …" he paused.

"Tell her about your other theory," Tom said, looking out over the water, not meeting Kurt's eyes.

"What other theory?" Vanessa asked.

Kurt set his beer in the holder beside him and cupped both knees with his palms, his reticence obvious in the sudden tightness of his face. He gave the back of Tom's head a look Tom couldn't see and said, "That one is a little more complicated. The guy's dead now, so it won't go anywhere even if we tried."

Vanessa leaned forward, curious. "Who is dead?"

"Patrick Lewis," Tom answered for Kurt and Vanessa screwed up her face in thought.

"Refresh my memory," she said. "I didn't remember seeing the name in your reports, but it sounds familiar. Someone from the church, right?"

Vanessa flipped through her notebook as Tom spoke. "He wasn't in the reports I gave you. Most of our interviews are confidential, remember?" Tom said. "But Kurt's retired and though he would be bound by confidentiality in some instances, he's a little more free than I am to disclose information. At least, he won't lose his job over it, since he's already retired. In any case, it's just a theory, nothing more than talk, which you could have heard anywhere else, right?"

"Right," Vanessa said, understanding.

"Go on and tell her, Kurt."

Kurt didn't hesitate now. "Patrick Lewis was one of Father Pauliuk's assistants at the time. One of the altar servers, along with Rick Beecher and Agnes Clarke, all teenagers. Father Pauliuk might be able to tell you more about all of them and Rick would know, too, that while Patrick was an altar boy, he was by no means a good kid, at least in my experience. The public is not privy to juvenile records so you wouldn't have found any of his history in Tom's reports, but I had enough run-ins with him to know he was no sweet-cheeked church angel. Patrick was what you might call a delinquent, or swiftly on his way to being one. A few minor run-ins with Tom's people, then two with me."

"He set fires?" Vanessa's eyes grew wide with revelation.

Kurt nodded. "First one was just a patch of dry grass out near the Paxton summer house, you know the one out on Tindy and Doddswell?"

"My aunt and uncle live near there," Vanessa said.

"All the richies like that area," Tom put in.

"Well, if we didn't have a call in when we did, they might not have had any homes there at all." Kurt sipped his beer. "Some passerby didn't like the look of a couple of kids goofing around just offside the ditch and called in. One of Tom's people got there first and she got our asses there before it could spread. It was hot and windy, much like this," he gestured to the wide sky around him. "We put the fire out and the boys, three eleven year-olds including Patrick, got a warning because at the time, we, that's Tom and I, felt that it was basically kids discovering they could make fire, they were goofing around with it. We warned them and left them to their parents, who gave them worse punishment than we ever could have. I think one of the kids was sent to some reform school down south afterward and Patrick's parents took his PlayStation away and made the kid volunteer at Southbridge for the summer."

"The nursing home?" Vanessa asked.

"None other," Kurt said. "His aunt or uncle was some kind of administrator there and they had him reading and playing games with the residents almost every day of the week, but it didn't help. He set a school trash can on fire not four months later. By then, Patrick was almost twelve. He'd scored his father's matchbook, which he happened to have on him when he rammed a pile of tests from the teacher's desk into the garbage and watched it go up. He was the only one in detention and it was after-hours so just the teaching and janitorial staff were aware. The science teacher that sent Patrick to detention had only stepped out for a moment to use the washroom and by the time he was zipping up his fly, the alarm was ringing. He managed to put it out with an extinguisher but there was quite a bit of damage. Patrick was expelled."

"Did he face charges for it?" she asked Tom.

Kurt shook his head. "I said he was almost twelve."

Vanessa wrote in her book. "So you couldn't do anything about it?"

"Nope," Tom answered for him, patting his calf to call the dog over. Flick responded by bounding onto his lap. "We can't charge a child under twelve of a crime, no matter what they do. We can force them into treatment for mental health, but that's about it."

"Did you do that?"

Tom coughed. "We tried, but his parents thought they could manage that one themselves. They were very adamant they could fix it and they took his punishment—and rehabilitation, if you will—very seriously so we agreed to it on the condition that if he set another fire, there would be no more opportunity for them to keep it in the family, if you understand me. Anyway, their solution was to throw him in front of Father Pauliuk, and it actually seemed to work. It's hard to be bad around someone so good, you know?" Both Kurt and Vanessa agreed. "But I don't think he was done with it. The way he held those candles in church, the way he looked at them, it's like the flames were calling him."

Vanessa emptied her own beer and accepted a bottle of water from Kurt. "Did Patrick set any more fires after that?"

Kurt let out a slow breath. "None that we know of but I can tell you from experience that pyromania is hard to cure without treatment and his parents refused it. Even then, it's a hard bugger to get rid of."

"And none of this would have been in the reports because he was a minor at the time," Vanessa looked at Tom, from whom there was an almost imperceptible nod.

Tom said, "But, and there's a *big* but, Patrick was nowhere near the church at the time of the fire. He was at a sleepover birthday party on the other side of town with five other kids playing video games until all hours of the morning; a 'Zelda marathon' they called it. He was fourteen by then, mind you. Anyway, his alibi was air-tight." He felt that heaviness come upon him again but he took his own bottle of water and drank it back quickly, abhorring the heat that was doing him no favors today. Tom clenched his teeth, wishing for just one day of rain or wind, anything cooler that might make his condition more bearable.

Kurt regarded Tom with unveiled concern. When Tom turned away from Kurt, Kurt's tone became slightly annoyed. "Patrick's got an alibi but he's also dead, so we couldn't talk to him if we wanted to anyway, which is convenient for him, if you ask me." He pulled an empty tube of sealant from his back pocket, wrapped it in a dirty rag and put it in a plastic bag, along with their empty bottles. "I'll sort this later," he said.

The sun bore down uncomfortably on them and soon they were unpleasantly sweating. If they sat on Kurt's boat much longer, heat stroke was almost a certainty, so Vanessa closed her notebook and tucked her pencil into its coiled binder. "I know I heard this before but I can't remember how he died. A fishing trip, right?"

Tom said, "Uh huh. You shouldn't get in a boat if you can't swim."

Vanessa gave Flick one more pet before gathering her purse. Standing, she said, "Does Phil know about Patrick?"

"Of course," Tom said, getting to his feet.

"And what does he think about it?"

Tom shrugged. "He's not convinced. Ray taught him to be a realist and that's what he is. The boy had an alibi we can't dispute. His mother played hostess for the boys until quite late and his father took over for a while after his shift at the hospital. They were covered from eight until almost two in the morning, when they went to sleep. The fire was started *and* almost out by then. That was enough for Phil to quit chasing up that tree but he still hasn't found another one to circle."

Vanessa stepped off the boat. "Then who put the shovel through those rings that night?"

It was Kurt who spoke, leading them back toward the shore. "The goddamn devil," he said.

12

Hours later when the day began to cool and the sun shrunk to a low simmer on the horizon, Vanessa wobbled up Betty Lurman's wide Victorian steps with two bags of Chinese food and a bottle of wine tucked into the crook of her arm. The food was heavy and cumbersome and she could feel something leaking over her left hand. At the last step, the food shifted in the paper bags and she had to lurch forward to keep the bags upright but the movement loosened her hold on the wine. The bottle fell with a hard clunk and rolled with the pitch of the slightly sunken porch toward a large bay window off to Vanessa's right. Thankfully, the bottle didn't break but the food was still on the verge of slipping from her hands as the paper containing it disintegrated. Suddenly, the front door swung open and Trevor appeared. He swiftly collected one of the bags, at once grimacing when hot slime hit his hands. "They never close these things properly," he said, and led her into the house.

Inside, Betty was asleep on the couch, mouth open in a peaceful snore, with a blanket tucked up to her chin and an arm dangling in the open space over the floor. "She's been passed out since I took her home," Trevor said with a slight laugh. "But I think the food will help." At this, Betty snorted and licked her lips, but her eyes remained closed.

"Sorry I'm late," Vanessa said. "The interview took longer than expected and it was so hot I needed a shower afterward."

He noticed then that her hair was still damp. She looked fresh and smelled softly like soap, her skin slightly pink from too much sun. He guided her into the kitchen where they unpacked containers of fried rice, ginger beef, chop suey, and spring rolls. The tubs of wonton soup had both spilled open and were now significantly emptier than when Vanessa first saw them being placed into the bag. Trevor wiped what he could with a cloth while Vanessa found bowls, plates, and cutlery. Her stomach growled as Trevor ladled their soup. "I haven't eaten since I saw you earlier, so I'm starving."

"You didn't have to wait for me," Vanessa said as she sipped her first spoonful of broth.

He shrugged. "I was busy taking care of her, anyway."

"Taking care of who?" Betty grunted, shuffling into the kitchen, hair askew. She was wearing a thin nightdress over which she wore a heavy sweater, her slippers scratched at the floor as she walked.

"I wonder," Trevor said, stuffing his mouth to keep from saying more.

"Smells dee-liscious." Betty stuck her nose into one of the containers of soup, grabbed a spoon, and began eating.

"We have bowls, Grandma."

"You washing dishes?"

Trevor wiped his mouth. "Like always."

Betty pointed her spoon at him, dripping soup onto the counter, onto the floor. "Then make me a plate, will you?" she ordered with a mouth full of noodle. Obediently, Trevor spooned hot portions onto a plate and they ate their first bites in comfortable silence. "Those old farts teach you anything today, dear?" Betty asked Vanessa now.

Vanessa warmed to Betty's acknowledgement of Tom and Kurt, both of whom were almost two decades younger than Betty herself. A little trickle of soup erupted from the corner of her mouth when she laughed. "People sure liked Ray," she said, chewing.

"Psssft," Betty flung her napkin in her empty soup container and shoved it away, then tugged her plate close. "Ray the Saint, tell me something I don't know, something the whole world doesn't know. You'd think he's got daisies growing out his ass underground." She began toothlessly grinding on a strip of beef, favoring one side where, in the far reaches of her mouth, a few stubborn molars rubbed the meat into a fine pulp. Her old eyes drew up and she set a hand over Vanessa's. "Loved the bastard like family, dear. I just don't want him to think I've gone soft when he looks down on me from up there." She pointed upward with another piece of ginger beef. "It might confuse him."

Vanessa laughed, then pushed back her chair, deflating from the long, hot day. "Well, my notebook is almost filled. A lot of it is more of the same, although Kurt had an interesting theory."

"About the altar boy?" This came from Betty, who didn't look up from her plate as she dug deep into her food.

"Did you know him?" Vanessa asked, wondering what the old woman knew; already, it seemed like a lot.

"He was a troubled kid but he had a reason to be. Daddy went out for milk when he was three and never came back and then his mom got into that crowd around Mitton." Their collective cringe shook Betty's time-worn table. "When she wasn't using, she was being used, if you know what I mean. That poor boy never had a chance. Started stealing from Merle's shop around the time he learned to read. Just candy, mostly, and Merle was really good about it. He knew the boy's situation so he tried to help him, even offered him a job, money under the table for sweeping up and keeping out of trouble, but that just pissed his mother off and she came in a gave Merle the what for."

This struck Vanessa as odd. "But it seemed like he came from a reasonable family. Quite involved, even."

"His *adopted* family was involved," Betty said. "The Lewises fostered him from the time he was six and made it official by the time he was nine. I'm telling you; he was a good kid. Terrible start, sure, but he was bright and couldn't have gone to a better family. Dale and Charlotte did him right. There's no way the boy did it."

"You don't think so?" Trevor stood and replaced their empty plates with glasses of wine. "Didn't he set the school on fire one year?"

Betty shrugged. "He burned some tests. So what? What kid hasn't wanted to do the same at some time?"

"But most kids don't," Trevor said.

Vanessa sipped her wine, thinking. "Do you think Patrick might have had a reason to start a fire at the church? I mean, churches around the world have been in the news for years …"

Betty slapped a thin hand on the table. "Not Father Pauliuk!"

"I'm just saying—"

"Absolutely impossible!" Betty roared with renewed vigor. Suddenly she was strong, her bones seemed straighter, her parchment-thin skin seemed to thicken, her blue veins sunk inward so that her pallor went from grey-blue to lively pink, even red. "Never on God's green earth!" She pushed away from the table, brooding.

"Okay," Vanessa ventured softly now, "let's say we forget about that one for the moment. Who else could have done it? Who would have had any reason to? If the shovel was just a prank gone wrong, then Kurt's initial theory about the fallen candle and Donna's attempted rescue of Stu would explain everything. But if the shovel and the fire are related, then it's a whole different story. It would mean that someone either had something against the church or Donna or Stu or both. We're going to get nowhere by following the first theory, and it will never explain who barred the door, so I say we focus on the second. Did the church have any trouble that we don't know about? Or maybe Donna or Stu had some secrets?" This latter part she knew to be true because Donna Pauliuk had been pregnant at the time of her death, which Father Pauliuk only discovered through the investigation.

"Get me some strawberry tea, will you hun?" Betty pushed her wine glass aside.

"You feeling okay Grandma?" Trevor filled the kettle with water and set it on the stove.

"Like a thousand pesos," she replied. "I'm good, I'm good. I just don't like to drink when I get to the serious stuff. It's best not to ruffle the brain when it's working or your wires get crossed and this isn't a time for crossing wires. God love Robert, bless him, bless him. You couldn't ask for a greater man in any community but I'll tell you that there was something unnatural between him and his wife. What kind of woman gets pregnant and doesn't tell her husband? Yes, I know. People around here know more than Tom lets on and Ray had ears like a damn gramophone. He knew everything that ever happened around here but part of what made him so good is that he barely shared any of it, except with Kathy, of course, and she with me. But who am I going to tell? And who would believe a batty old woman if I did? No, some secrets are best kept but not between a husband and a wife."

Trevor said, "But what if she didn't know she was pregnant?"

"Are you suggesting someone else stuck that test between Donna's legs?" Betty scowled. "Or maybe it was some other woman's pregnancy test in the Father's trashcan?" Trevor opened his mouth to speak but Betty put a hand up to stop him. "Look, everyone knew that they were trying for a long time and would have been thrilled about it. It wasn't a secret how much they wanted a baby." Betty's eyes swung to Vanessa and saw that the girl was working something over in her mind. She said, "Spit it out, girl."

A lingering thought broke Vanessa's lips. "Father Pauliuk is convinced Donna was so concerned about the church's finances that she left their house in the middle of the night to talk to Stu, who would have had little to do with the money. Unusual behaviour for both of them and too urgent. It doesn't make any sense at all, given that Ed Norman ran the books and she could have easily met with him the next day. Also, the church wasn't anywhere near as bad off as others have had it, unless someone was stealing, but there was no evidence of that. Tom showed me the reports." She paused. "As his assistant, what would Stu's normal responsibilities be?"

"Much of the same as Father Pauliuk's," Betty said.

"Did he ever hear confession?" Vanessa asked. Water hissed on the stove as the kettle spit and bubbled. Hit with this new possibility, the whistle rattled their ears, the walls, the air until Trevor finally pulled himself to the stove and removed the kettle from the heat.

Betty put a hand to her mouth. "I never thought of it, but yes, yes he did."

"Do you think Donna was trying to confess something to Stu?" Trevor poured hot water into their mugs.

"I don't know why she would confess to Stu. She was married to a priest. Unless—" Betty's hands seized the edges of the table.

"Unless she had something to confess that her husband wouldn't like," Trevor finished for her. "But it couldn't be. They would have thought of this for sure when they were investigating."

Vanessa leaned in. "Would they? Donna was revered just as much, if not more than Ray was and Father Pauliuk had a plausible explanation for her visit that night. Betty, did you ever hear what Father Pauliuk thought about why Donna might have been delayed in telling him about her pregnancy?"

"I did hear of a miscarriage a few months before but I can't be sure about it," Betty said. "They never announced they were pregnant before then but I heard that was because she lost the baby early. Don't quote me on that. You'd have to ask Robert about it."

Trevor cleared the table off and ran a sink full of soapy water. "Maybe she was hormonal. If she was pregnant, that could have given her more reason to be concerned with the books." Suddenly, the clink and clang of dishes in the sink was the only sound as both women stared at him in silence.

"What? Think about it. If she miscarried before, she might have wanted to keep her pregnancy a secret until she was past her first trimester, when it would have been safer to share and they were at less risk of losing the baby. How far along was she?"

Betty's hands went to her hips, full of interrogation. "And just how do you know so much about pregnancy, mister? Are there any grandchildren I don't know about? If so, God help you before I wring your neck." Her bottom lip protruded, her chin jutted, and her glasses slid to the end of her nose as she scowled.

"Grandma, I'm almost thirty." He shrank as she glared at him. "My ex-girlfriend was an obstetrician, okay? I never brought her to meet you because we weren't together long." He gave Vanessa a quick glance and she looked away before Betty could sink into it.

"Donna was about seven weeks pregnant," Vanessa offered, trying pull their attention back to the subject. "That would have put her in the first trimester. Very early in the pregnancy."

"With whose baby?" Betty wondered.

13

The heaviness on Nick's head was unbearable. Crushing, smashing, debilitating force threatened to split his skull and expose the delicate inner meat of his poisoned brain. An aortic thrum hit him just above the temples, now behind his eyes, now in his ears, deepening with each pulse into a heavy thickening of his nerves, his skin, his veins. His tongue had been replaced by sandpaper, his eyes had withered and dried in their sockets and his stomach—his stomach! That part of him which felt no longer part of him at all because it was too sour, too mouldy, churning first upward then viciously out of his mouth and through his nose and onto wherever it was Nick sprawled. His eyes were too dry to open, but open they did when a voice he did not recognise called, "Penner. You're out." The clang of metal echoed inside Nick's overburdened head as he pulled himself up. "You might want to clean yourself up before you see your wife," an officer said to him, handing him a towel and a bottle of water. Nick followed the woman along a corridor where she pointed to an institutional bathroom.

Nick stumbled inside, retched in the toilet, and looked for his liver in the mess. With effort, he opened the bottle of water and filled his mouth with it, sloshing the fetid upheaval from his cheeks and his teeth then spit it all out, flushing while drinking the rest of the water in three solid gulps. He went to the mirror where he saw his insides on his outside, half-digested, splattered in his hair, over his face and down his shirt and pants. He considered the towel then took his shirt off and threw it in the garbage. Nick opened the taps and rinsed his face and the rest of his skin, hastily rubbing at his jeans. Sadly, he couldn't say he looked any better for the effort. He left the towel in the bathroom and followed the officer, bare-chested, to the tightly crossed arms of his wife, who had his paperwork clutched in one hand.

Lynn scowled and Nick had to quicken his step to keep up with her. "Public nuisance? Public intoxication? Trespassing? Indecent exposure? You've really set a new low, Nick." Nick said nothing not only because there was nothing to say in this argument, which wasn't entirely all that new, but because his mouth couldn't form the words and the sound of his own voice would likely make him retch again. When they got to her car, Lynn thew an old t-shirt at him. "I'm not driving with you looking like that. Put it on." The door flew open and Lynn dove inside, anger pouring through her so hotly Nick wondered for a moment if it was safer to walk. His knees buckled without him having taken a single step away so he grudgingly got inside the car where, if he got sick again, Lynn would deserve it.

Lynn drove angrily, taking sharp turns, slamming on the breaks, gunning the gas so that Nick's useless body was thrashed this way and that. His head banged off the window and the seatbelt bit his shoulder and cut into his already delicate stomach. After a time, he managed to speak. "What happened?" Nick asked, for he truly couldn't remember.

The car screamed to a stop at the curb two blocks from their house. "What happened, Nick? What happened? Do you not remember pissing all over the Johnson's front door? Do you also not remember pissing on Ned's feet when he opened the door to see what the racket was? And what about the fucking library, Nick? When did you feel it was okay to scratch it up with your car keys? Was that before or after you thought you could outrun a cop car with your cock sticking out of your fucking jeans? You really outdid yourself this time, Nick. Nothing but class."

He had no concept of time except he thought it might be morning because the sun was just beginning to cut its path into the sky, hurting his eyes. "I'm sorry, Lynn. I—I must have had too much." He leaned his head onto the doorframe and squeezed his eyes shut.

Lynn gripped the steering wheel, staring ahead at the static road. "I can't do this anymore, Nick. I want a divorce." Maybe not now, and maybe not in the sorry state for which he had no excuse, but Nick expected this. Though it was a long time coming, it still surprised Nick the way his body constricted, the way his throbbing brain skipped, the way his heart momentarily stopped when Lynn finally worked the words from her mouth. He opened the door and vomited. "Say something," Lynn's voice was faint. But Nick couldn't say anything, and if he did, it wouldn't be right, could never be right. Instead, he unbuckled his seatbelt and fell onto the sidewalk. "Nick," Lynn said, but didn't stop him when he got to his knees, gently shut the door, and began walking.

His pace was slow and soon the car passed him. Nick saw that Lynn did not turn into the driveway but passed it without so much as a familiar pause. The short distance was torture. Chorals of crickets and honeybees and birds of dawn scraped at his ears and scratched his head. The thump of papers hitting doorsteps grated his nerves and Nick momentarily thought of drumming the paperboy, but it wouldn't be fair. Nick would just get caught. When he finally reached the steps, he realized that he had lost his keys. Grunting, he bent over the small pot of flowers Lynn kept near the door and rooted underneath it for their spare key. Inside, Nick passed out almost immediately.

His dreams were of that terrible night, of shoves and sirens and screams, of a city's collective cry, and of his own ragged breath in the shadows of his front porch, steadied only by the last vapors of his own sobs, when he had nothing left inside him to expel. The last touch of her skin before their eternal separation still haunted Nick, for in the moments before they parted that day, he actually believed he loved her. He woke in a thick sweat on the couch sometime later. Before he knew it, a mug of coffee was thrust in front of his face. He sat up.

"Mom told me what happened," Vanessa said, sitting on the coffee table.

Nick rubbed his face. "What time is it?"

"Almost four."

"Uggh," Nick accepted the cup. The coffee stung his dry lips.

"When are you going to stop, Dad?" She asked it simply and Nick knew she was right to ask it but he had no answer now.

"I'm sorry, Vanny," he said, regarding for the first time the new shade of her skin and the freshness of her face. He knew in that sobering instant that his daughter was happy and that something was making her happy but that her happiness was shrouded in her bitter disappointment of him.

"You need help, Dad."

"I know."

"And you need to shower because you've been invited to dinner and I'm not taking you like this." Unnecessarily, she gestured to the entirely of him.

Every movement of his body brought fresh pain and he slowly shook his head. "I can't, Vanny. I need Tylenol and twelve hours of sleep."

Vanessa pulled the blanket off him and an unpleasant coolness gave Nick the sudden shivers. "I'll get you Tylenol but you're getting your ass in the shower and you're going to get dressed and make yourself presentable for me, Dad. We've been invited to the Beecher's for dinner tonight and I said you would be there so you're going to be there."

Nick froze. "Phil's?"

Vanessa shook her head. "Rick and Gloria's."

"I'm not going." The declaration was sudden and angry.

Vanessa's eyebrows shot up. "What's wrong with them?"

"Nothing," he said and yanked the blanket out of her hands, covered himself, and laid back down.

She jerked the blanket off him again and threw it far in the corner. "You're coming, Dad."

"I'm not." Eyes closed, Nick turned over and away from her, digging his face into the cushions. She stomped to the kitchen and tramped back, then she was pouring cold water over his head. He flailed and fell off the couch, swiping at his face and bracing himself for more. "What the fuck Vanny? Stop it! Stop it!"

"I don't ask for much. I don't need money. I've never had you bail me from fucking prison. I've never gotten knocked-up. I've never done drugs. You're doing this for me because you're my father and we were invited as a fucking family. Don't be an asshole and make me beg." Vanessa's arms were stiff at her sides, her face rigid, her eyes deadly. Nick's jaw, sufficiently oiled with indignation, now dropped. His eyes sprang wide. Never had she used such language before him or against him.

"What's gotten into you?'

She threw up her hands. "Oh, I don't know! Maybe my father pissing his way around town? Maybe my friends texting me about my father hitting on a bartender? Maybe everyone else worried about you getting arrested? What's wrong with you, Dad?" The last came out as an accusation.

If Nick was anything, he was smart enough to know when to give up but this one he would not, could not relinquish. He slid his tongue over the grit on his top teeth and said, "I've been doing some thinking, Vanny. That job ain't right for you. It's not what you do and it's not who you are. I've got something else for you."

"What are you talking about?" She followed him to the bathroom where he located a bottle of Tylenol. He popped three into his mouth and swallowed them as he drank from the tap.

"I told you. You don't have to work for Beecher anymore. I got you something better through Gus. Advertising. You like that, right? Advertising is what you do, Vanny." Vanessa winced at Nick's breath as he passed her in the doorway, then he made his way toward his bedroom where he would sleep his pain away.

"I don't know what you're talking about, Dad. I like working for Phil."

"Well, *I* don't like you working for Phil. That god-damned church story? It's not for you, Vanny. It's not for you. People died there. You don't need to go messing around with something like that."

"You have no right," her voice quivered.

His head wobbled as he bent to pull clean underwear from the drawer. "You're my daughter and you'll do what I tell you to, Vanny. That's it. End of discussion." He swerved around her, needing a shower to rid himself of the smell.

"No!" Vanessa stomped her foot.

Nick turned. "What did you say to me?"

Vanessa hesitated, then her jaw stiffened and her chin went up. "I said no. I won't let you treat me the way you treat Mom."

Her eyes were suddenly wet and when he touched her arm, she recoiled. She had never recoiled before. Never. His baby girl, the child he loved more than life itself, afraid of him. *This* was the lowest he could go, he realized, and sank within himself. "I'm sorry, Vanny. I'm not right. I'm tired and I've got a headache and I just can't seem to stop fucking up. Please forgive me. I'll go to your dinner. I'm sorry."

"I'll get you another cup of coffee," she said quietly, and left him to clean up.

The water stabbed at Nick's scalp, pricked his back, and needled his stomach as he resisted the urge to turn the temperature up. Then his teeth chattered, his skin rose with gooseflesh, and his body convulsed, but Nick held on. He would suffer a cold shower that felt like a drenching in dry ice because he needed to wake up, needed to think. Mostly, he needed to prepare himself for whatever Rick might say. Had Rick seen him racing away that night? Had he known? Never before was there an indication but Nick couldn't be sure. He toweled off and put on jeans and a t-shirt, feeling less like roadkill and more like a cornered man. His nerves pulled and yanked at him, picked at his already weak stomach, and quickened his pulse. A quick search through Lynn's makeup kit and he found her not-so-secret bottle of Xanax tucked away in the bag that held her makeup brushes. Nick popped two of these and found Vanessa, coffee in hand, waiting for him in the kitchen.

"Feel better?" she asked.

"Much," Nick said. "I'm sorry, Vanny."

"You should be." She looked at him then with eyes that were too wise and he felt for a moment Lynn's exasperation in that stare.

Nick sipped his coffee. "I deserve that."

"You do, but you also deserve help, Dad. Whatever you are when you're drinking, you're not a terrible person. You're good when you're sober. I just wish you could stay that way."

He went to the cupboard and opened a bag of potato chips, downing a handful and letting the salt fortify his emaciated state. Two tall glasses of orange juice washed it down. "Forget what I said about the job, Vanny. Do what makes you happy."

"I was going to anyway," she said.

"That's my girl," Nick hugged her and he was glad she hugged him back.

With food and drugs in stomach and time doing its slow heal, Nick finally convinced Vanessa that, no, he would not start drinking while she got ready and, yes, that he would still be there when she was finished. Kindly, she allowed him a nap if he was able to take one. Though he was dog-tired, this was something he could not do. For the first time since the night of the fire, fear had once again gathered around him and Nick found that even with the Xanax, he was still a bag of nerves. A tide of memories surged at him and for only a moment, he conjured a different ending with a different life for himself without fear or regret. Now he compressed all of this, put it away in the stores of his other self where it would hopefully remain hidden until his last breath.

They drove and by the time they pulled up to the bustling house, Nick felt almost like himself again. Cars were lined along both sides of the street. Women in summer dresses and men in light shirts flowed toward the house carrying ribboned wine bottles and cases of beer. Not an intimate affair. Nick relaxed a little. "You never said it was a party."

"Phil told me it was a small get-together."

"Nick! Hi!" The door of a Mini Cooper slammed and then Sheena Blisinger, Lynn's best friend and orthopaedic surgeon was skipping toward them. "Vanessa, you look lovely."

"Thanks. You do, too."

Sheena was brilliant in an off the shoulder white jumpsuit and Nick admired the way it plummeted low on her back, almost pointing to her ass. He tried not to look at it but she caught him. "I guess I'll see you two inside?" she said, and then she was off, drifting away into the arms of a muscled, ebony-skinned man in a yellow shirt. He raised his arm in greeting but his smile dropped once Sheena, on tiptoes, whispered into his ear.

Nick slowed his pace so he wouldn't have to meet the pair again. "Looks like your mother beat us here," he said, gesturing to Lynn's white SUV.

"If anyone asks, *I* wanted to drive," Vanessa murmured and then it dawned on Nick that his truck was still in the parking lot at Shooters.

"How did I ever deserve you?" He nudged her with his elbow.

"Just try to have fun tonight, okay? And no drinking. Promise?"

In his slow state of recuperation, the idea of a drink nauseated Nick. No. He would not be drinking tonight. He would be on his best behavior because he damn well needed to be. Nick squeezed her hand. Inside, gold and white decorations adorned the walls, the tables, from the high vault of the ceiling to the low dip of the floors, unnecessary illusions of grandeur on an already impressive house. It was no secret that both Rick and Phil had received sizable inheritances in Ray's will and where Phil naively sunk the money into the Gazette, Rick's investment in his house definitely showed. Death did have its benefits, Nick reflected, and then he was shaking hands and patting backs, for he knew the Tuckers and the Landers and the Bollygottens and the Greens, all happily regaling each other with stories of Rick and Gloria over the ten years of their marriage. It was an anniversary party.

"Nick!" Gloria Beecher floated toward them, champagne in hand. A fitness instructor, Gloria radiated health from her liquid skin to the bend of her limbs. Honey brown hair tumbled over a long loose dress the hue of the sky. She gave Nick a quick hug, spilling her champagne down his back. It seemed there was no way Nick wasn't going to smell like alcohol tonight. "Oh! Gosh I'm sorry!" Gloria sprung away, returning at once with a napkin. She dabbed at his back.

"No worries," Nick said jovially. If the rest of the evening went this way, he figured he could breathe.

In an extravagant display of over-reaction, Gloria's hand flew to her chest. "Where are my manners? You need drinks. Whatever you want, just name it. Rick went all out today. We've got everything," she tittered. "And I thought he was incapable of surprises!"

From the periphery, Nick saw that Lynn was coming toward them. He brushed a nervous hand through his hair as she approached. Color saddled over her nose and cheeks the way it sometimes did when she was bothered but her smile was large and believable. "I thought you two would never make it." She squeezed Vanessa's shoulders with her free hand and gave Nick an air kiss beside his cheek that he did not much care for.

"Wouldn't miss it for the world," Nick said, feeling Lynn feed on his discomfort.

"Drinks! We need drinks over here!" Gloria thrust a braceleted arm in the air and with a flick of her fingers, a thin man in white shirt and black tie appeared at her side. Gloria cozied up to him with a shake of her shoulders. "Jovy! Our friends here are desperate for a drink." The man named Jovy acknowledged them with the slanting of his chin. They ordered. A gin and soda for Lynn, red wine for Vanessa, and club soda for Nick. "Aw, now Nick! There'll be none of that! At least have a beer!" Gloria encouraged.

"Wish I could but I'm driving these two beauties home."

Gloria melted. Lynn, on the other hand, looked almost nauseated. "Good man. At least keep him hydrated, Jovy." The waiter disappeared into the small crowd and Gloria used this opportunity to gush. "A waiter! In our house! You

162

know, I thought Rick was up to something but nothing like this. And just wait until you see the food! All our favorites in mini and even a poutine bar. You have to help yourself before Rick eats it all." She led them into the kitchen where white linens draped the Beecher's island and dining table, transforming the area into a chic dining spot. Petite pork sliders, mini crab cakes, garlic-sautéed mushrooms, goat cheese pizzas, marble-sized meatballs, smoked meats, gourmet cheese, bruschetta, breads, and colorful spreads of all kinds were artistically arranged on oversized white platters. The poutine bar, a hot mountain of fries sided with bowls of salty gravy and cheese curds and a colorful assortment of vegetable and meat toppings, would be exactly what Nick's stomach needed. He started making himself a plate when Rick entered the kitchen.

"There they are!" Rick hollered, his long arms outstretched. He carried a beer in each of his hands. "Don't worry! Don't worry! It's not that kind of party. I'm just making sure I don't go dry, you know?" From the far side of the room, Jovy inched upward on his toes, locating them over the throng of hungry guests that now congregated in the kitchen. They received their drinks with great relish, then Jovy departed with a slight bow of his head. Rick touched both of his beers to Nick, Lynn, and Vanessa's glasses. "Quite the spread, huh?" Rick threw an arm over Nick's shoulder and Nick felt as though he would be sick all over again. Was there a slight squeeze? A tightening of Rick's fingers on Nick's chest? The threat of an indent from Rick's nails? He tensed and then Rick was releasing him and slapping his back. "Don't let me stop you. Help yourselves."

For a moment, Nick forgot that Gloria was still with them but now she was flashing her jewelled hands at the food again. "Eat seconds, thirds. We don't want anything left over. Rick's been attached to the fridge lately so it's better for his waistline if it's all gone. Love you babe." She kissed Rick's offered cheek then skirted away to other conversations in other parts of the house.

Rick leaned in conspiratorially, elbowing Nick in the ribs. "She doesn't know I've already saved some for later. Ha!"

Nick stepped away. As he collected a plate and a roll of cutlery, he heard Vanessa say, "I wish I would have known it was a party. I was hoping to talk to you about the article." This would have been the perfect time to collapse, convulse, fake a sudden stroke or poisoning. Yet for a moment, the consideration was almost a reality, for Nick did feel so faint he had to hold the table to keep himself from falling over. Lynn eyed him curiously but said nothing and went on to fill her own plate.

"That!" Rick exclaimed. "Yes. Sorry, Vanessa. I should have told you we were having a bit of a celebration today but no worry, no worry. We can talk. Better sooner than later, though, while I still can, huh?" He jiggled his bottles of beer.

"Are you sure? We can meet later on in the week if you'd like." Yes, Nick thought. Later on in the week. Or the next month. Or never.

Rick set an empty bottle on the stove and it was dutifully scooped up by Jovy who seemed to have some ingrained radar for deserted beverages. Rick waved Vanessa toward the hall. "We can chat in the office. I don't think there's much I can add to what we already talked about with Phil and Father Pauliuk but whatever I know, it's yours."

Nick, who by now had abandoned his plate, followed them out of the room. "This is not the time, Vanessa," he said. Hoping to sound fatherly, Nick realized too late that after their earlier tussle at the house, his advice would not be welcome.

"Never mind that." Rick led them through the house to a closed door at the end of the hall. "Come, come. We'll get this over with and then we can party, huh?" That he was an interloper on Vanessa's interview was something Nick couldn't concern himself with. His fear pushed him down the hall and his anxiety simply would not let him leave no matter how unwelcome he was. Behind Rick's back, Vanessa's eyes squeezed with annoyance but she said nothing. They followed Rick inside to a predominantly white room with large bookshelves and a back wall fashioned entirely of glass. Modern grey couches sandwiched a magazine-clad glass table that Rick now used as a footstool as he sat. Taking seats across from him, Vanessa observed the room with wonder while Nick picked at a loose thread on his jeans.

"Wow!" Vanessa said appreciatively.

"This room is Gloria's baby," Rick told her. "I got my shop in the garage and she got her office so we're both happy." He chugged his beer. Were his eyes on Nick? Was the flicker of Rick's jaw muscle aimed at him? The too long swallow an avoidance tactic or a sign of the other man's virility? Nick sipped his soda, taking an ice cube into his mouth. He bit down, sensing Vanessa immediately stiffen beside him.

"I'll try to make this quick," she set her drink on a coaster and removed her notebook from her purse, turning pages for some time until a blank one appeared. "So far,

I've talked with Tom, Kurt, Kathleen, and, of course, you and Phil and Father Pauliuk at the church. I'm going to reach out to Southbridge and see if I can set up something with Ed Norman in the next few days, but I'd like more information on the other two altar servers, Agnes Clarke and Patrick Lewis before I do."

Was that a pause? The pushing of memory come to open the gates? Nick bit the inside of his lip until a tooth tore through the soft flesh near the inner corner of his mouth. Quickly, he took in a mouthful of soda to wash the blood down before either of them could see. "Well," Rick fingered his beard, "Patrick has passed and from what I hear Agnes is not too far behind."

"She's dying?" Vanessa slid to the edge of her seat.

"I'm not too sure. At least, I don't think so. All I know is that Agnes has been under psychiatric care since not too long after the fire. It was hard on all of us but especially Agnes. She was close with Mrs. Pauliuk—I still can't bring myself to use her first name, we were just kids, you know— anyway, Agnes looked to her like a mother so she took it really hard when Mrs. Pauliuk died. She started … cutting herself, and then there were the pills …" He looked away. Vanessa gasped. Nick chewed more ice. "Her mom died when she was just a baby, so maybe that was part of it, but her dad is a great guy. I've seen him every now and then with my boss, they've been friends for a long time, and he says she's doing okay in there but I don't think she talks much. She went catatonic or something. So sad."

Vanessa said, "I wonder why the Father didn't mention this when we spoke to him at the church."

"That's easy," Rick explained. "He's a man of faith. He believes she's going to get better, but from what I hear, I'm not too sure the doctors would agree."

"Hmm," Vanessa readied her pencil. "Do you think she had anything to do with the fire? Maybe that's why her reaction was the way it was?"

Rick shook his head. "Agnes? No way, I mean, it's possible, but she was always such a nice girl." He thought for a moment. "Now that I think of it, she did have a few quirks, but who doesn't?"

"What kind of quirks?" Vanessa asked.

"Well, she did scoop from the offering plate once, said it was for a pack of smokes but I told her I wouldn't say anything if she put it all back."

"Did she?"

Rick nodded. "Yeah. There was no argument about that. She didn't want Patrick to know. She was into him, I mean *really* into him, teen hormones and all that, so she didn't want anyone to find out, especially the Father or Mrs. Pauliuk."

"Because she was afraid they would kick her out and she wouldn't be allowed to be an altar server anymore? Where she would see Patrick on a regular basis?" Vanessa reasoned.

"I think so," Rick agreed.

"Do you know where she is staying right now?"

"Some hospital, I guess, but I'm not sure where," Rick's shoulders lifted as he thought.

Nick's knees jittered. For a brief moment, he considered faking a heart attack, anything to end the conversation. He clenched his stomach, hoping to appear sufficiently hungover, and when Vanessa's eyes slipped over him, she seemed to understand his unease. To Rick, she said, "One last thing. I'm working on a theory. It might be nothing but it might be everything."

"Go on," Rick swung his feet from the table and leaned in.

"Up to this point, much of the investigation has focused on Donna and Stu's meeting that night."

"Uh-huh. There were money issues."

"Not really, though," Vanessa said. "They weren't in enough trouble to warrant a secret late-night meeting, especially since Ed Norman, not Stu, ran the books. My understanding is that Stu would have carried many, if not most, of the same responsibilities that Father Pauliuk had which means that he would be an appropriate person to hear confession."

For a moment, Rick's eyes bored into Nick. This was it. This was the moment Nick dreaded. Here, now, all would be said and Nick would be on a swift train to hell. Instead, Rick's eyebrows shot up. "You think she was going to confess?" Vanessa nodded. "What would she have to confess? The woman was practically a saint."

"I'm not sure but I think it might have had something to do with her pregnancy."

"She was pregnant?" Rick set his bottle down. Nick watched the actor feign surprise, a pitiful but passable attempt. "I mean, I've heard rumours, but nothing ever concrete, you know. My dad kept most of that stuff to himself. If he knew, at least he never shared it with me. Widlow tell you this?" Vanessa said nothing but it was obvious Rick knew where she'd gotten the information. "Man, that's terrible." He stood then, and they knew the conversation was over. This was okay with Nick. What was not okay, however, was Rick's offer of meeting Vanessa again as he peered over her shoulder and leered at Nick. The message was clear.

14

An unfortunate uptick in temperature made the following days miserable. Rain that refused to come was now but a reflection in the suffering of burnt lawns and withered gardens, parched songbirds, and lifeless streets. August's burn had even begun to strip leaves from trees, with those lucky enough to still have them now tinder dry. The assisted living home seemed to bake in the heat, with pots of wilting flowers appearing just as downcast as the several residents now displayed on wheelchairs in the shade of the front veranda. Lingering indignities of the Covid epidemic were still prevalent at Southbridge; the handful of residents outside were spaced widely apart and the two mask-clad visitors that were present were situated on far away chairs directly beneath the sun. Vanessa adjusted the mask over her ears and went inside to the reception desk where a sign warned ill visitors away and insisted on the sanitization of hands. Vanessa complied, rubbing the gel over her palms, between her fingers, around her thumbs and the back of her hands until the gel had dried and her skin smelled strongly of alcohol. "How can I help you?" asked the sitting nurse from behind her mask.

"I have an appointment to see Ed Norman."

The nurse checked first her computer and then a clipboard. "Ah! Yes. Eddie. He's going to be so happy to have company. Come this way." She led Vanessa through a set of double doors, down a long corridor to another veranda on the rear of the building where a scattering of benches and tables waited for company that would seldom come. "I'll have to ask you to keep your mask on and try not to sit too close. Even with the vaccine, we're still careful about things around here, but visits do a world of good for them, more than we ever could, the Lord knows."

"I'll keep my distance," Vanessa said, and took a seat on a bench on the far side of the veranda that overlooked a small pond with what appeared to be a miniature fairy garden and several orange and white koi fish. She waited while the nurse collected Ed, rolling him outside with a small blanket on his lap.

The nurse whispered. "He gets cold even in this heat." Then in a louder voice, "But you'll be okay, Eddie, won't you? A pretty girl and some fresh air are every man's dream, isn't that right? Isn't that—"

"I heard you the first time," Ed said.

"I'll leave you to it, then." The nurse's soft shoes were almost soundless as she departed.

A flashing of mist quivered over the lawn as the sprinklers engaged and both Vanessa and Ed followed their wake, each of them involuntarily smiling as the ghost of a rainbow appeared in the low fog. "So you're here to talk about the fire," Ed scratched the shoulder of his checkered shirt and shifted in his wheelchair to face her.

"I am. If you're okay with it, that is."

"You a journalist?"

"Trying to be."

"Why try? Just be. Life's too short for anything else."

"I suppose so, but if you don't try then there's no be-ing at all, right?" She pronounced the word with slow emphasis on the first syllable and smiled at him.

"You're all right," Ed said simply, and looked out over the lawn again. His high-waisted trousers gave the impression of a shrunken torso but then Ed filled his lungs with summer air, and he stretched and extended and inflated to the full allowance of his skin, seeming to grow two sizes before her eyes. His white hair flapped in the wind.

"Do you get many visitors?" Vanessa asked. "I mean with the epidemic and everything." She instantly regretted saying this but Ed didn't seem to mind.

"Some. More hassle than some of them are worth, though. They do everything but delouse us after every visit. Don't mind the grandchildren coming, but their parents I can sometimes do without. Seems all I'm worth sometimes is whatever's written in my will." Ed sighed. "But I suppose I'll have to suffer those visits until I'm gone because the trick's on them—I'm broke." Rustling laughter blew out of him until he was bent over, coughing, when the concern on Vanessa's face caused him to settle. "I can assure you I'm not dying, however much some days I wish I were. Sorry, that was a terrible thing to say but when you get to eighty-five years the other side doesn't seem so unpleasant. Are you a believer, young lady? Vanessa?"

Vanessa nodded. "Yes. I used to go the old church with my family when I was younger."

"And you stopped after that?"

"No. We still went to those services Father Pauliuk had in the community hall while the new church was being built, then we attended the new one once it was done. I moved away for a while."

"Ah," Ed said. He wetted his dry lips. "Would you be so kind as to get me some water? It's a devil of a day and they keep me in blankets because they think I'll freeze without them. That's what happens in these places. They cocoon you once you enter the door and you don't emerge until your last breath when you take a different kind of flight." He cleared his throat.

Vanessa excused herself and found a nurse who gave her a tray with plastic tumblers and a pitcher of ice water. She carried it to the bench and set it down. By now, Ed had slipped the blanket off and was shuffling barefoot on the grass as she sometimes saw Father Pauliuk do.

"You Holy Redeemer men seem to lose your shoes a lot."

"Nothing frees the spirit more. Come! Join an old man and we'll talk." Vanessa removed her sandals then poured glasses of water which she shared with Ed. The tendons on Ed's neck pulsed as he drank, the bumpy sag of his skin suggesting a far away prehistoria that Vanessa preferred not to focus on. She told him what she knew as they walked together, feeling the cool wet grass while they migrated between tracts of oak shade and dogwood cover. The pace was slow and the conversation was thoughtful while Ed listened intently, occasionally clarifying what he could.

"Do you think it was an accident?" Vanessa asked after a time. "Was the shovel just a coincidence?"

Ed said. "I don't believe in coincidences. No. It was not bad timing, it was not bad luck, it was not some God-awful prank. We'd never had our doors blocked before that night. Whoever put the shovel there knew what they were doing."

"What makes you think so?"

"Timing, mostly, but also because it wasn't an easy thing to do. It didn't just slide like butter through those loops. They were old, imported from Europe, a gift from one of our German counterparts. Tight craftsmanship, over-built to last a thousand years. That handle had to be *pushed* through that metal."

"What about the back door? It wasn't locked or blocked. Had the fire or smoke not been so bad in that area, they might have gotten through there. Maybe it's just another meeting of bad timing and disaster."

"Maybe," Ed said, wiping his forehead with the back of his hand, his steps slower.

"Do you know of anyone who would have had a reason to set the fire?" she followed Ed back to his wheelchair and they sat.

Ed groaned as he settled in. "I don't know. They were all good people back then. Best church community I've ever been a part of. Devoted. Involved. Hard-working. I don't know a soul who didn't like Donna, though there were a few old birds who didn't much care that the Father's wife could bake them under the table." He laughed. "But people respected them. Stu was quieter, of course, and I don't remember there being any issues with him. A bit of a serious fellow, didn't often open up but I suppose that's why everyone trusted him."

"Even with money?" she asked.

Ed recoiled slightly. "Especially with money. We could have given him every red cent and he would have guarded it wisely. The church doesn't permit its clergy to manage such affairs without a committee, or Stu would have willingly and competently governed our funds. As it was, he quietly dipped into his own pockets to spare the church during a few cold snaps when our power bill shot through the roof and again on numerous occasions for repairs. Bless him."

"That day, when you discovered the roof was leaking, you found the Father and his wife in the vestry."

"She was crying," he nodded.

"Do you have any idea, any idea at all what it could have been about?"

It took some time for Ed to speak. "When I first found water in the entry, there were only the three of us there. Robert and Stu were always early as they had to prepare for the services but Stu had car issues and was running late so I came early to help out, I was usually early anyway.

Typically, Donna arrived just before the services because she prepared food for the fellowship afterward. She used the kitchen in the basement for our bigger events or when we were expecting more people but sometimes she cooked at home and just walked it across the field. They had a small house on the opposite end of the grounds."

"Were you expecting a lot of people that day, Ed?"

"Not any more than usual."

"So were you expecting to see Donna so early that morning?"

Ed thought. "No, but I also wasn't surprised to see her, either. What struck me was the look on her face. I'd never seen her like that before. She looked rather upset."

"Any idea why?"

The wind whipped up, snatching hold of Ed's blanket. Vanessa hurried to catch it before it was carried away. Great swaths of dust whisked from far away fields, wheeling over the sidewalk this way, that way, through the veranda, hot as the Sahara, and they had to shut their eyes until it rushed upon other bodies in other towns, in other cities. Ed's lids creaked open. "It was not my intention to pry but I had come down the hall to tell Robert about the roof. I paused for a moment outside the vestry door not to listen, mind you, but because there was water outside the door so I suspected another leak. I must stress that it was only a moment so I didn't hear much, but it did sound like Donna wanted to tell Robert something."

Vanessa folded the blanket and tucked it between the wheelchair and Ed's leg so it wouldn't blow away. "About the finances? Is that what she wanted to talk about?"

"I don't believe so, however much Robert believes it. Donna was not shy in matters of money. If she or the Father had any questions or issues, I was always notified without hesitation. Our books were open for anyone to see, and the repairs would have forced us to squeeze a little more than normal but they were not a death knell, by all means. The initial repairs that day were covered by our parishioners, with pledges to relieve us of the rest."

"Gil, Roger, and Wayne, right?"

"You've done your homework," Ed looked at her fondly.

"Were any of them there by the time you found Donna and the Father in the vestry?"

"I wish they were. Their hearing might have been better than mine. I was sixty-three back then and though I was in much better shape than I am now, I can't say I could hear a church mouse in a far field. Far from deaf, mind you, but far from my twenties when my ears could pick up a Beatles song playing in Mexico. Even so, I knew at once by the tone of the conversation that only one of them was upset. Robert was trying to reassure Donna of something but she did not seem to console easily. She turned from me when I came in and again when I returned to report on another leak. I had never seen her like that."

Vanessa scribbled feverishly as Ed spoke. "If she wasn't upset about the cost of the repairs, can you think of anything else that made her upset?"

His voice was low and soft as he reflected. "Nothing specific, but those who knew Donna knew her to be extremely empathetic. She routinely took on others' problems as her own. If someone had troubles, they were Donna's troubles. She was sensitive to other people's emotions, especially with children since she wanted her own so badly. The youth ministry was a personal project that she took very seriously. When she wasn't with those children, she was with our altar servers, trying to help them weave a clean, Christ-like way through adolescence, no drugs or alcohol sort of thing. She would have been terribly disheartened to hear about young Mister Lewis and Miss Clarke. They were such good kids, they had so much promise. I still remember the day when we took our youth ministry out to Roy Botcher's farm. He had this wild strawberry field in the back quarter and he invited the kids to come pick strawberries before he worked it up for hay. You'd have never known the teenagers weren't years younger, the way they took to that field with the little ones. You'd never seen such life. Jumping and yelling, tearing things up like miniature tornadoes everywhere they went. They gathered on that field and left jam in their wake. Got more on them than in their buckets, red fingers, red faces, stained shirts, and then they banded together and went after the adults. Then we were all thrashing around, flinging berries. It was one of those moments where the world faded away and there was just a group of people enjoying God's bounty." He sniffed. "That was the summer before the fire. Patrick was alive and Agnes was still our Agnes. I still think of all of them as ours, no matter what the circumstances are."

"Do you know where Agnes is staying, Ed?"

He nodded. "St. Dymphna's. It's a long-term care home outside of Fauville, about thirty-five minutes west of Toronto. Her mother writes me letters from time to time. It seems us old folks just like the feeling of pen on paper. She still believes Agnes is going to come out of it, you know." Vanessa said nothing. "And maybe she would if she had more of a reason to. She had quite a thing for young Patrick, I'm not sure if you've heard."

"I have."

"Teenage love," he grinned. "It was harmless, of course, but as things go, they drifted apart. The fire was no help, but she wasn't the same after that and I don't think he appreciated the change. I could never be sure about that, but it's an assumption I think is more or less correct. One minute, they were flirting, hauling gravel to the window wells with young Mister Beecher, and the next, there was a distance between all of them, but that's what the fire did, everyone so desperate for answers that they filled in the blanks for themselves. He did this, she did that, mistakes here, blunders there, indiscretions everywhere; none of it substantiated, of course, the police reviewed everything, everything."

The doors behind them opened and a thin, stooped woman lead a young family to a set of benches on the grass near the pond. Ed waved. "I have a theory I want to run by you," Vanessa said.

Ed's waving hand slipped back to his lap. "Please, go ahead."

"You mentioned indiscretions. Whether unsubstantiated or not, I'm leaning toward a theory that might be uncomfortable for you."

"Go on."

"I believe that Donna went to the church that night to confess something to Stu, maybe whatever it was she was trying to tell Robert when you heard them in the vestry." She paused. "I know I have no proof of anything, and it will put Donna in a bad light but—"

"You believe she was pregnant with a baby that wasn't Robert's." This was a statement, not a question, something that seemed to whisper from a long-held vault. The downturn of Ed's mouth was reflective. "Ten, fifteen, five years ago, I would have taken great offense to that theory, as was gossiped, but time has this way of shorting wires and softening nerves and mixing recollections, and maybe that's what's got me these days. Maybe my wires have crossed or maybe I've already got a foot on the other side and it's letting me look not as a bystander or observer but as a sophisticate with a malleable mind capable of possibility." On the grass, laughter clanged from the old woman's tin throat as the young girl and boy attempted lopsided cartwheels and ended up knee-deep in the koi pond. Ed said, "Today, I believe that child was not Robert's but tomorrow I may harden again and refuse to believe anything but."

"Who would you say the father is today?"

"Could be anyone."

"No hunches, no gut-feelings on this?" Vanessa nudged.

"I'm afraid not. She certainly wasn't a person who presented herself as a philanderer and our parishioners were not the type to be 'chasing skirts', as some might say. She seemed to be a happily married woman. If she wasn't with Robert she was with our kids, but that malleable part of me also believes that Jekyll was not whole without his counterpart Hyde, that order and chaos are inseparable from the human experience, so I couldn't rule out a different self for her however much I wish against it."

Sweat had budded on Ed's forehead, his cheeks, on the soft flesh of his ears. To keep him outside any longer would be cruel, so Vanessa thanked him for his time and began wheeling him back inside. She said, "Can you tell me anything at all about how the altar servers got along? You mentioned they sort of fell out after the fire. I know they were young, but it makes me wonder how strong their friendship was. I know Agnes and Patrick had a thing going but I wonder if there was any jealousy there, if maybe Rick had some unrequited thing for Agnes, too?"

This seemed to make Ed laugh. "Oh no, no. There were no glances there, at least none apparent to me. I'm not sure he looked at any of our girls, to be honest. I have to admit that I once thought he might have had affections for those of his own gender because he never regarded girls the way the other boys in our parish had." His eyes squeezed with amusement. "They thought we were too old to notice their flirting but we always knew, we always knew. We had to separate Agnes and Patrick several times, if I remember correctly, but none of that seemed to bother Rick. He'd just go and read his Bible or his comics, or keep to himself in the cold storage near the kitchen if things were too busy for his liking. Of course, he's been married for years now so I must have been mistaken."

"Ten years this week," Vanessa said as Ed pointed toward his room. She manoeuvred his wheelchair through the doors. "We went to their party."

Ed rose and shuffled to the window beside his bed. He fingered the curtains and looked outside, where the sun was still bleaching everything it touched. "His father would have been proud. That was another one gone too soon."

"I wish I would have known Ray."

"If he were alive, he probably would have said the same about you. He said everyone had a story and he lived trying to find it for them. Strangers, friends, old, young, he'd march across that aisle to learn about the people around him. 'Hold up!' he'd holler," Ed chuckled, "'I need to meet you! Tell me a story!' People sure took to him." Ed dabbed at his eyes. "There's a lesson here, Vanessa. Pay someone else to put up your Christmas lights for you." He turned to his bed and inched onto it. Vanessa plucked his blanket from his wheelchair and set it beside him. "Thank you for the visit today, young lady."

"Thank you for letting me pick your brain," she smiled at him. "I appreciate it."

"Better to pick now before it all goes to seed, eh?" Ed winked. "Come back any time. With chocolate." He pressed his index finger to his lips. "But don't tell them." He pointed out the doorway.

"I won't," she whispered back, giving him a thumbs up. She left Ed then, signed herself out at the reception desk, and hurried toward the much-needed air conditioning inside her car. But there, in the glare of the parking lot, Vanessa caught her breath. Blood oozed down her door and flies were accumulating around dark material tied to the handle. Her hands went to her face as she inspected the dripping thing, and the realization of what the material was brought a sourness to her stomach so violent, she turned her head and gagged. Then Vanessa called her mother to see if the cat was still inside the house.

15

Pain. Phil hadn't been this sore since his twenties, but here in the dusty wreck that was the Baldwin's kitchen, Phil felt every day of his inactivity slam his muscles, his bones, the uncalloused skin of his palms, and his stalled joints were not fondly recalling his previous work. Another slow day at the Gazette where subscriptions were down and no ads were bought and where even the website wasn't free enough for readers afforded Phil the latitude to accept another renovation. He knew the Gazette's impediments weren't temporary. At one time, he could easily convince himself of this, but no more. The paper was dying and he couldn't save it. Renovation income would help the Gazette last only a little longer and the two jobs would likely be the end of him, but here he was, sweating and swearing as he tore their cabinets down and split drywall into nothingness. Tanya cried when he took that first job a few weeks ago, as they both knew it was a sign of their desperation and that their time for dreaming had long passed. Though he pressed upon his clients his renewed desire for physical creation, he convinced no one, let alone himself. Everyone in Garrett knew and everyone in Garrett tried to help. Bathrooms suddenly needed updating, living rooms needed expanding, kitchens needed opening, decks needed lengthening, fences needed new gates, windows needed walls, walls needed lookouts. Maybe as a favor to his father, maybe the same for himself, but Phil felt at once both undeserving and excruciatingly humbled by Garrett's patronage, with every hammer blow and plier pull a conflict he couldn't resolve. His trade during his university years, which he used to supplement his student loans, had not only been convenient, but necessary at the time. Mentally, Phil was now prepared for the old work but by the end of last week his body, strained, tired, spent, had almost totally seized. Hot baths and painkillers helped him get to today.

His phone vibrated. He unwound the last screw on the cabinet above the old stove and carefully pulled it down, then he gave his hands a cursory wipe on his jeans before taking his phone from his back pocket. There, a message from Vanessa asking to meet. He typed the Baldwin's address and put the phone back in his pocket, regretting his earlier proposition. There was definitely not enough money to keep her through the summer and he would have to use some of his renovation money to pay her for her work on the church story, which he was still determined to see through. She hadn't exactly asked to be paid yet, but Phil knew it was coming. No one worked for free, yet everyone wanted news for free; it was an irony that crushed him. He took at long swallow of water and leaned against a wall that would be down by the end of the day, thinking of his father again.

Shame was never in his father's repertoire, yet Phil felt it creeping within himself. Yes, he could say he tried, and that it was not a feeble attempt, but that it was perhaps a bit foolish and who better to sail a sinking ship than a fool? His father would have dismissed these thoughts as purposeless, as counter-productive, as the rupture of a fragile ego but

Phil couldn't help it. He was not his father, however much he tried to fill his footsteps. The doorbell rang and Phil navigated around stacks of laminate and unopened boxes of custom cabinetry, finding Vanessa, surprised, at the door.

"Oh," she said, clutching her notebook to her chest, taking in his coveralls and the drywall dust on his face.

"Side job," he said simply and he was thankful she did not ask him to explain further.

"Would you like to meet later?"

"You allergic to dust?"

"No."

"Then I've got all the time in the world."

He dusted off a chair for her to sit but she hesitated. "I've left something in my car. Give me a moment?" She set her notebook on the chair and dashed out the door before Phil could respond. A few minutes later, her dress had been replaced with an old pair of grass-stained jeans and loose t-shirt and her sandal-clad feet bore a shabby pair of runners, her loose hair now knotted up. He looked at her. "I was pulling weeds for my grandmother before I came here. Had them in the car. Maybe I can help you while we talk?"

His regret intensified. "Ever tear down drywall?" She hadn't but that didn't matter. Phil found her a pair of safety glasses and before long, Vanessa was scoring the edge of the ceiling with a blade and Phil was jamming a drywall saw through the wall, carefully negotiating around the studs. Then they were prying, knocking, yanking away, each jerk a burst of fine white powder onto their hands, faces, shoulders, until the frame was exposed, its wooden bones revealed like a skeleton in a sandstorm. "You're pretty good at this, maybe I hired you for the wrong job," he said, then, feeling she might take it as a slight, he added, "Anything new for me?"

She sat, accepting a glass of water. "Maybe not new, since you probably know more about the fire even than Tom or Kurt, but there's a direction I'm leaning and I want your thoughts before I go any further with it."

Phil's eyebrows, white with dust, inched up. "I'm interested."

"I think that Donna was at the church for confession. I have no proof of any sort, but I believe that there is a chance she was going to confess to Stu that she was pregnant with a baby that wasn't Father Pauliuk's." She waited. "You don't look surprised."

He shook his head. "I'm not."

"There was nothing in your files …"

"There didn't have to be," he said. "A distraught wife. A secret pregnancy. However angelic she appeared to be, she wouldn't be the first person to stray from a marriage, no matter how holy the rest of us perceived it was. I remember when my dad told us about the baby. That's part of what tore him up so badly. 'Three lives, not two', he would tell us. I sometimes wish that Tom didn't share everything with him, you know?" Vanessa nodded as Phil looked out the window. Then he said, "I'm glad you're thinking about this and considering all angles. I didn't want to lead you in any direction but your own. That file is a trove of facts. No matter what we believe, we can't print something that isn't grounded in truth. Other papers might bend this a bit, hell, some get rich off theories and fabrications but that's not what we do. First, it opens us up to litigation, and second, it's just not right. Then we might as well be a gossip mag or, worse, Fox News." He rolled the stiffness from his neck, stretching his shoulders, shaking out his arms. "If your gut tells you go there, then go there, but just remember that the story is not an opinion piece."

"I'll be careful," she said. "As long as you're okay with it."

"It's what I hired you for," Phil said. "And I think you're doing pretty good so far."

She tucked a foot beneath her thigh, massaging a sore calf. "Tom and Kurt seemed to think that Patrick Lewis might have had something to do with the fire."

Phil nodded. "He set fires before."

"Do you think he could be the father?"

Phil's head snapped up. "I never thought of it. No. I don't know. Maybe. You know he was only fourteen, right?"

"Old enough to father a child. From everything I heard, he was with Agnes but my understanding is that they had a falling out after the fire. Why then? When most people would come together to console each other? I can't understand why and Ed doesn't know why, either. I know Patrick had an alibi, that he was at some gaming party that night with a bunch of other kids, but maybe Agnes was upset because Patrick had something going on with Donna? Maybe they knew Donna was pregnant."

"Are you suggesting that Agnes set that fire?" That the theory would also make Donna a child molester he did not say.

"I don't know. I don't want to suggest anything at all until I have proof." The corners of Phil's mouth slightly rose as she said this. "I hadn't put it together like that but now that you say it, it's a hunch I'd like to follow. Quietly, of course. I'm driving up to St. Dymphna's tomorrow."

"You know she's catatonic, right?" Phil said. "At least that's what I last heard. Rick's boss is friends with her dad, from what I understand."

Vanessa nodded. "I'm not expecting to get much but anything at all would be more than I have now."

When she left, Phil had the sensation of a bomb being dropped on him, a bomb with a long timer. He couldn't place the feeling, he only knew that at some point, there would be a disruption, perhaps so big the slabs of Garrett's quiet existence couldn't be pieced back together. And what that meant for him, Phil was nervous. Donna a child molester? They would have to tread carefully on that one. It would be terrible for the community, horrifying for the church, and potentially lethal to Father Pauliuk, whose teetering stability would be irrevocably felled should it be true. The damage it would have done to the Lewis boy ... Phil shuddered, thinking. Had Patrick Lewis displayed any signs of abuse? Had he withdrawn or acted out? Had his childhood ended before its time in the arms of a woman over twice his age? Phil sighed and took to cleaning up, his concentration eroded. He pulled out his phone and called his brother. "I need a drink," he said, and because it was too early for scotch, agreed to meet Rick at their parent's nearby cabin for a mid-day beer.

The day had cooled somewhat but the residue of the sun's punishment was evident in the droop of the flowers, the crunch of the grass, the crackle of insect corpses Phil crushed as he went from his truck, past the small cabin and onto the deck, taking his favorite chair opposite his brother overlooking the lake. Rick, already a beer in hand, passed a cold bottle to Phil. "Not working today?" Phil asked, looking out over the water.

"Took the day off. Can't handle a hangover anymore." His sunglasses were dark but didn't quite cover the puff beneath Rick's eyes. He raised his beer. "The whole hair-of-the-dog thing isn't working as well as it used to. Might take me a month to recover."

"It was a good party," Phil said.

Rick grinned. "Gloria's still in bed. Ended up wanting to skinny dip in Fosner's pool at three this morning but she passed out before she could get her dress off so I carried her home. She's still sleeping in it." He tossed a bag of sunflower seeds to Phil and they sat, spitting shells into Solo cups, drinking beer in the shade of the awning. The lonely cries of loons haunted the water, opening their throats first low, then high, then low once more, fading to the ensembles of honking geese and busy ducks. Mariners in sail boats and speed boats and rowboats and even those on paddle boats and jet skis took to the great lake slowly, slowly, so that they were all almost still and need of a sudden, collective nap under the rare canopy of clouds. The air smelled of moss and earth and musty lake water, then sweet with tobacco when Rick lit a cigarette. Somewhere, a child cried, and their silent contemplation broke. Rick said, "You sounded rough on the phone."

Phil emptied the last of his shells into his cup and washed the seeds down with beer. "Just tired, I guess. I have to rewire the Baldwin's kitchen before I do anything else. It's a bigger job than I wanted."

Rick turned to him. "You know you don't have to do this anymore. Dad wouldn't have wanted you to burn yourself out like this. It's not healthy."

His shrug felt almost painful, a timely and unwanted reminder of his age. "I'm going to let the Gazette go after we're done the story." As he said this, he felt the great weight that hung over him for so many years now lower, heavier, pressing to the point of pain.

187

"Dad would have been proud of you," Rick said, an unexpected catch in his voice. He tapped his cigarette.

It struck Phil that his own escape would be safer than his father's that fateful day. Though he would surely feel the heat of his professional defeat, there would be no smoke and no flames, but also there be no hero to save him, and no redeeming breath on the other side when he closed his paper's doors. There would only be the pitiless tear of his family business, a long-coming perforation, the separation of what he hoped for from what he knew was realistic. So he would leave the Gazette, bury it, and store it beside other failings, other regrets. The fire, though, that was something he couldn't step away from. He would always be beside his father in those flames and Phil wouldn't step away until the person who put them there was in prison. He said, "There's a new theory."

"Do tell," Rick said.

"You know how Agnes and Patrick broke it off after the fire?"

Rick huffed. "I heard she wouldn't put out, but don't tell Vanessa I said that."

"Maybe, but what if that wasn't it?"

"What do you mean?"

Phil fidgeted. "Doesn't the timing make you think?"

"Not really. They were kids. We were all just a bunch of runts back then. Fire's got nothing to do with it. Pat couldn't keep his cock in his pants and she definitely didn't want it in hers, so they split. Happens all the time."

"But what if that's not what happened? What if—now, I know you're going to think I'm crazy for saying it, believe me, I know it's out there but it's something we haven't thought of. Hell, I'm not sure anyone else around here would have thought it, but what if," he paused, "what if Donna was having an affair with Patrick." Phil braced himself, waiting for the argument.

Rick sat up. "I … no … I mean—"

"It's not impossible."

"Do you really think so? Really? The priest's wife? No, man. I can't see her doing that. No way." He spat in his cup and took a long drag of smoke, releasing it through his nostrils.

"Why not? Think about it. She shouldn't have been in the church at that time of night. She was confessing something, Rick. I'm damn sure of it. It just makes sense. I think it was her pregnancy. What if Patrick got her pregnant and Agnes found out? Do you think she would have been happy about it? He might have an alibi, but where was *she* that night?"

"You think she set the fire?" He was watching Phil now.

"I think it's possible. That's all I'm saying. There really wasn't much attention on her. How long was your interview? Do you remember when Tom's team questioned you?"

Rick shrugged. "I don't know, maybe twenty minutes, maybe more."

"Exactly! Who would suspect a kid? And if they were going to suspect anyone, it would have been the kid who'd already had a history of setting fires, not his girlfriend. Don't you think it's a bit strange how she was institutionalized so soon after? Think about it."

Rick's tongue dragged behind his lower lip, the bristles on his beard rising, falling, rising. Then he ground something between his front teeth, looked out over the water, and let out a long breath. "Widlow know about this? It'll kill the preacher, you know."

"I know, that's why we're keeping it quiet for now. Just you and me and Vanessa. She's driving out to see Agnes tomorrow."

"Waste of time. She doesn't talk."

"You said, but no stone unturned, right?"

"If it's true ..." Rick's voice trailed to a whisper. His palm went to his face and he pressed his eyes shut, sliding his fingers wide to rub his temples.

Phil looked his brother, at the uneasiness he had brought, and gave Rick's foot a gentle kick. "Let's hope it's not, huh?"

16

It was a rare summer day when Nick Penner turned on the porch lights before dinner but the clouds were ugly and the sky was dark as soon as the last plate was set on the table. Uglier, though, was Lynn's mood as she stormed upstairs with the laundry basket and slammed Nick's clothes in the drawers so loudly it could be heard from Vanessa's room in the basement, where Reggie was coiled up on Nick's lap, purring. Evidently, Lynn's temper had not cooled since she picked him up from the police station because she could not look at him without scowling and could not talk to him without reminding him of what a louse he was. Now, she trampled down the stairs and peeked her face in Vanessa's doorway, adopting a nauseating singsong voice that repulsed him. "Clothes for me, hun? I'm putting in another load right now." She spoke as though Nick was not in the room.

Vanessa, busy her desk, leaned over and plucked a pair of jeans and blouse off the floor. "Only these," she said. "I'd like to wear them for my drive tomorrow." Lynn stepped inside, avoiding the space Nick occupied as though it might burn her, and scooped Vanessa's small bundle into her arms.

"Oh?" Nick asked causally, for he had been in Vanessa's room, avoiding Lynn for over an hour, and hadn't heard of any trip. He pet the cat, waiting.

"After getting you worked up over Reggie today, I thought you needed a break. I didn't want to say anything," Vanessa hesitated.

Nick forced an easy smile. "I'm just glad we found him in one piece. You had us scared there for a while, but I wouldn't worry about it. Kids around here do some stupid shit, you know. They're just lucky they didn't get caught." Reggie purred loudly, leaning into Nick's hand with his cheek. "So where are you headed tomorrow?"

"Nowhere special," she said, though as she spoke, he noted that she couldn't quite look at him.

"Come on, Vanny. We're all done with that, now. I told you I'll stay out of it, I'll stay out. You're happy, I'm happy."

She gave him a reassuring smile that he didn't quite believe. "I'm driving up to the hospital to see Agnes Clarke. She was one of the altar servers at the church."

"You're going to a hospital? Is she sick, Vanny? You have to be careful, the way everything spreads around here. Those places are germ holes." Though Nick's face puckered in disgust, he knew the situation in that hospital with Agnes Clarke. He knew that, tucked away in those bleach-smelling corners, the girl chewed her own hair and picked at her skin and said nothing to no one.

"She's in a long-term care home, Dad. She's not sick."

"Those places are filthy, Vanny."

"Not the one I was at this morning."

Nick bristled, knowing that if inquired who she saw, she would tell him it was none of his business. That, or she might wonder at his curiosity, might start looking a little too close to home, anything to validate her already low opinion of him. He felt his skin crawl, his gut clench, his nerves tense. He said, "The writing thing not working for you, Vanny? You got to go cleaning bedpans now?" Then Vanessa's jeans stung his face and Reggie's nails cut into him as he bolted away.

"Cut it out, Nick," Lynn warned, her free hand now resting on Vanessa's heavy lamp.

"Stop it!" Vanessa shouted. "Just stop, okay?" She snapped her laptop closed, yanked out the power cord, and shouldered past Lynn into the hallway and up the stairs.

"That's your fault," Nick pointed at her.

"Grow up Nick," Lynn snatched the jeans back up and slammed the door.

Alone but for the angry sounds of Lynn packing the washing machine (with rocks, he thought), Nick reflected on his depreciation within the household. His baby girl had turned into that part of Lynn that despised him. Was hate hereditary? He thought it could be, for he loved her as he should, took care of her as he should, but still she turned away, measuring him not by the nature of his fatherly role but by a standard that was unrealistic and unattainable. He was no deity, no totem of moral standing, but neither was he a low-life or a monster. Those things he'd done were done and he would protect Vanessa's ignorance of them with his life. He would let her despise him for all of Lynn's reasons but he would not let her despise him for the fire because she wouldn't just despise him if she knew, she would *disown* him.

Agnes Clarke. Agnes Clarke. Nick rolled the name, the face, over in his mind, trying to recall the sound of her voice, the way she stuttered, "ick, ick, ick, ick, ick," over and over, spitting and drooling down the front of her gown when he last saw her. Agnes Clarke, whose hard-on for the Lewis brat was noticed by everybody. Agnes Clarke, who had known, of course she had known, because she lost her fucking mind right after. Although he knew she wouldn't say anything to Vanessa, Nick felt a spotlight on him, oversized and blazing like the sun. He drummed his fingers restlessly, jigged his knees, and grinded his teeth until they crackled and his jaw stung. Rick hadn't outed him yet but what if Agnes did? What if she was recovering? Would there be a moment of clarity that saw Nick on a speedy trip to prison? He couldn't lock Vanessa up, however much he wished, and if he took another day off work Simon might tell him to hand in his work boots. That would just give Lynn another reason to hate him. Besides, there was no way in hell Vanessa would let him tag along. It would be too suspicious, and his complaints would inevitably broil out matter how much he tried to suppress them. He stewed, tossing her pillow aside, silently raging to the empty room. A neat pile of books lay on her shelf and Nick leafed through them mindlessly. Poe. Gaiman. King. Irving. Bradbury. Some guy named Cheever. All ammunition in their ambition to depress Nick further, make him feel stupid, make Vanessa and Lynn feel that much smarter. He was smart, too. Twenty-two years without so much as a sniff could only be accomplished by someone clever, fucking brilliant, even. He tipped the books over, one by one, and watched them fall to the floor. *How's that for intelligence*, Nick thought, and then beamed, for below the shelf, in the clutter of Vanessa's desk, lay her open notebook.

Nick listened for footsteps. The washing machine was humming now, Lynn's storming abated, and he thought he'd heard her tramp up the stairs but he couldn't be sure. A few quiet strides brought him to the door where he pressed his ear. He'd go flying if it flew open now, so he pressed his shoulder against it to cushion the blow, just in case. He could hear them upstairs, validating each other, and took the moment to nudge open the door and peek down the hall. Left. Right. No company except the cat, whose hackles raised the moment Nick looked at him. Nick silently shut the door and moved back to the desk where the notebook lay. There, in his daughter's handwriting, were her observations, thoughts, and theories about the church fire. He skimmed the open pages, not for a second feeling that he was invading Vanessa's privacy because most of what she had written was common knowledge. This wasn't the secret cache of her deepest desires or dreams or wonderings, this was work and Nick did not see that as being private at all. At least, this is the excuse he prepared should they barge in on him.

He saw her first notes, brief and monosyllabic. *Rain. Church. Dark. Ray. Two. Front. Door. Locked.* Quickly, though, his daughter had formulated the affair into something that made sense and involuntarily played out in Nick's mind. The rain was worse than Vanessa described and while he could say nothing of the water damage to the church or the assistance that came, Nick knew that in the time after the help left and the fire started, that at least three people were in the church and that three people were still in the church when Ray Beecher arrived. Only, one had been able to run away. Vanessa's notes had missed this, as he knew they would.

There were tears in the pages. Not only could Nick feel the public sentiment pouring through the paper, but he could see little watermarks, little dimples that he was sure had fallen from his daughter's eyes. He touched the paper, knowing that it was his fault, that Vanny's tears could have been avoided had Nick done what he should have done all those years ago.

Steps. Voices.

Nick pulled away from the desk and scooted to the bed where he pretended to nap. He was not surprised when the door opened but when he felt a blanket being pulled over his body, Nick wanted to cry.

At the side of Nick's bed in the morning, Vanessa screamed. "How could you!" She slammed her hand on the blanket beside Nick's leg. Then she tore open the curtains and Nick's hands flew to protect his eyes from the sun that was now pouring through the window. Since his arrest, he had taken the spare room so he knew Lynn would not be beside him to calm their daughter down, whatever her problem was. He snatched the clock beside him, pulling it to his face so he could see. Barely after six. Definitely not time for Nick to wake up.

"I thought you were better than this, I really did," Vanessa fumed, sounding much too much like her mother for Nick's liking.

"What the fuck, Vanny!" Nick growled, pulling the blanket over his head.

Then she tore it off and Nick was assaulted by light and over-eager air conditioning and what he thought was his daughter's spit hitting the skin on his back as she screamed at him. "You could have talked to me. You could have fucking talked to me!"

Nick rolled over, his hands in front of his face in case she decided to strike him. "What are you talking about?"

"My car!" she wailed. "You slashed my tires! How could you?"

That woke him up. He sat up and rubbed the sleep from his eyes. "What are you talking about?"

Then Vanessa's arms flew up in a great woosh of frustration. "Right. Like you don't know what happened. Anything to keep me from going today. My own father. My own FATHER! You know what? I wonder if it was *you* who put that fucking cat tail on my door yesterday. Anything to keep me scared. Anything to keep me home. I can't believe this."

Her screams, now in the periphery as he tried to get focused, raged on while Nick pulled on a shirt and pair of jeans, then he ran outside. There, parked in the driveway, was Vanessa's Echo, clean and white and at least half a foot shorter. The tires had not just been slashed but shredded, each of her four rims now resting on a thin layer of flat rubber against the concrete. Beside it, Nick's truck sat undamaged, as whole now as it was when he parked it the night before. Lynn's car would be in the garage and there was no sign of entry so Nick thought damage there would be unlikely. He definitely hadn't done this. "This wasn't me, Vanny," he whispered, his voice caught in confusion. Crouching beside the tire, Nick touched a strip of rubber. He picked it from the ground like a rope, tightening it inside his fist. "I swear to God this wasn't me."

"Oh my God!" Now Lynn was rushing out the front door, barefoot in her robe. "Your tires!" Her hands drew to her cheeks, where her mouth sprung open. She circled the car, looking for other signs of damage. "Who could have done such a thing?" she asked no one in particular but Nick was glad she said it because it suggested she did not suspect it of him. At this, Vanessa seemed to soften. She finally turned away and went into the house. Lynn said, "What about your truck? My car's in the garage, but ..." she checked the truck for damage, both relieved and confused. "Who would do this, Nick?"

Nick dragged his hands through his hair, clasping them together at the back of his head. "I don't know, Lynnie, but when I do, I'll tear the motherfucker apart."

Lynn did not blanch at his language. Instead, she looked at him and said, "See that you do," and followed Vanessa inside.

He took a cigarette from his hidden can behind one of the porch chairs and lit it, then walked the perimeter of his front yard, his back yard, the garage, and everything in between, looking for something, anything, that might point him to the culprit. That it would undoubtedly spoil her travels today was not an advantage for Nick, for it only served to point Vanessa's suspicion further toward him. Maybe, though, that was the point. His truck was untouched, as was Lynn's car. No windows had been broken, no doors had been keyed, there was no harm anywhere but for the obliteration of the tires, the very things cars could not do without. He knew it was no accident. There were no neighbours out screaming about their own cars, no community report out on the sidewalks, or on the streets, or through their windows. There was just Nick Penner and his daughter's wrecked car.

Outside, clouds from the east began to weave with those from the south, layer after layer, saturating the sky with an impenetrable haze that hid the morning sun. The wind started to whisper, hinting at a coming storm so Nick went inside, where he called a tow truck with instructions to deliver Vanessa's car to Eddie's Tire Shop once it opened. By the time he had made the appointment, Vanessa was back in the kitchen with a thin leather jacket over her blouse and her purse on her shoulder. A moment later, there was a light knock on the door. His daughter walked past him without saying a word and Nick silently followed her to the front of the house where his only child opened the door and threw her hands around a stranger's neck. The stranger seemed just as surprised as Nick, for his eyes went wide, looking at Nick as Vanessa hugged him. "And who's this?" Nick asked, crossing his arms.

The guy quickly released his daughter (*a good move*, Nick thought) then outstretched his hand to Nick. "Trevor," the guy said simply.

Though he looked familiar, Nick could not place him. He only knew that his daughter would use any means possible, including this *Trevor*, to piss him off. Nick introduced himself, shaking Trevor's hand with enough gusto the guy stepped back slightly. "You came quickly," Nick said, "Or was this always planned?"

Trevor pointed to his ballcap. "Morning hair but I was up helping my grandmother with yard work. She likes to get it done early or she gets too hot." His smile was easy.

As they turned to leave, Nick said, "You can't leave without coffee. I'll make it to go," adding the last part to mollify Vanessa, who was already halfway out the door. They reluctantly trailed him toward the kitchen where Lynn, dressed for a run, was cutting up strawberries and oranges.

"Trevor! Hi!" Knife in hand, Lynn whirled around to embrace him.

That Lynn was familiar with the guy was a sign that Nick had no handle on his house at all. He frowned, turning his back to focus on the coffee while Lynn and their daughter's fuck buddy carried on, then he pushed the tumblers into their hands and excused himself to take a shower. There, Nick chewed on the possibility that he wouldn't be missed should he end up in prison. He might not have a single visitor, save for Tommy Guthrie or Steve Rikkes, but even those two assholes tried to avoid places like that. Having come this far, Nick knew that prison could be avoided if he could only stop the two people who knew. One was in a home and less likely to spew anything coherent but the other—

Nick stopped his lather, recalling Vanessa's tires.

17

Forty minutes later, Trevor pulled off the highway toward a rest stop for gas and fresh coffee after Vanessa refused to drink the cup her father made. The air was muggy with humidity and by the time they were back in the car, their clothes were sticking to their damp skin. Vanessa bought bottles of orange juice and two toasted bagels, one of which she passed to Trevor after he edged back onto the highway, and now winced as her coffee burned her lip. She removed the lid, blew the liquid to cool it, then took a tentative sip, then another and another. She was two-thirds through the cup when Trevor said, "I'm sorry about your tires."

"Thanks for driving me," Vanessa said as she looked out the window, watching early morning commuters zip between lanes, hurry down on-ramps, and ease onto exits. A multitude of semi-trucks blasted past them, shaking their vehicle, but Trevor was disinclined to accelerate. He maintained an easy pace a few kilometres over the speed limit, yielding to drivers with lead foots and, sometimes, lead brains, while Vanessa shared her suspicions about her father.

Trevor listened attentively, quietly, while she talked. "You really think he did it?" He asked. "I can't speak to your situation but I can't imagine a father doing that to his child. The tires and the bloody tail? I mean, I know it's not a perfect world and families can get be quite dysfunctional, but even so, you're his flesh and blood. And it would have been a very expensive point to make regardless of how he feels about your job. Expensive and insanely cruel to you and that poor cat, whosever animal that was."

Vanessa shrugged. "Maybe, but you don't know my dad. He can be vicious sometimes. He was always terrible to my mom, and since I've been home he hasn't been so great to me, either."

"Sorry to hear that," Trevor said. "My family is just the opposite. My parents are happy and Grandma is about as hostile as you get with us and she's not all that bad."

"Not at all," Vanessa agreed.

They listened to the sounds of the road, the working of engines, the chugging of mufflers. Trevor finished his bagel and glanced at her. "I know you're hoping to get something today but don't be disappointed if it doesn't work out. If she's catatonic like they say she is, there's no use in pressing. At least you can say you tried, right?"

"I guess."

He saw the slump of her shoulders and touched her arm. "But we'll stay as long as you like, don't rush it for me. I've got all the time in the world today so I'm at your service."

"If this goes nowhere, I don't know where else to look. Maybe I shouldn't have taken this job and wasted everyone's time." She leaned her head against the window and sighed.

"Don't say that."

"I don't even write, not really, not since university, at least. I don't know what Phil was thinking when he convinced me to take this job." She rubbed her forearms.

Trevor depressed the accelerator and made a rare pass, overtaking a smoking Chevy Blazer, whose driver shot them a venomous look. This, they ignored. Vanessa couldn't be bothered with cranky drivers when there were more important things to think about. Like whether to concede or keep going. At the moment, both options sounded fine.

Trevor said, "You might not have ever been employed as a writer before this, but you need to stop saying that. Think of all the people who don't take university-level writing classes, huh? Lots of them go on to write and some even make careers of it." He nudged her and she smiled reluctantly. "Besides, you seem to be asking the right questions. At least I think so. The theory about Patrick fathering Donna's baby is new, right? Was that mentioned anywhere in the files they let you look at?"

"Well, no, but—"

"But it's something. Maybe more than Phil even suspected. You shouldn't be so hard on yourself. Phil asked for a new take on an old story and, right or wrong, that's exactly what you've given him. It might not solve the case, but it might, and even if it doesn't, you should be proud of yourself for how you've managed to steer your way through it. You've done more than you know."

"I guess so," she said without much conviction.

"*Know* so," he pressed, and soon they were merging off the 401 and onto the 403, just outside of Woodstock, now about twenty-five minutes to the care home. She reviewed her notes as Trevor drove, flipping backward, forward, setting the book down and closing it only to open it seconds later when she had another thought or question. There was something there, Vanessa was sure; something she wasn't seeing, something nebulous. She moved it around in her brain, trying to coax the fragments together, trying to make sense of them. Whatever it was, she could feel it close; close enough to reach to those floating things that were powerless on their own but were no doubt dangerous when they interlinked. How dangerous, she couldn't be sure, but it chilled her, and she sensed it growling at her like a prowling animal.

Soon, they were off the highway, dipping from the push of traffic toward a yawning community where a wooden sign with a pair of red and white beach umbrellas flanked the greeting: *Welcome to Fauville, Canada's Tropic of The South.* Here, the gathering of grass gave way to banks of sand dappled with soft footprints disintegrating in the wind. Beach dwellers with towels and buckets, air-filled tubes, lifejackets, boards, bags, and coolers of all sizes padded lazily alongside the road, where Trevor's speed was now reduced to a crawl. "Wow," he said, stretching his arm out of his lowered window, "I didn't expect it to be so nice."

"Me neither," Vanessa said, feeling the air moving through her fingers, too.

They moved slowly, languidly, through the throng of sandaled pedestrians crossing the road to secure their spots along the water. Spaces between coffee shops and restaurants offered brief views of the beach, where the sounds of children and birds and waves blended into a harmonious, steady hum, and Vanessa was disappointed she hadn't brought her swimsuit. The clouds were not as dark as earlier, but scattered and lurking in the periphery as though waiting for the perfect moment to emerge. Nevertheless, summer activity filled the sidewalks, the streets, the shops that had just opened for the day. Lines outside coffee houses wound beneath awnings and around corners, while others threaded near pancake restaurants and all-day diners. Past the touristic main street, a number of small inns and bed and breakfasts huddled along a handful of inlets, sentimental with fairy tale architecture and European styling. Beside this, quaint storybook homes with long lawns and tall trees offered a glimpse of fanciful living Vanessa could only dream about.

Trevor said, "My parents have friends that grew up here; they talk about it all the time but I never thought it would be like *this*. Who would ever think there would be an institute here?" The GPS directed them to turn at the end of the street. Here, they proceeded away from the water through a scattering of simpler homes and small apartment buildings, over a wooden bridge, in the direction of Fauville's baseball and soccer fields.

"It's not really an institute. Their website says it's a long-term care home. It's small, they only have something like thirty or so patients so maybe it doesn't attract much attention."

He whistled. "I'll bet there's a lot of money here funding it."

Vanessa agreed. It was a few minutes before the fields gave way to a large brick building with a tin roof, robin's egg blue. Before the glassed front entrance, yellow and purple flowers dangled from overhead baskets under cedar pergolas where an older couple patted the shoulders of a woman strapped to a wheelchair. Her head twitched to the right, to the right, and still right even as they passed in front of her. The couple smiled warmly, tiredly, at Trevor and Vanessa, and then each grasped and unfurled one of the woman's tightly curled hands, soothing the woman when she squeaked at their touch. Inside, the air was cool and smelled faintly of antiseptic. Tangerine sofas and teal armchairs and low ivory tables were assembled off to the right near a wall-wide bulletin board, and the left, near the windows and water cooler. Behind the half-moon reception desk, a portly man with a grey moustache and a wide smile said, "Howdy Folks! How can I help you?" Vanessa gave him her name and then they both showed the man their drivers licenses. He clicked quickly at his computer and said, "Miss Clarke! Of course! Of Course! Glad you could drive all the way out from, Toronto, is it?" He slid his finger under Vanessa's address, holding her card close then at arm's length. He peeked over his glasses, squinted, and typed their information, handing their licenses back with a friendly double-tap on the plastic.

"We came up from Garrett," Vanessa said.

"Boy! That's a long drive for such an early morning, But, as I always say, I say, 'Glen, the world ain't going to wait for you so don't wait for it.' And look! It's a beautiful day and our Agnes has visitors. Mighty fine day, this is." His round cheeks went wide then he pointed to the area near the bulletin board. "You two wait right there while I make your tags and call Angela. Protocol around here requires a nurse for most visits but not to worry, you won't even see her." He picked up the phone and soon he was sending his cheer through the line. They went to the bulletin board, glancing over tacked-up posters, pamphlets, brochures, and various sheets with an assortment of prevention hotlines and mental health advice. *Caregivers Support Meeting, Tuesdays, 6:00 p.m., St. Anne's Catholic Church, Refreshments provided*, one read, the perforated tabs with phone numbers at the bottom all torn away except two. Below this was a purple and pink poster featuring a grouping of stick figures holding hands in an enclosed circle with *Care for Caregivers* italicized in the glossy middle. The poster closest to Trevor, *Alzheimer's Fun Run, Sign Up Today!* flapped gently from one unpinned corner as he took a seat directly below it. Vanessa herself had just sat down when Glen poked his head up from behind the desk. "Here you are," he said, sliding two *Visitor* lanyards across the pale surface, then he pointed to a door at his left. "You go on over there and Angela will meet you. Take as long as you like. We usually like to have our residents together for mealtimes but if you're still here at lunch, you're welcome to stick around. Plenty for everyone. Also," he passed them a bottle of sanitizer, "no masks required but we'd like you to have clean hands. Can never be too careful."

They took the gel in their palms and rubbed vigorously, then pulled their lanyards over their heads and proceeded to the white steel door. A nurse appeared in its vertical window, a small gap in her front teeth visible as she grinned and held a finger out, indicating for them to wait. She turned then, tapping a card to a square key reader on the wall. With a click, the door opened and the nurse stuck out her hand. "Vanessa?" Vanessa nodded. "I'm Angela but you can call me Ang. One of my patients has a thing about two syllable names so Ang it is. And, Trevor, right? I'm going to have to ask you to remove your hat, if you don't mind. We find they tend to invite paranoia in some of our patients and we do everything we can to keep them in an environment that they feel comfortable in."

Trevor removed his hat, smoothing his hair as best he could. His eyes went up to where he knew there would be a fine mess. "Rushed out of the house this morning," he said, following the two women.

"You don't have food in it, so I'd say you're better than half the people in here." Angela shrugged. "But at least it's interesting." She chinned toward the common area where a dozen slumped bodies were collected around a small television on which a Donald Duck cartoon was showing. Donald was making pancakes but, in Disney fashion, was foiled from eating them. A drooling man whose head rested on his chest guffawed as Chip and Dale arrowed a fork at Donald's pancakes, drawing them away before he could take a bite. A woman with closed eyes laughed too, but at what, Vanessa wasn't sure. In the corner, someone snored. Angela led them past this group to a bright, artificially lit corridor with a stretch of doors interspersed on both sides all the way to a set of closed double doors at the end. "This is our chronic wing," Angela explained. "We have twenty-six patients that will live in these walls for the rest of their lives. Eleven with dementia, five who've suffered strokes, one with Parkinson's, three with complicated diabetes, and six with various cognitive disabilities or disorders. Our Agnes has been diagnosed with conversion disorder. It's a technical term that says she is experiencing neurological symptoms for reasons we can't figure out."

Trevor asked, "So you don't know what's actually wrong with her?"

"The short answer is no. She's been in a state of paralysis, on and off since she's been admitted. Early on, it even appeared she was experiencing episodes of transitory blindness, but that has since cleared up. Physically, everything seems normal. We've run every test in the book and, truthfully, we're stumped." Ang slowed as they reached the last door on the left. Here, she stopped and pointed inside the little window at the thin figure on the bed.

Vanessa peered inside. There, a body as insignificant as mist under a sheet. "Is that normal? I mean, how often does this happen?" she asked.

Angela shrugged, her long black ponytail swaying along her back. "More often than you imagine. We have another resident like Agnes but he's only been with us for not quite a year now. The condition is believed to be caused by extreme stress, though not always. The events leading to her admission would have affected even the most resilient mind. We know she was close with the church community and in times of tragedy, individuals may reach out to that type of support group but sometimes they draw in and deep, perceiving a continued threat even if non-existent. They're not comforted by contact, no matter how well-intentioned, but hide from it because they believe it's safer within themselves. Our doctors think this is likely the case with Agnes. Our role is to support her and help her try to find her way back but," she sighed, "it's a process. We *have* had success with others. With treatment, these symptoms resolve in weeks, sometimes months. For others, it's years. Not many go on like this for decades but it's also not something we haven't seen before." She held her key card to a reader outside Agnes' door and led them into the room. She said quietly, "You can talk to her just like you would anyone else. Hold her hand, give her a hug. We try to keep things calm and we like to let her know what we're doing before we do it. There's no reaction, of course, but we can't be sure how her brain processes the activity so we try to keep her aware as much as we can." When Angela turned to leave, Vanessa and Trevor's eyes went wide. A reassuring smile touched the nurse's lips. "I'll just be outside the door. You'll be fine. Her parents love it when she has visitors. We just moved her so take as long as you need." Her footsteps were silent as she left the room.

Alone, Trevor and Vanessa silently edged toward the bed. Under her short tawny hair, Agnes' eyes were closed, her skeletal jaw undulating with slow breath. The dim light shone sickly on her skin, jaundice yellow on her face, liver grey on her arms, bile green on her fingertips. Somewhere under the thin sheet was her body, though it was not certain which lumps were limbs and which swellings were filled with cotton. "She's sleeping," Vanessa whispered.

From outside the door, Angela whispered back, "She may not open her eyes but can hear you."

Unsettled, Vanessa looked at Trevor and together they came upon the same side of Agnes' bed. There were teddy bears printed on her pillow, frolicking cats on her gown, a stuffed dog set in the crook of her arm and posters of flowers puttied to the walls but there was no mistaking the room, or the girl inside it, for part of common experience. A series of monitors were hooked up to Agnes and there was an intravenous bag hung high over her shoulder and a urinary drainage bag, half full, hung from a bedframe pin below her mattress. On the side table to her right, Agnes' chart lay open on a clipboard with rows of incomprehensible treatments that Vanessa dare not copy into her notebook. Unwillingly, her eyes caught on Agnes' face where a light froth accumulated in the corners of the woman's mouth. Instinctively, Vanessa plucked a tissue from a box beside the clipboard, wrapped it around her finger, and gently blotted Agnes' mouth. "You know," she said timidly, "if I were in the same situation I would want someone to do the same for me, but I drool quite a lot and wouldn't look as pretty as you." She dropped the tissue in the wastebasket beside the bed. "There, that's better. My name is Vanessa and I brought my friend Trevor with me. If it's okay with you, we'd like to stay and visit for a while. We both grew up in Garrett, just like you."

Trevor said softly, "I live in Toronto but I'm back in Garrett for the summer. It's so much better there, not like the city."

If Agnes heard, she gave no response. Not a flutter of an eyelash, not a quickening of the breath, not a twitching of muscle. "I'm going to hold your hand if that's okay. I know that we don't know each other well, but my mom is a pediatrician and she always told me that touch can tell us just as much as words do, sometimes more. I think we can talk this way, or at least you can get a feel for who I am." She didn't know why she said it, but the words felt natural. Again, Agnes gave no indication of hesitation or resolution so Vanessa reached with her fingertips and brushed the cold skin on Agnes' wrist and took Agnes' fingers into the palm of her hand. The woman's fingers were as fine as sparrow bones, so light that they felt almost empty, void of marrow, bereft of nerves, syphoned of everything but the thin membrane of her skin. Vanessa felt that if she squeezed too tightly, Agnes' hand might fall to dust.

Trevor reached for Agnes's other hand, then pulled away. He said, "Angela tells us you've been here for a while." Immediately, Trevor cringed at his own uneasiness. He spread his hands wide in an unsure manner, then he silently mouthed an apology to Vanessa. She mouthed her reassurance back to him, but his smile was nervous.

"Agnes, we're here because I'm working on a project that I'm hoping you can help me with." She was speaking Phil's words now but, under the circumstances, they were the right words, maybe the only right words Vanessa could think of. For a moment she paused, but then Trevor nodded encouragingly so she said, "I guess I should tell you first that I'm a graphic designer by trade. I lost my job in Toronto and moved back home a few weeks ago, where I started looking for work." Agnes' skin seemed to warm slightly as Vanessa brushed it with her thumb. "Well, you know Garrett, it's not easy finding work there unless you're in construction or a realtor, and who needs another one of those, huh?" She laughed awkwardly. "Anyway, my dad wanted me to work for a car dealership, but I wasn't into it so I took a position with the Gazette. The funny thing is, I wasn't even looking for a job like this, but I guess we surprise ourselves sometimes, right?" Agnes' heart rate beat steadily on the monitor. It seemed she was in a deep sleep but Vanessa was determined, so she went on stroking Agnes' hand, talking. "It was terrible about the fire. My parents say it was one of the saddest days they can ever remember but they also say it brought the city together. Since then, they say that people watch out for each other more, that they're ... well, I guess the right word is *neighbourly*. I think that's why I took the job. My boss, Phil, was nice to me from the moment I met him. A lot of people tell me he's a lot like his father, Ray. You know him? Ray was the one who tried to save Donna and Stu that night, and Phil wants to honor his memory by figuring out what happened." She gave Agnes' hand a gentle squeeze. "I was hoping you could help me with that, Agnes."

From the doorway, the top of Angela's dark head leaned inward as she listened. She gave another thumbs up to the room. To Agnes, Trevor said, "I'm going to pull a chair here for Vanessa so you can talk while I wait outside with Ang." Vanessa glanced at him and shook her head to indicate that she did not want to be alone in Agnes' room but Trevor opened a palm and stroked her back before wordlessly joining Ang in the corridor.

Suddenly, the room felt warm, too warm, and Vanessa began to sweat. Where before her thumb rubbed dryly, smoothly, against Agnes, it now caught, her sweaty thumb sticky as it tugged the woman's skin and gathered it up like wet dough. She coughed and shuffled where she stood, then squirmed down into the seat Trevor brought for her before he left. Settled, she worked to slow her breath, to show the quiet woman that nothing had changed, that all was as it should be. She kept a hand over Agnes' wrist and fetched her notebook from her purse. "I'd like to read you something," she said, and for the next forty-five minutes, Vanessa read Agnes Clarke everything in her notebook during which time, the other woman didn't respond. When she finished, Vanessa rose and touched her lips to the clammy skin on Agnes' forehead. "Thank you for listening to me, Agnes," she said, and left the room.

Back in the corridor, Angela's eyes were admiring. "You know, I've never heard it put that way before. I thought I knew the story quite intimately, but it almost seemed new the way you said it."

"Since I have no idea what I'm doing, I'll take that as a compliment," Vanessa blushed.

"You should," Angela said, then she pointed to the area outside the door. "Give me a moment? A quick check and I can walk you back." She turned, and they watched her readjust Agnes' arms and read her monitors and smooth the sheet over her body. Angela took the medical file off the bedside table, turning for one last look at Agnes when she stopped, pressing a hand to her heart. Her mouth dropped open and she leaned in toward Agnes, observing the woman's face. Quickly, she reread Agnes' monitors and pressed two fingers to the inside of Agnes' wrist as she watched the clock on the far side of the room. Then Angela made notes on the clipboard and scurried out of the room, walking swiftly in front of them.

"What happened? Did I do something wrong?" Vanessa jogged to keep up with Angela.

"Is she okay?" Trevor asked.

Breathlessly, Angela said, "She's okay, she's okay. At least I think so. Her stats are good but ..." she hesitated, still hurrying down the hallway.

"But what?" Vanessa begged. The fear that she had somehow hurt Agnes barrelled upon her like granite, squeezing and clamping at her conscience, and she suddenly found it hard to breathe.

Angela stopped outside the main entrance to the corridor and Vanessa and Trevor had to pull back sharply to keep from running into her. She said, "Agnes has been here for over twenty years. In all that time and with all of her visitors, few as they were, she ... has never cried before."

"I'm sorry?" Vanessa was stunned.

"There were tears on the side of her face," Angela said, a small hitch in her voice.

"We didn't mean to—" Trevor started but Angela quickly cut him off.

"No, you didn't, but I don't want you to think this is a bad thing. Not at all. It's a *reaction*, you see, and that's not something we get from Agnes."

"My God!" Vanessa was breathing hard as Angela led them back into the reception area where Glen greeted them, his smile faltering as he saw their faces.

"Hey, now, something the matter?" Glen asked.

"Page Dr. Bauchman," Angela insructed and without another word, Glen had turned serious and was on the phone.

Vanessa said, "I'm so sorry. I didn't mean for this to happen."

"Please," Angela reached out and took Vanessa's arm, pressing firmly. "There is no fault here, but it's something we must take note of and possibly action on. Her parents will want to know. I don't know what you said that reached her, but whatever it was, it got through. No one else has been able to do that."

Vanessa felt those nebulous parts coming together again, gathering, almost shaping into something recognizable. How had she gotten through to Agnes? What was it that she read from her notes that breached the woman's defences? How had the words of a stranger gotten through when interactions with other, more familiar faces hadn't? She straightened. "You said Agnes had only a few visitors since she's been in here. May I ask who they are?"

Agnes shrugged. "I don't see why not. It's not confidential or anything, save for medical professionals." She went to the desk. "Glen, can you pull up Agnes' visitation records, filtering out the usual suspects, staff, and all that?"

"Sure can," he said and then he was madly typing, his moustache twitching as his mouth worked the words of his search quietly to himself. "Let's see here, we've got her parents, the Clarkes, siblings too, they're quite frequent, and then a David, Huddy, Pauliuk, McKinley, Foster, Rand, Beecher, Penner, Grant, and then you two."

"This is my first visit," Vanessa said.

"Pardon?"

"You said Penner before, then me and him," she thumbed toward Trevor, "But I've never been here before today."

Glen checked the computer, clicked once, twice, then he shook his head. "Sorry Miss, we've got a Penner down for an April visit in … let's see … in oh-one."

"That can't be right. Nineteen years ago I was only eight."

"Computer don't lie, Miss," Glen looked at her apologetically.

Trevor leaned over the desk, squinting at Glen's screen. "First names?"

Glen swivelled his screen to face Trevor more clearly. "Last names only back then, I'm afraid. We're more thorough now. See that?" He pointed to a column at the far right of his screen and scrolled the spreadsheet downward, slowing after a few moments. "The first names start *here*. We didn't start collecting first names or addresses of visitors until about six years later, after an audit recommendation. We scan licenses now but back then we just took their last names and their cities so we knew where people were coming from, but not for any real reason besides curiosity, I suppose. There's some deep pockets around here and, between you and me, I wonder if this building was supposed to be the right distance from what you call *riffraff.* They like to keep things quite local, at least local with etiquette, if you know what I mean. No druggies or lowlifes. I think they might have closed it down had people started visiting from Timmins or somewhere like that." Glen's tongue clicked with disapproval. "But there's more oversight now, so it's changed quite a bit. For the better, if you ask me."

Whatever Glen said, Vanessa hadn't heard. Instead, she asked, "Where was the Penner visitor from?"

One of Glen's short fingers touched the monitor. "Garrett," he said.

"Male? Female?" The idea of her mother or father visiting Agnes sat in Vanessa's stomach like spoiled milk. With a sour certainty, she suddenly knew it couldn't be anyone else.

"Doesn't say, Miss."

"Any visits from a Penner after your system changed? Besides today?"

"No ma'am."

Trevor said, "And what about from the others? Beecher or Pauliuk?" Vanessa looked at him as he said this, realizing she had too quickly focused on finding fault within her own family, excluding the possibility of others, no matter how unlikely those options seemed.

Glen went back to his keyboard and they all watched as new information populated his screen. "Father Pauliuk comes out at least once a month, see here?" They saw the regularity of Father Pauliuk's visits as Glen's finger slid down the column of dates. "He's been coming since she was admitted but he doesn't just see Agnes. He blesses every one of our residents before he leaves. Staff too."

"And Beecher?" Vanessa asked.

Glen batted the keys and soon they were seeing a record of Phil Beecher's visits. "He's an annual kind of guy. Every year, end of August."

Just then a small, spectacled man in a tan shirt emerged from the door connected to the other wing of the building, his tan cheeks flush with excitement. "Angela?" he said, taking a few quick strides toward the nurse.

Sensing a conversation for which she and Trevor weren't prepared, Vanessa extended her hand to Angela and said, "Thanks for everything today. You've been a big help, but we should be going."

Angela took Vanessa's hand and pulled her into a hug. "Thank *you* for everything today, Vanessa. Come back any time. Please. We'd be thrilled to have you."

"You're sure everything is alright?" Trevor asked, unsure.

The man, whom Vanessa assumed was Dr. Bauchman, raised an eyebrow at Angela, who looked over him to bid the two of them safe travels. Before the doors closed behind them, they heard the doctor exclaim, "What!"

Back in the truck, their desire for visiting the quaint little city had completely evaporated and it took some time before Trevor found the words to raise to Vanessa. He said, "You don't know your dad had anything to do with it." When she began to protest, he interrupted, "Just hear me out, okay? That name could have come from anyone. Are you the only Penners in the city?"

"Well, no, but—"

"Do you have aunts? Uncles? Cousins that live there?"

"Yes—"

"So you can't be sure."

"No," she paused, waiting for him to interrupt her. When he didn't, she said, "But come on, Trevor, you know it doesn't look good. Doesn't it seem strange how much my dad hates my working for the Gazette? Only, I don't think it's really that; I think it's the *story* I'm working on. He doesn't want me close to it … maybe because he had something to do with it."

Trevor looked at her, then swung his eyes back to the road. "You think your father is a murderer?"

She shuddered, thinking of the bloody cat tail and of her slashed tires and of all the times her father raged at her mother. With a heaviness she hadn't felt before, she frowned at Trevor and said, "Maybe."

18

Clouds rolled overhead as Phil raked dead grass from his lawn. It came up like hay, dry and stiff, even with the daily waterings he'd timed every evening. The heat had been bad, so very bad, Phil knew of more than one local farmer whose crops would be the duty of insurance or federal payouts and Phil recognized that even with his failing paper, he was better off than the growers around him. At least this year. He arched his aching back and called his children out to bag what he gathered in piles. They groaned out of the house, trudged across the lawn, and made slow work of the bagging until Phil snuck up behind them and belly-flopped onto the bag they were filling. Grass blew from the bag onto their faces, their hair, into their cheering mouths and even Christopher, sensitive to excitement, laughed gaily until tears moistened his face. Then Josie and Andrew flung armfuls of grass and soon Phil's hard work had been confettied back over the lawn. The kids made such a carnival of the unbagging that Phil hadn't realized the truck pulling in front of the house until the kids pointed at it. Phil stood, dusting the grass off his clothes, and went to see who the visitor was.

Vanessa sprung from the truck as soon as it was parked and the guy Phil knew as Trevor bounced out shortly after.

Phil heard him hastily warn, "Remember, be calm, okay?" and then she was standing in front of Phil while his children clambered around his legs peek at their visitors.

"This doesn't look like good news," Phil observed.

"Maybe you tell me," Vanessa's voice was incongruent with the smile on her face. She waved at the three small heads poking from behind Phil.

Phil looked at the sky and then his face fell to his children. "Looks like rain," he said. "Why don't you go inside and ask Mom to put coffee on?" The scramble back to the house became a mad dash to be the first to touch the stairs and it was Josie who screamed victoriously, having reached them before her brothers. Vanessa and Trevor giggled. Phil said, "Have a few minutes? Tanya's coffee is famous around here."

"Why didn't you tell me you've seen Agnes at St. Dymphna's? You acted like you didn't know she was catatonic when I told you I was going to see her."

Phil nodded. "That's right."

"But why?" The question had come from Vanessa but the wonder was written Trevor's face, too.

"Because I wanted you to see everything fresh, like I told you," Phil explained, and continued when neither Trevor nor Vanessa looked convinced. "I didn't want to feed you anything, I didn't want my own expectations or assumptions to take root in your investigation, subconsciously or not. You're not the first writer I've hired to do a story on this. I didn't share it with you because I was afraid it would make you feel pressured and because nothing ever came of it. This was maybe seven or eight years ago. Hired a greenie, just like you, and I hadn't realized how much I inserted my own beliefs in his search until I got the story back. I tell you; I could have written it myself, every single word. It was nothing I wanted because it was everything I expected. Absolutely not a speck of anything different, and I didn't want to make the same mistake this time around. Maybe I should have said something, I'm sorry." He sighed and they followed him to where the children had left the bags on the lawn and began raking again.

The indignation previously on Vanessa's face had calmed into something more of understanding. She knelt and began pushing grass into a bag and soon Trevor was doing the same. She said, "How am I doing so far?"

Phil grinned. "With the story, Agnes could have been on the moon as far as the other writer was concerned, so I think you're doing better. With the grass, you missed a spot." Together, they cleared the lawn as the sky got thick with humidity. After a time, Phil said, "How was Agnes when you saw her?"

Vanessa stopped and sat on her knees. "I don't really know, to be honest. She was exactly like you said ... but something happened before we left." She looked to Trevor, who acknowledged this with a nod to Phil.

"Did she talk?" Phil asked.

"No. No, there was no talking, at least on her part. She just laid there while I read her my notes."

"And?" Phil gripped his rake tightly in his hands.

"She cried," Trevor said. "And it was a big deal because they called the doctor when it happened."

The news hit Phil with such ferocity that he had to sit. He moved to the front steps where he turned and rested, rolling the strain from his neck. He whistled out a long breath. "I've visited that girl every year for ten years now and I never got anything like that. Never even opened her eyes; not so much as a sneeze or a twitch out of her. They told me not to expect anything and I shouldn't have. I know that. I swear it's not the only reason I visited, honest to God, and I guess I feel a bit ridiculous telling you, but I always *hoped*, you know? That maybe she'd just wake up and talk, maybe she'd somehow snap out of it and tell us what happened, maybe—what? Why are you two looking at each other like that?"

Vanessa cautioned, "I'm glad you're sitting down." Color flooded her cheeks and she bit her lip as she took a seat across from him on the stairs.

"Tell me," Phil urged.

"I can't be sure," she started, "but I think I'm close. A name came up."

The weight that hovered over Phil these long years seemed to compress him now. He felt his stomach roil and his chest tighten. He held the railing, readying himself. "Whose name?"

Unbelievably, Vanessa shook her head as she faced him. She said, "Not yet. I don't want to say anything until know for sure, and I don't want to get your hopes up if it turns out to be nothing."

It didn't pay to press, if anyone knew that it was Phil and his decades of journalistic acuity, so he didn't press now. Presently, he calmed himself, breathing long, slow breaths, then said, "Someone we know?" When Vanessa nodded, he asked, "How did it come up?"

"We can't say yet, especially if it's the person we think it is," Trevor told him, then hastily added, "But let's hope we're wrong, huh?"

Phil saw him regard Vanessa with something like pity on his face and as they stood and bagged the rest of the grass, Phil's mind sought a clarity that just couldn't be found. It gave him a headache. Finally, as they tied the bags and brought them to the back of the house, Phil said, "You know, I don't think I'm going to sleep until I know what you're up to."

"That makes two of us," Vanessa told him. "But I don't want to plant something or give you ideas that shouldn't be there. Something like this could ruin a person's life and I wouldn't want to do that if I'm wrong."

"How soon?" Phil prodded, leading them toward the house, his entire body trembling with curiosity. "How soon until I know?"

"I don't think it will be long," Vanessa said, and was interrupted by the vibration of her cell phone in her back pocket. Surprised by the number on her screen, she answered, "Maury?" Then with a finger held up to excuse herself, she walked away to continue the call.

Alone with Trevor, Phil thought he might wrangle the name out, but the man was just as disinclined to answer as Vanessa was. "I think it's better if we wait on this one," Trevor said, looking off to the truck where Vanessa was pacing. His avoidance told Phil that he wouldn't like the name, that maybe it was close, too close, maybe even right under Phil's own nose. In a moment, Vanessa walked back across the lawn, returning her phone to her pocket. "Everything all right?" Trevor asked.

"Yeah, yeah," Vanessa said strangely. Her face was twisted with surprise. "That was my old boss. Three people I used to work with just up and quit to work for Farm Boy and he wants me to come work for him again."

"Farm Boy?" Phil scrunched his face in thought.

"It's another grocery chain. They focus on fresh pro-duce, meats, lots of local, farm-to-table sort of thing," Vanessa told him. "They're expanding and just swiped two of our designers and one of category managers. I can get my job back if I want it. They got a new contract last week, so they're getting busier, too. If the other three didn't quit, they would have been more than fine but Maury's freaking out now. He said he would make me a manager of my old department."

"What did you tell him" Trevor asked.

Vanessa looked at Phil uneasily. Phil said, "Don't let me hold you back. You have to do what you have to do. It's not my philosophy to keep my staff tethered to me for the rest of their lives." The encouragement on his face was real, for the dictum that ran through his blood was the same as his father's when he was alive: help others rise. The inward disappointment that came at Phil, however, he would keep to himself. Moving on was simply part of life, whether he liked it or not. He said, "But can you finish the story first? I'd sure love to see that, if you have the time, of course."

"I haven't said yes yet and there is no way I'd leave without finishing what I started. My parents did teach me some good things." As she spoke, Phil noticed Vanessa's thumbs fidgeting with her belt loops.

"We haven't spoken much about your compensation, Vanessa, but I know I can't match what they're able to give you." Phil was embarrassed to admit this but he saw no reproach on their faces; instead, there was such overwhelming sympathy, he felt a knot in his chest.

Vanessa shrugged. "I know, and if I stayed, I wouldn't expect you to match it. I'm just not sure I'm ready to go back to Toronto. Maybe if ever. There's something to be said for small towns, and I'm really not hurting yet since my parents won't accept rent from me anyway."

"It's a great opportunity, though. Just don't turn it down because of me. I'm definitely not worth it."

From the kitchen, Tanya heard Phil's acquiescent chuckle through the doorway and called to them. "Come on in. Everything's ready."

Phil led them into the house where the rich smell of coffee and warm cinnamon buns met them in the mudroom. The busy, playing sounds of children filled the space around them and soon they were each dragged by a child eager to get to them to the table. "Mom said we had to wait until you guys came in," Josie, the eldest, whined to Phil.

"My stomach can't take the wait anymore!" Andrew, the youngest, thew himself onto a chair, licking his lips. "Finally! They're here! I'll take the biggest one, please."

Trevor accepted a mug from Tanya and the coffee sloshed over the side and onto the table as Christopher grabbed her arm, trying to convince his mother that the first cinnamon bun was his. Trevor said to the boy, "Sorry to keep you waiting."

Tanya took a cloth and wiped the small spill under Trevor's cup. "They didn't wait long. I just took them out of the oven as you walked in."

"Well then, I guess we're right on time," Phil winked at his wife and the conversation for the next hour was easy because there was no mention of Vanessa's writing assignment or her job offer in Toronto or the fire. Later, when Phil waved at Trevor's departing truck, the weight that previously compressed him now pulled again at his nerves. He felt nauseous, crippled with an anxiety he hadn't felt since his father's precarious recovery from the fire. His knees jittered, his fingers trembled and he hadn't realized he bit his nails to the quick until he tasted blood. As he sat in his dark living room later that evening, it struck Phil that he never expected to know what happened the night of the fire and

226

that his existence ever since had foolishly been fashioned on an elusive target. Now, the idea that all his searching might come to an end simply wasn't something Phil was prepared for and he shrank from the anxiety it stirred.

Hours later, when Phil hadn't moved from his chair, Tanya opened his palm, kissed it, and closed his fingers over his car keys. "You need to get out of here," she said. "Go have a drink with your brother. It'll do you some good."

When Phil arrived at Shooter's, however, the splash of urine on the outside wall of the bar from a pair of wobbly drunks almost made him get back in his car and return home. But with the shake in his fingers, the keys nearly flipped out of his hand and Phil didn't much believe he should be driving in his condition. So he pocketed his keys, gritted his teeth, and held his breath as he marched toward the building. Neither of the drunks noticed Phil's wide berth around them until he was opening the door, when they quickly turned their private shows and accidentally peed on each other. Inside, the breath Phil had been holding came rushing out and he was somewhat thankful for the smells of alcohol and perfume and sweat as he found his brother in his favorite seat at the bar, two pints of beer in front of him. Overhead on dusty screens, the Blue Jays were down 9–2 in the last inning against the Marlins and the Roughriders were up 33–17 in the second half against the Lions. Both screens had just cut to commercial break as Phil smacked Rick's shoulder. "Thanks for meeting me."

Rick slid a beer toward him. "You sounded like shit on the phone. Something's going on if you've lowered your standards like this." He gestured vaguely to the entirety of the bar.

"Can't a man enjoy a beer with his brother?" Phil wiped a smear from his glass and took a tentative sip.

"Come on, man, this isn't your place. Things all right at home?" He spoke to Phil but Phil noticed his brother's eyes on the rear end of the bartender, whose slender body was stretched out and reaching high for a bottle on the top shelf.

Phil coughed. "When'd you get here?"

"Right after you called," Rick answered, winking at the bartender who was now facing the two of them. He shook his head as if to tell her something then swung toward Phil. "What's going on? Your girl find anything on her little trip?"

"She did," Phil nodded. "At least I think she did."

"What's that supposed to mean?"

"They said a name came up but they wouldn't tell me whose."

Rick scowled. "Why not? Isn't that part of her job? Aren't you paying her for it?"

Phil took another sip from his glass, winced, and pushed it aside. "Of course I am, don't be like that."

"Then why won't she tell you? It's her job to tell you these things. Don't get soft, now, it's not good for business, you know that."

Again, anxiety tugged at Phil, so he swung his eyes to the screens where unimportant things were happening. He said, "It's someone we know, Rick, but she wants to be sure before she tells me. I can understand that."

"Patrick?" Rick asked, now straightening to face his brother. "Did he and Donna ...?"

"I don't know."

Rick emptied his glass in two long swallows and hailed the bartender for another, shrugging off Phil's refusal of joining him. "Sounds funny, if you ask me. That girl's no detective, Phil. What if she barks up the wrong tree and ruins someone's life? Or gets hurt or something? You have to rein her in, man."

"You think?"

Baseball and football returned to the screens, along with a bar full of shrieking fans. Through the noise Rick said, "Maybe. I don't know. You know Dad would have been all over this, right? He wouldn't have taken no for an answer. He would have made her talk."

Phil disagreed. "That wasn't his style."

"He wasn't one to quit, you know that. When he caught on to something, he was a pit bull, no matter what those awards say." Rick scanned the bar menu, ordered a dozen hot wings, and passed the menu to Phil, who inattentively scanned it and ordered a sparking water. "Can I ask you something?"

"Not going to stop you." Rick howled at the screen as the Jays scored a double.

"The thing I keep coming back to is Donna. I think everything revolves around her. I'm not sure Stu had anything to do with it. Maybe he was just in the wrong place with the wrong woman, and I'm not sure he would have known it if he was. He's squeaky clean. But Donna … do you think she would have slept with Patrick? He was just a kid."

Rick smoothed the hair on the back of his head, letting his hand rest there as he considered. "I'd like to think not," he said. "She was … she was *good*. I just can't see her doing that. But maybe the *thought* of Donna and Patrick together would have been enough for Agnes to be upset. I still think it has something to do with Agnes or Patrick, or both. He might have had an alibi but what's *she* doing in a mental institution? Whatever the case, I think justice has been done. One gone, the other mostly gone, it's karma if you ask me."

The finality of Rick's statement made Phil even more restless. "I'll be glad when this is over," he sighed.

"That makes two of us," Rick agreed, and plunged into his food.

19

Another day, another morning where Nick Penner was the pariah of his own household. He woke early after a restless sleep, showered, and ate his eggs in silence as the two women who cohabited with him cleared the area once he entered. No *thank you for fixing my car, Daddy*. No *thank you for helping our daughter, Honey*. Just a giant *fuck you* with every bat of their over-made lashes. At first, he felt he'd done nothing to deserve the treatment. A drunk tank pick-up wasn't worth this kind of room-clearing punishment, so Nick quietly drank his coffee and finished his toast as he prepared to eventually clear out their bank account, bid goodbye to matrimony, and shout hello to bachelorhood. As for fatherhood, well, Vanny still wasn't responding when he tried talking to her. If anything, she'd gotten worse since her road trip. It was near midnight when she tried tip-toeing through the front door, yet Nick had still readied popcorn and their favorite movie as an attempt to ease her recent hatred of him. But then the coldness in her eyes told Nick everything he needed to know. His daughter, his lifeblood, *knew*.

But …

But as much as Vanessa despised him, she *loved* Lynn; loved her so much that any harm to her mother was harm to herself and Nick knew that Vanessa didn't want such a thing. No, his daughter would keep quiet because of the damage it would cause her mother. He was as sure of this as of the Clarke girl dying in the institution. *There's no coming back from oblivion*, he thought to himself, watching the morning clouds hover low and dark over the streets he passed. He lit a cigarette and opened the window to let the smoke out, thinking. Could Vanessa toss his guilt at him to garner a more equitable, if not lopsided, divorce settlement in Lynn's favor? Possible, possible, but he would play that game when the time came. Now, however, he had to think, plan, strategize. A song came on the radio and Nick whistled, appreciating for the first time how good it was to be the smarter parent.

By the time Nick reached his parking spot under the small stretch of Oak shade on the other side of the city, Simon was outside waiting for him with a stack of papers in his hand. His boss said, "I thought I'd give this to you out here. Penny took Lynn's call and her spidey sense got her stalking me now. I swear I can't piss without that woman wanting a fucking report. It's all here I think." Simon thrust the papers into Nick's hands and yanked up his sagging pants, a half-smoked cigarette dangling from his lip.

"What's this?" Nick asked. In his pocket, Nick's phone vibrated.

"Those papers Lynn wanted," Simon said. "It was a bitch of a job, I tell you. Penny worked late trying to get this for her and I took over this morning. They're really threatening prison for tax evasion? You know better than that." Simon shifted his smoke, sucking it inward from the corner of his mouth, then finally pinched it away, tapping the ashes onto the sidewalk in front of him.

Nick juggled the heavy bundle, slapping and snatching papers back as the wind gusted. His phone vibrated again but he ignored the buzz. "Tax evasion? I don't know what you're talking about, Si. I haven't missed a goddamn year."

Simon's eyebrows crested upward in surprise. "It's nothing to be ashamed about ..."

"Of course there's nothing to be ashamed about, Si. My goddam taxes are done. What the fuck is this?"

"No need to get angry, Nick." Simon frowned, the calm, good-natured manner fell off his face and pricks of color bloomed on his cheeks.

The quick rage that festered under Simon's skin threatened to manifest should Nick push the man any farther, so he stood and inhaled deep until his lungs were full and his chest was tight. He tossed the pile of papers on the floor of his truck and pinched the bridge of his nose. Nick closed his eyes, silently counting to himself. *One, one thousand, two, one thousand. Three.* "Sorry, sorry, Si. I just don't know what this is. What exactly did she ask for?"

Simon shifted his jaw, left, right, left, right, the way he did when he was close to boiling over. He snorted and said, "She called me just after you left last night, said you were too embarrassed to ask but that she needed a list of contracts you've been on since '97; dates, locations and all that. She told me that they were threatening prosecution because you hadn't done your taxes. I'll tell you, Nick, twenty-three fucking years wasn't easy to dig up."

"Are these the only copies?" Nick asked quietly.

Simon shook his head. "I sent Lynn maybe thirty emails this morning with attachments. These are the copies. I just didn't want Penny to see them because she would have opened that yap of hers and I didn't want that shit in the office again. You know how she was when Gary was audited. It was a fucking shit show."

"You should have called me, Simon."

Simon threw up his hands. His cigarette fell to the sidewalk and he stepped on it, dragging it with his toe and leaving a dark skid mark across the cement. "Look, I don't want any trouble, Nick. I don't know what you've got going on with your wife but I was trying to do you a favor. You should thank me."

Nick regarded Simon's red face, the shuffle of his hips, the jut of his elbows, the swell of veins at his temples and knew that if he told the man the papers weren't needed he might erupt in a public fury that Nick had neither the patience nor the time for. Nick said, "Thanks Si. I'm sorry. I—Lynn—she's going to leave me. I didn't know it until now. I'm sorry she got you involved."

Simon's anger foundered. He pulled a pack of cigarettes from his shirt pocket and tipped it toward Nick, who also accepted a light. The men smoked, venting their troubles and their grey exhalations upward and out. "I'm damn sorry to hear that, Nick. Didn't see that coming to tell you the truth. Is there another rooster in your house? Damn. I shouldn't have said that. Sorry about that." Nick gave Simon a look that he hoped expressed to the other man that, yes, yes there was another rooster in the fucking henhouse. That sweet Doctor Penner was not the model citizen she purported to be— quite the contrary—and that maybe, just maybe, Lynn would need an obstetrician of her own some months from now. Simon sucked in his breath. "Oh Nick, man, I'm—I'm sorry. Terrible news. Let me tell you something, they all seem good until they're not. Know what I mean? It's going to suck, Nick. It'll fucking suck and then it will get better. Maybe even better than before. You don't want to hear that now, but you need to. Look at me! Second time was a charm."

Gotcha, Nick thought. That Simon was actually on his third marriage, Nick figured Simon didn't need a reminder. "I need the day to get things organized, Si."

Simon grunted, "Take it. Need you back tomorrow, though. Gotta get shit done before the weather turns. We're so backlogged there's shit in our throats. Fucking virus. A day, okay? Can't give you more. Scut'll kill me."

"Thanks again," Nick replied and didn't pound his gas pedal until Simon was out of earshot.

Nick took the shortcut home, down the backroads, past the old police station and the funeral home until his neighbourhood suddenly bloomed before him like stadium lights on an autumn night. He was nowhere and then suddenly there were clots of children darting, running, tagging this way, that way, over every sidewalk and street corner and then one, two, seven times Nick had to slam his brakes because a child had tumbled out in front of him. When there were no children, there were dogs on leashes and women on skates and young men on skateboards all demanding Nick to stop, slow, stop, wait, stop. So busy was the scurry on the streets that Nick's quick route took even longer than his long route and it chafed his nerves until he could stand it no longer and stuck his head out the window to curse anyone and anything he passed. He brooded, filling his cab with another smoke finished to the filter by the time he pulled into the driveway. Again, his phone vibrated and he yanked it from his pocket to see Steve Rikkes' number. Probably had a few too many and left his car somewhere last night. It wouldn't be the first time Steve would need

Nick to drive him to work, but not today. Definitely not today. Nick bent to scoop the papers from his floor but they spilled as he touched them. He fisted a few of the top sheets, flung the others aside, spat on them, and marched into his house.

Coming into the front room, Nick heard Vanessa and Lynn talking in the kitchen. With a heave, Nick slammed the door, passed the hallway, and went to them. He held the crumpled papers up high above his head. "What the fuck is this? Tax evasion, Lynn? Fucking tax evasion? Do you know the shit you caused?" His eyes whirled off Lynn, to Vanessa, back at Lynn.

There, on a bar stool at the island where Nick had long ago ravaged her, Lynn said, "One more step and I'll call Tom Widlow." She held her phone so that he could see Tom's name at the top of her screen. Lynn's finger hovered close over the icon. Beside her, Vanessa had her own phone out with *911* already typed and ready to be summoned. Nick balled up the paper in his hands and threw it at them. It missed horribly. "Sit down Nick," Lynn ordered.

Nick withered onto a chair. "Lynn—"

"You don't get to talk, Nick. You don't get to open that lying mouth of yours," Lynn eyed him tensely. "Your daughter discovered something interesting yesterday." Nick's glare swung back to Vanessa, who had the good sense to look away. "You know, Nick, I've known you were an asshole for years but now I know you didn't just grow into it. I'm just sorry our daughter was the one to figure it out." Before his eyes, Lynn grew with hardened assurance. She seemed taller and tougher.

Nick's felt his throat dry up. When he spoke, his serrated words caught in his mouth. "Tell me."

Lynn's eyes narrowed. "What were you doing visiting the Clarke girl?" Heat flushed Nick's face. His fingers trembled but he stayed silent, unsure if Lynn was testing him. "Don't try, Nick. Your lies won't work this time. They have records. Did you not think of that? Really, Nick?"

Nick frowned, his resolve collapsing. "I didn't do it," he said simply.

Lynn threw a glass of water at him and it found his face, where he let the water drip. Her steady voice now boomed through the house. "No, Nick! You don't get to do that! You were *there*, Nick! The home, the church. You were there!" She seethed, shaking her head, flapping her arms, spitting her venom at him. "It wasn't me at the hospital, Nick. It wasn't your mother or father or fucking sister or anyone. It was *you*, Nick. You were off the day you drove to see Agnes. I have proof!" She shook her phone in front of him.

"Mom," Vanessa said so quietly it was more shocking to Nick than if she had screamed. Lynn turned to her, breathing hard. Vanessa put a hand to her mother's leg. "Let me," she insisted. Reluctantly, Lynn nodded.

Vanessa held her notebook in front of her, so close as though afraid Nick might snatch it away. Her voice quavered. "The week of the fire, you were working on a road near the Gazette but one of your excavators hit a line that cut power to the Gazette's parking lot and security cameras. You knew this because you sent Steve Rikkes to notify them. I didn't know this until your name came up at the care home yesterday, so I asked Mom where you were working that week. When she got the emails from Simon, I called Katherine Beecher and asked her if she remembered who notified them of the outage and she gave me Steve's name. It was on a notification letter he gave her. So I called him."

Nick gulped. "I swear I didn't do it."

"You knew the cameras weren't working," Vanessa told him.

"I can explain. It's not— it's not good, but I can explain." He paused, expecting them to interrupt, but when they didn't, he went on. "That night ... I did something that I know was wrong, unforgivably wrong. I won't expect you to understand ... but I was afraid, just afraid, and I didn't know what to do and then I held it in for so long that it was too late. I just want you to know that." Nick saw that Vanessa and Lynn were holding hands now, their pressure-white grips held tight against Lynn's knee. "I was there that night. I saw what happened, but I didn't say anything all these years because ... because I was with another woman, Lynn. God, I'm sorry. I was there but I didn't want you to know that I was with Celeste Zimmerman."

Lynn blinked. "The pharmacist?"

Nick's voice croaked, his words were tentative and fearful. "We were in my truck, parked in the field across the street. You know where the league plays?" A sound escaped Lynn's lips that Nick took as an acknowledgement. He looked down at his fingers. "We were there for maybe fifteen, twenty minutes when I saw the flames. I thought the building was empty. Honest to God. It was almost midnight for Christ's sake. I should have called 911 but ... I don't know. I panicked. I know they track numbers and I didn't want to call and hang up and then have them think that *I* set the fire so I had Celeste wait in the truck while I ran across the street to the paper. I knew their cameras were down but I also knew their internal alarms *were* working because it was in Steve's report."

Nausea crept from Vanessa's stomach and spread through her body. "So you threw a rock at the window to get someone's attention? Because you didn't want to get caught cheating?" she asked unsteadily.

With a nod, Nick said, "Celeste didn't want her husband to know, either. We didn't know there were people in the building until later. I swear, we didn't know."

With a strength Nick didn't suspect Lynn had, she said, "And when you realized that two people died, neither of you said anything? Nothing, after all this time? For Christ's sake, Nick, is that why she—?" Lynn's eyes grew large with realization, recalling how Celeste Zimmerman's suicide fifteen years ago made waves throughout the city.

"I think so," Nick convulsed with regret as tears stung his eyes. "We stopped talking about a month after, but I know it bothered her." He bit his lip and looked at his wife.

"Oh my God," Lynn sobbed, and then she was crying, taking in great, choking breaths, looking at Nick like he was the devil, and seeing the hurt on his wife and daughter's faces as they wept in front of him, he supposed he was. Vanessa's chair screeched across the floor as she went to the window ledge above the sink. Then she returned and pressed a tissue into Lynn's hand, taking another for herself.

Nick buried his face in his hands and steeled himself for the rest. "There's more," he muttered through his fingers.

"Oh?" Lynn shrieked. "You ruined another family, Nick? Any other murders you witnessed? You fucking coward!"

Nick braced himself for Lynn's glass to bullet toward him but her hands were securely girdled by Vanessa's own. He dragged his hands up his face, cupping his forehead with the tips of his fingers to stare down at the table again. "On my way back to my truck, I ... saw someone come down the front steps of the church. He was at the doors and I'm sure he put that shovel through those loops. Celeste saw him, too."

Vanessa stiffened. "Who?"

Nick breathed slowly, speaking the name he'd held for over two decades. "Rick," he mouthed, then said aloud, "Rick Beecher."

20

Robert had just finished preparations for the midweek service when his phone rang. Ten minutes later, his found himself clumsily making a cup of chamomile tea. His first kettle didn't boil because he'd forgotten to fill it with water, his second kettle didn't boil because he'd forgotten to switch it on, and when he finally had the water ready, his hand was shaking so badly the counter was flooded after he missed the cup entirely. He quickly mopped up the mess, managed a half-cup pour, and dipped two tea bags into the water before retreating into his thinking chair in the bright front entrance of the church. On the other side of the windows, clouds gathered darkly and wind wheezed leaves and rubbish over the church lawn, but a small spot of sun found his face, which Robert took as a timely sign of God's grace. Alone in the vestibule, Robert was thankful for the solitude. Not thirty minutes ago, the building was busy with the women's group and the youth ministry but now it was silent while Robert waited for his guests. It were times like these, when he was forced to remember that day, that memory spiked Robert's heart so deeply his agony manifested into physical pain. It spread from the center of his chest and knotted along his shoulders and he could do little but rest. He touched above his breastbone where his nerves lanced into him and winced. Then Robert prayed silently for a moment, so deeply aligned with the Lord he hadn't heard the footsteps until they were right beside him. He opened his eyes.

"Father?" Vanessa touched his shoulder and Robert gave a little cry. "Sorry Father, I didn't mean to startle you."

Robert waved her apology away. "No, don't be sorry. My mistake. It's the first bit of quiet I've had all day and, well, I guess I must have dozed off." He smiled, standing now to properly greet his guests. "So good of you to come." It was a rare sight to have all three of the family members in front of him at the same time and, judging by their demeanor, Robert suspected he might not like the reason for their unified presence. He sought the crucifix on the far all as he embraced them and led them to his office where Nick pulled a side chair to the two others in front of Robert's desk. The family was fidgety and looked strangely at each other and Robert noticed that the two women sat slightly apart from Nick. Vanessa and Lynn had their shoulders to Nick, who was turned away with his knees facing the door. "Coffee?" Robert asked politely.

"Thank you, Father, but I don't think I could stomach it right now," Lynn told him.

"Oh?" Robert took his chair in front of them. "Not a bug I hope?"

"Why don't you tell him what's wrong with me, Nick." The tone of Lynn's voice was not often witnessed within such sacred walls so it took Robert aback. He felt himself involuntarily leaning away from them, tipping his chair so that it was balanced only on the back two wheels as his knees hit the underside of his desk.

"Mom." Vanessa nudged Lynn.

Lynn's grip on her purse loosened and her shoulders fell slightly as she said, "Sorry Father."

Robert smiled at them. "Please, let's start with where the trouble is, huh? On the phone you said you might have some new information about the fire?" The last word crumbled out of him. He sipped his cold tea and cleared his throat.

"I'm glad you're sitting down, Father," Vanessa told him, her breath so long and heavy that Robert squeezed his mug. "I believe we know someone who was involved that night." Robert opened his mouth to speak but Vanessa interrupted, "Before I tell you who it is, I need answers on a few things, so I can be sure, at least surer than I am now. I hope you understand that I'm trying to be fair and that I don't want to blame someone who could be innocent."

Robert said, "How sure are you about this … person?" The family volleyed furtive glances at each other and Robert knew at once that the family wasn't guessing. Suddenly, he pulsed with apprehension and his voice escaped him. "Wh-wh—" he started and then Vanessa was on the left side of him and Lynn was on the right, their hands clasped over his.

"I know, I know, Father," the women soothed him, though with the jar to his faculties, Robert wasn't sure who was actually speaking, maybe Nick, maybe the two beside him. He gave his head a shake.

"I—I need a drink. I'm sorry, but I need a drink. May the Lord forgive me," he stuttered.

Lynn shot a look at Nick and then Nick stood. "I'll get it, Father. What do you prefer? Wine or something a little stronger?"

Robert momentarily thought of the sacristy wine. "Scotch please."

"I'll be quick," Nick said, his keys out of his pocket before he left the room.

Robert sniffed. "Father Bonner would laugh if he could see me like this, worrying over a silly drink. Lord knows how many he's had over the years. It's not forbidden, I know, but it's a weakness to seek comfort that way. Heaven help me."

"No judgement here," Lynn slid a box of tissues toward him.

"I'm fine, I'm fine. The Lord has seen me this far and I believe He'll see me through the rest. Thank you for your concern, ladies. You don't know how much I appreciate it." Robert righted his chair. "Now, your questions. Please, let's proceed."

Vanessa swallowed. "This may be uncomfortable for you, Father."

"*Do not grieve, for the joy of the Lord is your strength.* Have you ever heard that one? No? A verse from Nehemiah. His name means comfort and hope and I have leaned on his words many times, as I do now, but I have to remind myself that it doesn't mean I won't feel sorrow or heartache. The human condition does not allow us to shut those feelings off, however much we try. We cannot fence ourselves away from discomfort, it does no good even if it seems the most sensible thing to do. Since my wife passed, hardship is all I know, and there would be no benefit if I resisted the discovery of its origin, despite the pain it may cause me. And there are few questions that would be a surprise. The devil has seen to that." The faint light that managed to seep through Robert's window was obscured by the passing of clouds, which Robert saw as shadows on the two women's faces. The shade softened their expressions as though a kindly veil had been draped over them and he felt the sudden rush of the Lord's tenderness.

Robert tipped his head to signify his readiness but it was Vanessa who spoke. "What can you tell me about your altar servers back then?" she asked.

"You think it was one of them?"

Vanessa shook her head. "That's not what I'm saying, Father, but I do need more information about them."

Robert leaned backward and swiveled his chair so that he could look out the window. "I don't know what I can tell you that you don't already know. We had Agnes, Patrick, and Rick. Good bunch of kids. I know that Agnes and Patrick had affections for each other but it wasn't anything we hadn't seen before. The behaviour was very normal for teenagers, as they tend to be. They knew we were watching so they more or less kept it appropriate inside the building, but I couldn't comment on anything they did when they weren't around me. I just don't know. I might hear confession but people, especially teenagers, aren't eager to share their misdeeds with me outside of the confessional. As for Rick, he was quiet. Kept to himself. A helpful boy. Read a lot of comics, superhero type of stuff. Nothing out of the ordinary for him either. He was really helpful. Donna said she couldn't have asked for a better group. Those three were amazing with the little ones, you know." When he turned back to them, he pointed to a picture on a console at the back of the room. "See that middle one there? That's them, three weeks before. Didn't they look so happy?"

Lynn stood. "May I?" she asked.

"Please," Robert nodded agreeably.

Lynn crossed the room and carried the heavy frame back to the desk, gently laying it flat so they all could see the picture. She pressed a hand to her chest as she studied the group. "My, I haven't seen these faces in so long, I'd forgotten how little they all were. Look, hun! There you are." Lynn pointed to a small girl with a long golden braid sitting cross-legged and clutching a stuffed cat.

Vanessa slid her finger over the glass. "Is that Agnes?"

Robert shook his head. "No, that would be her mother. Fiona found the fountain of youth, as some of our members say. She was helping out in the kitchen that day and the kids snagged her for the picture." He pointed to a tall, pink-cheeked girl in the back row. "*That* is Agnes. And there is Patrick beside her and there is Rick. See those kids at their feet? We had a camp day that day. Hotdogs, games, evening campfires, songs, stories, and all that. This was right before their parents came to collect them. Donna won the three-legged race that day," Robert smiled at the memory.

"Who was her partner?" Vanessa asked and it did not escape Robert that Lynn's eyes seized on her daughter.

Robert shifted in his seat. "That would have been Iris, the little one ... here." He tapped the face of a dark curly-haired girl with braces. When he looked at them, his jaw twitched. "There was a time when I had not the fortitude for what I believe your question insinuates but faced with it often enough, you know to prepare yourself that it will come again and again, regardless of how much pain it causes."

"I'm sorry Father, I didn't mean to —"

Robert held a palm up. "I'm just being difficult. Forgive me."

Footsteps hurried down the hall and Nick entered the room carrying two damp paper bags. "It's starting to rain out there. Might even get a good storm." From the bags came three bottles, which Nick proffered on Robert's desk. "I wasn't sure what kind you liked so I bought a few of them." He shook water from his head and removed his jacket, setting it on the back of his chair. "Got any ice?"

Robert said, "In the freezer, and glasses are in the upper cupboard to the left of the sink, though don't bother with a glass for me. I don't mind using my teacup." He sipped the dregs of bitter tea from the bottom of his cup and tossed the bags into the wastebasket under his desk. When Nick departed to the kitchen, Robert said secretly, "If I didn't know any better, I would think your husband is trying to get me drunk."

Lynn laughed politely. "You've had a rough day, Father."

"I have, though, if I may be so bold, I don't believe I'm the only one who needs a drink today?" His wise eyes crossed the distance to the occupied chairs. Both women blushed uncomfortably and looked at each other.

"It's been … unusual … to say the least," Lynn's words were hesitant, as though Robert had squeezed her and they were reluctantly disgorged out into the open.

"I'm assuming it has to do with why you're here?"

"Partially," Lynn admitted. "But it's been a long time coming, Father."

"Ahh," Robert said sympathetically. "Those problems tend to be the trickiest, they really like to hang on, don't they?"

Glasses clinked in the doorway as Nick entered carrying a tray with three tumblers and a bowl of ice. "Now, what will it be, Father?" he asked.

"Whatever you're pouring at," he checked his watch. "Ten forty-eight in the morning." Nick twisted the cap on a label Robert didn't care to read. The amber-gold liquid that filled his teacup to the middle smelled slightly sweet and considerably spicy. He waited while Nick filled the other three glasses and then he tinkled his cup against theirs. "To rainy mornings. May we never again need a drink before lunch."

"Hallelujah," Lynn trumpeted a little too loudly, and then quickly emptied her glass while Nick looked on. It didn't take a fool to suspect marital strife, so Robert said a silent prayer for them.

"So," Robert began, his tongue now pleasantly numb. "I believe we were skirting the question of any extramarital relationships my wife might have had." Nick's drink sprayed onto the carpet. "Now, now, it's alright. You missed a little while you were away."

"Let me start by telling you I have no evidence of … an affair," Vanessa paused, avoiding Nick's gaze, "but the further I get down this thing, it's becoming difficult to refute. I believe I have it narrowed down, but this is where I need some clarification."

"I'll do what I can," Robert held his cup against his body, letting the smell of the alcohol anaesthetize him.

Vanessa set her glass onto the desk. "How close was your wife with your alter servers?"

"She was like a mother to them," Robert said. "I'm not just saying that; she really was. We'd been trying to conceive for some years by then and when it didn't happen the way we hoped, she took to the children and prepared for motherhood sometime in the future. The little ones gathered naturally as they tend to do but with adolescents you have to work for their affection. You have to earn it.

Donna felt that if she could reach them on a personal level, it would be a testament to her readiness, if that makes sense, so she spent a lot of time with them."

"Privately?" Vanessa ventured cautiously.

Robert reddened. "With the others and, yes, privately, as you say."

"What sorts of things would she do with them?"

"Lots of preparation and education for the youth services, mostly."

"Anything else?"

The three faces waiting for Robert's answer collectively leaned forward. He reached deep into the reserves of his strength and said, "They would help her in the kitchen sometimes and sometimes she would minister to them if they needed guidance."

"*In* the church?" Lynn asked.

"Usually," Robert said. "We had a room dedicated to the youth ministry, as we do now, but pretty much every part of the building was at their disposal, except for the vestry and my office. There was a storage closet that Agnes and Patrick liked to escape to, for lack of a better phrase, but after the first few times we caught them there, I believe they were inclined to take their activity off the premises."

Vanessa wrote furiously in her notebook. "And Rick?" she asked.

Robert's shoulders rose and fell. "Like I said, the boy was a reader. If he wasn't with the ministry, he would be with a book in the cold cellar."

"Why there?"

"It was the only place that the little ones wouldn't go because they said it spooked them. It was quite dark in there but Rick used a flashlight, said he thought it was *funner* that way. The building was old, mind you. Our ladies' auxiliary stored their tomatoes and pickles and peaches in the room but there was a small area with a bench."

"Did Patrick or Agnes ever use the cold storage?" Vanessa asked. "For whatever purpose?"

Robert thought, taking small sips from his cup. "I don't believe so, no. Agnes was just as scared of that room as the little ones were and Patrick was quite a bit taller than Rick at the time, eight inches, maybe nine. The ceiling was low and he had a hard time stacking the jars without bumping his head so Rick did almost all of that for us." The glance between Vanessa and her parents was almost imperceptible but Robert caught it. "What?"

Nick, who had been an observer until now, said, "What do you know about Patrick's death?" That he spoke at all seemed to startle them. Lynn pursed her lips into a tight line and Vanessa buried her face in her glass so that Robert couldn't tell if she was looking at him or warning her father, but Robert suspected it was the later.

"Well," Robert scratched his chin. "I don't know all that much, just that he was on a fishing trip and the boat tipped but he wasn't wearing a life jacket. Terrible accident."

Lynn regarded the picture on the desk again. She patted Patrick's green t-shirt with the tip of her finger. "You were good friends with his parents, No?"

"Dale and Charlotte? Of course. They never stopped attending, you know."

"Did they ever tell you who he was on that fishing trip with?" Lynn asked.

"Well, Rick, of course," Robert said confidently. "If anything, it was a blessing that he was there to pull Patrick out of the water. They'd been drinking and when the canoe tipped, Patrick was too drunk to swim but Rick was able to pull him to shore and give him CPR. By then it was too late. Rick had a tough time after that."

"I never knew that," Lynn's voice cracked as she spoke.

"The Lewises wanted to thank Rick publicly for getting Patrick to shore but he wouldn't hear of it. If anything, he wanted to keep it private because it was so hard on him. I presided over the funeral. It was small, mostly immediate family and a handful of friends. After the fire, there was a lot of suspicion around him and a lot of folks kept their distance after that, so it was handled privately out of respect for the family."

"But you never suspected Patrick," Vanessa stated.

Robert shook his head. "Never. He had his troubles, sure, but he was a good boy and he had an irrefutable alibi. I wanted answers more than anyone but who am I to doubt the authorities?"

"Hmm," Vanessa thought aloud. "Do you think that Agnes' condition has anything to do with Patrick's drowning, if she is even aware?"

"I don't believe so," Robert said. "She was in St. Dymphna's years before Patrick's accident and I don't believe she would have understood if anyone had told her about it. You know I've been visiting her?"

"Every month since her admission," Vanessa acknowledged. "They told us you bless all of the patients."

"I do."

"Do you ever wonder about the timing of her admission there, Father? If she was somehow involved or maybe even saw something that she couldn't cope with?"

Robert sighed. "Of course. Before the fire, Agnes was a bright girl with lots of potential. If she was struggling internally, she certainly didn't show it. But in my experience, I've learned that people tend to manage their problems in their own unique ways. Some bottle it up, some let everything out, others yet run away. Could I be convinced that Agnes has something to do with the fire? Possibly, but Fiona said she was home that night and I believe her. If anything, I think it's more likely that she couldn't handle the loss of her mentor in the manner it happened. I try not to think of my wife locked inside while the flames … you understand. I am only sane because I am strong enough to push those images aside, even if they are very real, but a sensitive youth like Agnes was as the time might have greater difficulty doing the same. I'll tell you, I could have easily wound up in my own bed at St. Dympha's had I not chosen the Lord as my guidepost. Even for me it was touch and go for a while and, who knows, there's a chance I end up there yet."

They drank in silence, reflecting on the conversation, on each other. Nick had barely touched his drink but Lynn was in the middle of pouring herself a third when Vanessa looked up from her book and gasped. "Father! I—I'd like to check something in the old building but I'm going to ask that you don't come with me. I promise I'll tell you what I know when I can but for now, I'm asking for your trust … and the key to the gate." She stood, looking at her parents. "My mom will keep you company."

Lynn said, "Vannyyy—" but cut her slurred protest short when Vanessa shook her head in warning.

"Dad?" Vanessa gestured toward the door and Nick quickly got up.

Robert opened his drawer, removing a small keyring with silver cross dangling beside a square-topped gold key. He handed them to Vanessa. "As you wish. I've no desire to stop your progress, though I admit curiosity is playing tricks with my nerves right now."

"Thanks Father. We won't be long," and before he could respond, Vanessa and Nick were out the front door, jogging toward the old church.

21

Outside, the hesitant rain became decisive, coming quick and heavy as it fell on Nick and Vanessa as though the pent-up arid month finally breached an opening that allowed it to rage with uninhibited fury. They ran with the field sucking at their shoes and splashing up their legs so that by the time they reached the gate, their clothes were soaked through to their skin. Vanessa wiped at her eyes trying to spy the lock but the wind-whipped rain and sunless sky made it difficult to see and she had to bring the lock to just a few inches from her face to locate the keyhole. "Tell me again why we didn't get umbrellas?" Nick pouted beside her.

"Do you have one in your truck?"

"Well, no, but—"

"If you want to go home—" Vanessa started, wiggling the key.

Through the rain, Nick's sigh was wet and garbled. He said, "I'm not leaving Vanny. Not this time."

The lock clicked. "Then get your ass in here and try to help me figure this out." She swung the gate open and stepped inside while Nick scrambled after her, his jacket flapping over his head. Vanessa whacked her way through waist-high weeds and came to what used to be Holy

Redeemer's vestibule. Her first step onto the rotting porch punched through the wood and caught her ankle but the scratches were superficial so she withdrew her foot and tentatively took another step.

"Careful Vanny," Nick warned from behind. "Maybe you should let me go first."

She pretended not to hear, deciding instead to hurry back past him, running to a patch of nearby trees. Vanessa jumped, pulling at a branch which swung heavily until it snapped. She jogged back, stripping the branch of leaves and smaller shoots until she had a thick and singular rod. Nick stood as she passed him again, this time prodding at the spaces before her, testing for stability. "Smart girl," Nick observed.

"No thanks to you," she spat back, stepping for the first time in twenty-two years onto Redeemer's blackened aisle. She pushed aside a small pile of fast-food wrappers and overturned waxed cups before halting at a section of the fallen roof, charred and decayed but too heavy to move and too dangerous to walk on.

Nick brushed past her, using his jacket-wrapped hand to shift the sharp and dangerous juttings around them. "Let me," he said, and reached deep beneath the underside of the roof. Something tore into his palm and he winced as he pulled his hand free, carefully feeling with the tips of his fingers the length of a rough nail. Vanessa eyed him but Nick took no notice as he heaved the water-logged weight of the roof onto a collapsed bench. As Nick slid his hands away, splashes of crimson fell down the length of his left palm. He quickly wrapped his jacket around it and asked, "Can you at least tell me what we're looking for?" Vanessa's hesitation told Nick that she had seen his injury and, more importantly, that maybe all was not lost for him. "Please," he added.

Vanessa's eyes darted from Nick down the aisle, toward the broken windows, past the remains of the altar, along the benches, up to the ceiling, around the floor. Her wet hair was plastered to her face and she combed it back with her fingers, speaking loudly so he could hear through the wind. "Both Kathy and Phil say Ray felt that someone else besides Donna and Stu was in the building that night, but it never made sense to me. I think we all figured it was the smoke, but what if it wasn't? What if Rick was there all along? What if he'd somehow managed a way out, maybe through the cold storage? If the building had been leveled, they would have found any exit from the cold storage, right?"

Comprehending, Nick said, "You're suggesting that Rick *made* an exit no one else was aware of?"

Vanessa nodded. "Maybe. If he was the only one to spend some real time in there, do you think it's possible he dug a way out, something he would use for when he didn't want anyone to know he was in there with Donna? He was smaller than Patrick but he wasn't weak, right? Is it possible?"

Nick's eyes grew saucer-wide. "It was an old building with an old foundation. Something like that could cave-in …" his voice faltered.

"But it's possible?"

"Maybe," he said, "but it would have been hard to hide. If no one went into the storage because it was dark, it's possible they wouldn't have seen a tunnel there, but on the outside people would have seen an exit."

"Unless he hid it well or the opening was far enough away," Vanessa reasoned aloud.

"I don't know," Nick scratched his head and it brought a fresh stab of pain to his hand. "The firefighters would have combed through the place."

"But what if they missed it?"

Nick sighed, following Vanessa down the length of the aisle, testing the floor with their heels, listening to the wooden skeleton groan as it woke, creaking in protest against their weight. "The cellar was off the kitchen," he pointed to the left of the aisle, down a short hallway open to the sky. Wet ash and old growth made a putrid slush that stuck to their feet as Nick led Vanessa to a scorched doorway sloped by decomposition. They lowered their heads, pushing past a clot of high rubble that tangled the otherwise clear space in front of them, then shoved an overturned fridge aside. Nick pushed a doorless oven to the right, and then flipped a graffiti-covered cabinet onto its side where it promptly burst through a fault in the floor. It came to a rest with a spray-painted 'wuz here' defiantly poking up at them. "I think we found the cold storage," Nick said.

"Does it run the length of the kitchen? I thought it was *beside* the kitchen in another room."

"It was," Nick said, "but most storage areas like that are a little deeper underground than a main floor because it's cooler there. If they had a storage that extended from the kitchen, it would make sense that it would run beneath the surface of the ground, maybe by a slope or even a ladder. Grandma had one like that, remember?"

"I hated that place," Vanessa shivered.

"You were just claustrophobic; it wasn't so bad if we kept the mice out." Vanessa poked the floor with her stick, listening. Nick scanned the cluttered room and saw at the far end a narrow opening where a short door hung crookedly off one hinge. He waded through the dregs of crushed cigarettes, broken glass, discarded underwear, crippled drawers, and wet cardboard and found the door, up close, to be no taller than his own navel. "Did dwarfs use this?" he pinched the top corner of the door and swung it open, revealing the dim, shelf-lined dirt walls, all but one jar broken below. An upturned splintered bench hung from a wide recess behind a thin metal pillar along the right wall.

"No wonder nobody wanted to go in there," Vanessa gulped.

"I'm sure it was better before," Nick offered optimistically. "A lot of times rooms like this are an afterthought so they make do with what they've got." He crouched low and reached for his pocket. A moment later, the light from Nick's phone illuminated the room. "A cold storage doesn't have to be pretty, just functional. Something like this would have worked for them because the walls are just dirt. Feel that?"

Vanessa carefully ran her fingers over sides of the entrance. "It's cold."

"If they'd dug a little deeper it would have been even colder." They bent low and inched into the room, Vanessa trailing her father at his insistence. Something scurried in front of them and Nick pivoted the light along the floor but found nothing. "Cover your mouth, Vanny. Could be mice in here." He pulled his shirt over his nose but the rain made the fabric impossible to breathe through so he reluctantly yanked it back down. "Let's just make this quick, okay?"

Vanessa acknowledged him with a cough. "See anything?" She squinted, trying to look wherever Nick aimed his phone. The space was narrow but long with an earthen floor, walls and ceiling, the length of which was intermittently supported by thick wooden beams. Air that previously was fresh and wet and manageable was now muggy and the old kind of humid that smelled of stale dirt, must and mold. Several times they croaked as their lungs took in the foreign air and soon they were covering their noses and mouths with their hands, trying to filter out the decay.

Above, Nick's light shone on a rectangular ventilation shaft dug into the wall. Nick reached to feel for a breeze but no air touched his fingers. "Closed up," he reported. "Get your phone out and help me look for another opening."

"It's in my purse," Vanessa answered.

"In the church?"

"Sorry. I wasn't thinking this far ahead."

Vanessa's regret polluted the small room. It fermented the heaviness already between them so quickly that Nick stopped his advance and turned around, pressing his phone into his daughter's hand. "It's alright. Just keep the light on me, Vanny." Without another word, Nick spun sideways and, using the side of his fist, began pounding the wall, listening for a change in pitch.

"The walls are solid, Dad—"

"It's worth a shot," Nick protested, continuing his double-bumps against the dirt every time he took a footstep. It was fool's work, Nick knew, but he had a lot of making up to do and if that meant banging around a rotting old church, then so be it. He finished his self-torture and stepped back as the light withdrew. "There's a fault in the ground, Vanny. That cabinet proves it. It's just not *here.*"

Back in what was left of Holy Redeemer's kitchen, Vanessa's rotation of Nick's phone into the cold storage yielded nothing but disappointment. She sighed, "I thought we were going to find something here. I really did. Help me pull the cabinet up."

Navigating the spoil of too many trespassers, Nick bent next to the half-sunk carcass of what he suspected was formerly a massive storage cabinet. The vestigial wedge now caught in the floor was split and splintered on all sides. With a thrust of his boot, Nick severed the topmost shards. Again he kicked, again, again, winnowing the wood until it would give no more. "Wrap your hands, hun," Nick instructed and tossed her his jacket.

A long burgundy stain streaked across the material and Vanessa recoiled. "Dad!" she sputtered and threw his jacket back at him. "You're hurt. You need to get that looked at—"

Nick held up his palm on which not one but two angry wet holes were bleeding fast enough that when Nick put his hand down, the movement sent a spray of blood onto the cabinet stuck in the floor. "Not as bad as it looks, Vanny. Didn't break through to the other side or anything. I just need to wrap it and get a tetanus shot. Grab the other side, will you?" He tied a tight knot with his jacket over his hand and reached into the hole to grab the bottom of the structure. His fingers searched for nails or glass or arrows of wood that could snag him but the surface was clear of detectable danger so Nick readied his hands while Vanessa investigated the area she was to place her fingers. Carefully, she managed a steady grip, and together their muscles orchestrated a rare cooperative feat, Nick pulling, Vanessa pushing, both forcing the leaden thing out and over and away. Several syringes fell out from somewhere inside and rolled onto the floor, coming to a rest against Vanessa's shoe. She squealed, kicking them away.

They followed the track, watching the needles reel forward and drop through the hole in the floor. Two heads peered down into the cavity, where they saw another dozen needles scattered over what appeared to be a collapse in the dirt under the floor. Cautiously, Nick got to his knees and drew his head past the floorboards. Above, Vanessa aimed the light of his phone into the pit. "Careful," she instructed.

"Look at that," Nick said aloud to himself, his jaw and eyes gaping and taking it in, all in. "There's your tunnel, Vanny. A goddamn room. How the fuck did he manage that?"

22

After another torrent of Irene's tears, Tom slept poorly. His own tears aside, he knew he'd done her wrong since his diagnosis by refusing to resign. It was what he knew, he told her; the real reason being cowardice of facing the only woman he'd ever really known and watching her wither alongside him. His death warrant was a sentence on both of them and however much judgement on others was part of his own professional tool house, he much preferred distance when it came it his own demise. Death itself wasn't what he feared, exactly, and it wasn't what gave him ulcers or held him awake at night. It wasn't what made him tremble, it wasn't what clutched at him or toyed with his brain, it wasn't the thing that made routine activity now difficult for him. Exceedingly, his disintegration was induced by Irene. Her tears infiltrated him more deeply than the cancer itself and he knew without a doubt that *that* would be the death of him. Her trembling every time he left the house. Her skin so pale as though Tom was already six feet under and had taken all of her blood with him. His thin wife, always delicate, now so small and insignificant, Tom thought of her bones like saltine crackers every time he hugged her, afraid she would break apart and fall to dust. Now, as they sat at the kitchen table drinking tea and stroking their old golden retriever, Molly, with her head dutifully tucked into Irene's lap, Tom read his resignation letter to Irene one last time. This time, he didn't cry.

"It's perfect, Tom," Irene covered Tom's hand with her own. Her cold skin gave him the shivers so he poured more hot water into their cups.

"Not bad for an old fart like me," he sighed, smiling at her. "It is what it is. Hey, Molly? What do you think?" The dog's head whipped up and she looked at Tom expectantly. She wagged her way toward him and he scratched her head taking comfort that the dog, at least, would be here to console Irene after he was gone. All was not lost.

"How about some lunch? What do you feel like?" Irene's flight to the fridge was soundless, as though she was afraid any sound might cause Tom to tear up his letter.

Tom considered the dog, his wife, his now delicate stomach, only one of which could be satisfied. "Why don't you get some potatoes going while I grill us some steak?" Tom said, knowing the activity would help keep them busy and momentarily sane.

"Salad?" Irene asked, her hand already on the romaine.

Tom's nose bustled up, thinking of what the last salad did to him. "Got anything else? Asparagus maybe?" He could stomach the butter, at least so far.

Irene did a quick inventory of the lower drawers and said, "I'll pop over to Grenner's and get some. Won't be but fifteen minutes. If you want to come for a ride …" her voice receded when, over the door of the fridge, she saw Tom eyeing his buzzing phone.

Tom held a finger up. "Just a moment," he said gently to her, then he drew his phone to his ear. "Hello? Vanessa, hi. I wasn't sure when I'd hear from you again. I was won—"

Tom stopped. "Yes, I'm sitting down but—" he looked at Irene as she slammed the fridge door and crossed her arms indignantly. "—slow down, slow … I don't understand. No. No—I … are you sure? Uh-huh. Uh-huh. Yes, I can meet you. Can you go to my office now? Okay, let's make it," Tom looked at his watch, "sometime after lunch. Two or three work for you? Five? I'll be there." By the time he disconnected the call, Tom was breathless and it brought him into a coughing fit so violent, it shook the table and scared the dog. Small drops of blood fell from his lips and Irene quickly swooped to get him a tissue.

"What happened?" she asked, dabbing at his mouth.

"The church," he breathed heavily, taking the tissue into his own hand if only to have something to hold on to. "They think they've got something, Ri. After all these bloody years. All this time. She's convinced. Can you believe it? I've got to check it out, Ri."

Irene's hand went to her lips. "No." Her words were whispered, faint, like an exhalation. "No, not now, Tom. Not …" she struck his chest, slapping it with her bird bones. That he could barely feel it bothered Tom more than if she had dealt him actual pain. "… now." Tears spilled into the trenches of her cheeks, into the hollows beneath her eyes, the water magnifying her emaciation so that she appeared skeletal and sicker than even Tom was.

He caught her wrists as she struck again, restraining them together inside one of his big hands and used the other to pull her in, where he folded her into himself. "The fire—" Tom began.

"Was years ago, Tom. But I'm right here! I'm right here for goddsakes! Don't you see me, Tom? Don't you? Look at me! Look at *you.*" The last word extending the length of her breath, Irene sobbed into him.

Tom sniffed her hair, trying not to cry. He breathed heavily, slowly, calming himself for her benefit. "The letter will go in today, Ri. That's not going to change. I promised you." He used her pet name to soften what he said next. "I'm going to the office. If it means we figure out what went on that night, then we owe it to everyone do this. I need this, Ri. *You* need this, even if you don't know that you do. Don't you want to stop wondering? Feel safe? What about Ray? What about Donna and S—"

"Don't give me that crap, Tom!" Irene spat into him, trying to push him away. "Don't give me that. You know I want justice as much as the next person but not at your expense. You can't do this to me, Tom. You can't." He held her and she mumbled something else into his shirt that he couldn't make sense of.

Tom stroked her head, feeling her once thick hair now sparse and coarse against his fingers. He said, "I'm going to do this, Ri, and I want you to come with me. We can finish this together if that's what it takes. I want you with me." Never before had his wife accompanied him at the station for anything other than lunch or the times he'd forgotten his wallet or phone, so he knew she would see his sudden invitation as insincere. He would worry about the appropriateness of Irene at the station later, if he even lived to worry about it, but in the dependent state she was in, Tom knew she couldn't be without him. "Together, Ri, and then we're done. I need you to do this for me. I *need* it."

She stiffened in his arms then seemed to unravel, melting with resignation. Irene wiped her eyes, used her sweater to dry her nose, and tugged her hair into place. "I need you to peel the potatoes while I get the asparagus," she said stiffly. A moment later, he heard Irene's car pulling out of the garage.

Alone but for the company of the dog, Tom went to the pantry and fished two Russets from the bucket on the floor. Then he took a handful of Milk-Bones from their red box and set them in front of Molly and watched her swallow them whole. With her tail wagging, she looked up at him for more. "Sorry old girl," he patted her head, "you have an important job to do and we need you healthy for that." Molly's head tilted sideways, waiting, so he slipped her one more treat before closing the pantry door. He washed and stabbed the potatoes then wrapped them in foil and put them in the oven while Molly retreated to her bed in the corner, underneath his medals hung near the back hallway. Briefly, Tom considered calling Phil but then recanted the thought as premature and undisciplined. He was getting ahead of himself and that made for bad police work. Tom had never been sloppy and here he was on the verge of it. He shook his head as though to rattle out all his competing thoughts but there they remained, in him, mashing against each other like wrenches in a dryer. Tom sighed and brewed himself a strong cup of coffee while he waited for Irene, but all he could think about was what awaited him at five o'clock.

23

Phil's face hurt. Somewhere inside, he clung to that comfortable darkness that promised nothing at all and that was exactly what he wanted. Nothing. No voices telling him strange things. No rush of faces trying to calm him. No memories. No worries. No musts. He dug deeper as the pain intensified, trying to crawl into that space, that alone space that spoke of peace and the lifting of bad things. It was the space where his father was still alive and the Gazette wasn't in jeopardy and his body wasn't breaking down because he wasn't working two jobs. Another smack of pain. Something was trying to get him. Phil fought against it. "—alone …" he muttered feebly.

Tanya slapped him again. "Phil! Wake up, Phil! Honey, it's okay, wake up now. Come back to me. Come on!" She pinched his chin and shook him then pulled his eyelids up and bore into them. "That's it. That's it. Come on." She encouraged, poking and jiggling all parts of his body.

Suddenly, Phil was sucked from the place he wanted to be and thrust somewhere with bright lights and big sounds. He felt his tongue slide back into his mouth and his fingers curl with movement as his pupils woke. He recognized at once that he was lying on the floor, still in his jeans, the front of his polo shirt radiating sweat. "What happened?" he asked groggily.

Tanya answered slowly, choosing her words with care. "Vanessa … called."

Phil grasped for the memory but then at once it accelerated toward him, finding him halfway so that he was struck by it. He swallowed and sat up. "She knows. She knows who did it. That night, someone … someone *saw*." His eyes reached for his wife and what he saw told him she wasn't convinced.

"Okay," Tanya said with a melodic uptick of the word so that it was pronounced in three skeptical syllables: *o-kay-ee*. "Maybe that's true but we always hoped this day would come. That's what we were working for, right?" She patted his knee once, twice, like he was a child whose hopes she was trying to temper.

Phil shook his head, needing her to understand. "You don't get it. The way she was on the phone—she's certain. She swears she's certain, Tanya. There was a name, and now she's figured it out. And—" he stopped, his hair now prickling on his arms and legs.

"And what?"

He swallowed and then the words rushed from his lips. "She says it's someone we *know*." He linked his hands between his knees and looked up her while he took several great breaths. He said, "Can you believe it? They've got evidence. She's meeting Tom at the station later today but she wants to meet me before she goes. My God. Can it be real? You think? My God." He dug his fingers into his hair. "My God." Tanya rubbed his back, steadying him as he got to his feet. Phil wobbled and she drove her hands under his armpits, just in case, but he quickly stabilized and walked toward the kitchen to get a glass of orange juice. When he turned to face her, there was a look on her face that he knew too well. "I know what you're thinking but you don't have to say anything. It's real this time, I can feel it."

"I just don't want you to get your hopes up Philly," Tanya bit her lip and looked at him with such pity he felt foolish.

He shrugged and said, "It's what I do." Then Phil located the orange juice at the back of the fridge and tilted it horizontally to extricate it from the tangle of leftovers packed in precarious heaps. A bowl of something red and saucy without a lid wobbled when he nudged it, but to his great relief it didn't spill. Phil closed the door and put the bottle on the counter. "Kids pack this thing again?" He quipped, if only to change the subject.

"You need rest," Tanya told him finally. "What you're doing ... the contracting, the paper, it's too much. You need to slow down. It's doing a number on you." He started to protest but she didn't let him speak. "I know you say you enjoy it, but it's too much. You're overworked, no, don't say you can handle it. We see you for five minutes a day since you started the other job. The kids miss you. I miss you. And you look ... unwell. Sometimes I think there's going to be a day where I can't hug you because there won't be anything there to hug, just bones."

Phil took two glasses from the cupboard, filled them with ice and splashed orange juice into them. He slid Tanya's glass across the counter and thirstily drank his own. "You're just jealous because I can fit into my jeans from high school," he teased.

"You can fit into *my* jeans from high school," she retorted, making a face at him.

"Don't they call that meth-chic?"

"Phil," she grew serious again. "This has got to stop. We need you healthy and present and right now we have neither of those things. You fainted for chrissake. One phone call and you're on the floor."

Sugar pumped through system and the haze that shrouded his mind a few moments ago now dissipated. He felt clear. "I know, and you're right. I am tired. God I'm tired. But it's almost over. If Vanessa's right, well, then this is the end of it. There's no more searching, no more investigations, no need losing our asses hiring people we can't afford. I should have wrapped it up a long time ago, I know that. I know. I do. I just … couldn't. I'm sorry I put you and the kids through that."

She smirked. "It wasn't as bad as you make it out to be. I knew what I was getting into when I married you. You're as stubborn as your father, God love him."

"You know that if you'd married another guy your mortgage would probably be paid off by now, right?" Phil reflected openly.

"If I married another guy I would have been divorced by now. Screw the house." She threw her arms around him and kissed him deeply.

"A woman turned on by poverty. Who knew?" Phil appraised her.

They were silent for a time and then the rain that had stopped began to fall again, she drew her arms around his waist and looked up at him. "Journalists are not known for being rich, my dear. I knew that when I married you."

Phil squeezed her shoulders as his eyes drew downward. "About that. I think it's time. I hate to admit it, but I don't think even my father would have held on as long as I have. You know that? He was persistent but he wasn't stupid. He had so much more sense than me."

"Sense is subjective, wouldn't you say?" she hugged him but he didn't speak. "Are you sure about this? Fifty-one years in the family is a long time. Maybe I can figure something out ..." she trailed off, knowing his distaste at what she was suggesting.

"We talked about this." Phil cringed, hating the words as he said them. Tanya was her own person and Phil would support any venture she chose but, the idea that she would burden herself just so he could continue sinking his ship was not something he was prepared to endorse.

"*You* talked about this," she said. "I can do it. They'll take me back at the office. You know they will."

"Tanya, the kids—" On cue, Christopher, Josie, and Andrew ran into the house, soaking wet and giggling as though all three were on the verge of wetting their pants. Their feet were caked with mud, their soiled bottoms were sagging with filth, their shirts clung to their thin chests like ointment on injury and nowhere could Phil see a space that revealed the true color of their clothing, skin or hair.

"You were in the dirt pile again!" Tanya cried. "Stay right where you are. Don't move. Don't you dare move." The children looked at their mother, unable to temper their delight. They tittered and giggled and snorted and chortled while she ran to fetch towels.

Phil waited until Tanya was out of earshot then faced them with his hands on his hips. He winked. "Well, was it fun at least?"

Christopher regarded his father naughtily then he elbowed Josie and Andrew and before Phil knew what was happening, he was under siege. Six arms attacked, rubbing against him. They snuggled his ankles, pressed his knees, coiled around his stomach, leaned against his back, and tugged at his shoulders. His sweaty shirt became brown, browner, black here, grey there; in the eye of the filthy tornado he became the color of clay, silt, swamp and of course, "Poop!" Josie howled. "Looks like Daddy pooped his pants!" She pointed to Phil's own bottom and soon four dirty Beechers were leaking joy.

Tanya collected the children with strict orders to stay on the towels and away from the walls and furniture, but while Phil made his way to the bedroom for his own shower, he heard her voice from across the house. "I said— Christopher! You two stop egging him on like that! No. No! C'mon guys!" Phil laughed, closing the door. He twisted the tap, waiting while the bowels of his old house stirred, groaned, and finally began to spit water, taking an elder's time to warm to comfort. He retrieved his phone from his pocket, wiped an accumulation of dirt from the top half and called his brother. After the seventh ring, Phil was greeted by the beginning of Rick's short voicemail so he hung up and messaged him instead. *Call me. Big news.* But twenty minutes later when he was showered and dressed, Rick still hadn't returned his call or his message. For a guy that practically lived by his phone, even at work, the delay struck Phil as unusual. He typed *Where are you?* then mindlessly scrolled through the day's news as he stood by his phone. Fifteen minutes later, he wrote *Can you meet me and V at Betty's at 2:00?* However, by one o'clock, more than an hour after his first message, he gave up and called Gloria at the house.

"Big brother!" her high voice trilled over the line. "To what do I owe the honor? I tell you, I think I'm *still* hung over from the party. I just can't handle it like I used to. You know it's bad when the detox doesn't even work. Holy shit I'm old." The sound of her giggle was a squeaky chirp.

"Hey Gloria. Is Rick home?" Phil asked.

"You're funny!"

"Did I miss something?"

"Good one, Philly." She waited and Phil felt that she was expecting him to divulge something. When he didn't, she said, "Oh come on! I know what you boys are up to. I might have been fooled once but now I know when there's a surprise coming my way. Oh! Look at me ruining everything for you. I think I just need more coffee. Forgive me, dear." Something clicked in the background and then there was the too-loud sound of their specialty coffee maker pumping water through what Phil knew was Gloria's espresso sump. Water hiccupped and burped and steamed over the line and then she was apologizing. "Sorry hun. Where are my manners? Pretend I don't know anything at all and I never said anything. We never spoke, right?" He could practically see her winking at the phone.

"I'm not following you, Gloria."

"Riiiight," she drew out the word. "You're good, Philly. You Beecher boys, when you commit to something, you're in all the way."

"Gloria," Phil paused to reign his frustration in, "I know your birthday is coming up but—"

"The big four-oh," she reminded him, sipping loudly.

"The big four-oh," he repeated. "And you deserve one hell of a celebration but if I were in on something with Rick, he'd kill me if I let it slip. Right now I just need to know where he is. It's important."

Phil cringed at the crack of Gloria's mug hitting the counter. "Well, he's with *you*, of course. Or am I not supposed to know that either?"

"Say that again?"

"If you really don't know where he is, Philly, then I don't know either. He was supposed to be with you all afternoon, at least that's what he told me."

"Where were we supposed to be going?" Phil asked. "Maybe it slipped my mind. Sorry, Gloria, I've just had a lot going on and I don't know my way left from right lately." Even if the Gazette closed, Phil's journalistic skills were by now so ingrained they would die with him. Persuasion. Humility. Persistence. The ability to zero in on what made his subjects tick. He drew from the latter weapon now, knowing that Gloria would be persuaded to talk if he gave her an opening, any opening to counsel him on his contracting work. If she felt pity for him, if she felt like an insider to his business, he knew Gloria could be softened in such a way that she would tell him whatever she knew, and therefore lead him to Rick without offense. In a different world, Phil might have explained the true reason for his call but Gloria was of the here and now, so much so that she avoided any talk of the Redeemer fire. She was born and bred in Garrett, but she withdrew whenever Phil and Rick had recalled that night, as though she had reassembled Garrett's history and created her own, albeit incomplete, cache of memory and the Redeemer incident had happened at another time, in another city, to other people.

She said, "You doing okay lately? I hear you've been pretty busy putting in some fancy kitchen for the Baldwins." Of course, Phil knew she knew, Gloria always did.

"I am. Just a side job, though."

"You must be exhausted."

"A little. I'm not as young as I used to be."

"None of us are, dear, that's why you have to take it easy. I know you love that paper of yours but everything is online now, you don't even need to print the stuff. Sure, your little website has quite the following with the older generation around here, but you need to get creative if you want to get the younger ones, and that's where all the money's at these days. It's terrible but in small cities like this, if you don't innovate you get swallowed up by the giants who don't care about *local* or *personal* or *community*. They say they do but they don't, they just pander to Toronto, the center of the universe, because anything outside of that airlock is nothing to them. It doesn't *sell*." He imagined her flicking her braceleted wrists as she schooled him on an industry she knew little about. "Have you ever thought of expanding? Not physically, like the building or anything, but what about stories outside of Garrett? Maybe change your focus?"

He palmed his face so that his words were muffled as he spoke. "Like Toronto?"

"Exactly." He knew she was nodding as her jewelry jangled against the phone. "When Covid hit, I would have been lost if I didn't take my gym online. And you know what I found? There was a whole other sphere of clients just waiting for me, and almost all of them were in Toronto. I had no idea it was going to be the success it was but there it is for you. There's more money to be made if you just reach a little further. I know I sound preachy, Philly, but I just want the best for you and Tanya and the kids."

His chair squeaked as he leaned backward and looked at the ceiling for salvation. "Thanks Gloria. It's good advice. I can't change anything overnight but it's something

I'll look into; I just need to sort some things out. That's why I was originally calling. I was hoping Rick could come help me install the Baldwin's new countertop. It's too heavy for a one-man job. Solid granite." While this was not exactly true (the granite component was only a replacement for their small guest bathroom), Gloria thrived on the idea of being indispensable and Phil knew if he needed help she would go to great lengths to rescue him, if only to *feel* she did just that.

"Oh gosh, look at me keeping you like a Chatty Cathy. Sorry hun. Rick said he was going to help you with something, but he didn't say what, and when you called asking for him, I just assumed something was up with you two. You know how he gets all secretive around all our special days, the planning and all that. Let me think … you might try Max's number. What time is it? Quarter after one … you know, he might be at Boomer's. He's big on their steak sandwich special and it's on today. Can't go wrong for a lunch like that for nine bucks."

"I think you just sold me on my own lunch today."

"Before you go, you want me to call him, Philly? I'll give him a ring and tell him you're looking for him." She did and a minute later Phil's phone lit up with Gloria's number.

He answered quickly. "Any luck?"

"No, but I'll keep trying. It could be that Scut's got him near the river again. You know that new development they're planning? The one near Fischer's? He gets terrible reception out there. I've been telling him to get a new phone but you know how he is."

"Thanks Gloria. I'll try him at Boomer's and maybe take a drive out to Fischer's if he's not there."

"It seems like a very important countertop," Gloria observed slyly.

"Just want to get the job done. One piece waits on the other like dominoes. Can't get the sink installed if I have no counter to put it into." Phil bid Gloria a very welcome goodbye, snatched his keys and gave Tanya a quick peck on his way out the door.

"No more fainting, you hear? Remember to breathe and that we like it better when Daddy is conscious."

"What's *conshus*?" Josie asked from behind them, tugging at her ponytail.

"It means ready to snuggle, baby." Tanya picked her youngest up. "When Daddy gets home we're all going to— is that gum in your hair? You just had a bath!" She dramatically crossed her eyes and blew upward at hair that fell over her forehead.

Before she closed the door, Phil blew her an air kiss and captured the moment in his mind, committing it to that part of his memory where all the good times lived. He called Rick again, messaged him twice, and when he started his truck toward Boomer's, he felt certain that Rick would be there, too busy eating his steak to answer. Despite his hurry to find Rick, Phil drove slowly as the humidity in the truck made it difficult to see the road. Fog covered the windows and the old truck was slow to warm up so he first moved at a crawl, then a slow amble, until the mist dilated like a pupil and he was picking up speed and passing River Retirement, Temple Baptist, Finn's Produce, St. Matthew's, and the North Central Fire Station. Too soon, he slowed when the rain quickened and his time-worn wipers were unable to keep up with the barrage of water. At the intersection in front of the Blundy and Ashurst Funeral Home, he stopped at a red light.

The squeak of his wipers sounded formidable, like they were working hard, but in effect only cleared half of what they touched; the lower half of the left wiper and the upper half of the right. Outside, the wind grew stronger and pushed against the passenger side of the truck so that the window rattled and oozed inward from every poor seal. The truck cooled and Phil shivered, waiting for a light that seemed to want to stay the color it was, as though it had just realized the proximity of the funeral home and was dead set on progression. Leaves unfurled from trees and shot over lawns and across the street and along Phil's windows until a clump of foliage caught in his driver's side wiper. Like a snowball, the clump grew and grew as the wind tucked in more leaves here, another there, until a mass the size of a dinner plate was swinging metronomically across the window. Phil opened his door and stood on the running board. He leaned over the window and timed a quick pull at the leaves but it took another two beats before he could completely free the wiper.

The light turned green and he proceeded, wet and frustrated, the rest of the way to Boomer's, finally pulling into the parking lot half past the hour. As he was expected at Betty's at two, this would leave him only fifteen minutes. Phil hurried inside. The building was warm and nearly every seat was taken with rain-soaked lunchtime patrons either already eating or waiting on nine-dollar steak sandwiches. In the far corner near the hallway to the restrooms, a group of big teenage boys, squished elbow to elbow, were just receiving their sizzling plates while an older couple in the booth next them were finishing the last bites of their own. Some pop song was playing through Boomer's dozen or so high-mounted speakers but the chatter of the diners overtook the sound so that only the sopranos could be heard. Phil shook the water from his hair as he neared the front counter. Presently, the pie display under the glass was receiving a fresh deposit of generous apple, cherry, lemon, and pumpkin slices from a cart that the wizened cashier, Bonnie, arranged by flavour. She slid the door to the counter closed and finally looked up. "Phil! My you've come at a busy time. No seats except at the grill, unless you want to grab it and go again?"

"I don't have a lot of time, Bonnie. I'm actually looking for Rick. Is he here by chance?" He looked over Bonnie's low head and scanned the room, recognizing many of the faces that were turned his way. Of the handful that weren't facing him, Phil regarded their companions that he could see and knew he wouldn't find his brother among them.

"Sorry, hun," Bonnie shook her head sympathetically. "He's usually here by now whenever we have our steak special but he hasn't been in yet. Maybe hang around for a few minutes? A cup of coffee won't take long."

Phil briefly considered driving to Jack Fischer's farm to look for Rick but it was a twenty-minute drive one way and it would make him late for his meeting with Vanessa. If he waited fifteen minutes at Boomer's on the off-chance Rick appeared, nothing was lost. Plus, the smell of steak and potatoes and hot coffee and onion rings got his stomach grumbling. Maybe he *would* take an order to go. "Coffee it is," he said, "and whatever everyone else is having. It smells too damn good in here."

"I'll tell Griff you said that," Bonnie winked and led him to the lone unoccupied seat just off center of the grill.

Before he even sat on the stool, Nina had a coffee in front of him. "I was told you're in a hurry," she said. "One special to go. That all?"

"You're good," Phil smiled.

"Don't give me that much credit. You look like a drowned rat," she eyed the length of him, "but so does everyone else in here. We can barely brew the coffee fast enough and Griff has already cooked up ninety-two eight-ouncers." She put a little bowl of creamers in front of him and gave him a spoon from the side pocket of her apron.

"Must be a record," Phil said admiringly.

Nina shook her head. "He did a hundred and seventeen the day after the vaccine blitz was over. In two hours." Her eyebrows knit upward. "People sure like to be together. I'll tell Griff you're in a hurry, hun. Just holler if you need a top up." She sped away, inserting herself between diners, through the swinging doors to the kitchen, behind the grill, flashing her teeth here, there, everywhere, owning her work with great pride.

Though it hadn't vibrated or rang, Phil scanned his phone again and saw nothing from Rick. Then he put it in his pocket and warmed his hands around his mug when a creamer came whizzing over his head. A second later, another little tub splashed right into his cup, sending a wave of hot coffee over his hands and toward his face. "What the—"

"Hey asshole!" cackled a slow voice. "You too good to sit beside me? Don't be like that, man. Don't be like that."

Phil's head snapped three spaces to his right, where Rick's best friend looked ready to fall off his stool. Tommy Guthrie burped, the pendulum of his head swinging low over the counter, watching while Phil pulled a handful of napkins from the silver dispenser to wipe his hands. "Shouldn't you be at work Tommy? Want some coffee?" The diners between them looked left, right, left, and decided between themselves to stand and shuffle their plates one space over so that Phil and Tommy could sit together. That they wanted space from the drunk was apparent on all of their faces but they smiled congenially at Tommy and moved away from him and ate quietly, if only so they could hear what Phil and Tommy were saying. Seeing the disturbance, Nina quickly made herself available.

Beside Tommy, Phil settled on his new stool and waved Nina over. "Top up for me and a cup for my friend, here," Phil said, patting Tommy on the back.

"I don't want no coffee, man. You wanna have a drink with me? Have a drink with me." Tommy's head was propped heavily on one of his thick fists, slitting the side of his mouth open from which he now drooled.

"It's cold out there, Tommy. Let's have some coffee first." Behind the man's back, Phil circled his index finger to indicate to Nina to keep the coffee coming. It was too early for drinking, even for a guy like Tommy, so Phil regarded him with concern.

Nina set another cup on the counter and poured carefully. "Tommy's been warming that seat since ten, ain't that right, Tommy?"

"If you say so," he grunted, taking his coffee to his lips but failing miserably to keep the flow confined to his mouth.

The waitress set a stack of napkins under his cup. "Our boy is having a rough day so we're taking care of him. You sit right here with Phil, G-man, and let that coffee sober you up."

"One more, Nin, just one. I'm not driving. I swear I'm not." With a thumb and forefinger, Tommy pinched his keys from his hip pocket and slid them over to Phil. "See?

Straight shooter's got my keys." His red eyes pleaded for another drink.

"You're not walking either, my friend. The coffee'll help you more than the booze, trust me." Nina scurried away before Tommy could protest.

When she left, Phil said, "Aren't you supposed to be working, Tommy?"

"Not anymore. They laid me off this morning. Raylene's going to be right pissed. There's going to me one hell of a mighty fight in the Guthrie house tonight."

"Sorry to hear that."

Tommy shrugged. "Ain't your fault. Blame the virus. At least that's what they said but that goddamn shit's over now and business is good. Scut's just got his ginch in a knot."

"Why's that?"

A sly smile came across Tommy's face. He leaned in and whispered conspiratorially, "Before I got with Raylene, Scut and his wife were having problems. Let's just say I fixed them for her." He winked as his hips gyrated on his creaking stool. "But you know how it goes. One minute they're good and the next minute they're using you to get back at another guy. She found Bobby Jo Harrison's panties on the floor of Scut's SUV and she was so pissed she told him about me. Ain't that fucked up? Eighteen years I worked there. They're going to be screwed without me. Let him find another manager who'll put up with his shit."

Phil recoiled as Tommy's breath hit him. He recovered with a long inhalation over his mug and checked his watch. "Sorry about your luck, Tommy, but you're smart and you'll find something soon and you won't have to worry about Scut anymore. How many got laid off?"

"Rick's okay, man. Don't worry about that. He's got his head so far up Scut's ass he's not going anywhere. Bro's smart. The fuckers just laid me off. No one else. Can you believe that?"

"Sorry," Phil said again, unsure what else to say.

Tommy sniffed. "It's going to be weird not working with him, though. Eighteen years of seeing your bro's ugly mug every day ... going to be strange. He's my best friend, man, my best fucking friend, a brother, even." He threw a heavy arm around Phil's neck. "That makes us brothers, too, don't it? I remember you in school, all smart and shit, and there's me and Ricky, little shits getting into stupid shit and you'd always set us straight like you were our father. An old man even then, eh? Eh? Father Phil!" He snorted and swayed unsteadily against Phil.

"I don't know about that ..." Phil started.

Tommy squeezed his neck. "It's true. Once a goodie, always a goodie. How many times did you drive our stoned asses around? That's one thing; we always knew no matter where we were and no matter what shit we got into, you'd always be there bailing our sorry asses out. Fuck, those were great days." He winced as he drank his coffee. "Heh, remember the time when Rick took those brownies to that church BBQ? When he realized it was the wrong fucking batch, I swear he just about shit himself!" he slapped the counter. Three heads looked left and four heads looked right, spooked by the commotion at their counter. "Your dad was so mad, but not the kind of mad *my* dad would have been. Yours got real quiet and Rick wanted to run away. I said, 'shit Rick, is that all?' And Rick said your dad's silence was the worst thing of all. Like he was the goddamn pope or something."

"Careful Tommy," Phil warned.

"Whoa man. It's alright. All right. I don't mean nothin' by it. He was a good man but everyone acts like he was a king. The king of Garrett." He laughed into his coffee and it spurted from both sides of his mouth.

Phil wiped his face. "Tommy—"

Tommy put his hands up. "I'm drunk. Don't listen to anything I say."

"I got to run Tommy." Phil stood.

"I'm sorry, okay? I'm not thinking straight, the way that I am. Sit and have a drink with me, Philly. Coffee. You want coffee? I'll get you coffee." Tommy tried standing and his thighs hit the underside of the counter. Plates jangled and mugs and glasses and silverware shook until Phil set his hands on Tommy's shoulders and guided him back down.

"I've got to run once my food gets here," Phil said. "You should probably order something, too." From between a bottle of ketchup and the tumblers of salt and pepper, Phil retrieved a bar menu and gave it to Tommy who pushed it away and patted his stomach.

"Already ate two of them. Both sides of the cow's ass, man," Tommy hooted and burped then his face got serious. "I have to tell you, Philly, let's get real here for a moment. Really real. You got me? I don't want you to forget this. Never ever. You listening?" Phil nodded, chancing a glance over Tommy's shoulder to see the progress on his order. "Look at me now, Philly. This is important. There was no one like your old man, you know that? No one. He was a good shit, I wasn't even his son but sometimes I wish I fucking was. That day when he died ..."

Phil said, "It's alright, Tommy. You don't have to say anything."

Tommy slapped the counter. "No, man! No! That's where you're wrong. I do have to say something. I do. I tell you, when I got that call from Rick that night, he was all freaking out and shit, he was real sad, man, real sad like a puppy dog. He was crying and it made me cry, which I never do, but I just couldn't help it. My best friend lost his dad and I was a wreck. I had to get back to him. My mom saw me and cut our shopping trip short and I swear she must have ran a dozen lights to get me to him. At least that's what it felt like. It was like my own dad died when yours … you know."

Behind the grill, Phil saw Nina packaging what looked to be his order. By now, he knew that if he hit any red lights on the way to Betty's he would be late. "It was a terrible day," he said, recalling the moment he had first seen Rick when he drove to pick him up at Tommy's house. That was the instant the auto-pilot that had taken him from his father's body to the other side of the city wore off and it was Tommy's mother who held him while he cried in their living room and explained what happened.

"It was, man. Just terrible. You know your brother was curled up in a ball when we got to him? Right on our front step, like a baby. I'll never forget it." Tommy sighed.

Seeing Nina come toward him with a bag in her hand, Phil rose and stepped back from the counter. "I don't remember it like that."

Tommy said, "You weren't there yet. You got there maybe, I don't know, an hour after, maybe more."

Phil reached for his wallet and stopped. He looked at Tommy. "No, that can't be right. You two were at your house getting stoned on something you got from the Asher kid. Jacob? Jake?"

"Jake, but no, man, my parents made me go shopping with them. Every year, third week of November like clockwork near Dorville for all those Black Friday deals. Mom, Dad, grandma and two aunts come with us. We came back because of Rick."

"But I picked him up at your house," Phil insisted, exchanging cash for the bag Nina wordlessly slid onto his outstretched fingers.

"Yeah, of course you did. He was waiting for us on our steps in such a fucking state ... we had to give him a drink to calm him down."

Obviously, the man had more to drink than Phil initially thought but his sincerity had Phil doubting his own recollection. "I have to go, Tommy. I got your coffee and I'll give your keys to Rick. Take care, okay?"

Tommy reached to shake Phil's hand but then canted forward and gave him an awkward one-armed hug. "You're a good shit, Philly."

On his way out the door, Phil dialed Rick's number. He let it ring until Rick's voice message came on, then disconnected the call. Before he even reached the truck, Phil sent three more messages and wondered for the first time if his brother was in trouble. Worried, he slid the key into the ignition, jerking from the wheel when his phone finally rang.

24

Betty Lurman's porch lights shone dully in the haze of the afternoon rain. In the driveway where she had been parked for a quarter of an hour, Vanessa stared upward at the house where she was to tell what she knew, the thought of which corroded her stomach to the point of incapacity. So here she sat, unable to open her door yet unable to start the car and return home, nauseous with the poison of knowledge. Something hit her window and she yipped uncontrollably, embarrassed to see Trevor's face pressed up against the passenger window, when she unlocked the doors.

"You coming in? You've been out here for almost twen—," he stopped, considering her for the first time under his umbrella. "You're shaking." She gave him a weak smile and he quickly ducked inside, closing the umbrella fast but not fast enough. Rain came in sideways, soaking his t-shirt and jeans and when he finally managed to pull the umbrella into the car, he was much more wet than dry. "What's wrong?"

Vanessa bit her lip. "Can I ask you something? Would you want to know the truth if it was worse than not knowing?"

"We're talking about the fire, right?"

"Uh-huh," she said, her chest heaving from the pressure of keeping everything inside.

Trevor's lips went sideways as he thought. "Well, if I think about it, I suppose I would, mostly because it would hang over me as long as I live."

"But what if it hurts you?"

"That's what they say: *truth hurts*. It isn't always meant to be kind, it's a snapshot of reality and not everyone takes good pictures, right? Some are downright terrible. Whatever you have to say to them, it's going to be the right thing if it's the truth, and they're much tougher than you think." He took her hand and squeezed her fingers. "Is it that bad?"

Her phone rang and awakened her from her pause. On the glowing screen she saw Maury's number and she dismissed his call, sending him a stock message that she would reach him later. She finally pulled the keys from the ignition and faced Trevor. With deliberate slowness, she said, "Rick set the fire. He killed Donna and Stu."

Trevor lips fell open. For a time, he was silent, then he cleared his throat. "W-what?" The sound of his voice was an inaudible whisper, as though it had been trapped in his throat. He said, "Are you sure?"

Vanessa's nod was slow and subtle. "Almost certain. It's possible there was someone else with him, but I don't think so."

Just then Betty's front door swung open. She waddled out onto the porch in her thin nightdress carrying a banana which she promptly threw at Vanessa's windshield. Startled, Trevor opened his door far enough to hear Betty holler through the rain. "If you're not making me grandbabies, get your asses inside. I'm old and I'm not getting any younger waiting for you to pour me a drink." At that, she shuffled back inside, leaving the door open.

"Wish me luck," Vanessa said, grasping her door handle.

"Wish *her* drunk. She's so much calmer that way." Trevor counted to three and Vanessa raced him to the porch. Wind and rain tore at their backs and pummelled their heads and it was not until Trevor had reached the shelter of the porch did he realize he had forgot to open his umbrella and, worse, that he had not insisted Vanessa take it instead. "I think the shock destroyed my manners," he said weakly. "Sorry I didn't give you the umbrella."

She raked her hair back from her face and shook the water from her hands. "In the state I'm in, I wouldn't have been able to open it, so don't worry about it."

Inside, Betty lounged impatiently on an overstuffed sofa, patting a floral cushion. "You can't call me and tell me there's news and then expect me to wait. I might be dead by then. Come sit and spill your guts, girl." *Jeopardy* was playing on the TV in the corner but Betty grabbed the remote and switched it off as Trevor hung their coats and Vanessa tossed her phone on the table and sat beside her. "Want a towel?" Betty asked.

"Kleenex, maybe." Vanessa shrunk a little as the old woman's eyes bored into her, waiting.

Then Betty's eyes narrowed and she thrust a finger at Vanessa's face. "A bottle of rye will fix you. Trevor? Get us some rye, will you?"

Without a word, Trevor dutifully departed to the kitchen where the pantry, fridge and freezer doors opened and closed. He returned quickly. "You're out, Grandma."

"Then be a dear and get us some. Wine, too. The good stuff. Something at least over ten dollars. My purse is on the counter."

"I got it," Trevor insisted, then to Vanessa he said, "Want anything? Wine okay or something stronger?" He dug into the pocket of his wet jeans and pulled out his keys.

"A case of anything," Vanessa replied seriously.

"You got it," he winked, removing an umbrella from Betty's coat rack.

The door had not yet closed behind him when Betty said, "I have a sip of tequila left in the side of my purse if you want it."

Vanessa laughed, and covered her face with her hands. She wished she could stay in the dark of her fingers, where she wouldn't have to look as she spoke, where she wouldn't see firsthand the pain she was about to bring. She said, "I haven't had tequila since I was nineteen. I got sick from it on my birthday and haven't been able to stand the stuff since, but thank you."

Betty shifted in her seat, tucking her thin legs beneath her body. "I think I know why you didn't want Kathy here," she said softly.

Vanessa's hands fell from her face. "Why?"

"It's someone we know, isn't it?"

Slightly, Vanessa's head shook once up, once down. "I'd like to wait until Phil gets here so I can explain it to you together. I don't think I have the strength to tell the story twice." She reached for her phone and dialed Phil's number while Betty waited. "No answer," she reported after a while.

Betty covered Vanessa's hand with her own cold one and tightened her slim fingers around it. "You know, I think Philly was mighty lucky when he hired you. It hasn't been easy for him. Ray's death almost killed him and the paper hasn't been what it was for years now. I think he held on because you were coming, whether he knew it or not. That Guy up there," she pointed upward, "He knows what He's doing. Don't forget that. There's a reason it's you, dear. He knows you can handle it."

A tear fell down Vanessa's cheek. "I don't know that I can."

Betty hugged her then, taking Vanessa into her outstretched arms, holding her against her delicate body, then left to the kitchen to make chamomile tea for the both of them. When she returned, Vanessa was dabbing at her eyes with a crumpled tissue. "We'll take this to calm us down then we'll toast to the end of that fiasco when Trevor comes back. Alright?" Vanessa nodded, accepting a warm mug which she promptly sipped. Outside, a crack of thunder upset the already angry sky. Lightening lit the window once, twice, and then small pellets of hail tapped the glass, the roof, at first gently as though testing the durability of the house and then roughly, brutally, coming down with such force the window behind the TV cracked. With impressive gracefulness, Betty bounced to the front door, slipping on an old pair of boots. "We'll need to close the shutters." She stroked the wall admiringly. "That's the thing with these old houses. They might not look as pretty as the new ones, but they're so much more useful. After storms like this, I'm usually the only one on the block who doesn't need a face lift. Come get drenched with me." She took what looked to be a man's raincoat off the coat rack and tossed it to Vanessa.

Through the clattering of the hail, there was a knock at the door. "That was quick. Poor boy must have his hands full." As the door opened, the old woman stepped back, surprised. "Oh! Ricky! Get inside! Come in, come in, boy, you look like a drowned rat. But where's your car, Ricky? You can't have walked?"

Rick towered over Betty as he stepped into the house, folding an umbrella. Droplets of water fell from his beard and onto the porch rug. "I was at Tommy's house when Phil called and told me to get over here. It wasn't hailing when I started walking," he said. In the living room, Vanessa froze. She hadn't yet got the rain jacket on and now she found herself rolling it up, twisting it in a ball, gathering layers with which to put between herself and Rick.

"I'm glad you came," Betty said warmly. "But can you be a dear and close my shutters since you're already wet?" Gray eyelashes batted up at him as Betty nudged Rick toward the door.

"Sure," he said, his eyes on Vanessa, "no problem."

And then he was gone, back outside where the storm sheathed the city in chaos. The shutters clicked against the siding while Rick worked to secure the windows. Like a receding tide, the hail abated as the shutters cloaked the house in darkness and Betty's small face spun back to the couch. "My dear!" Betty said, pointing. "I think you've wet yourself." Vanessa felt it, too, spreading down the inside of her pants, the heat of which stung her skin. She looked down, at once crossing her legs, then let her eyes tell Betty what she held close only moments ago. All color drained from Betty's face, her body still as she brought her fingertips to her quivering mouth. "No," Betty breathed, "it can't be. It can't. you don't mean—" But Betty knew exactly what Vanessa meant. She grabbed the bannister to steady herself, clutching her chest.

"Betty!" Vanessa ran toward her but then the woman was hushing her, urging Vanessa to sit on the step beside her.

"Tell me it's not true," Betty's voice cracked. "It can't be true. No way, not him."

Vanessa tugged her shirt over her thighs, hiding the wetness, knowing that Rick and Trevor would soon be back inside the house. She said, "My dad saw Rick leaving the church that night. He was across the field in his truck with Celeste Zimmerman. He didn't say anything because he didn't want my mom to know that he was having an affair. He was the one who broke Ray's window that night. I just found out this morning."

"B-b-but it could have been a coincidence, no? Did he actually see him set the fire? It could have been someone else. It could have been. It could have."

Vanessa swallowed. "My dad saw him come down the steps, and then the shovel was … you know. But that's not all. You know the cold cellar near the kitchen where he used to read? There is a small recess behind the bench, almost impossible to see, but he tunneled from there and built himself another room almost directly under the kitchen. My dad and I found it this morning. There were some of his comics there … and other things." Betty arched her eyebrows and then Vanessa said, "Underwear. Men's and women's. It could have been from the looters—there were tons of needles and garbage there— but I don't think so. The area collapsed under a cabinet that we moved, that's how we found it. After we left there this morning, I went back through all of my notes and there's something else that I think was missed before. You remember Ed Norman?"

Before Betty could respond, the front door swung open and Rick rushed in. "It's hell out there!" He brushed small white pebbles from the crevices of his jacket, the cuffs of his shoes.

Vanessa's nerves shocked her to the point that she visibly shook. She looked from Rick to her phone on the table and back to Rick. "I should see where Phil's at," she said unsteadily. "He was supposed to be here by now."

"He's going to be late," Rick told her, removing his shoes and hanging his jacket beside Vanessa's on the coat rack. "There was some issue with the kitchen he's working on. I don't know, rot or mold or something, he said to start without him. Anyone want coffee?" He strode past them to the kitchen and turned on the tap.

Betty whispered. "Put the jacket on. No one will see." Vanessa did and together they snuck back to the living room to retrieve Vanessa's phone. She was reaching for it when Rick came into the living room.

"Coffee's on," he told them, his eyes latching onto Vanessa's grip on the pink phone case. He dropped into Betty's armchair and looked at them. "I just called Rick to ask him to hurry. He's going to try to be here soon. Let me tell you, I'm dying to hear what you've come up with."

Vanessa felt Betty's hand on her wrist, guiding her onto the sofa against the wall where the exit to the front porch was partially blocked by Rick and the exit to the back of the house would be too far to reach should Rick come after them. They were trapped. Betty said, "Let's wait until Philly gets here. It's a long story so we're not going to make the girl tell it more than she has to."

"Give me the Cole's Notes version, then. The long and short of it," Rick insisted.

"Let's at least wait for the drinks," Betty offered. "Trevor should be back soon. We sent him on a run. The rye will help."

"Nonsense," Rick protested. "I'd like to be straight when I hear it, Aunty."

From the kitchen came the beep of the coffee maker. Betty's demeanor now took on a chiding, motherly tone. "Calm yourself, Ricky. The girl's been working her tail off to help us and it won't do any good to push her. You can wait a moment while she helps me in the kitchen. What do you want with your coffee? Cheese? Crackers? I might have a little lasagne left if you want some." The old woman pulled Vanessa off the couch and slid an arm around her shoulders, leading Vanessa past the chair where Rick sat, frowning.

He threw up his palms. "Fine, fine. We'll wait. Just coffee, then. Black."

In the kitchen, Betty made a great display of opening drawers, getting cups, retrieving spoons and plates. She shot a glance down the hallway toward the porch to see if Rick was listening then, leaning in, whispered, "Dial 911. Kathy will forgive me eventually."

But when Betty drew away from Vanessa's ear, it was Rick's face she saw behind them. He had some in so quietly, neither of them had noticed his presence in the back entry. "What's the secret?" he asked.

"Girl stuff," Betty smiled tightly. "I took the lasagne out for you."

Rick sighed theatrically. A long puff of air came from his nose as he faced the ceiling. He closed his eyes and pinched the bridge of his nose, dragging a hand over his chin. "Look. I've got to get back to work and I don't know when Phil is going to be here. Can we just get this over with?"

"I'm sorry," Vanessa said, unable to look at him.

"You two want to tell me what the fuck is going on? You're getting me angry. Just tell me already and I'll be out of your hair."

"Ricky!" Betty scolded.

Rick's face reddened. "Why aren't you telling me? I shouldn't have to beg, goddamnit. You know the paper is still a family business, right? You work for Phil, you work for me. I can fire you just like that." Two inches from Vanessa's face, Rick's fingers snapped.

"You stop that right now!"

"Enough, Aunty. You two are playing some game with me and I don't like it. Tell me what you know. Is it that hard?"

Vanessa raised her phone. "I'll call Phil and—"

Rick slapped Vanessa's phone from her hand and Betty jumped as it crashed to the floor. "Ricky!"

With a quick bend, Rick scooped the phone off the floor and tossed it into Betty's sink, where it sunk beneath old suds. "I was hoping this would go easy. We could have talked, you know. We could have figured something out together, but it's obvious we can't." Rick pulled a lighter from his pocket, igniting it with the turn of his thumb. He stared into the flame as he said, "There's such a double standard with child abuse. Did you know that? If a girl is assaulted by a man, even if she's a willing teenager, then the world comes down on him. He gets vilified, she gets sainthood, it's pretty much the same for both genders when their abusers are male. Nasty, right? But what happens when a teenage boy gets assaulted by a woman? Are his hormones to blame? Is that it? The world doesn't look at it the same way; we're just horny little bastards so why wouldn't we want it? We're jacking off anyway." Rick hissed as the flame warmed the switch, burning his thumb. He shook his hand wildly then stuck his thumb in his mouth to suck away the pain. Betty took the moment to reach out to him but Rick struck her hand away, unconcerned with her yelp. "I was thirteen when it started. She caught me my first time smoking a joint. Tommy got it from his older brother and we were all planning to try it together but the little scrub that I was, I wanted to be big. I wanted to practice first so I could handle it. Be a big man! Isn't that funny? Little puke like me trying to keep up with Harlan. There was no fucking way I was going to look like a wuss in front of him." He laughed, igniting the lighter again, observing the flame. "I thought I was smart about it. You know? Everyone had gone home but that was the day I offered to clean the place up because I knew I would be alone. No one ever came into the storage before so I was surprised. It was literally my first puff and there she was; Donna could smell it from the kitchen. She forgot her purse and came back to get it."

"I think we should sit," Betty said, backing away.

"Don't tell me what to do!" Rick roared. Spittle erupted from his mouth and fell on his beard where the droplets stayed as he spoke. "Don't … tell me what to do. Not you. Not her. Not anyone. You're going to listen because if you listen it will make sense. If you listen, you'll understand. A boy deserves that. He … I … deserve that. Don't I?" He pulled a flask from his back pocket, proceeding to splash the contents around the kitchen. The strong smell of gasoline invaded their noses as, in a flash, Rick sloshed the liquid on the floor, the table, the chairs, Betty's magazine rack, coming at the two of them with slasher rage as he spattered their clothing with the rest of it.

Betty's mouth fell open. "W-what are you doing? My God!"

"I'm making you listen!" Rick shrieked, spreading his arms wide, spinning his insanity around the room. "I closed the shutters so it would be easier for you to hear me but I also doused them in gas. Your shutters. Your porch. Those god-awful fucking ornaments you should have thrown out sixty years ago. They're all ready to go poof if you don't hear me out. Poof! Isn't that a funny word? A little boy's word, isn't it? An innocent little boy's word." Seeing them tremble, Rick bit his lip, his eyes appealing to whatever deity was above him. "See that? Don't you see what you've done to me? I didn't want it to be like this. This isn't what I wanted." He suddenly seemed to grasp the gravity of the situation and dropped the lighter. Rick knelt before them, curling inward with grief, scrabbling toward their feet. He kissed the toe of Betty's slipper and raised his hands to her. "I'm sorry. I'm so sorry. I'm sorry. Sorry. Sorry." His beard was wet with saliva now and it was dripping down the front of his shirt.

Betty put a hesitant palm to Rick's head, setting her hand gingerly on his hair as though any quick movement might spark flames. "T-there's no harm right now, Ricky. We can help you out of this. Just let us wash up." Under her fingers, Rick nodded. "And we should call someone and get you the help you need." Betty gestured to the phone mounted beside the pantry and Vanessa shuffled sideways toward it. "Maybe Gloria—"

Rick went still. "No. Not Gloria. *Not* Gloria. You keep her out of this." His eyes raged up at Betty. Then he took the bottom hem of her nightdress, clamping the material in his hands, pulling at it, ripping, and tearing until the old woman's thighs and the smooth brown silk of her panties was exposed. "Do you get it now? Do you? This! This is what it feels like!"

Betty cried out and Vanessa moved to pull Rick away but he snatched the lighter from the floor, bolted up and struck Vanessa across the face. Her ears rang and the pain in her cheek thrummed exquisitely. For a moment Vanessa could not see, could not speak, because the lighter's wheel had cut her deep and blood began to seep down her face. She reached to touch it and found a gash from her nose to her temple, open and oozing blood. Stumbling back toward the oven, Vanessa cried, "We won't say anything. I'll change the story. I'll—"

"I don't believe you," Rick sneered as the women cowered together. "You're just like Agnes. She said the same thing."

Vanessa stiffened. "You … you put her in there didn't you?" She thought again of the dead woman who was still alive but imprisoned by fear on a hospital bed hours from home.

Rick shook his fists, clenching the lighter tight, tighter, until it cut into him and his own blood dripped. "She *saw*. They sent her looking for fucking peaches and the nosy little bitch heard us. She knew and she was going to tell just like my fucking father."

"Ray was a good man. He was good man, damn you," Betty insisted, though her voice had grown small and fragile.

"Ah! That's the problem with this place. Everyone thinks that. *Ray's a good man. Your father was the best thing that ever happened to this city. All hail king Ray*," Rick intoned like a whiny child then spat at their feet. "He wasn't any of that. What fucking father turns his own son over to the police? Makes him feel like he was the one at fault? What? Surprised? That's what he was going to do to me! I confessed to him, my father, the guy who was supposed to help me and protect me and keep me safe and you know what he said? You know what he fucking said? He didn't ask if I was alright. I was molested by that woman for two years and my own father didn't ask me if I was okay. You think *I* wanted to be a father? I was fifteen for Christ's sake! But he didn't care. He didn't protect me. He told me he was going to drive me to the police station so I could turn myself in. Can you believe it? Saint Ray, he was the fucking devil."

"Are you saying that you … you—" but Betty couldn't finish.

"It was a very merry Christmas for me that year, I'll tell you," Ray cackled.

"No! Noooo!" Betty sobbed, collapsing in anguish. Great rivers of tears fell from the woman's eyes and Vanessa held her then, smoothing and hushing into Betty's hair as Rick rolled his shoulders and cracked his neck.

"If you don't want to fall off the roof, then don't put up decorations after it snows. Everybody knows that," he said.

"Your mother—"

"Should thank me. She got a nice settlement."

In Vanessa's arms, Betty stiffened. "How could you! After all he did for you! You would be nothing if it weren't for your father."

But Rick didn't answer, because at that very moment, Vanessa grabbed Betty's frying pan from the stove and whacked him on the side of the head. The steel cracked against Rick's face and he went down in a heap of pain. Vanessa clasped Betty's hand and dragged her from the kitchen but before they could reach the front door, a knife jetted past them. Behind them, Rick had snatched Betty's knife block from the counter and was now cradling it against his chest. An angry red welt erupted where Vanessa hit him, but Rick gave it no attention. Instead, he lumbered toward them, yanking a knife from the block then firing it into the hallway where the two women huddled. He threw another and another and yet one more before Vanessa and Betty knew that if they went for the door, Rick would get them. They looked at each other and raced for the stairs, with Vanessa pushing the older woman up, up, up, further into the chambers of the house and away from Rick.

"Oh no you don't!" Rick howled, scrambling out of the kitchen, over the bannister and up the stairs after them.

Up they raced, past Betty's bathroom and sewing room, down the hallway to her bedroom where Betty slammed and locked the door. Then Rick's fists began pummelling the wood, smashing it with his fists, his shoulders, his whole body. "Here! Here!" Betty cried, guiding Vanessa to her closet where inside there was a narrow staircase. "The attic! There!" They flew past the bed, the rocking chair, Betty's beige and cream dresses, taking the stairs two at a time. At her heels, Vanessa urged Betty on as Rick's pounding grew manic. The door rattled, the hinges reverberated against the wood and then, suddenly, the house was quiet.

25

Nick straightened his collar and smoothed the front of his jeans as he rang the doorbell. Beside him, Lynn pulsed with fury, anger, resentment; a tangle of emotions Nick could not fault her for. As they waited, her pinky finger brushed the side of his hand and he reached for it but she pulled it away and took another step further from him. They had just come from the house, where she had thrown her wedding ring at him among other, heavier things, the bruises from which were already forming. He pulled his sleeve over the purple mark on his arm and rang the doorbell again. Footsteps light as feathers fell inside the house, barely audible in the heavy rain until they were just inches away on the other side of the wood. Irene Widlow, in a thick navy sweater buttoned tight to her neck, answered. "Lynn!" the small woman exclaimed, observing Lynn and Nick and the incensed sky behind them with bewilderment. Quickly, she welcomed them inside and brought them to the kitchen where Tom was opening the dishwasher.

"You two look like wrecks," he said jovially. "Coffee? Tea? Something stronger? I'm thinking this must be important, by the looks on your faces."

"Tea for me, please," Lynn said, taking a seat at the table where the remains of Tom and Irene's lunch had yet to be cleared away.

"Nothing for me," Nick said, declining because although he could use a glass of water, he knew that once he told Tom and Irene of his involvement in the fire, his touch would irrevocably soil whatever he handled.

Tom removed his and Irene's half-eaten plates from the table and set them on the counter. He took a cloth and wiped the table while Irene prepared tea for all of them. "What can I help you with?" he asked once he had the dishwasher running.

"Nick—" Lynn started but Nick held up his hand.

"I got this, Lynnie," he said, noting with regret the way she flinched at his use of her nickname. By now, both Irene and Tom were eyeing Nick warily so he waited until Irene had set all of the cups on the table and she was seated to begin. "I—" he ventured but then found his mouth dry, so very dry. With a grunt, he cleared his throat and continued, "I should have come forward years ago but I was a coward. I have no excuse except that I wasn't man enough to do the right thing when it needed to be done. That's on me. I know what I'm going to tell you is going to hurt a lot of people and I want to say I'll never forgive myself and I don't expect anyone's forgiveness because I don't deserve it. My actions were terrible." He stopped then to rally that part of him that was still strong and right.

Over the table, Irene took Tom's hand. Tom looked from Nick to Lynn then back to Nick. "Is this a confession, Nick?" Tom asked carefully. "Should we do this at the station?"

Nick shook his head. "It won't matter if I tell you here or there, I promise my story will be the same. You need to know it."

"I'm listening," Tom said.

"It's not a secret that I've been a terrible husband. I've never deserved someone like Lynn and I know she has always deserved better than me. You do, Lynnie. You always have. I was wrong to treat you the way I did." Tears formed in the corner of Nick's eyes as he sniffed, looking at his soon-to-be ex-wife. With the back of his hand he wiped his cheeks then faced Tom. "I was parked in my truck with Celeste Zimmerman in the field across from the church the night it burnt down. I was the one who threw the rock at Ray's office."

There was a great pause in the room as though time itself had ceased to exist, then Tom said thoughtfully, "Celeste committed suicide a few years after. Was she aware of what happened?"

Nick picked at a loose string on the cuff of his shirt. "She knew."

It was Irene who spoke, her voice coming softly like a breeze across the table. "Both of you? But why?"

Nick sighed. "I didn't want Lynn to know about Celeste. That we … that I … you know. I didn't have the balls to tell her. Pardon my language, Irene. And Celeste couldn't bring herself to tell her husband, either. She had two young kids and Vanny was only in kindergarten back then. We made a pact. It was wrong and we should have said something years ago, but it always felt like we were too late for it."

"You saw the flames, then?" Tom asked.

"I did," Nick admitted. "But I didn't realize anyone was in the church then. I swear. Had I known those two were in there, it would have been different. I would have done something."

Tom leaned back in his seat, considering. "Why are you telling us now? Why now, Nick?"

The string on Nick's cuff was longer now as he pulled it taut. "Because the person who did it slashed Vanny's tires last week. I'm sure of it, and I think he killed a cat and tied its tail to the door of Vanny's car to scare her off," he said as Lynn's mouth fell open. "I think he knows that I know and wants me to keep quiet, and he doesn't want Vanny working on that story."

"Come again?" Tom scratched his head.

Nick sighed and looked at his hands. "After I threw the rock, I saw someone come down the front steps of the church. I can't say he came out of those doors because I didn't see that but I did see him run from the entrance. Back then, I wasn't sure if he saw me, but now I'm sure of it, with all the trouble Vanny's been having."

"Who are we talking about?" Concern was stitched all over Tom's face.

Under the table, Nick's knees shook and as they waited for his answer. A loose floorboard squeaked continuously beneath his toe. "It was Rick. Rick Beecher," he finally revealed.

26

From the recesses of the stale attic, Betty and Vanessa scavenged boxes and chairs, two old televisions and a long oak storage chest to barricade against the door. Inch by inch, the pile grew until not a speck of the door could be seen. The handle hidden, the top and bottom rails covered, all four of the panels protected, they stood back and examined their urgent work. "Your face!" Betty cried, really seeing for the first time the cut Rick tore into Vanessa's skin. A curtain of blood draped beneath her right eye, down her chin and onto her neck.

"It's really not that bad," Vanessa told her, though the wound stung deep, and then she took in Betty's nightgown, lacerated and grey with dust. "Are you okay?"

The old woman's eyes went down to the veins on her thighs, the folds of loose skin on bone and smiled. "It would have been much worse if he got me naked. For both of you. Let's get the windows open, huh?" She set a composed and motherly hand on Vanessa's back, then she stopped, her nose high in the air. "Do you smell that?"

Vanessa did. "Smoke!" she said too late, for just then thick black clouds were venting up from the bottom of the door. Smoke rushed from the top, ballooned from the sides, coming fast, faster, so thick the room was soon a midnight haze. "Oh my God, no! He did it! Betty, your house is on fire!" Another ream of panic clutched at her so that instead of running, instead of fighting, Vanessa found she was unable to move.

Betty slapped her hard across the face. "Get a hold of yourself, girl!"

The shock did it. Vanessa reached for her other cheek, her fingers lifting over the small swell where Betty hit her. "What are we going to do?"

"Let's get to the window!" Betty yelled, as the house had begun to groan and creak and snap, voicing its peril first calmly, then bitterly and sharply. They advanced to the side window with low heads. Betty reached for the latch, twisting it the width of an eyelash when the glass exploded inward. Glass invaded Betty's eye, her mouth, as Vanessa dragged her away from the window.

"He's throwing rocks!" Vanessa cried.

"Not rocks," Betty wailed, spying the red and blue ceramic remains of a birthday present through her better eye. "My garden gnomes! He's throwing them! We have to get out of here!" She swung back to the window where the air was good and clean but the opening was billowing smoke, outward from inside and inward from flames just below. Another ornament shot inside. Another. Another. Two stones. Three more. They cowered, trying to break from the attic. Vanessa tried to push the woman out, tried lifting her up and over but then Betty fell backward as something hard connected with her skull.

"There! There!" Vanessa pointed to the other window, calling to Betty, for the terrible sounds all around them made her ears ring. Betty held her head, faltering through the smoke. Far, too far, Betty tumbled sideways. Vanessa tried to catch the woman, tried to pull her back, but Betty was disoriented and drifted further from the opening. Smoke filled the room. The vapor thickened and soon they could not see. Coughing, choking, Betty and Vanessa could hear yelling now, Trevor and Rick, Rick and Trevor, shouting and wailing louder than the fire, roaring with war. The sirens came next and then their ears were filled with splintering and cracking and blazing, their eyes watered and they felt the room heat their skin, their insides until both women dropped to the floor.

It was bright when Vanessa woke in the hospital three days later. Beneath her eyelids, Vanessa's vision was pink and yellow and as her eyes fluttered, she felt something warm on her hand. She struggled with the suction of her eyelids then lifted them hesitantly, at once wincing at the overhead light, taking her time to adjust to the change. "Vanny?" Her mother's voice, soft and breaking, came from nearby. Vanessa searched with her eyes, up, down, around, until they came upon her mother's face. "Vanny! Oh Vanny! Thank God. You're all right, hun. Everything's going to be all right. You're going to be just fine. I love you sweetheart." She smiled up at her mother and grimaced as she felt a small pain in her face. She reached to touch her cheek but her mother gently guided her hand back down. "Don't touch your stitches, hun. They look really good right now but you don't want to move anything just yet."

She was reminded then of her terrible dreams that lurked in dark places with sinister people. Until she opened her eyes, she was chased and cornered, this way, that; hunted underground where vile things lived. Now, with her mother beside her, she had to speak, had to say what she had to say, in case the darkness took her again. "I love you, Mom," Vanessa whispered, for that was all her throat allowed.

"I love you baby. Oh, I love you!" Soft lips touched Vanessa's forehead and then she heard the familiar sound of her father clearing his throat. She swung her eyes back around the room, finally settling on him at the foot of her bed.

"Hi Vanny," her father croaked. His face was lined with cuts and his hands and arms were bandaged. Unable to restrain himself, he went to her side and put a gauzed hand on her arm. He, too, kissed her head but then Vanessa felt his tears on her skin. When he pulled away, his face was wet. "This was all my fault, Vanny. I'm so sorry." He convulsed with emotion, damming his tears with gravity as he looked upward. "I'm so sorry, Vanny," he said again.

Something in her room beeped or had been beeping all along but she just now noticed it. The steady chimes came quicker as Vanessa tried to move her arms, her legs, anything that would allow her to make sense of the room, her parents, her condition. Someone in pale blue hurried beside her and then motes of silver scattered her vision and she once again succumbed to darkness.

When Vanessa woke again sometime later, her recovery from sleep was quicker and it took her little time to orient the faces in the room. Her parents wore in the same positions as before as if they had not moved, but there was a new presence between them, smiling sympathetically down at her. "Well, good morning," Tom Widlow said softly. "It's good to have you back, Vanessa."

"Tom?"

"Yes dear," her mother said. "He's been here all day waiting to talk to you again."

"Again?" Vanessa asked, confused.

"You wouldn't be the first woman to have forgotten me," Tom chuckled, coughing with closed lips.

"I—you—," she waited for her memory to come from the far reaches of her brain. It was lethargic and sloppy as she recalled it, then she felt its resistance wane and come away from its station and she was able to formulate some sense. "Betty's dead," she whimpered.

Tom nodded. "I'm sorry to say that she is. She was a good woman, gutsy to the end, God love her, but she will be with her husband Stan now, giving him a run for his money." His smile was reminiscent when he came forward.

Vanessa parents retreated to a pair of chairs near the window, staying close and steady beside her bed. She bit her lip, apprehensive. "Trevor?"

"Was discharged this morning. He has a few scrapes but he will be fine. It would have been much worse for everyone if he hadn't wrestled Rick's gun from him. I told him you'd think he'd look sexy with stitches, anyway." Pain rippled through her side as she laughed. Then she thought of Trevor, of Betty, of the smoke that woke her screaming. Now, she assembled that night in her head, trying but unable to shut out the terrible vision of Betty reaching for her, of the old woman's hands scraping the floor when a cabinet came down and trapped her leg, then of the ceiling as it crumbled onto her spine. Sucking the last dredges of air on the ground, Vanessa was so close to giving in that she crossed herself and asked the Lord to take her. Instead, a flash of clarity engulfed her and took her to the front window, an operation of divine automation, she believed.

Burning her hands, she used Betty's pub chair to break the window—where she fell into her father's arms on the roof of the porch. Then the sounds of the dying house and of the sirens and of the shouting men faded. "If it weren't for you, I don't think we'd ever know what really happened those twenty-two years ago, Vanessa. I have to thank you for that."

Vanessa regarded her father's profile as he stared out the window, away from them. "I couldn't have done it without my Father. He was late," she wheezed, "but he made it right." Now her own eyes were wet and flowing but the release felt good and she let her tears run over her cheeks, down her chin, and into the hollow of her neck.

Tom pressed a tissue in her hand, using another one to dab his own face. "It's never too late," Tom said.

27

In the quiet of the morning light, Robert looked out over the renewed fields of his parish. The week's rain had blessed the fields and now, as Robert strode barefoot across the soft grass toward Holy Redeemer, he slipped the little pill into his mouth and swallowed it with a sip from his tumbler of green tea. He waited for the little saviour to work its miracle and settle his nerves and by the time he reached the old building, the knots in his neck relaxed, the pain in his back ebbed, and his tight coils of anxiety unwound and eased into to a pleasant numbness. He took in the Lord's grace, His air, His light, His mysterious ways, and breathed heavily with new awareness. Donna was a … a pedophile. That terrible, evil word. He couldn't put the blame on her impatience to become a mother. He couldn't put the blame on his physical ineptitude. Fault, that ghastly, inseparable demon, was Donna's alone. That Donna's positive pregnancy tests were of Rick Beecher soured his soul. Tom's investigation, though not conclusive, now zeroed in on Ed Norman's first encounter with Rick in the vestibule. The boy was quick to arrive when they called for help and though Ed couldn't be sure of the timing of Rick's arrival, his certainty of the boy's expediency suggested Rick might have been there all along. The water outside the vestry, the police now believed, was not from the leaking roof but from Rick as he stood outside the door listening in on their conversation. In the cold cells of Garrett's small jail where Rick awaited his coming transfer to Millhaven, Robert knew the man was less than forthcoming and it would be a decent length of time until Robert knew more, if anything at all. He sipped his tea again, regretting calling the boy in that day, regretting his disillusioned marriage, and his own inattentiveness to the occurrences in his church. He begged the Lord for forgiveness but his penance for his failing would be lifelong, carrying him to his grave and marking him darkly when he bowed his head in front of his Father. Robert wouldn't beseech the Lord for mercy, as he felt undeserving of it. Rather, he would accept his Divine punishment and trust the Lord to make him useful, should the devil not take his soul instead.

A sudden rush of birdsong affixed his eyes to the crumble of his old parish and as Robert finished his tea, he heard footsteps coming up behind him. "Father," Tom Widlow said respectfully, "we're all here, if you're ready for us."

Robert adjusted his collar and turned to his old friend and sighed. "I've presided over hundreds of funerals in my time and they're never easy. Reconciliation with the Lord should be a time of celebration but it so rarely is. We like to hold on to our existence, and when it finally escapes our mothers or fathers or sisters or brothers, we're so busy raging at the injustice of it that we fail to remember it was never ours to begin with. I *know* this. In my soul I know this, but even with me it's a herculean weight on my shoulders. Especially with this one. I fear this one will be the worst of them all."

Tom put a hand on Robert's stooped shoulder as they walked to the waiting congregation, slowly, because in the days since Betty's death, Tom's energy had plummeted to the point all activity exhausted him. "Her death was not your fault, Robert."

"I may not have set those fires, Tom, but had I been as astute as I should have been, I suspect none of this would have happened."

A clever smile came upon Tom's face. "*Trust in the Lord with all your heart and lean not on your own understanding.* Proverbs. I would think that applies here; don't you think?"

"Either you've been reading your Bible or you took that one from our bulletin board," Robert said.

"Guilty of the first," Tom said.

"There is no sin in that," Robert told him.

"I should have been at it years ago. There's some good stuff in there."

As they neared the sidewalk that would take them inside the church, Robert stopped. He put a gentle hand on Tom's arm. "How are you feeling these days? Treatment going all right?"

Tom pressed his lips together. "Makes me too sick to do anything but lie in bed. Today's the best day I've had since last week and I'll need a long nap after this but I had to be here." He paused, looking at the quiet blue sky. "You know, Robert, when I'm ... when I ... when it's over for me, I want you to be too busy sunning yourself in Hawaii to preside over my funeral. You need some time away and I don't want you to worrying yourself over me. I'm serious."

"A vacation?" Robert asked.

"That thing people take to get away from it all, sit back and relax," Tom said. "Ever hear of it?"

Robert scratched his chin. "Can't say that I have, and I don't think I will for a very long time. You're covered, when the occasion arises a long time from now." He winked and pulled Tom in for a hug and they embraced briefly but tightly, both men loosening when the music started and they walked on.

As expected, the service was a somber affair until Robert invited the mourners to gather for a reception in the hall where, as per Betty's directive, a full bar awaited their arrival. He waded through the room, offering condolences, sharing memories, dispensing blessings, taking his time with the weepers and the laughers and the silent bewildered until at last he reached the prayer closet, where Phil and Vanessa awaited him. Somehow, Phil had managed to squeeze Vanessa's wheelchair inside the narrow doorway and there she sat near him, a mist of melancholy under both their eyes. Though they had seen him, Robert knocked gently, so as not to disturb their reflection too abruptly before entering the room. "They're getting quite rowdy in there, sorry for the delay."

"They were already through three bottles of vodka before I came here," Phil said knowingly.

"Add four bottles of tequila and two of rye to that," Robert cringed slightly. "Not necessarily my cup of tea but I believe it would have made the woman proud." He took a seat opposite them and leaned inward with great concern. "How is your mother doing?"

Phil shrugged. "Right now she's drunk with the rest of them and I think that's a good thing."

"Maybe so, maybe so," Robert said. "Definitely can't blame her."

"Or you," Phil looked at him deliberately now. "You need to stop apologizing, Robert. This is not on you."

It was Robert whose eyes misted now. How to admit he didn't have the slightest idea of how to move on, that he wasn't sure that he could, that strength had escaped him and he wasn't sure if it would ever return. "I've been praying for your brother," he said weakly. "Have you spoken with him?"

"Don't want to," Phil admitted. "Is that wrong? It sure wouldn't feel right."

"The Lord does not ask you to be Rick's refuge," Robert said, patting Phil's leg. "But he does ask us to help take care of the ill and injured. How are you feeling Vanessa? Can I get you anything? Tea? A motor on that thing?" He pointed to her wheelchair.

"My mom is making me use it," Vanessa confessed. "I can walk just fine but I get a little tired and you'd think I was dying, by the way she reacts." She bushed a bandaged palm over her the wisps of her shorter hair, carefully manicured to cover the bald spots. "And I've had so much tea I'm going to explode, but thanks, Father."

For a time, they quietly reminisced about Betty, while the sounds of the party eventually faded. Sad with reflection, Phil shifted sentiments to his paper, apprising Robert of a substantial print contract the Gazette recently received from Vanessa's old employer. "Just fliers," he said, "but it seems I'm quite a bit cheaper than those big city outfits."

"Sometimes it pays to be the little guy. Congratulations," Robert said, then appraised Vanessa admiringly. "You are full of surprises, Ms. Penner."

She shrugged. "If I'm going to be a writer, it doesn't help if the only paper in town closes down, right?"

From the back of his hand, Phil said, "She needs all the practice she can get. She's terrible at it." They laughed and together they exited the back door of the church where Trevor waited, then Robert shared with them the comfort of bare feet on soft grass.

Manufactured by Amazon.ca
Bolton, ON